LADY OSBALDESTONE'S CHRISTMAS INTRIGUE

LADY OSBALDESTONE'S CHRISTMAS CHRONICLES
VOLUME 4

STEPHANIE LAURENS

ABOUT LADY OSBALDESTONE'S CHRISTMAS INTRIGUE

#1 New York Times *bestselling author Stephanie Laurens immerses you in the simple joys of a long-ago country-village Christmas, featuring a grandmother, her grandchildren, her unwed son, a determined not-so-young lady, foreign diplomats, undercover guards, and agents of Napoleon!*

At Hartington Manor in the village of Little Moseley, Therese, Lady Osbaldestone, and her household are once again enjoying the company of her intrepid grandchildren, Jamie, George, and Lottie, when they are unexpectedly joined by her ladyship's youngest and still-unwed son, also the children's favorite uncle, Christopher.

As the Foreign Office's master intelligencer, Christopher has been ordered into hiding until the department can appropriately deal with the French agent spotted following him in London. Christopher chose to seek refuge in Little Moseley because it's such a tiny village that anyone without a reason to be there stands out. Neither he nor his office-appointed bodyguard expect to encounter any dramas.

Then Christopher spots a lady from London he believes has been hunting him with matrimonial intent. He can't understand how she tracked him to the village, but determined to avoid her, he enlists the children's help. The children discover their information-gathering skills are in high demand, and while engaging with the villagers as they usually do and taking part in the village's traditional events, they do their best to learn what Miss Marion Sewell is up to.

But upon reflection, Christopher realizes it's unlikely the Marion he was so attracted to years before has changed all that much, and he starts to wonder if what she wants to tell him is actually something he might want to hear. Unfortunately, he has set wheels in motion that are not easy to redirect. Although Marion tries to approach him several times, he and she fail to make contact.

Then just when it seems they will finally connect, a dangerous stranger lures Marion away. Fearing the worst, Christopher gives chase—trailed by his bodyguard, the children, and a small troop of helpful younger gentlemen.

What they discover at nearby Parteger Hall is not at all what anyone expected, and as the action unfolds, the assembled company band together to protect a secret vital to the resolution of the war against Napoleon.

Fourth in series. A novel of 81,000 words. A Christmas tale of intrigue, personal evolution, and love.

Praise for the works of Stephanie Laurens

"Stephanie Laurens' heroines are marvelous tributes to Georgette Heyer: feisty and strong." *Cathy Kelly*

"Stephanie Laurens never fails to entertain and charm her readers with vibrant plots, snappy dialogue, and unforgettable characters." *Historical Romance Reviews*

"Stephanie Laurens plays into readers' fantasies like a master and claims their hearts time and again." *Romantic Times Magazine*

Praise for Lady Osbaldestone And The Missing Christmas Carols

"Lady Osbaldestone's rambunctious grandchildren are back and hoping for a repeat of the previous year's Christmas capers. Brimming with the sweet sights and sounds of the season, this book hits all the right notes in a most charming and nostalgic holiday tale."
Angela M., Line Editor, Red Adept Editing

"Recalling their sleuthing triumph of the previous year, Lady Osbaldestone's grandchildren have returned to Little Moseley in hopes of finding another Christmas adventure. They haven't long to wait: a music book has gone missing, without which the church organist will not be able to play the village's traditional carol service. They undertake the search, eager to produce a Christmas miracle—one that includes nurturing new love along the way."
Kim H., Proofreader, Red Adept Editing

"Lady Osbaldestone's Christmas Chronicles has just what Stephanie Laurens's readers enjoy about her stories—engaging characters, a mystery or two, and budding romances, all in an authentic Regency setting. It's enjoyable to read about the competent matchmaker and grande dame of the ton attempting to play the role of grandmother. Laurens has created a new favorite Christmas tradition—seeing what Christmas has in store for Therese and her grandchildren."
Laura B., Proofreader, Red Adept Editing

OTHER TITLES BY STEPHANIE LAURENS

Cynster Novels

Devil's Bride

A Rake's Vow

Scandal's Bride

A Rogue's Proposal

A Secret Love

All About Love

All About Passion

On A Wild Night

On A Wicked Dawn

The Perfect Lover

The Ideal Bride

The Truth About Love

What Price Love?

The Taste of Innocence

Temptation and Surrender

Cynster Sisters Trilogy

Viscount Breckenridge to the Rescue

In Pursuit of Eliza Cynster

The Capture of the Earl of Glencrae

Cynster Sisters Duo

And Then She Fell

The Taming of Ryder Cavanaugh

Cynster Specials

The Promise in a Kiss

By Winter's Light

Cynster Next Generation Novels

The Tempting of Thomas Carrick

A Match for Marcus Cynster

The Lady By His Side

An Irresistible Alliance

The Greatest Challenge of Them All

A Conquest Impossible to Resist

The Inevitable Fall of Christopher Cynster

The Games Lovers Play (March 18, 2021)

Lady Osbaldestone's Christmas Chronicles

Lady Osbaldestone's Christmas Goose

Lady Osbaldestone and the Missing Christmas Carols

Lady Osbaldestone's Plum Puddings

Lady Osbaldestone's Christmas Intrigue

The Casebook of Barnaby Adair Novels

Where the Heart Leads

The Peculiar Case of Lord Finsbury's Diamonds

The Masterful Mr. Montague

The Curious Case of Lady Latimer's Shoes

Loving Rose: The Redemption of Malcolm Sinclair

The Confounding Case of the Carisbrook Emeralds

The Murder at Mandeville Hall

Bastion Club Novels

Captain Jack's Woman (Prequel)

The Lady Chosen

A Gentleman's Honor

A Lady of His Own

A Fine Passion

To Distraction

Beyond Seduction

The Edge of Desire

Mastered by Love

Black Cobra Quartet

The Untamed Bride

The Elusive Bride

The Brazen Bride

The Reckless Bride

The Adventurers Quartet

The Lady's Command

A Buccaneer at Heart

The Daredevil Snared

Lord of the Privateers

The Cavanaughs

The Designs of Lord Randolph Cavanaugh

The Pursuits of Lord Kit Cavanaugh

The Beguilement of Lady Eustacia Cavanaugh

The Obsessions of Lord Godfrey Cavanaugh

Other Novels

The Lady Risks All

The Legend of Nimway Hall – 1750: Jacqueline

Medieval (As M.S.Laurens)

Desire's Prize

Novellas

Melting Ice – from the anthologies *Rough Around the Edges* and *Scandalous Brides*

Rose in Bloom – from the anthology *Scottish Brides*

Scandalous Lord Dere – from the anthology *Secrets of a Perfect Night*

Lost and Found – from the anthology *Hero, Come Back*

The Fall of Rogue Gerrard – from the anthology *It Happened One Night*

The Seduction of Sebastian Trantor – from the anthology *It Happened One Season*

Short Stories

The Wedding Planner – from the anthology *Royal Weddings*

A Return Engagement – from the anthology *Royal Bridesmaids*

UK-Style Regency Romances

Tangled Reins

Four in Hand

Impetuous Innocent

Fair Juno

The Reasons for Marriage

A Lady of Expectations An Unwilling Conquest

A Comfortable Wife

LADY OSBALDESTONE'S CHRISTMAS INTRIGUE

This is a work of fiction. Names, characters, places, and incidents are either products of the writer's imagination or are used fictitiously and are not to be construed as real. Any resemblance to actual events, locales, organizations, or persons, living or dead, is entirely coincidental.

LADY OSBALDESTONE'S CHRISTMAS INTRIGUE

ISBN: 978-1-925559-43-9

Cover design by Savdek Management Pty. Ltd.

First print publication: October, 2020

Savdek Management Proprietary Limited, Melbourne, Australia.

www.stephanielaurens.com

Email: admin@stephanielaurens.com

Created with Vellum

Little Moseley, Hampshire

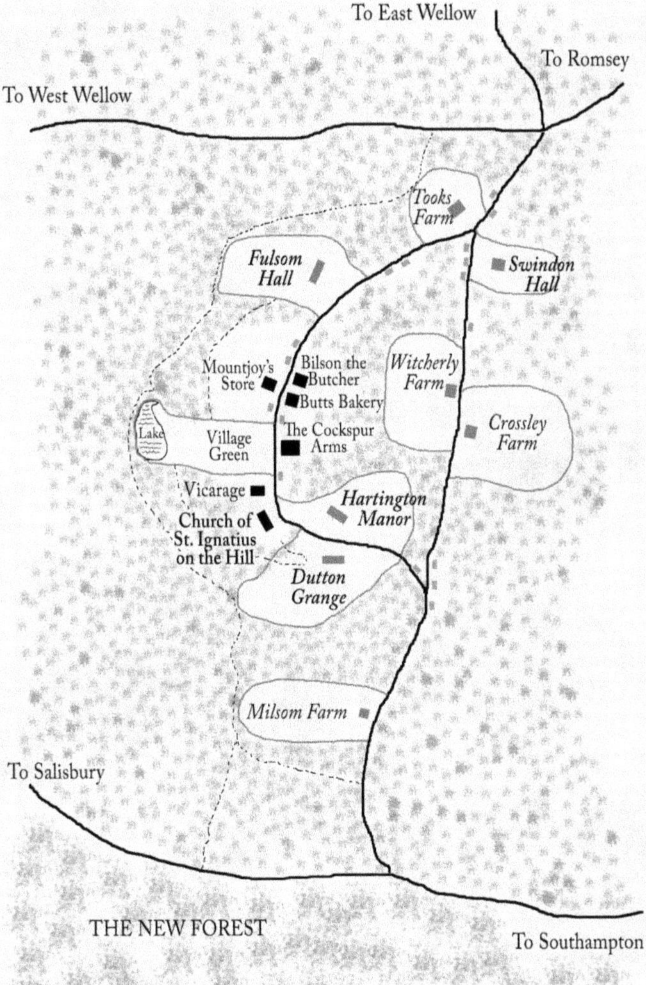

To East Wellow
To Romsey
To West Wellow
Tooks Farm
Fulsom Hall
Swindon Hall
Mountjoy's Store
Bilson the Butcher
Butts Bakery
Witcherly Farm
Lake
Village Green
The Cockspur Arms
Crossley Farm
Vicarage
Hartington Manor
Church of St. Ignatius on the Hill
Dutton Grange
Milsom Farm
To Salisbury
THE NEW FOREST
To Southampton

THE INHABITANTS OF LITTLE MOSELEY

At Hartington Manor:
Osbaldestone, Therese, Lady Osbaldestone – *mother, grandmother, matriarch of the Osbaldestones, and arch-grande dame of the ton*Skelton, Lord James, Viscount Skelton (Jamie) – *grandson of Therese, eldest son of Lord Rupert Skelton, Earl of Winslow, and Celia, née Osbaldestone*
Skelton, George – *grandson of Therese, second son of Lord Rupert Skelton, Earl of Winslow, and Celia, née Osbaldestone*
Skelton, Lady Charlotte (Lottie) – *granddaughter of Therese, eldest daughter of Lord Rupert Skelton, Earl of Winslow, and Celia, née Osbaldestone*
Osbaldestone, the Honorable Mr. Christopher – *third son and fourth child of Therese, a senior intelligence officer with the Foreign Office*
Live-in staff:
Crimmins, Mr. George – *butler*
Crimmins, Mrs. Edwina – *housekeeper, wife of Mr. Crimmins*
Haggerty, Mrs. Rose – *cook, widow*
Orneby, Miss Harriet – *Lady Osbaldestone's very superior dresser*
Simms, Mr. John – *groom-cum-coachman*
Drummond, Mr. Charles – *masquerading as Christopher's valet-cum-groom, in reality, a Foreign Office guard*
Daily staff:
Foley, Mr. Ned – *gardener, younger brother of John Foley, owner of Crossley Farm*

Johnson, Miss Tilly – *kitchen maid, assistant to Mrs. Haggerty, daughter of the Johnsons of Witcherly Farm*
Wiggins, Miss Dulcie – *housemaid under Mrs. Crimmins, orphaned niece of Martha Tooks, wife of Tooks of Tooks Farm*

At Dutton Grange:
Longfellow, Christian, Lord Longfellow – *owner, ex-major in the Queen's Own Dragoons*
Longfellow, Eugenia, Lady Longfellow – *née Fitzgibbon, older half sister of Henry*
Longfellow, Cedric Christopher – *elder son of Christian and Eugenia*
Longfellow, Edgar Harold – *second son of Christian and Eugenia*
Hendricks, Mr. – *major-domo, ex-sergeant who served alongside Major Longfellow*
Jiggs, Mr. – *groom-cum-stable hand, ex-batman to Major Longfellow*
Wright, Mrs. – *housekeeper, widow*
Cook – *cook*
Jeffers, Mr. – *footman*
Johnson, Mr. – *stableman, cousin of Thad Johnson of Witcherly Farm*

At Fulsom Hall:
Fitzgibbon, Sir Henry – *owner, younger brother of Eugenia Longfellow*
Mrs. Woolsey, Ermintrude – *cousin of Henry and Eugenia's father, widow*
Mountjoy, Mr. – *butler, cousin of Cyril Mountjoy of Mountjoy's Store*
Fitts, Mrs. – *housekeeper*
Phipps – *Henry's valet*
Billings, Mr. – *Henry's groom*
Hillgate, Mr. – *stableman*
Terry – *stable lad*
James – *footman*
Visitors:
Dagenham, Julian, Viscount Dagenham (Dags) – *eldest son of the Earl of Carsely, friend of Henry from Oxford*
Kilburn, Mr. Thomas – *friend of Henry from Oxford*
Wiley, the Honorable Mr. George – *heir to Viscount Worth, friend of Henry from Oxford*
Carnaby, Mr. Roger – *friend of Henry from Oxford*

At Swindon Hall:

Swindon, Mr. Horace (Major) – *owner, ex-army major, married to Sarah*
Swindon, Mrs. Sarah (Sally) – *wife of Horace*
Colton, Mr. – *butler*
Colton, Mrs. – *housekeeper*
Higgins, Mrs. – *the cook*
Various other staff

At the Vicarage of the Church of St. Ignatius on the Hill:
Colebatch, Reverend Jeremy – *minister*
Colebatch, Mrs. Henrietta – *the reverend's wife*
Filbert, Mr. Alfred – *deacon and chief bell-ringer*
Moody, Mr. – *choirmaster*
Moody, Mrs. – *wife of Mr. Moody, organist*
Hatchett, Mrs. – *housekeeper and cook*

At Butts Bakery on the High Street:
Butts, Mrs. Peggy – *the baker, wife of Fred*
Butts, Mr. Fred – *Peggy's husband, village handyman*
Butts, Fiona – *Peggy and Fred's daughter*
Butts, Ben – *Peggy and Fred's son*

At Bilson's Butchers in the High Street:
Bilson, Mr. Donald – *the butcher*
Bilson, Mrs. Freda – *Donald's wife*
Bilson, Mr. Daniel – *Donald and Freda's eldest son*
Bilson, Mrs. Greta – *Daniel's wife*
Bilson, William (Billy) – *Daniel and Greta's son, Annie's twin*
Bilson, Annie – *Daniel and Greta's daughter, Billy's twin*

At the Post Office and Mountjoy's General Store in the High Street:
Mountjoy, Mr. Cyril – *proprietor, cousin of Mountjoy, butler at Fulsom Hall*
Mountjoy, Mrs. Gloria – *Cyril's wife*
Mountjoy, Mr. Richard (Dick) – *Cyril and Gloria's eldest son*
Mountjoy, Mrs. Cynthia – *Dick's wife*
Mountjoy, Gordon – *Dick and Cynthia's son*
Mountjoy, Martin – *Dick and Cynthia's second son*

At the Cockspur Arms Public House in the High Street:

Whitesheaf, Mr. Gordon – *proprietor*
Whitesheaf, Mrs. Gladys – *Gordon's wife*
Whitesheaf, Mr. Rory – *Gordon and Gladys's eldest son*
Whitesheaf, Mr. Cameron (Cam) – *Gordon and Gladys's second son*
Whitesheaf, Miss Enid (Ginger) – *Gordon and Gladys's daughter*

At Tooks Farm:
Tooks, Mr. Edward – *farmer, keeper of the village's flock of geese*
Tooks, Mrs. Martha – *Edward's wife, aunt of Dulcie, Lady Osbaldestone's housemaid*
Tooks, Mirabelle – *eldest daughter of Edward and Martha*
Tooks, Johnny – *eldest son of Edward and Martha*
Tooks, Georgina – *younger daughter of Edward and Martha*
Tooks, Cameron – *younger son of Edward and Martha*

At Milsom Farm:
Milsom, Mr. George – *farmer*
Milsom, Mrs. Flora – *wife of George, works part-time in the bakery with her sister Peggy Butts*
Milsom, Robert – *eldest son of George and Flora*
Milsom, William (Willie) – *younger son of George and Flora*

At Crossley Farm:
Foley, Mr. John – *farmer, brother of Ned, Lady Osbaldestone's gardener*
Foley, Mrs. Sissy – *wife of John*
Foley, William (Willie) – *son of John and Sissy*
Various other Foley children, nephews, and nieces

At Witcherly Farm:
Johnson, Mr. Thaddeus (Thad) – *farmer, father of Tilly, Lady Osbaldestone's kitchen maid, and cousin of Mrs. Haggerty, Lady Osbaldestone's cook, cousin of Johnson, stableman at Dutton Grange*
Johnson, Mrs. Millicent (Millie) – *wife of Thad, mother of Tilly*
Johnson, Jessie – *daughter of Thad and Millie, Tilly's younger sister*
Various other Johnson children

Others from farther afield:
Stewart, Robert, Viscount Castlereagh – *Foreign Secretary, in Whitehall*

Powell, Jerome, Lord – *Foreign Office mandarin, reporting to Castlereagh*
Carter, Mr. Gordon – *undersecretary in the Foreign Office*
Selkirk, Lady – *diplomatic hostess in London*
North, Henrietta, Lady – *eldest daughter of Therese and wife of Lord North, another Foreign Office mandarin in London*
Sewell, Miss Marion – *daughter of Sir Nathaniel and Emily Sewell*
Camden, Mrs. Glennis – *Marion's maid, widow*
Foggarty, Mr. John – *Marion's coachman*
Griffiths, Mr. Simon – *Marion's groom*
Leonski, Gregor, Count – *personal envoy of the Russian Emperor Alexander I*
Solzonik, Sergei, Kapitan – *military attaché accompanying the count*
Coles – *butler at Parteger Hall*
Kincaid, Mr. Stephen – *Foreign Office operative*

CHAPTER 1

DECEMBER 3, 1813. THE FOREIGN SECRETARY'S PRIVATE OFFICE, WHITEHALL, LONDON.

"We need you to leave London and keep your head down until we get to the bottom of this." Across the width of his desk, the Foreign Secretary, Lord Castlereagh, bent a stern look on the Honorable Christopher Osbaldestone. "You, sir, are far too valuable an asset to the government, let alone the war effort, to court the slightest risk of Napoleon's agents getting their hands on you."

Ensconced in portly splendor in one of the armchairs angled before the desk, Lord Powell, Christopher's immediate superior, huffed in agreement. "Especially at this crucial stage in the campaign. Were he aware of the threat, Wellington himself would insist you go to ground."

Elegantly seated in the second armchair, Christopher managed not to grind his teeth, instead adopting the bland, uninformative mask perfected by all who served the powerful in Whitehall. "Are we sure the man was a French agent?"

Powell snorted. "Fredericks saw him watching your house, then the blighter followed you all the way from Hill Street to Whitehall—and he spoke to the street sweeper in French, then caught himself and spoke in heavily accented English. What more proof do you need?"

Castlereagh met Christopher's gaze and arched a cool brow. "Do you have an alternate explanation that would account for those facts?"

Christopher inwardly grimaced. He owned a town house in Hill Street, and Fredericks—an old friend and a still-active field agent for the firm—was his lodger. That morning, as Christopher was about to quit the house, Fredericks had happened to glance out of the window and had spotted the man in question lounging in a recessed doorway across the street. Instantly alerted—presumably in a case of like recognizing like—Fredericks had watched and seen the man straighten just as Christopher had stepped outside and shut the door. When the man had left the shadows and headed off in the same direction Fredericks knew Christopher would take, Fredericks had hurriedly set out in pursuit.

Apparently, the man had followed Christopher from Hill Street, around Berkeley Square, down Berkeley Street, across Piccadilly and south on St. James to Pall Mall, then around into Cockspur Street and past Charing Cross into Whitehall. When Christopher had gone into the building housing the Foreign Office, the man had halted. After several moments, he'd approached and spoken to a street sweeper, then turned back toward Trafalgar Square, apparently unaware that Fredericks was on his tail. Unfortunately, Fredericks had been unhelpfully impeded by a passing carriage and had lost the fellow in the increasing crowd in Pall Mall.

"The damned man looked French, too," Powell declared as if that settled the matter.

Fredericks also reported to Powell, and Christopher had been in Powell's office when his friend had appeared, grim-faced, to report. Fredericks had described the man as tall, dark-haired, faintly swarthy, well-built, with a noticeably military bearing, and wearing clothes of a distinctly Continental cut.

The immediate assumption everyone had leapt to was that, somehow, Napoleon had learned of the network of informers Christopher had established through his earlier years of working as a field agent throughout Europe, a network that now fed Christopher and his masters a steady stream of secret intelligence, not only from deep within the French state and its currently claimed dominions but also from the higher levels of the various courts and palaces throughout Europe, including those of Britain's allies currently fighting alongside them in the so-called Sixth Coalition, intent on defeating the Corsican upstart once and for all. The subsequent assumption was that Napoleon's agents had decided to kidnap or otherwise remove Christopher from the game.

Christopher drew breath and, speaking to Castlereagh, ventured, "Nevertheless, my lord, with the campaign entering such a critical phase…" He trailed off because Castlereagh, lips tight, was already shaking his head.

"I appreciate that this is a highly inconvenient time to insist you leave your desk, Osbaldestone." Castlereagh held Christopher with his gaze. "However, the investment of years that has gone into the establishment of the network of informants that you—specifically you and no other—oversee, and the vital nature of those contacts not just in the immediate campaign but even more in what will come afterward, make it imperative that we take whatever steps are necessary to ensure that you and your network remain intact, in place, and operational for the coming year."

Castlereagh glanced at Powell, who nodded determinedly, then the Foreign Secretary returned his compelling gaze to Christopher. "I agree with Powell that the best way to achieve that is for you to make yourself scarce while the department does its damnedest to flush out this agent and his friends. Immediately we have them in custody or have evidence that they've fled, you may return to London and your desk."

Maintaining his impassive expression, Christopher bit back a sigh and inclined his head. "As you wish, my lord."

Despite his best efforts, his unhappiness over the unpalatable order had seeped through. Castlereagh hesitated, then in a less hard tone, asked, "Given the season, can you suggest a suitable bolt hole?"

Christopher recognized the sop for what it was, a consolation for accommodating Castlereagh's wishes.

Powell shifted. "We could dispatch you somewhere north, I suppose—to the Midlands, maybe? Somewhere they would find it more difficult to follow."

"No." Frowning slightly, Castlereagh tapped a finger on his blotter. "There can be nothing formal or organized about this—you need to simply vanish. You're here today, but you won't be anywhere to be found tomorrow. However, I would prefer you to remain within a day's reach of the capital. If any urgent matter arises, I want Powell to be able to contact you, and you to return if needed."

Rapidly, Christopher mentally canvassed all the places he might go. He hadn't been in the field for the past five years, but the instincts of an active agent never died, and he felt them stirring now.

"It needs to be somewhere no general acquaintance would think to look for you," Powell helpfully suggested.

An idea occurred; Christopher narrowed his eyes, assessing the prospect, then said, "My mother owns a small manor house tucked away in Hampshire, near the New Forest. It's her dower property and was inherited from an old aunt decades ago, so few people alive know it's hers. She retreats there in autumn and is there now, prior to heading to Winslow Abbey for the family's Christmas gathering."

Christopher looked at Powell, then Castlereagh. "Aside from Hartington Manor being within a day's reach of town, the reasons I suggest it as a suitable bolt hole include that Mama and her staff will understand the situation and know what to look for and how to react should anyone turn up looking for me."

Both Castlereagh and Powell were well-acquainted with his mother and her extensive experience of Foreign Office business; both had been juniors in the firm when his father had reigned as the head of the department.

"In addition," Christopher continued, "in such a tiny, out-of-the-way village as Little Moseley, anyone who doesn't belong stands out and is immediately viewed askance. While I'll initially be noted as a stranger, within a day, everyone will learn that I've come to visit my mother, and no one will wonder about that. However, anyone without an obvious reason for being in the village will be considered suspicious and watched." He paused, then added, "On top of that, none of my friends and acquaintances know of the place, nor would they imagine that I might take refuge with my mother."

"You haven't visited there before?" Powell asked.

Christopher shook his head. "Mama started using the house only about four years ago, so from the locals' perspective, it will be perfectly believable that, having some time on my hands, I might come to visit and see the place."

"Little Moseley, heh?" Castlereagh sat back. "I confess I've never heard of it, which suggests you might be right in proposing it." He glanced at Powell. "Given our requirements, it seems an excellent choice."

Powell nodded. "Indeed." He skewered Christopher with a sharp gaze. "You need to vanish yourself down there. Keep your destination to yourself, and if you haven't heard from me before, check in with me in the new year."

"Yes, my lord." Resigned, Christopher rose and nodded to Powell, then bowed to Castlereagh. "My lord."

With that, he walked to the door, already enumerating all the things he would have to do before he quit the capital.

Lady Selkirk's soirée, held that evening at Selkirk House, was an event Christopher had to attend if he wished to preserve the illusion that all in his life was progressing as usual. Quite aside from the fact that her ladyship had sent him a gilt-edged invitation and would notice if he didn't appear, her soirée was the sort of gathering at which men like him were expected to be seen, a sophisticated event during which diplomats and functionaries of all stripes mingled and chatted, affording unrivaled opportunities for acquaintances and contacts to brush shoulders and exchange a quiet word or two.

Such events were a master intelligencer's playground.

After greeting her ladyship at the door and bowing over her hand, Christopher confidently moved through the guests, progressing from one group to the next. Smiling urbanely, greeting most ladies and gentlemen by name, and exchanging news with the facility of one born and bred to the ton, he absorbed, catalogued, and stowed away all snippets of potential interest uttered within his hearing.

Snippets such as that a senior Spanish general's nephew had recently joined the staff at the Spanish embassy. Also that a count from Liechtenstein had arrived in London, but was not present that evening; Christopher made a mental note to set one of his juniors to find out more about the count and what had brought him there.

"I say, Osbaldestone." Harry Plummer from the War Office paused by Christopher's elbow as they were about to pass each other. Without looking directly at Christopher, who obligingly paused as well, Harry murmured, "As you've no doubt heard, Schwarzenberg's marching his men through Switzerland, but a little dicky bird told me he's finding his supply lines stretched. Any chance of some help from our trade boys now that Wellington's dug in for the winter?"

"I can't say," Christopher replied in the expected noncommittal style, "but I'll pass the information on."

Harry nodded and resumed his ambling. Christopher did the same, making a mental note to direct another of his junior staff to ferry a request to the Ministry of Trade, where it would, no doubt, support a War Office memorandum. With Wellington dug in in the foothills of the Pyrenees, facing Soult and Suchet, similarly snowbound, it was possible those involved in supplying the country's armies might have time to have a natter with the Swiss about how much importance Britain and its allies attached to the defeat of Napoleon.

He was diligently circling the room when he realized that a niggle of awareness had been dancing along his nerves for the past fifteen minutes. He was being watched.

His nerves leapt. After being followed earlier in the day, he had to wonder if the two episodes were connected.

He was far too experienced to turn and search for the culprit, even in that setting. Indeed, especially in that setting; such an action would alert others present, others who didn't need to know anything about his current difficulties.

Keeping his relaxed smile firmly in place, he continued to move from group to group, surreptitiously watching from the corners of his eyes, especially when he quit one group and moved to the next.

Finally, he spotted his stalker—and yes, she was definitely following him in a manner that suggested she was angling for a moment in which to pounce.

Damn! His lips tightened in annoyance combined with disbelief; he immediately forced them to relax into an easygoing line again.

Why the devil was Miss Marion Sewell dogging his steps? He supposed he could guess; given his oh-so-close call only three nights before, he was starting to feel as if he had a target blazoned on his back, one that proclaimed him a thirty-six-year-old bachelor of excellent family, significant wealth, and sound prospects.

On Tuesday evening, he'd learned just how dangerous ladies who focused on such criteria could be. He'd attended a highly select ball and had, as usual, been trawling for information—he had long ago learned that the mothers and sisters of young men posted overseas often possessed and readily shared more military and diplomatic details than most men would ever imagine they even knew—when a young lady had paused beside him and, eyes downcast, whispered that she had something of a highly sensitive nature to convey to him.

He'd shown his interest, and she'd suggested they meet in the small gazebo set in the extensive gardens. His mind wholly focused on his job, he'd agreed; her approach had been so very similar to one many of his contacts used that the request and arrangement hadn't triggered any suspicion.

Indeed, he'd swallowed her lure—hook, line, and sinker. At the appointed time, he'd set out to meet her via the direct route—a path giving off one end of the terrace—but several couples had been standing by the windows overlooking said terrace and studying the night sky, thus forcing him to take a roundabout route and approach the gazebo from the rear.

He'd turned the last corner in the path, looked ahead, and seen, clearly illuminated by the moonlight, three older ladies—the minx's match-making aunt and two of her bosom-bows—hiding in the bushes that crowded the railing of the gazebo on that side. Their attention had been avidly fixed on the interior of the small structure.

He'd been walking silently, a blessing from his past. He'd halted, stared at the scene for half a minute, then turned on his heel and walked away.

He'd been rattled to his boots by the realization of how close he'd come to being snared, all because he'd been so caught up in his work that he'd trusted a young lady intimating that she had a secret to impart. That, he'd sworn, was one mistake he would never make again.

And now, mere days later, here was Marion Sewell, of all the young ladies in London, following him with what, to him, was transparent intent. He had to wonder if the matchmakers of the ton had declared open season on him.

Over the months since she and her family had returned to London, he hadn't caught more than a glimpse of Marion. He'd been introduced to her long ago, when she'd first made her come-out. Now he thought of it, that had to have been ten years ago; she must be all of twenty-eight and, he believed, still unmarried.

That said, in her case, being unwed at such an advanced age was more a reflection of where she'd spent the decade since her come-out. In that same year, her father, Sir Nathaniel Sewell, had been posted as ambassador to the Imperial Court of Russia, and Marion and her twin brother, Robert, had accompanied her parents to Moscow. For a lady of Marion's ilk, eligible beaux would have been thin on the ground in the imperial court and also in the Hapsburg court, which had been her father's subsequent posting.

Sir Nathaniel had returned to London permanently only a few months ago. He now occupied a similar position at the Foreign Office as Powell and Christopher's brother-in-law, North, reporting directly to Castlereagh.

Determined to avoid creating the sort of momentary opening he suspected Marion was waiting to seize, Christopher drifted toward the middle of the room so that, when he moved to the next group between him and his hostess, stationed near the door, he was surrounded on all sides by other guests.

From the corner of his eye, he saw Marion, who'd been unobtrusively drifting in his wake, check, then halt by the side of the room. She was of above-average height and somewhat more than passably pretty, with an alabaster-and-cream complexion that set off the lustrous golden-brown waves of her hair, currently swept up into an elegant knot on the top of her head. She was too far away for him to see her eyes, but he knew they were a curious shade of aqua blue, quite mesmerizing in the way they reflected her moods.

With her strong yet ladylike features—large eyes set under well-arched brown brows, pale rose-tinted lips, straight nose, and firm chin often set in determined lines—exuding an indomitable, intrinsically feminine resolve, in his younger mind, she'd featured as a slender and elegant Amazon.

He hadn't forgotten how he'd viewed her then, or that he'd wondered whether the nascent attraction he'd felt for her—quite different to what he'd ever felt for other ladies—had been reciprocated. Regardless, that had been ten years ago and was surely water long under the bridge; they would both be very different people now.

Still, he had to admit he was surprised to find her hunting him; he wouldn't have thought her the type.

Then again, an unkind observer might point out that she was twenty-eight and still unwed and he was more than eligible. Conversely, and possibly even more dangerously, her twenty-eight years notwithstanding, as Sir Nathaniel Sewell's diplomatically experienced daughter, she would be considered an excellent match for him.

Now, she stared at him as if willing him to notice her and come to her; he could feel the compulsion in her gaze as it bored into him, but determinedly ignored it.

Step by step, group by group, he adroitly edged closer to the door. Finally, he crossed to Lady Selkirk's side. When she turned to him, he took his leave of her with his customary flair.

Her ladyship smiled on him, then tapped his arm with her fan. "Do remember me to your mother when next you see her."

Blithely, Christopher swore he would, reflecting that he would be able to discharge that promise sooner than anyone might suppose.

Without glancing at the room—at Marion, who he felt certain was still watching him—he walked out into the hall and started down the stairs. If his banishment from London held any silver lining, it was that he wouldn't need to remain constantly vigilant against the wiles of the matchmakers and Marion Sewell. At the very least, he could forget such irritations existed until he returned to London.

The thought of appealing to his mother for advice rose in his mind and provoked an immediate, self-protective shudder. If his mother discovered that the matchmakers had started targeting him…it was entirely possible she would step in, take charge, and organize a campaign he wouldn't be able to defend against. There was a reason she was still regarded throughout the ton as not just a grande dame but something of a social general.

No. He would have to make sure she didn't get wind of the Marriage Mart's sudden interest in him.

He collected his hat and greatcoat from a footman and made good his escape.

~

Reluctantly dismissing the notion of marching after Christopher and chasing him down the street, Marion Sewell drew in a deep breath, then released it in a slow exhale. It didn't really help; her temper continued to smolder.

She felt frustrated and thoroughly exasperated. She was fairly certain that Christopher had been aware of her wish to speak with him and had chosen, instead, to avoid her. She was—now—loweringly aware of how her careful pursuit of him around the room might have appeared to anyone who had noticed and, most especially, to him. From his reaction, she assumed that, in the years since they'd last interacted, he'd grown sensitive over having ladies chase him; for all she knew, he might have cause to feel so. He remained an undeniably attractive man—handsome in a conventional way, with his tall, lean, ineffably elegant figure and a sophisticated aura that didn't quite mask an underlying hint of sharpened steel.

From years past, she knew he was intelligent, with an incisive mind, quick wit, and a ready, often-honeyed tongue. Despite the impact of his physical attributes, it had been his intellect that had captured and fixed her attention all those years ago.

She could, therefore, readily imagine that, over the years, other ladies had pursued him with matrimonial intent. Not until some time after she'd embarked on her plan to stalk him—until she could engineer an apparently purely social encounter during which she could murmur her request in his ear—had she realized how he might interpret her behavior.

Bah! Bad enough that I'm committed to surreptitiously engaging with him, but now I've managed to put the wind up him.

She glanced around, then without any rush, made her way toward her hostess. Drawing on her extensive experience as an ambassador's adult daughter, she paused to exchange farewells with several ladies and traded gracious nods with various others along the way. Given her age and said experience, her presence in Lady Selkirk's drawing room without her mother or father in attendance was accepted without remark; most would assume she was attending in her parents' stead.

Without conscious thought, she allowed polite words to trip from her tongue, while inside, she dwelled on the abject failure of her evening. Clearly, the simple plan of approaching Christopher at a social event wasn't going to succeed, at least not without attracting attention from others, which, in the circumstances, was to be avoided at all costs; she suspected that, in the social sphere, Christopher would prove adept at avoiding unwanted encounters.

So she would need to find some other way of crossing his path, preferably in an unthreatening fashion—such as encountering him in the park—or alternatively, in a way he couldn't avoid.

She finally found her way to Lady Selkirk. After thanking her ladyship and complimenting her on her event, head high, her customary serene mask in place, Marion glided from the room.

Apparently, accomplishing the task her absent twin had begged her to undertake wasn't going to be as straightforward as he—or she—had supposed.

~

At five o'clock the next morning, Christopher walked out of his front door, closed it behind him, paused on the porch to tug on his driving gloves, then descended the steps to the pavement. His curricle stood waiting by the curb, the reins of his blacks in the ham-like hand of his recently acquired valet-cum-groom, Drummond.

After Lady Selkirk's soirée, Christopher had returned home to find Fredericks and Drummond waiting for him. Fredericks had introduced Drummond as an operative with the firm who had been sent by the powers that ruled them to watch Christopher's back.

"Just in case the Frenchies try to kidnap you," Drummond had dourly informed him.

Christopher had exchanged a long-suffering look with Fredericks, then studied Drummond.

The middle-aged man—tending to portly, brown-haired, brown-eyed, the sort of man who would pass largely unremarked by most—had caught Christopher's eye and opined, "I don't think that's at all likely, any more than you do, but we all know better than to waste breath arguing with Powell, especially not when he's got Castlereagh behind him."

Fredericks had handed Christopher a glass of whiskey. "You've grown too damned valuable to the firm, my friend. In the circumstances, they're not going to let you venture anywhere without protection."

Christopher had snorted and downed the whiskey. He'd savored the glow, then asked, "Have you given Drummond the description of the man you saw?"

Fredericks had nodded. "I'd swear he has a military background, possibly even still serving, but beyond the word of the street sweeper, I don't know that he was French."

"Was the boy sure it was French the fellow muttered and not some other language?" Drummond had raised the glass he'd held and sipped.

"He was. Apparently, there are émigrés living near the boy's home, and he's familiar with the language—enough to be sure."

"Well"—Christopher had carefully set down his glass on a side table—"all we can do is keep our eyes peeled for the man, but if by chance he does follow us into the country, it sounds as if he'll stand out like the proverbial sore thumb."

With nothing more to be said, Christopher had informed Drummond of the hour at which he wished to depart, causing Drummond to shudder, but he hadn't otherwise complained. Adhering to his orders, Christopher hadn't mentioned where he intended to go, and neither Fredericks nor Drummond had asked. The three of them had retired to their beds, with Drummond taking the spare room Christopher kept prepared to accommodate Foreign Office agents on temporary furlough, those he and Fredericks knew.

Now, Christopher reached the curricle and climbed to the seat, then accepted the reins from Drummond. He waited until the heavy man had hauled himself up to the perch behind the seat, then flicked the reins, setting the blacks trotting.

With London still slumbering, they made good time to Vauxhall

Bridge. After clattering across, Christopher turned his horses' heads sharply right and sent them pacing smartly down the Wandsworth Road. The day looked set to be overcast, with gray clouds obliterating any hint of blue, but there was no scent of rain on the nevertheless chilly breeze.

Finally, Drummond stirred and asked, "So where are we headed, then?"

"To my mother's dower house in a tiny village by the name of Little Moseley, by way of Guildford, Winchester, and Romsey." After a moment, Christopher added, "I didn't see anyone watching us or even taking note of our passing."

"No more did I," Drummond rumbled. "No doubt everyone who can is still sleeping."

Christopher grinned at Drummond's aggrieved tone; clearly, the man was not an early riser.

~

"He's *what*?" Stunned, Marion stared at Gordon Carter, a friend of her brother's she'd persuaded to help her.

A sharp breeze flicked the dangling ends of the ribbons of her bonnet into her face—almost as if the elements were laughing at her. About them, only a few hardy souls had braved the dismal afternoon to stroll on the lawns leading down to the Serpentine.

Gordon raked a hand through his hair and repeated, "Gone. He's not there. He should be at his desk, but he isn't, and no one knows where or why he's gone or when he's expected back." He paused, then added, "Given it's you—or rather, Robbie—who's asking, I did a little nosing around. It seems Osbaldestone was called into a private meeting with the Foreign Secretary yesterday afternoon. Powell attended as well, but no one else, and everyone's being terribly tight-lipped over what the meeting was about, but the gist of it is that Osbaldestone came out after the meeting, issued various orders to his underlings—essentially putting his desk in order—then he left the building and hasn't come back."

Marion struggled to keep the depth of her consternation from showing, with mixed success.

Gordon sighed. "Before you ask, I checked at his house, and he's not there, either. His housekeeper was in, and she said she thought he left before dawn in his curricle with another man, who had stayed overnight."

Marion drew in a deep, deep breath, then released it on a muted yet explosive "Damn!"

Realizing she'd shocked Gordon, she explained, "He attended Lady Selkirk's soirée yesterday evening. I was there, but he proved difficult to pin down. In retrospect, I should have tried harder." Even if it had meant chasing him down the street.

Clearly, she'd made a strategic error in following her brother's, the count's, and her own assumption that approaching Christopher in a social setting would be the easiest and least remarkable way of making contact. She should have had the sense to send a note via Carter to pave the way for such a social encounter, and now, it seemed, she'd missed her chance.

Yet she couldn't fail; Robbie, let alone everyone else, was counting on her.

She glanced at Gordon. "Do you have any idea where Osbaldestone has gone?"

Gordon grimaced. "Not the faintest. I asked around, and no one seems to have the slightest inkling. It's a complete mystery." He paused, then lowering his voice, added, "Everyone assumes that, for reasons unknown, he's been ordered into hiding. He's rather central to the war effort, you know."

She blinked. "He is?"

Gordon nodded. "He's…well, I've heard people say he's a master intelligencer, that he operates a network more widespread and comprehensive than that of any of our enemies—or our allies, come to that. He's the sort of fellow the higher-ups are inclined to protect at any cost."

She frowned. "I see." She wondered whether Robbie had known that. She doubted it, for it seemed that Christopher's true position in the firm was shaping up as a very real hurdle.

After a moment, she asked, "Do you know who the man who left with him is?"

"Not exactly, but I suspect he's one of ours, ordered to stick to Osbaldestone's side."

"A guard?"

"That would be my guess." Gordon reached into his pocket and drew out the letter Marion had given him that morning. He held it out. "In the circumstances, I didn't think you'd want this lying on Osbaldestone's desk until he got back. Given the season, that might not be until the new year."

She grimaced and took the letter. "That was sound thinking. Thank you for attempting to deliver this and for learning all you have." Where that left her…

"I wish I could have been more help." Gordon glanced around, confirming that there was hardly anyone about. He turned back to her and studied her face. "So how are you going to get Robbie's message to Osbaldestone now?"

She allowed her frustration to show. "To be perfectly honest, I really don't know."

CHAPTER 2

Therese, Lady Osbaldestone, sat in her favorite wing chair in her private parlor, her gaze resting fondly on the bent heads of three of her grandchildren. Jamie, George, and Lottie had bowled up to the manor two days before, and now, the trio were clustered on the rug before the fire, playing a game of spillikins in rather desultory fashion, much as if their mood matched the weather—overcast and damp.

As they had in years past, the three had arrived to spend the weeks preceding Christmas with Therese, her household, and the denizens of Little Moseley. This was the trio's fourth such visit, and if their enduring enthusiasm was any guide, the village's Christmas events continued to exert a powerful attraction, one Therese and the children's parents—Therese's younger daughter, Celia, and her husband, Rupert, Earl of Winslow—were happy to accommodate, deeming the time the youngsters spent interacting with and appreciating the ways of ordinary village folk to be an excellent preparation for their subsequent, more exalted roles.

In truth, other than during their visit to the village each year, the three had little contact with those outside their elevated social circle.

Therese watched as the three reached the end of the game and started to count up their points with a notable lack of their customary eager energy; it appeared that they were already bored. Accepting, as she had in years past, that she would be wise to find some quest into which she could direct their energies, she cast about for some task that might suit. In the first year they'd spent with her, there had been missing geese to find, while the second year's task had been to hunt down a missing book of Christmas carols. Last year, they had assisted in locating the local Roman hoard. Unfortunately, this year, she found herself at a loss for a suitably distracting project that would interest and absorb them and keep them amused.

Admittedly, they were all a year older—Jamie, more correctly Lord James, was nearly eleven years old, while George had recently turned ten, and Lottie was an inquisitive eight years old. But from Therese's memories of her own brood, an extra year only meant that, if left to their own devices, the adventures they might dream up and the resultant scrapes would simply be of a greater, potentially more disruptive magnitude.

The three were setting the last of the spillikins back in the box and Therese was still casting about for inspiration as to what to suggest next when the sound of gravel crunching under carriage wheels reached them.

All three youthful heads rose, rather like hounds alerting.

Therese looked at the window facing the front lawn. "That sounds like a carriage coming up our drive. Apparently, someone has come to call—I wonder who."

Jamie, George, and Lottie leapt to their feet and rushed to peer out of the lead-paned window.

Therese smiled at the three and shook her head. She should tell them that it was really not acceptable for young gentlemen and ladies of their class to evince such rabid curiosity as to press their noses to the glass, but she had to admit, she was curious herself. She wasn't expecting any visitors, and aside from the discouragement of the louring skies, it was a trifle late for any incidental callers.

"It's a bang-up curricle with a pair of neat blacks between the shafts," Jamie informed the room at large.

Of course, the boys' eyes had gone first to the carriage and horses.

Predictably, it was Lottie who observed, albeit uncertainly, "Isn't that Uncle Christopher?"

Therese blinked and sat up. "Christopher? Great heavens!" She'd had no inkling her third son might be in the area, much less that he would stop by.

She got to her feet as George confirmed, "Yes! That's him!"

Knowing Christopher was a firm favorite with the children, Therese wasn't surprised to see all three quit the window and, in a headlong rush, make for the door. "Wait, children!"

They pulled up and looked at her inquiringly.

"Give the poor man a chance to get inside and hand over his coat before you mob him."

All three grinned at her and waited, transparently impatiently.

From beyond the door, the sounds of arrival drifted to their ears, then Crimmins opened the door, and Christopher strolled in.

To give them their due, the children glanced at Therese. She nodded, and like a pack of puppies let off the leash, they cheered and rushed Christopher, milling about him, clamoring, bouncing, and eagerly welcoming him and, in the next breath, asking why he was there.

Therese fought back a grin of her own as she watched Christopher deal with the now-rambunctious trio; his arrival had transformed them, reigniting their customary eagerness and keen interest in everything around them.

Christopher bent to talk to them, and she let her gaze travel over him. Although she never would have voiced the thought, in her eyes, he was the handsomest of her three sons, elegant and graceful in a way neither Monty nor Lionel had ever been. She took note of the cut of his coat, pristine linen, and subdued waistcoat and approved. Although her son-in-law Lord North was more senior, to her mind, it was Christopher who was destined to carry on the Osbaldestone legacy at the Foreign Office; if her husband, Gerald, had still been with them, she felt sure he would think the same.

Eventually, Christopher managed to satisfy his nephews and niece sufficiently for them to allow him to come forward and buss her cheek. "Good afternoon, Mama. You're looking well."

Therese reached up and patted his cheek. "Thank you, my dear." She waved to the chaise facing her chair. "Do sit, and you may tell me and the children to what we owe the unexpected pleasure of your company."

She resumed her seat and watched him settle on the chaise. The children immediately swarmed him, with Lottie wriggling into place on his left and George on his right. As befitted his position as eldest of the three, Jamie sat beside George.

Once the three had stopped squirming, Christopher looked at Therese. "Castlereagh and Powell are concerned that Napoleon's agents might be taking too great an interest in me, and despite the current state of affairs on the Continent, they've ordered me away from my desk and out of London until they've convinced themselves the agents have been rounded up or been dissuaded sufficiently to leave the country."

"Ah," Therese said. "I see. They're more concerned with ensuring they have your input for the negotiations that will come once the Corsican is removed."

Christopher grinned. "Just so."

"And how close are we to that moment?"

"Much closer than we were a few months ago." Enthusiasm flowed into Christopher's voice, and his eyes lit with the same sort of devotion to a subject that Therese often saw in his niece's and nephews' gazes. Without prompting, he went on, "Since October and the Battle of Leipzig and the surrender of Pamplona, the action has fallen very much our and our allies' way. On the Peninsula, Wellington is currently dug in for winter in the foothills of the Pyrenees—meaning the Peninsula itself is now essentially entirely in allied hands. Courtesy of directives from above, Wellington had to split his command. He's currently with the major force, including the majority of the Spanish and Portuguese armies, at the northwestern end of the Pyrenees, facing Soult, and he left a sizeable force at the southeastern end, facing Suchet. Word is that neither force will be able to move until sometime in January."

Christopher barely paused to draw breath; Therese noted how avidly all three children, even Lottie, were hanging on his every word. "Meanwhile, on Napoleon's eastern flank, after the Battle of Leipzig, the allied armies split. Von Bulow, Wintzingerode, and Bernadotte are commanding the Army of the North—they're currently spread along the west bank of the Rhine between Wesel and Frankfurt and aim to eventually press toward Brussels and then sweep south. In the center of the line—roughly due east of Paris—Prince Blücher led the Army of Silesia to a position somewhere near Wurzburg. I believe he's set his sights on taking Mainz and eventually Metz. Somewhere south of that, about level with Dijon, Prince Schwarzenberg is in command of the Army of Bohemia—word is he's swung through Switzerland, which is not making the Swiss happy at all, but Napoleon is mustering his army somewhere between Reims and Troyes, and Schwarzenberg is looking to attack from the southeast while Blücher strikes head-on, as it were, from the east. While Wellington, the Spaniards, and the Portuguese hold the south and keep Soult and Suchet occupied, and Bellegarde is in position to challenge Eugene in Northern Italy, the others—von Bulow and Bernadotte, Blücher, and Schwarzenberg—plan to press on and drive Napoleon back into France and, this time, all the way to Paris."

Therese smiled. "I'm sure that will make Emperor Alexander happy." Her correspondents had told her that, immediately after Leipzig,

Alexander had wanted to continue and push Napoleon all the way back to Paris, but the other commanders had insisted on regrouping first.

Christopher grinned. "It will, indeed. I believe Blücher and Schwarzenberg are itching to move, but of course, they have to consider the weather. My information is that von Bulow and company won't be ready to sweep south until somewhat later, but I suspect that won't matter. The fact they are there and threatening all along the northern section of the Rhine is enough to keep the French command stretched over an impossible-to-hold line."

Eyes wide, Jamie asked, "Does that mean Napoleon will be defeated soon?"

Christopher glanced down and met his nephew's eyes. "That, my lad, is everyone's fondest hope."

"But when is soon?" George asked.

Christopher tipped his head and considered, then ventured, "It won't be in the next two months, and Napoleon won't surrender without a fight, so…possibly late April, most likely May, possibly even into June. But by the middle of the year, I would say."

"Yay!" the children cheered.

For her part, Therese nodded decisively. "Given that, I can certainly see Castlereagh's point in wanting to keep you safely tucked away. If he's going to be negotiating within months with Alexander, Bernadotte, the Prussians, and the Hapsburgs, let alone the Italians, then he'll want your network operating at full capacity."

"Indeed. My contacts in the various allied courts will be crucial." He glanced at her and smiled. "Some of them, I'm sure you'll know." He named several informants, and Therese responded with her recollections of what position each had held when she and Gerald had known them.

As Therese spoke and Christopher responded, she noticed that, far from losing interest, all three children were avidly drinking in the information—information that was, as it happened, of the highly secret sort. It occurred to her that perhaps she should warn Christopher about saying too much before the three, yet it was exceedingly likely that she would need to employ the children's observational skills if she wished to keep apprised of what Christopher got up to about the village. Especially if any foreign agent managed to track him there.

She decided it was arguably more sensible for the three to learn what was at stake directly from Christopher's lips. Consequently, she kept hers shut and let him speak freely.

Eventually, Christopher grimaced and ruefully admitted, "After hearing myself relating all that, it's impossible to argue that, strategically speaking, ordering me out of London wasn't the right decision. My juniors can keep things ticking along for a few weeks, but when it comes to the negotiations, the subtleties will be critically important, and Castlereagh, Powell, and the others will need me there to identify and interpret those."

His mother smiled, transparently pleased and proud of his status within the department to which, as his father's hostess, she'd devoted much of her adult life.

Then she fixed him with an openly curious look. "While I'm pleased you chose to take refuge here, I own to being surprised you thought of this place. Was there some specific reason why Little Moseley called to you?"

He smiled and looked at the children. "Well, aside from spending the time being entertained by my favorite nephews and niece"—the children promptly beamed at him—"one of the attributes that indicated Little Moseley might be the perfect place to, as Powell put it, 'go to ground' was that I haven't been here previously." He looked at his mother. "There's no record in anyone's memory of me coming here, ergo no reason to suppose I would venture here now."

His mother nodded regally. "As I've been out of Foreign Office circles for so long, I doubt anyone currently in the firm would know about Hartington Manor. Although several of your father's and my peers contacted me around the time of his death, I hadn't, then, returned here, so this place wouldn't appear in anyone's address book."

"Quite. And as I explained to Powell and Castlereagh, you and your staff will readily comprehend my need for a bolt hole and what that entails. None of your staff are likely to spread the word that I'm here."

"No, indeed. And although my closest friends know of the manor, those in the wider ton do not." His mother arched her brows. "Given my closest friends are a highly select group, I doubt you need concern yourself about them sharing the information with anyone who asks."

He inclined his head in acceptance; his mother's closest friends were an extremely canny bunch—while they accumulated intelligence better than any spies, they rarely if ever shared what they knew, except with each other. "I can't think of anyone among my wider acquaintance who would think to look for me here. More than anything else, that was what influenced me to throw myself on your mercy."

"I will admit I'm looking forward to having you about, and I'm sure the children are, too." His mother looked at the children inquiringly, and they promptly cheered.

Christopher grinned.

His mother caught his eye. "How long do you think you'll need to remain?"

"If the matter's resolved quickly, Powell will send for me, but if I'm not summoned back by the week before Christmas, I'll stay and travel with you to Winslow."

"Yay!" the children cheered even louder.

"You'll be able to come to all the village events!" Lottie declared.

When Christopher looked unsure, George eagerly explained, "The village always holds at least three main events in the weeks leading up to Christmas—the skating party on the lake, the village pageant on the green, and the carol service in the church."

"And we always attend them all," Jamie said. "You'll have to come, too—it's great fun!"

The excitement in their faces and voices was impossible to miss.

"You won't be bored," Lottie said, leaning against his arm and looking cajolingly into his face. "I promise!"

Still unsure what such events might entail—what he might be letting himself in for—Christopher cast a questioning glance at his mother.

She smiled and confirmed, "The children return here every year to experience those events. I think you'll find it will be perfectly safe for you to be seen going about with them. It's a small village, and once the locals learn who you are, they'll consider you to be one of us—they will certainly not speak of you to outsiders, meaning those not known to them. And if any strangers do appear, I assure you these three"—she nodded to the trio surrounding him—"and their friends will be among the first to know." Her lips quirked, and she met his eyes. "They always are."

"I see." He looked at Lottie, then at George and Jamie.

Taking that as an invitation, the three immediately bombarded him with descriptions of the village, the people who inhabited it, and what they considered to be enjoyable outings and experiences to be had within its environs.

Watching the children's performance, and taking note of the increasingly besieged expression in her son's eyes, Therese stifled a laugh. Clearly, she need look no further for a task to keep her grandchildren amused.

When the children eventually ran down and, having finally comprehended that, in taking refuge in Little Moseley, he might have ventured into an arena of activity he hadn't foreseen, Christopher arched a wary brow at her, Therese smiled and inclined her head. "I second the children's enthusiastic notions. Now you're here and the festive season is upon us, you mustn't miss the chance to experience the full glory of Christmas in Little Moseley."

~

After sharing dinner with the children and his mother, Christopher retreated to the room he'd been given upstairs. A medium-sized chamber with a decent-sized bed, wardrobe, tallboy, and two armchairs angled before a cheerily crackling fire, it was a comfortable space. He closed the door, then checked and confirmed that his new valet-cum-groom had unpacked his clothes into the tallboy's drawers and hung his coats in the wardrobe.

Even his brushes were neatly aligned on the top of the tallboy.

Smiling, Christopher crossed to the armchair that afforded a view of the door and sat, relaxed, and waited.

Sure enough, five minutes later, a knock fell on the door. It opened, and Drummond walked in.

After closing the door, he walked to the other armchair and slumped into it—an action that was hardly in keeping with his supposed role, but Christopher didn't bother mentioning the lapse.

At Drummond's insistence, Christopher hadn't mentioned to anyone —not even his mother—that Drummond wasn't who he was pretending to be but a guard provided by the firm. During the drive from London, Christopher had voiced his doubts over Drummond being able to pull the wool over his mother's, her staff's, and even more, the children's sharp eyes, but Drummond had been arrogantly confident in his chameleon-like abilities, especially regarding the children, so subsequently, Christopher had held his tongue.

Now, surveying Drummond, who looked far more like one of the merchants he habitually masqueraded as than any valet or groom Christopher had ever seen, he wondered how long it would be before the children at least—highly observant and with an innate understanding of the relative behaviors of the different social orders—unmasked Drummond.

"So," Drummond said, fixing Christopher with a sharp look of his own, "what do you know of the staff here?"

"I know the Crimminses and Orneby of old and Simms, too. Those four hail from the time Mama was mistress of Osbaldestone House in London. The others are new to me."

Drummond nodded. "Those others are locals, and the lot of them are what one would term 'loyal to the bone' and, I judge, reliable. Very settled and with no tensions that I've noticed." He paused, then patted his well-rounded stomach. "I have to say that the cook, Mrs. Haggerty, is a gem."

Christopher hid a grin. "I take it you're finding the accommodations comfortable?"

Drummond nodded. "Comfortable and tasty. More than I expected, truth to tell. Now!" Drummond straightened in the chair. "I've had a quick gander up the lane and chatted a bit with the staff. The church—St. Ignatius on the Hill—is more or less opposite, as we saw when we drove in, and the graveyard and vicarage lie alongside. Going farther north on that side of the lane, next up is the village green, followed by a row of cottages with Mountjoy's Store, which is the main shop and also the post office, between. Haven't actually seen it yet, but that's what I've gathered. Opposite Mountjoy's is Bilson the Butcher and Butts Bakery. Nearer to here, opposite the green, is the village's public house, the Cockspur Arms. I gather there's a few more cottages scattered here and there, but essentially, that's the sum total of the village."

A map of the village forming in his mind, Christopher frowned. "What about the other houses, not cottages, associated with the village?"

"So far, I've heard of Dutton Grange—we passed the drive on the other side of the lane as we drove into the village. Seems the house itself is more or less south of this one. It's home to a Lord Longfellow, who it might pay to be aware of."

"Oh? Why?"

"Seems he was a major in the dragoons and fought in Spain—he was injured and sold out when his father died. He's been back for about four years. His sergeant, a man called Hendricks, and a batman, Jiggs, returned with him. Hendricks is now his lordship's majordomo, and Jiggs is his groom."

Christopher nodded thoughtfully. "If anything does blow up while we're here, Longfellow and his men might be useful allies. Not that I imagine anything will erupt, but it's comforting to know we have backup if needed."

Drummond huffed in agreement. "His lordship's married now, and he and his wife have two children, both boys, one a toddler and the other a babe-in-arms."

Christopher regarded Drummond with increasing respect. "You've collected a decent amount of intelligence in just a few hours."

Drummond shrugged noncommittally. "I'm good at playing curious and unthreatening, and people like to talk."

Christopher inclined his head. "Over dinner, the children—who have visited here for four years now and are a mine of local information—mentioned a Fulsom Hall, located at the other end of the village and owned by a youngish gentleman, one Sir Henry Fitzgibbon, who at this time of year usually plays host to three or four other young gentlemen. From what I could gather, those visitors all hail from well-heeled and established families. In a pinch, they might be useful as well."

Drummond nodded. "Duly noted. I'll see what more I can learn tomorrow. Anything else?"

"Yes. There's another largish house, Swindon Hall, which I gather is farther north along the lane toward Romsey. The owner is an older retired soldier known as Major Swindon. It seems it's just him and his wife there at present." Christopher watched Drummond absorb the information, no doubt slotting it into the map he, too, would be building in his head. For both of them, this was normal procedure when finding themselves in a new location—scout out the surroundings and learn who lived around about.

Finally, Drummond's gaze refocused on Christopher's face. "How are we going to play this, then? Me keeping you safe?"

Christopher arched his brows. "As far as I can see, the only time there could possibly be any danger is when I'm out and about the village."

Drummond snorted. "There's really no reason for you to go wandering about, though, is there? You could sit comfy here, inside the house, and wait out the time until we hear from London."

Christopher smiled wryly. "That might have been possible were my nephews and niece not here. I've already been informed that they're looking forward to showing me the sights of Little Moseley, and I gather there are several village events—a skating party, some sort of pageant, and a carol service—that the children believe it's obligatory I attend."

When Drummond frowned, presumably thinking to protest, Christopher blithely went on, "However, my mother confirmed that, as I hypothesized, no stranger, much less any foreigner, will be able to haunt the village without being noted and remarked upon."

Drummond grimaced, then somewhat reluctantly tipped his head. "While I haven't yet been over the ground myself, I admit that's the feeling I'm getting. I hadn't truly grasped how small this village is and how tucked away from everywhere."

Christopher left it at that; he couldn't imagine Jamie, George, and Lottie allowing him to remain indoors—not unless it sleeted and snowed continuously. They were an intrepid trio and so very eager to show him around a place they clearly viewed as special.

Drummond had slumped back in the armchair. "You know, I feel I'm here under false pretenses."

Christopher arched his brows. "You are here under false pretenses."

Drummond waved dismissively. "I don't mean my cover. But as far as I can see, there's really no need for me to be here at all. I mean, what's going to happen?" He raised his hands. "Even if a Frenchie shows up here, you're going to hear about it soon enough." Drummond eyed Christopher assessingly. "You may spend your days behind a desk now, but you were in the field for years. You know how to handle yourself—you don't need me. This assignment is a waste of my talents."

Christopher could understand Drummond's disaffection. "What's your usual type of mission?"

"Impersonation almost always," Drummond replied. "I usually go in as a merchant or businessman. Gentry-ish, but not quite. You know the sort—backbone of the country, self-made man of business, that sort of thing." Drummond shifted. "I was in and out of Moscow over the past six months, keeping an eye on their supply lines there. Before that, I was in Austria, doing much the same."

Christopher could see that Drummond's usual roles—those he was most adept at filling—wouldn't have prepared him for being a valet-cum-groom. He wasn't used to having staff, and he also wasn't used to being staff; he had little to no insight into how a man behaved in such a position. Christopher frowned. "Do you have any idea why they tapped you on the shoulder for this one?"

Drummond heaved a heavy sigh. "I was told that, although it's not my usual type of operation, they were shorthanded because it's the end of the year and the coffers were running low. They weren't about to call in extra agents in this season, not when I was sitting there, temporarily free and twiddling my thumbs."

"Ah," Christopher cynically replied. "I see." After a moment, he added, "I have to agree that expecting French agents to turn up here, chasing me, is altogether a waste of time. I seriously doubt we'll see any action during our stay in Little Moseley."

CHAPTER 3

After breakfast the following morning, Christopher returned to his room to collect his hat and gloves. When he opened the door and walked in, his gaze fell on Drummond, slouched in the chair he'd occupied the previous evening and reading yesterday's copy of *The Times*.

Hardly the picture of a proper valet-cum-groom.

Drummond glanced up as Christopher shut the door.

"What are you doing here?" Christopher asked.

"Hiding." Drummond shook the news sheet. "If I spend too much time downstairs, plainly without having a task to occupy me, I'm afraid Mrs. Crimmins will set me to work on some ordinary household chore that I have no idea how to do."

Christopher considered that scenario, then tipped his head. "A pertinent danger, to be sure." He walked to the tallboy, rifled through the drawers, and found his gloves. After shutting the drawer, carrying the gloves in one hand, he reached for the hat sitting on the tallboy's top.

"Here." Drummond sat up. "Where do you think you're off to?"

"Church." Christopher made for the door.

Drummond lumbered to his feet. "Surely your soul will manage if you don't attend for a few weeks?"

"Very likely." Christopher paused with his hand on the doorknob. "However, as my mother was quick to point out, in a village such as this, *not* turning up will attract far more attention and raise more questions than if I play the role of dutiful son and uncle and escort my mother and the children to Sunday service. Moreover, if I play least in sight instead, that will certainly raise eyebrows and suspicions with the staff here and make my mother wonder just how serious matters are. I would prefer to avoid that, if possible."

Drummond heaved a put-upon sigh.

Christopher grinned. "Console yourself with the thought that the usual gathering on the lawn after the service will be the perfect occasion for me to meet the other local families and establish my presence in the village as entirely unremarkable. Everyone will see me, learn who I am, and accept me as an innocuous visitor behaving in an entirely unsurprising way."

"All right." Drummond started toward the door. "Just give me a minute to get my hat and coat."

"We're walking. You'll be able to catch up." Christopher turned the knob, opened the door, and found himself looking at George, who had his hand raised as if he'd been about to knock.

For a second, George's expression remained blank, then his gaze cut past Christopher to Drummond as he lumbered up. Then George looked up at Christopher and smiled. "Are you ready, Uncle Christopher? We're all waiting in the hall."

"Yes, I'm coming." Christopher stepped forward, and George turned and trotted toward the stairs. Christopher shot a warning look at Drummond, hoping the man correctly interpreted it as an admonition to watch his behavior before the children. Christopher wouldn't wager against George having heard something of their conversation, and while the words might not have been all that revealing, the exchange hadn't been one between master and servant.

Pulling on his gloves, Christopher joined George at the head of the stairs, smiled, and nodded downward. "Let's go."

Christopher noted that Drummond caught up with the rest of the household staff as, in the wake of Christopher's mother, the children, and him, the group started up the path that wound up the hill to the church.

The day had dawned fine, a welcome relief from the gray dreariness that had held sway for the past week. Thin white clouds drifted across a pale-blue sky, and if the breeze was still cold, at least it wasn't icy. The pleasant weather put an extra brightness into people's smiles as groups nodded and greeted each other as, in an impressive stream, the congregation toiled upward toward the gray stone church.

A few carriages rolled past, heading for the area beside the church, but the bulk of parishioners walked, some, Christopher suspected, from the farms surrounding the village.

As he steadied his mother up the shallow steps, Christopher looked ahead and glimpsed the crowd already seated in the nave. He glanced back at those still approaching, then murmured to his mother, "This seems a very enthusiastic congregation. Is it always so devoted?"

"In this season, in general, yes." She met his eyes and smiled. "Farming families, my dear. Winter is their slow time, and at least in this village, attending church is a species of entertainment."

He wondered quite what she'd meant by that, but assumed he would learn soon enough. He duly escorted her to the second pew on the left; once the children had scampered in, his mother and Christopher followed, leaving him sitting at the aisle-end of the pew.

It was, he realized, a position of some prominence, leaving him easily seen by all as the congregation filed in and settled. Several of the local gentry exchanged smiles and nods, not only with his mother but, somewhat to Christopher's surprise, also with the children. In turn, the children beamed back, unabashedly confident and sure of their welcome. Of their place in village society.

Given that, as far as he'd ever heard, the trio spent only the weeks before Christmas in the village, that they were so well-known and patently well-regarded was…just a touch intriguing.

Then the minister appeared at the end of the nave, and the congregation rose and quieted. The minister, smiling serenely, paced down the aisle, followed by the choir, and in short order, the service began.

Although Christopher rarely attended services in London, he usually did when in the country, while staying with relatives or friends; somehow, the activity seemed to fit more appropriately in a pastoral setting. Consequently, he followed the prayers, sang the hymns, and generally participated without stumbling. He even found the sermon, mild and in no way radical, engaging in a gentle way.

By the time the last prayer was uttered and the benediction bestowed, he felt he understood the attraction that had lured such a goodly crowd to the church that morning. Despite his rather dithery appearance, Reverend Colebatch—Christopher's mother had whispered the minister's name—

was a sensible, benign, and quietly erudite man who was thoroughly in tune with the needs of his flock.

After the reverend had led the way up the aisle, Christopher offered his mother his arm, and they joined the rest of the congregation in filing out of the church. Along the way, his mother introduced him to Major and Mrs. Swindon, and they chatted as they shuffled toward Reverend Colebatch.

On reaching the good reverend, Christopher's mother introduced him, and he shook Colebatch's hand. "An entertaining sermon, Reverend. I look forward to hearing more."

"Excellent!" Colebatch beamed. "I take it you plan to remain in the village for the nonce?"

"Most likely for a few weeks, at least," Christopher confirmed.

"Well, you must make sure to attend the village Christmas celebrations." Reverend Colebatch smiled at the three children, who had assumed the demeanor of angels. "But I'm sure these three will ensure you don't forget, heh?"

The children beamed, and while her brothers nodded, Lottie slipped her small hand into Christopher's and piped, "We'll make sure Uncle Christopher comes along to everything."

Laughing, his mother drew him on and, with the children following, directed him onto the lawn.

They'd taken only a few steps when, from behind, Jamie called, "Grandmama, we're going to go and talk to the other children."

His mother didn't turn but raised a hand in acknowledgment. "Be sure to get back to the manor before lunchtime."

"Yes, Grandmama" came in three-part chorus.

Christopher glanced over his shoulder and saw the three dodging through the crowd in the direction of the graveyard. He faced forward. "What other children were they speaking of?"

"The other village children, of course," his mother serenely replied.

He glanced again toward the graveyard and saw the three being enthusiastically greeted by a bevy of other children, all of whom seemed to be farmers' or shopkeepers' offspring.

Intrigued, he slowed, captured by the sight of his high-born nephews and niece interacting freely with the village children. He saw no evidence of shyness or hesitation, not on any child's part.

Realizing he'd almost come to a halt, he faced forward and stepped out and found his mother eyeing him with her customary understanding.

He gestured toward the children. "They seem to fit in with the others remarkably well."

She nodded. "Indeed. And yes, I've encouraged the association. I've always believed that exposure to those of lower rank, especially during one's formative years, is invaluable in instilling an appropriate degree of understanding of others—of the feelings and concerns and anxieties felt by those of less power. That will stand all three of them in good stead in the future."

"Hmm." He couldn't help observe, "I have to agree that having that sort of understanding of others is a very valuable skill."

His mother cast him a smiling glance. "In our business, at least."

He tipped his head her way. "Indeed." Given the likely futures of Jamie, George, and Lottie, an ability to interact with others regardless of rank was a skill that would, indeed, be a definite advantage.

He and his mother continued across the lawn, and Christopher caught himself surveying the people, who were gathered in small groups, and scanning the shadows cast by the trees bordering the open expanse. He'd noticed that Drummond had left the church by another door and was now standing by one corner of the building, keeping watch over those assembled on the lawn.

In truth, he felt he and Drummond were overreacting. The scene before them was one of bucolic peace, and everyone he could see was readily identifiable as a villager—meaning that they were greeted by others and clearly belonged to the village community.

His mother steered him to a group standing not far from where Drummond lurked. Over the following fifteen minutes, he was introduced to and chatted with Lord and Lady Longfellow, of Dutton Grange, the house across the lane from the manor. They were a pleasant couple, easygoing and friendly. Longfellow was about Christopher's age and had served under Paget in Spain; he limped and bore bad shrapnel scars that had disfigured one side of his face, but clearly, he and everyone else had learned to ignore them. Lady Longfellow told a tale of the latest addition to their family, making the ladies laugh and the gentlemen smile, while Longfellow beamed with paternal pride.

The Swindons came up, bringing with them two older ladies. One was Mrs. Colebatch, the reverend's wife. A tall, plain-faced, but good-natured woman, she smiled at Christopher and gave him her hand. "It's a pleasure to make your acquaintance, Mr. Osbaldestone. Her ladyship's family are always welcome in Little Moseley."

"Hear, hear," Major Swindon echoed. "You'll be kept busy with the three scamps, no doubt." Turning to Christopher's mother, he asked, "What quest have they undertaken this year?"

"I believe," his mother replied in mock seriousness, "that they have yet to define what will be the object of their attentions this year."

Mrs. Swindon laughed. "Geese, a book of carols, and a Roman hoard. I can't wait to hear what this year's effort will be." Smiling, she turned to Christopher and gestured to the other older lady who had accompanied them across the lawn. "Pray allow me to present Mrs. Woolsey, sir. She lives at Fulsom Hall with her nephew, Sir Henry."

Mrs. Woolsey was rather older than the other ladies, perhaps even older than Christopher's mother. She cut a rather strange figure, well-wrapped in a warm winter coat, but with her head of fluffy white curls and her shoulders swathed in a plethora of colorful scarves. She smiled somewhat myopically at Christopher and held out a gnarled hand. "Such a pleasure, sir. Quite delightful to meet one of her dear ladyship's sons."

Christopher murmured the correct phrases and half bowed over her hand.

The instant he released her fingers, Mrs. Woolsey glanced around. "Have the children come this year as well?"

His mother smiled. "Indeed, they have. I've been assured that nothing would keep them away."

Mrs. Woolsey sighed happily. "Such a delight, to have children all aglow with the promise of Christmas running about under one's feet."

Christopher's respect for his three young relatives was growing apace; even the most unlikely adults seemed to view the trio with abundant goodwill.

"There you are, Cousin Ermintrude."

Along with the others in the circle, Christopher turned to see a bluff young gentleman come striding up.

Endowed with curly blond hair and blue eyes, he smiled good-naturedly at Mrs. Woolsey. "Thought I'd lost you, what?"

"Dear Henry." Mrs. Woolsey gripped the young man's sleeve. "You must meet Lady Osbaldestone's son." To Christopher, she said, "Allow me to present my nephew, Sir Henry Fitzgibbon of Fulsom Hall. Henry, this is Mr. Christopher Osbaldestone."

Henry smiled and thrust out his hand. "A pleasure, sir."

Christopher grasped his hand. "Likewise, Sir Henry."

Henry waved. "Oh, just Henry, please. We're all very informal here."

When Henry asked the Longfellows how his nephews were getting on, Christopher realized that Eugenia, Lady Longfellow, was Henry's sister. From the comments that subsequently flowed between Longfellow, Henry, and Major Swindon, it was clear that all three were engaged in managing small estates.

The conversation was winding down when four more young gentlemen—Christopher placed them in their early twenties—came strolling up and were greeted by all the others in the group.

Henry promptly introduced Christopher to Thomas Kilburn, heir to Lord Kilburn of Norwich, Roger Carnaby, heir to Lord Carnaby, George Wiley, heir to Viscount Worth, and lastly, Julian, Viscount Dagenham, who Christopher deduced was the eldest son of the Earl of Carsely.

From the corner of his eye, Christopher saw Drummond straighten and pay closer attention. While Christopher had discarded the notion of requesting support from either of the ex-majors, the younger gentlemen looked more promising. While he didn't foresee any actual action of the foreign-agent sort, it was second nature to assess who of those living nearby could be called on if needed.

Through the ensuing exchanges, Christopher learned that all four newcomers were friends of Henry, dating from their shared years at Oxford. "Although we're all down, now," George Wiley said, "we've decided to keep these few weeks as an annual get-together."

"A time to catch up and learn what we've each been doing through the year." Kilburn glanced at Henry. "We first came here for the weeks before Christmas…it must be four years ago, now."

Dagenham nodded. "This is our fourth year visiting the village." He glanced at Christopher and smiled, although Christopher noted the smile didn't reach the viscount's striking gray eyes. "There's always been something fresh to learn, some new experience to expand our horizons."

Christopher's instincts pricked, although he had no idea why, other than that he felt certain there was something specific behind Dagenham's apparently idle remark.

"Well." Mrs. Swindon claimed her husband's arm. "We must be away. Cheerio, all."

That triggered a general departure, with the Longfellows walking away along a path that wended through the trees bordering the lawn and the Colebatches heading through the graveyard to the vicarage beyond, pausing to speak with the large group of youngsters still playing between the gravestones. Henry and his four friends solicitously escorted Mrs.

Woolsey to Henry's curricle, then the others piled into two other carriages, and they drove off in convoy.

Christopher noticed his mother regarding the departing curricles with a considering eye. "What have I missed?" he asked.

She smiled and glanced at him. "I was just thinking how mature those five are becoming. They were anything but, the first year they were here."

He wound her arm in his and started them walking down the path toward the lane and the manor beyond. "Well, it is generally true that young men do, in the fullness of time, grow up."

"Indeed," his mother replied rather caustically. "But sadly, not all of them improve."

Deciding he didn't wish to attempt a riposte to that, Christopher kept his lips shut and walked on. He'd seen the staff go ahead, and a second later, the three children came pelting up and settled to pace and, in Lottie's case, skip alongside.

Christopher smiled at the three, then glanced briefly back and saw Drummond strolling in their wake.

Consulting his instincts, Christopher realized that they and he had relaxed to a quite remarkable degree.

Indeed, as he faced forward, he registered that even Drummond was ambling in a decidedly relaxed fashion.

The effect of Little Moseley, he supposed.

Smiling more definitely, he guided his small party across the lane and on up the manor drive.

~

Given Drummond's comments and the quality of the dinner Christopher had savored the previous evening, he'd been looking forward to Mrs. Haggerty's luncheon, and she didn't disappoint. The roast beef was succulent, the gravy tangy and savory, and the custard trifle a honeyed delight.

Christopher hadn't been surprised when, soon after the children had joined them at the table, Jamie had asked, "Have you had Drummond as your man for long, Uncle Christopher?"

"You didn't have a man last year at Winslow," Lottie had pointed out.

"No. Drummond is a recent addition to my small household." Christopher had looked at his mother, seated at the other end of the dining table

—reduced in size to comfortably seat six—and held up the butter dish. "Butter, Mama?"

She'd met his eyes for a second, then smiled. "Thank you, dear. George, please pass the dish."

Christopher ended the meal being even more grateful for Mrs. Haggerty's delicious offerings. As the children had brought their appetites to the table and Crimmins had kept the courses coming, the trio had been too busy eating to instigate an inquisition on Drummond.

Regardless, Christopher didn't make the mistake of thinking the three didn't harbor suspicions of his recently acquired valet-cum-groom. And if the look his mother had bent on him prior to deigning to aid his diversion with the butter dish was any guide, she, too, suspected Drummond wasn't quite as he was struggling to appear.

The instant the children's dessertspoons clattered into their empty dishes, Christopher asked, "Did you learn anything exciting from your friends?"

The three exchanged a brief glance. "Only that the first practice for the carol service will be held on Tuesday," Jamie said.

"We sing in the choir for the Christmas carol service," Lottie explained.

"But we won't join the Sunday choir until closer to Christmas," George added, "when they start singing the Christmas songs."

Christopher glanced at his mother. "I take it the choir for the carol service is a special one."

The children nodded, and Jamie said, "It's open to all the visitors to the village. We always join, and for the last two years, Melissa did as well, and last year, Mandy did, too."

"I see." Christopher vaguely remembered hearing that, the previous year, his sister Henrietta's daughters had also joined the manor household for these pre-Christmas weeks.

"Henry and his friends join, too—just for the carol service," George added.

"Viscount Dagenham and Melissa sang 'The Holly and the Ivy' as a duet." Lottie's eyes were wide. "It was really beautiful."

Christopher noticed his mother trying to suppress a smile, then her obsidian gaze rose to his face, and even at that distance, he sensed her amusement. He returned his attention to the children. "So what else is there to know about the village?"

The upshot of that unwise request was the children insisting he accompany them on a village tour.

He wasn't sure that was a good idea and looked at his mother, hoping for deliverance, only to see her glance out of the window at the pale winter sunshine bathing the manor's gardens.

"As the weather is obliging, I suggest you make the most of it." She smiled at the children. "In this season, one needs to take advantage of such days."

"Yes!" they chorused.

They all looked at him expectantly, and Christopher discovered he really didn't want to quash their enthusiasm—and perhaps it would be wise to use a Sunday afternoon, when most adults in the village would remain indoors, somnolent after their Sunday dinners, to get a better idea of the layout of the village and its immediate surrounds. Slowly, he nodded. "All right."

The children cheered wildly and leapt from their seats. Gabbling farewells to their grandmother, they raced upstairs to fetch coats, gloves, mufflers, and hats.

Grinning—unable not to—Christopher rose and, after nodding to his mother, followed them from the room.

He'd left his gloves and hat in the hall, along with his greatcoat, which Crimmins helped him don. While Christopher waited for the children to return, he remembered Drummond and told Crimmins, "Please let Drummond know that I'm being taken by the children to see the village sights. He can follow if he wishes."

Crimmins bowed slightly. "Of course, sir."

The children came clattering down the stairs, eager to rush outside. Laughing, Christopher let them take his hands and tow him out of the door that Crimmins held wide.

"Come on!" Lottie tugged him down the step and onto the drive.

George and Jamie had been conferring. Now, Jamie said, "We'll take you up one side of the lane, then down the other."

"That way," George explained, "you won't miss anything."

"Whatever you think best," Christopher returned. "I place myself in your hands."

That put wide grins on all three faces.

When they reached the lane, Christopher glanced over his shoulder and saw Drummond, his hands sunk in his coat pockets and his expression dour, plodding along behind them.

Facing forward, Christopher attempted to smother a grin of his own, but only partially succeeded.

The children steered him to the right, around the bend in the lane, past a small, neatly kept cottage and on to their first stop, the Cockspur Arms.

Halting in the small yard before the front door, Jamie informed him, "This is the only public house in the village, and it's used by everyone around about, including from all the farms and cottages farther afield."

"At this time on a Sunday, there'll be a lot of farmhands and some of the farmers and their wives inside," George said.

It was Lottie who gave him the most pertinent information. "The Whitesheafs own it. Mr. and Mrs. Whitesheaf are rather old now—we don't often see them working there anymore. Their sons, Rory and Cam, are usually the ones behind the bar, and Ginger, their sister, is the waitress."

The inn sat directly across the lane from the village green. Glancing in that direction, Christopher saw that Drummond had halted a few steps away, close enough to have overheard the children's comments.

"Come on!" Lottie towed him on. "We've lots more to see yet."

The three led him—and Drummond, who closed the distance to a respectful few yards—northward up the lane, past another small cottage to two freestanding shops—Butts Bakery and Bilson the Butcher.

"Mrs. Butts makes the best buns," George said rather reverently.

"Ben Butts sometimes plays with us, but he's a bit older, and Mrs. Butts tends to keep him busy these days," Jamie reported.

"And this," Lottie said, towing Christopher onward, "is the Bilsons' shop, where Mrs. Haggerty gets all her meats. Annie and Billie Bilson are twins. They're a bit younger than me, but we let them play with us."

Having apparently imparted all they considered noteworthy about the Bilsons, the children looked up the lane, then turned to Christopher.

"We could take you on to the end of the lane, where it meets the main lane that continues north, but other than a few cottages, there's not much to see on this side of the lane." Jamie indicated the right side of the lane. "And on the other side, all we'd see are the opening of the drives to Tooks Farm and Fulsom Hall."

"Farmer Tooks and his wife run Tooks Farm," Lottie said. "And Johnny and Georgie Tooks are great friends of ours."

George nodded. "Johnny will be minding the village's flock of geese up at Allard's End at the moment."

"We'll show you that later," Lottie assured Christopher.

"You've already met Mrs. Woolsey and Henry and the others who are staying at Fulsom Hall," Jamie said. "And Grandmama said she was thinking of calling there tomorrow, so there's no point going up there today." He swung to face the other side of the lane. "So we might as well turn around here."

Amused, Christopher allowed them to steer him around.

"This"—Jamie gestured to what appeared to be the largest shop in the village—"is Mountjoy's Store."

"Run by the Mountjoys," George put in, "both old Mr. and Mrs. Mountjoy and their son and his wife."

Christopher waited expectantly, then asked, "No children?"

"No," Jamie said.

"Well," Lottie amended, "there's Gordon, the younger Mountjoys' son, but he's only three so doesn't come out to play."

Christopher looked at the shop front. "So what do they sell?"

"Most things," George said. "All sorts of goods, as well as fruit and vegetables from the farms."

"There's also maps of the area pinned up on one wall," Jamie said.

Christopher glanced at Drummond, hovering nearby, and received a slight nod in reply. Maps were always useful; Drummond would no doubt return when the shop was open and see what he could learn of the area.

"The Mountjoys also run the post office for the village," Lottie said.

Christopher and Drummond took note of that as well.

They were turning away from the shop when a hail had them pausing and looking up the lane.

Henry and his four friends smiled as they strode up.

"Well met, young Skeltons!" Henry beamed at the children, then nodded to Christopher. "Osbaldestone. Are you being given the village tour?"

Christopher smiled. "I am."

Kilburn waved down the lane. "We're on our way to the Arms. Can we tempt you to join us?"

Seeing the looks of consternation that bloomed on the children's faces, still smiling, Christopher said, "I rather suspect I have more village scenery to take in first. Perhaps another time."

The children beamed at him, and Lottie gripped his hand more tightly.

"Well, we'll at least walk with you to the village green." Henry waved onward, and the combined party ambled on, with Drummond, ignored by all, bringing up the rear.

Henry engaged the children, asking about the skating party and whether they'd heard anything about the songs chosen for the carol service.

Viscount Dagenham fell in beside Christopher, pacing easily by his side. "I hope you won't mind if I pick your brains a trifle, Osbaldestone. The thing is, I've been with the Home Office for the past year—with Pritchard on the Irish desk—and I've been tossing up whether a move to the Foreign Office might better suit. I gather you've been with the FO for years."

Christopher chuckled. "I'm an FO brat—my father was FO before me. You might say I was born and bred to sit behind a desk there."

His hands sunk in his pockets, his gaze on the lane before his feet, Dagenham concluded, "So you know the firm inside and out."

"I'm happy to answer any questions you have." Christopher was often approached by younger men curious about what life in the service was like.

"I'm aware of the positions of Lords Castlereagh, Powell, and North," Dagenham said, "but I'm not sure of the internal structures, so have no idea if I would be a suitable fit. Can you explain how things are set up?"

Christopher understood what he was asking and, given it wasn't any great secret, readily outlined the hierarchy of the department. Then he paused and looked at Dagenham. "But having said all that, I believe you're your father's heir." When Dagenham glanced at him and nodded, Christopher went on, "All the aristocrats in the FO are second or later sons. They might have higher titles bestowed on them during their careers, but none of them sit in the Lords by birthright, which, one day, you will."

"Ah." After a moment, Dagenham nodded. "Yes, of course."

"The way things work," Christopher said, "given that you are your father's heir, were you to move to the FO, you would almost certainly find yourself tied to some desk in London—definitely not dispatched on exciting missions in foreign climes."

His gaze on the lane ahead of them, Dagenham gave a short laugh. "As it happens, there's talk of sending me to Ireland soon, and many would consider that a foreign land."

Christopher chuckled. "True."

The company had drawn level with the Cockspur Arms. They halted and, with good wishes all around, parted. The five younger men headed for the inn's front door, while the children shepherded Christopher—and with a look, Drummond as well—onto the green.

"The lake is on the other side of the rise." Jamie pointed down the green to the far end, where the ground sloped upward, forming a low ridge that hid the land immediately beyond.

As they trudged over the grassy sward, George pointed to a stone wall to their left. "That's the vicarage garden."

Christopher looked and spotted the tiled roof of the vicarage and, in the distance, the top of the church tower.

They toiled up the rise, and when they reached the crest, they paused, and Christopher and Drummond swiftly took stock. Before them, the land sloped down to a dip filled by a decent-sized lake, presently frozen.

Beside Christopher, Lottie jigged. "The village skating party is held on the lake—provided Dick Mountjoy, Mr. Mountjoy's son, says the ice is solid enough."

"He's already declared it is," George added excitedly. "The skating party is to go ahead on Wednesday afternoon!"

"It's great fun." Lottie stared up into Christopher's face. "You'll have to come."

Christopher smiled at her and didn't reply. In his mind, he could hear Drummond muttering against any such public activity.

"That path over there"—Jamie pointed to their right—"leads along the back of the Mountjoys' land and on, all the way to the Fulsom Hall shrubbery."

"And *that* path"—not to be outdone, Lottie pointed to an opening to the left, a little way down the slope—"leads through the woods to the Grange."

"You can also take the path that hugs the vicarage wall and leads to the rear of the church," Jamie said. "From there, another path leads on to the Grange stable yard."

Christopher took due note and noticed Drummond doing the same.

"And if you look hard," George said, pointing across the lake and to the right, "there's a path that runs all the way from the lane between West Wellow and Romsey, past the back of Tooks Farm and the Fulsom Hall gardens, down through the woods, and over the stream to the far side of the lake. And from there it goes on"—from right to left, he traced the line of the woods bordering the southern shore of the lake—"past the lake and on through the woods, past the back of the Grange and Allard's End, and on past the back of Milsom Farm until it reaches the highway to Salisbury."

Mentally slotting the information away, Christopher murmured, "You certainly know your way about the place."

"Well, this is our fourth year visiting here," Lottie said.

"Let's go this way." Jamie turned back to take the path that followed the rear wall of the vicarage garden. "We can show you Allard's End if we hurry." He glanced at the western sky. "It'll start getting dark soon, and Grandmama likes us to be home before then."

Christopher fell in with the children, and Drummond followed at their heels. Christopher saw the children take note of Drummond, but while they exchanged glances Christopher suspected were laden with meaning, they made no comment regarding the other man's presence.

Quite what to make of that, Christopher wasn't sure.

As he paced along, he scanned the woods ahead and thought of what else the children might know that could prove useful. "Are there many farms close to the village?"

"A few." Jamie thought, then offered, "Tooks Farm is the closest, but if, from there, you follow the village lane around to the main lane that comes up from the highway and turn south along it, you'll come to Swindon Hall, and there's a farm attached to that. A little beyond that, on the opposite side of the road, is Witcherly Farm—one of the manor's maids, Tilly, comes from there."

"And across the lane from Witcherly Farm is Crossley Farm," George said. "The manor's gardener, Ned Foley, comes from there."

"If you continue south," Jamie went on, "past the other end of the village lane, you'll eventually come to Milsom Farm, about halfway to the highway. Other than the fields attached to the Grange, that's really all the farms around about."

"Or at least the farms we think of as village farms," Lottie clarified. "Some people who live in the cottages scattered about work on other farms farther away, but they're still thought of as village people."

They reached the end of the stone wall and emerged into the rear section of the graveyard. The children immediately spread out, dodging and skipping between the gravestones. Christopher grinned at the sight and murmured loud enough for Drummond, now by his shoulder, to hear, "I can remember doing the same. There's something about graveyards that invites children to run and play in them."

Drummond huffed, but didn't disagree.

As they left the last gravestones behind, the children closed in around Christopher again. Lottie once more took his hand and tugged. "Come on. We'd better hurry."

Increasing their pace, the trio dragged him along the path. When they emerged from the woods not far from what he took to be the Grange stable yard, they turned right and chivvied him along a rising track that led upward past well-tended fields to another crest in the land.

The track ended before an ancient ruined cottage.

"This is Allard's End," Jamie said. "Come on—let's see if Johnny's still here."

The children led Christopher and Drummond around the side of the dilapidated structure. Rounding the rear corner, Christopher saw a plantation of old trees stretching out across a small field. "It's an orchard."

"It's the goose-fattening orchard." Lottie pointed excitedly at the flock of birds foraging and pecking in the litter beneath the trees.

"And this is Johnny." Jamie and George towed forward a young lad, who judging by his lanky limbs must have been about thirteen years old.

Christopher smiled at the boy. "Hello."

Johnny mumbled something and bobbed his head.

"It's all right," Jamie told him. "This is our Uncle Christopher."

The information seemed to relieve Johnny of his anxiety. He brightened and shot Christopher a grin. "In that case, pleased to meet you, sir."

Christopher let his smile deepen and nodded at the birds. "Are they your charges?"

"Aye. I keep watch over them 'til it's time to get them ready for the table."

"Farmer Tooks supplies the geese for all the village houses' Christmas feasts," Lottie said. She stared at the flock. "I wonder which one will be ours."

Along with Johnny, the children went to look more closely at the birds.

"If it's all the same to you, I'd rather we stayed where we are," Drummond rumbled. "Geese don't like me."

Christopher chuckled. "I'm not sure they'll approve of me, either, and I can't see any reason to find out."

He stood and watched the children chatter with their friend and noted the way the weak winter sunlight slanted beneath the nearly bare branches as the sun dipped toward the horizon. Despite the sunshine, the air had stayed cold enough to guarantee that the ice on the lake remained solid.

Now that the sun was almost gone, the temperature started to slide even lower.

Christopher glanced around. It must have snowed days earlier; the remnants of drifts could still be seen beneath some of the larger trees.

The children noticed the fading light, took their leave of Johnny, and came racing back.

"We can head home now." Lottie caught Christopher's hand and dragged him around. Laughing, he let her tow him down the track.

With his nephews flanking them, they hurried along, past the fields that now lay fallow.

Christopher drew the crisp air deep into his lungs and sensed his own memories of long-ago winter holidays pressing close.

Looking at Jamie's, George's, and Lottie's faces, he noted the glow of simple pleasure that gilded their features. It had been a long time since he'd been touched by the same magic, yet he felt it now.

They paused by the stable yard fence to exchange hellos with a wiry man the trio introduced as Jiggs, Longfellow's groom—the major's ex-batman and another veteran of the Peninsula campaign.

Although they didn't dally beyond the introductions and a few words of explanation, both Christopher and Drummond took note. If anything happened and they needed assistance, Jiggs would be one to remember.

They finally reached the village lane again, not far from the entrance to the manor's drive.

Christopher was relieved when Jamie merely waved at the cottages to their right, and between them, the children rattled off who lived there.

"But now, we'd better get back to the manor." George led the way. "It's almost dark."

Finally, they were striding through lengthening shadows up the manor's drive. Christopher glanced at Drummond and saw an expression on the man's face that suggested he was busy mentally annotating the map of the village he carried in his head.

Smiling to himself, Christopher looked at the children, pacing quickly along. "Thank you for your excellent introduction to Little Moseley."

They turned beaming faces his way.

"Did you enjoy it?" Lottie asked.

Christopher smiled at her, then at the boys. "Indeed, I did. It was fun."

He followed the trio through the manor's door and into the front hall and realized he hadn't lied.

CHAPTER 4

An hour later, Jamie, George, and Lottie huddled in the shadows of the small alcove beside the head of the servants' stair on the manor's first floor. With their eyes trained on the stairs, they waited patiently.

Eventually, they heard the thud of heavy footsteps ascending, then Drummond's dark head appeared in the stairwell.

The children froze and watched as Drummond, with his gaze fixed on the treads and a stack of laundered shirts and cravats carelessly balanced on the palm of one hand, continued to climb.

Failing to spot them, he stepped off the last stair and straightened.

"Mr. Drummond," Jamie said commandingly as he, George, and Lottie stepped out of concealment, blocking Drummond's path.

"Eh?" Startled, Drummond's eyes flew wide, and he nearly dropped the pile of linen. Scowling, he juggled the garments and settled them once more on his wide palm, then looked at the children. Belatedly, he remembered his position, wiped his face of all expression, and only then remembered to say, "Yes, my lord?"

Jamie, along with George and Lottie, frowned at Drummond. "You may as well give up pretending to be a valet," Jamie advised him. "You're not very good at it."

Drummond attempted to look hurt. "I'm learning, aren't I? I'm new to the position—Mr. Osbaldestone only just hired me to be his valet-cum-groom."

"You've never been a valet in your life," George said. When Drummond looked his way, George nodded at the linen. "Those aren't folded properly. Papa would have a fit if Grenlin—his valet—brought him shirts folded like that."

"Let alone cravats like that." Lottie poked a finger at the pile, which was definitely askew and faintly creased.

"You surprised me, miss." Drummond tried for dignity. "I jiggled them and rumpled them."

A far cry from the sweet-faced angel Drummond had taken her for, Lottie narrowed eyes like flint on his face. "They were rumpled already—and it's 'my lady.'"

Drummond blinked, and Jamie pounced. "If you were really a valet, that's something you would already know and would never forget."

Feeling distinctly cornered, Drummond eyed the three warily. To his discomfort, their accusatory gazes never wavered.

"So who are you, really?" Jamie demanded. "Or should that be what are you?"

Seeing any chance of brushing the three and their suspicions aside drifting away like smoke, Drummond set his jaw and tried to wait them out.

They didn't move, didn't shift, and continued to watch him with the patience of a three-headed sphinx.

Eventually, he drew breath and grumpily admitted, "I'm from the firm—the Foreign Office. I was sent to stick close to your uncle and guard him." He omitted saying against what.

Jamie nodded. "That's what we thought."

Lottie said, "Uncle Christopher told us some French agent had been following him in London, which is why he's here now."

Drummond blinked again, faintly shocked that their uncle had told them that.

"Does he truly need a guard here in Little Moseley?" His gaze on Drummond's face, George tipped his head. "It's not as if French agents are likely to appear down here."

Drummond frowned. "He shouldn't have told you about the French agent."

"Well," George said, "he didn't specifically tell *us*. He told Grandmama, but we were there, so we heard as well."

"Oh." Not knowing what else the three had overheard, Drummond felt on uncertain ground.

"Do you usually spend your days guarding people like Uncle Christopher?" Jamie asked.

Trying to figure out what he should do with the three and sensing no danger in the question, Drummond replied, "No, not usually."

"So what do you *usually* do?" Lottie asked.

How much should he tell them? "I usually pretend to be a businessman or Squire Jones or something similar."

"Here in England?" George asked.

"No. Usually somewhere on the Continent. I'm generally over there." More to the point, what was *safe* to tell them?

"But what about your family?" Lottie asked. "Wouldn't you rather be with them for Christmas?"

While trying to work out how much of a disaster the three knowing too much might be, Drummond heard himself reply, "I've only got a brother and sister-in-law, and with any luck, this nonsense with your uncle will be over before Christmas, and I'll be back in London in time to join them for Christmas Day."

Jamie studied him rather censoriously. "Why do you call the threat to Uncle Christopher 'nonsense'?"

Drummond hissed through his teeth. That was what came of trying to think while being interrogated by three children too precocious for their own good. "Look, the threat isn't nonsense—I assume it's quite real. When he was in London, it *was* real. But I can't see any foreign agent getting at him here." He dropped all pretense. "I admit I didn't think much of the idea of him hiding away down here, but now I've seen the place, they were right—it's the perfect place for him to sit and wait it out. All he and I need to do is sit tight here, and whoever was after him in London will give up and go away. With the current state of affairs on the Continent and how rapidly things are changing, they won't have time to hang about. They might try for someone else—although there isn't anyone with your uncle's particular expertise—but more likely, they'll slink back across the Channel, and that will be the last we'll hear of them, whoever they are."

The words falling from his lips registered, along with the children's intrigued expressions. *Damn—I've said too much.* He frowned. "Here, now, you'd better let me get on. Your uncle might be wanting to change his shirt for dinner."

The three didn't immediately move but, instead, eyed him assessingly—as if debating whether they might winkle more information from him.

"Indeed, ma'am." The butler lifted the precious jar from his mistress's hands. "I'll take it to Cook immediately."

Mountjoy turned and headed for the rear of the hall, and Mrs. Woolsey waved, intending to herd them into the drawing room, but halted as the clack of several pairs of boots approached from another corridor.

Everyone waited, then Henry, Dagenham, and the three other young men came striding into the front hall.

"Aha!" Henry's eyes lit, and a smile curved his lips. "I thought it might be you lot." He'd directed the comment to the children, but now raised his gaze to Christopher's face. "We saw the blacks the stable lad was leading off and couldn't imagine who else they might belong to."

"They looked to be a bang-up pair," Kilburn put in.

"Lovely lines," Dagenham added.

When the gentlemen gave every indication of plunging into a discussion of horseflesh, the ladies, young and old, grew restive. Recognizing the signs, Henry suggested, "I say, Osbaldestone, we were just on our way to the billiard room. Why don't you join us? That will make six of us, so we could play as teams. Always makes it more interesting, I think."

Christopher glanced at his mother and Mrs. Woolsey. "If you ladies will excuse me?"

"Yes, of course, dear," Mrs. Woolsey replied, while his mother, smiling, waved him away.

Standing between the adults, the three children shared a long look, then Jamie looked at Henry. "George and I would like to watch, if that's all right?"

"Of course, young Skelton," Henry assured him. "You and George might be too short to play, but you're welcome to watch and learn."

Jamie smiled brightly, as if that was all that was on his mind.

He glanced at Lottie, who nodded and shifted to their grandmother's side. "I'll go to the drawing room with Grandmama."

With that, the group parted, the males heading down another corridor to the billiard room beyond the library while Lottie went into the drawing room with the older ladies.

Jamie and George trailed after the men. Quietly, so only George would hear, Jamie said, "Lottie will keep track of anything Mrs. Woolsey says. She probably won't know anything about strangers being seen about the village—"

"But," George said, "one never can tell what Mrs. Woolsey might let fall."

Jamie nodded. "Exactly."

Just before they'd left the house, Drummond had caught the three of them in the upstairs corridor and, pointing out that this was one outing on which he couldn't accompany their uncle, had asked them to keep their eyes peeled and their ears open for any sign of or mention of strangers about the village.

As they neared the billiard room, George said, "I wonder if we'll get any scones."

Jamie and George followed their elders into the room and took up positions by the wall, making themselves as inconspicuous as possible. The six gentlemen divided themselves into three teams of two players and commenced a set of games, with each team successively playing against the other two.

Both Jamie and George were more than tall enough to watch the action on the table, making it easy to pretend to an interest in the game. Indeed, upon further consideration, Jamie couldn't imagine any foreigner being able to approach his uncle in the billiard room of Fulsom Hall. He jogged George's elbow and whispered as much.

"You're right," George whispered back. "So we may as well concentrate on the play."

Subsequently, both gave their attention to the games, watching the balls and even more the techniques and angles employed by the players.

They also listened closely to the quiet exchanges between the team members, which were, in the main, about tactics to defeat their rivals. The single exception was Dagenham's apparently idle question to their uncle about what life in the Foreign Office was like.

Jamie and George exchanged a glance. They knew that Dagenham had joined the Home Office at the prompting of his family. To the boys' minds, there was only one reason for Dagenham to be interested in Foreign Office matters.

Consequently, they listened avidly as the viscount asked several more questions, all apparently to do with how things were done, assignments decided, inside the Foreign Office.

For the life of them, the boys couldn't fathom what Dagenham was really trying to ask. In the end, Jamie whispered to George, "It's as if he's asking random questions so that when he asks the important one, Uncle Christopher won't realize and will simply answer, just as he's doing now."

After a moment, George whispered back, "Do you think we ought to tell Uncle Christopher? About why Dagenham's asking questions?"

Jamie thought, then shook his head. "Not when we can't be absolutely certain that Melissa is the reason he's asking them."

Over the past two years, their cousin, Melissa, younger daughter of their aunt Henrietta, Lady North, had spent the weeks before Christmas at Hartington Manor along with Jamie, George, and Lottie, and Melissa and Dagenham had grown close, although Melissa was far too young to be thinking of bestowing her hand on anyone.

Although neither Jamie nor George fully understood why, Lottie had declared that it was necessary that Melissa and Dagenham part, at least for the next several years until after Melissa made her come-out.

The crux of the matter—the reason Jamie and George suspected Melissa was the reason behind Dagenham's questions—was that her father, Lord North, occupied a position toward the top of the Foreign Office tree.

Jamie met George's eyes and shrugged, and the pair turned their attention back to the table as their uncle and Dagenham strolled forward to take on Kilburn and George Wiley.

That left Henry and Roger Carnaby standing and chatting quite close to Jamie and George.

"I enjoyed our ride this morning," Henry said.

Roger nodded. "It was a good idea of Thomas's to ride out every day that we can and see more of the countryside."

Jamie's eyes widened. He met George's gaze, then leaned forward and asked Henry and Roger, "When you've been out riding, have you seen any strangers around about?"

George amended, "Any foreigners, we mean."

Henry and Roger looked from George to Jamie, then Henry said, "Not that I noticed." He arched a brow at Roger.

Roger shook his head. "Nor me. All we saw were farm workers."

"But why do you ask?" Henry directed the question to both boys.

Jamie slowly blinked, then said, "Well, Uncle Christopher is with the Foreign Office. We thought it might be interesting to see him in action, as it were."

Henry smiled. "I don't think chatting to wandering foreigners is quite how Foreign Office gentlemen like your uncle operate."

Roger, too, smiled rather patronizingly.

Jamie ignored the insult to his intellect and made his eyes wide. "Oh. I hadn't realized."

A commotion on the table with balls tumbling into pockets drew everyone's eyes.

Once the ensuing crowing faded and the game resumed, Jamie met George's eyes. "At least we've learned that, so far, no foreigner's been seen lurking about."

George nodded and whispered back, "That should make Drummond happy."

~

After enjoying a late luncheon, Christopher quit the dining room, slipping away while the children were chatting animatedly with his mother. Intending to retreat to his bedchamber to read the London news sheets in peace, he paused in the front hall and looked around. He didn't spot any printed sheets, but Crimmins appeared, and Christopher smiled. "I was looking for the news sheets, Crimmins. I take it they've arrived?"

"Indeed, sir. Drummond has already taken them up to your room."

"Excellent!" With a nod, Christopher started up the stairs.

He opened the door to his room, stepped inside, and saw Drummond sitting in one of the armchairs before the hearth. He had one of the two news sheets in his hands and was carefully perusing it.

Christopher shut the door with a definite click.

Drummond looked up, then grunted. He waved the news sheet. "I can hardly read this in the servants' hall or even in my room in the attic."

Christopher huffed and went forward. Accepting the second news sheet that Drummond held up, Christopher sank into the other armchair, flicked out the sheet, and started reading.

Just as Christopher did, for his work with the FO, Drummond needed to keep abreast of developments in the ongoing campaign against Napoleon and also with any news from the courts of the various other members of the Sixth Coalition.

After reading and digesting the war report, Christopher lowered the sheet and looked at Drummond. "I forgot to ask, do you have anything of a local nature to report?"

Drummond lowered his news sheet, plainly ordered his thoughts, then said, "While you were off at Fulsom Hall, I called in at the Cockspur Arms and then stopped in at the village shops. Not so much to be learned at either the baker's or the butcher's, but Mountjoy's Store is what I'd call a gossip hub. Even over the few minutes I was in there, two of the local farmwives came in and chatted away with the young lass behind the counter. After the second one left, I asked the shop girl in a roundabout way if she'd heard of any foreigners lurking, but seems there's been no whisper of any strangers at all."

Laying the news sheet on his lap, Christopher sat back and steepled his fingers. "That fits with what I heard at Fulsom Hall. Apparently, Sir Henry and his four friends have decided to learn more about the surrounding countryside than they have in years past. In pursuit of that goal, they've been riding out every morning, taking a different tack each day. I didn't specifically ask, but I feel sure that if they had come upon any unexpected foreigners, they would have mentioned it—they know I work at the FO."

Drummond slowly nodded. "I'm starting to see that what you said—that any stranger in these parts will stand out, be noticed, and be remarked upon—is true." He shook his head. "I can't see any French agent sneaking up on us without anyone saying."

"Indeed. As I said at the outset, I expect our sojourn here to pass without incident."

Drummond grunted and went back to his news sheet.

After listening to the clock on the mantelpiece chime three times, Christopher returned to perusing the news as well.

~

The weather had turned nasty, with an icy wind blustering around the house, faintly howling about the eaves and tossing flurries of sleet against the windows. After luncheon, the children had settled by the fire in Therese's private parlor, each engrossed in reading a book.

After perusing the last of the letters the post had brought that morning, Therese laid the sheets aside and studied the three bent heads. A moment later, the clock struck for the half hour, and as one, the children raised their heads, then looked at her questioningly.

She laughed and nodded. "All right. Jamie, please ring for Crimmins."

Grinning, Jamie leapt to his feet and crossed to the bellpull. He was just tall enough to reach it. After tugging imperiously, he returned to sit cross-legged on the rug before the fire.

Lottie and George likewise closed their books and sat up.

Crimmins hadn't waited to hear an order he knew would be forthcoming; the door of the parlor opened, and he carried in a laden tray. "Afternoon tea, ma'am."

Therese smiled in appreciation. "Thank you, Crimmins. I believe we have three hungry children to feed." She indicated the low table to one side of her chair, and Crimmins carefully set down the tray to a chorus of oohs and aahs as the children's big eyes settled on the small mountain of Mrs. Haggerty's luscious crumpets, slathered and dripping with butter, that occupied pride of place on the tray.

Crimmins glanced at the three faces and struggled to keep his smile within bounds. "Will there be anything else, ma'am?"

"I doubt it, Crimmins, but I believe Mrs. Haggerty deserves a commendation for reducing these three to speechlessness."

"Indeed, ma'am. I will convey as much to her."

With that, Crimmins departed. The click of the door shutting had three pairs of pleading eyes rising to Therese's face. She smiled and waved at the tray. "Have at them—but don't forget your manners."

Within seconds, they had each taken a small plate, helped themselves to one of the golden delights, and drizzled it with honey. When they each took their first bite, Therese watched expressions of gustatory ecstasy pass across their faces.

She poured herself a cup of tea, ensured the three had glasses of milk, then sat back, sipped, and bided her time.

When the three were halfway through their treats, Jamie glanced at the plate, patently verifying that there were more than three crumpets left. He looked at Therese. "Shouldn't we let Uncle Christopher know it's teatime and there are crumpets?"

Setting down her empty cup and relaxing in her chair, Therese waved the notion aside. "For some strange reason, your uncle never took to crumpets." That was why she'd ordered them to be served that afternoon.

Lottie, too, had been regarding the remaining crumpets. "But Uncle Christopher has never tried Mrs. Haggerty's crumpets, has he?"

Seeing the indecision in all three faces and having her own reasons for wishing to keep their small gathering private, Therese firmly stated, "That may be so, but at this time of day, your uncle will be busy scrutinizing the news sheets—that's an important part of his work—and I suspect we shouldn't disturb him. Gentlemen do not appreciate being interrupted when they're working." She arched her brows at the three. "I'm sure you've noticed that with your own father."

From the quick looks they exchanged, they most certainly had. To further distract them from any thoughts of summoning Christopher, Therese encouraged them to help themselves to another crumpet each.

Once they'd reloaded their plates and started consuming the treats, she ventured, "Speaking of your uncle's duties and what led him to take refuge with us here, have you three anything to report?" She regarded them encouragingly. "Have you stumbled on any possible French agents? I'm sure you've been looking."

The three exchanged another glance, then Jamie licked his fingers and confided, "Drummond isn't really a valet-cum-groom. He's Uncle Christopher's guard."

"But Mr. Drummond doesn't usually guard people," Lottie explained. "He usually works for the Foreign Office by pretending to be a merchant or something like that on the Continent."

"Does he?" Feeling entirely justified in encouraging the children, Therese leaned back in her chair. "Fancy that." She had wondered about the rather strange addition to her son's personal staff and had suspected Drummond wasn't who he claimed to be.

"This morning, Drummond asked us to keep our eyes open while we were at Fulsom Hall, in case we spotted or heard about any stranger lurking around the village," George said.

Therese allowed her brows to rise in mild query. "And did you?"

"No," Jamie replied, "but we did learn that Henry, Dagenham, and the other three have been riding out every morning, taking different routes out and around the village each day, and they haven't seen any strangers at all."

"So no unexpected sightings of strangers about the village at all?" Therese clarified.

"We don't think Uncle Christopher or Drummond *expect* there to be any strangers about." Lottie frowned slightly. "I think they think that no one will find Uncle Christopher down here."

Busy devouring the last two crumpets, the boys nodded in agreement.

Jamie swallowed and said, "We have noticed that Dagenham seems quite interested in asking Uncle Christopher questions about his work."

"More about the way Uncle Christopher's office works," Lottie explained. "At least that was what he was asking on Sunday, when they met us in the lane."

"This morning," George said, "when he spoke with Uncle Christopher, Dagenham wanted to know about how assignments were given out."

The trio exchanged another of their wordless communications, then all three faced Therese. "We wondered," Jamie said, "whether those were the things Dagenham really wanted to know or if he was working his way around to asking something else."

"It's obvious that Dagenham has something to do with the Foreign Office on his mind," Lottie stated very seriously, "and we wondered if that something was Melissa."

"Given Uncle North is with the Foreign Office." George met Therese's eyes. "We wondered if we should warn Uncle Christopher about what might be behind Dagenham's questions."

"Only," Jamie countered, "we can't be sure that it *is* Melissa behind them and not something else entirely."

Therese regarded the three with burgeoning pride; they were so gratifyingly observant and quick-witted as well. Understanding the unvoiced question in their eyes, she admitted, "Like you, I suspect Dagenham's motives might be more personal than professional. However, as you say, we cannot be sure, and I don't believe attempting to explain the situation to your uncle is necessary. He will answer what he wishes to answer—feels he is able to answer—and nothing more."

She had wondered if Dagenham still carried a torch for Melissa; apparently, he did. "At this point," she went on, "I don't feel we need to intervene on that score. Once Dagenham's motives are clear, if they do involve Melissa, then perhaps I might drop a word in his ear, but for now, let's set that matter to one side."

Regarding the three children sitting before her, bright-eyed, keenly observant, and inveterately curious, Therese confided, "As you might expect, the situation with your uncle is of some concern to me. However, while I plan to be out and about the village in my usual fashion, the chances of me stumbling across French agents lurking in the vicarage garden or in the open on the green or inside Mountjoy's are, I venture to suggest, rather slim. Further to that, your uncle, perhaps understandably, is likely to be rather reticent over reporting any potential danger to me, his mother."

The three flashed her quick, understanding grins.

"Consequently," she went on, "I wondered if I could rely on you three to report on any new developments regarding your uncle and these French agents thought to be after him." She arched her brows at them. "Can I count on you to do that?"

"Of course, Grandmama!" The three-part chorus echoed through the room.

Therese smiled delightedly. "Thank you, my dears. Having you three acting as my eyes and ears in this will be something of a relief."

"We'll tell you anything we see or hear," Lottie vowed.

The boys nodded earnestly, then their gazes fell to the now-empty plates.

"Very good." Therese waved Jamie to the bellpull. "If you would, Jamie dear, ring for Crimmins to fetch away the tray."

Crimmins duly appeared and removed the remains of their feast.

The children returned to their books, sprawling like contented puppies on the rug before the fire.

Therese sat back in her chair and idly watched them, confident that, now that she'd recruited them, she would remain fully apprised of all that was going on involving her son without any risk of appearing to be directly poking her nose into his business.

It was tricky and not a little difficult, knowing as much as she did about his work and having her decades of experience on which to draw, to resist the temptation to stick in her oar; to that end, she usually maintained a wall of sorts between herself and Christopher's duties. And those of her son-in-law North as well. Neither gentleman would welcome her input, not unless they had asked for it.

In this case, however, with Christopher facing some nebulous threat, maternal instinct trumped her customary reticence to engage. If there was danger lurking, she wanted to know of it.

She focused on Jamie's, George's, and Lottie's gleaming heads and smiled. She was surely blessed to have such reliable agents to whom she could confidently delegate the task of keeping a close eye on Christopher while he remained in Little Moseley.

CHAPTER 5

Rugged up against the icy chill of early morning in his coat and gloves and with a muffler wound about his neck, Christopher slipped out of the manor's front door as the church clock tolled seven times.

The sleet had finally ceased, and although the sun had yet to clear the horizon, the pearly light of predawn cast the country landscape in shades of palest pewter and rose. Despite the chill, the air was fresh and crisp. Given how variable the weather had been, Christopher was determined to make the most of the clear skies, knowing beyond question that they wouldn't last.

Ducking his head against the light breeze, with his hands in his greatcoat pockets, he stepped off the porch and set off striding down the drive. Courtesy of the children's tour, he had a decent understanding of the paths about the village. He wanted to immerse himself in the quiet of the early-morning countryside and, free of all interruption, cast his mind over the catalogue of his army of informants and decide which of them it might pay to contact now that Napoleon's defeat was drawing ever closer.

While those in the War Office—like his brother Lionel—were adamant one could not take the Corsican's surrender for granted, a good part of Christopher's duties involved making contingency plans for all potential outcomes. A continuing conflict wouldn't require any great change, but the prospect of Napoleon's surrender and abdication—for surely that would follow—and the subsequent re-establishment of the

French monarchy, let alone the redrawing of the borders that the victors would demand, would qualify as change on a monumental scale, and Christopher and his Foreign Office masters would need to be prepared to manage all in the best interests of Britain. That, above all, would be the task before them.

Christopher hadn't informed Drummond, much less the children, of his intention to go out that morning. With so many details whirling through his mind, he needed to simply walk, one foot in front of the other, and let his mind sort through and evaluate his options and, from that, form a list of the informants likely to prove most useful in any post-triumph negotiations. From what he'd heard of the movements of the various Coalition armies, victory could come at any time after the end of January. He and the firm needed to be prepared. His present enforced absence from his desk would not be considered any real excuse, not by Powell and Castlereagh and not by himself, either.

While he mentally ordered and reordered a list of which of his informants scattered throughout the European courts he should contact first, he let his feet lead him where they would. He reached the lane and turned right. When he drew level with the Cockspur Arms, just opening its shutters to the morning light, he paused, looked around, and saw no other living being. Reassured, he swung on his heel and walked out onto the green.

Head down, he returned to refining his mental list as he walked to the rise, then trudged up it. On gaining the crest, he surveyed the frozen lake and its shores. Seeing no one about, he continued down the slope a little way, until he was far enough below the crest that anyone passing in the lane couldn't see him.

He halted and drank in the view before him—the silvery-green-gray expanse of the lake, the winter-brown grass, and the woods that stretched to either side and covered the rising hill beyond the lake, protectively embracing the area in the dark green of firs and pines—and felt a sense of peacefulness enfold him.

Little Moseley was definitely very different from London.

He recalled that the children had mentioned a village skating party. Was that tomorrow? He wasn't sure, but the ice certainly looked thick enough for the event to proceed. Studying the vista before him, he imagined what the party would be like—children shrieking as they whizzed about on the ice, their parents and older siblings skating more gracefully past, and the village elders sitting on the bank, watching, smiling proudly, and chatting. He found himself smiling at the image in his mind, and it struck him that this bucolic serenity and the unsophisticated pleasures of village celebrations were the embodiment of what he and all the others—the soldiers and officers under Wellington and even the commanders themselves—were fighting to preserve.

This was the true England, and the same would be so of Scotland, Ireland, and Wales. This promise of soul-comfort, this peace, this sense of recognition and belonging—of home—was what men held in their hearts when they went to war.

This was what men fought for.

Christopher considered that insight; in going into the post-victory negotiations, he would be wise to remember that the Swedes, the Russians, the Prussians, the Austrians, the Italians, the Spanish, and the Portuguese very likely felt that way about their countries, too.

After several minutes' deliberation, he softly huffed. Perhaps it was fated that he'd chosen Little Moseley for his enforced sojourn, just so that this view in this moment could remind him of that.

With his gloved hands sunk in his greatcoat pockets, he remained where he was as his mind swung to the information that would be piling up on his desk in town. But then the chill reached through his coat, and noticing the strengthening light, he turned and walked back up the rise, angling toward the wall enclosing the vicarage garden, intending to follow the wall along the side of the green to the lane.

He reached the crest by the corner of the wall and paused to catch his breath while pondering the prospect of what Mrs. Haggerty might deign to serve for breakfast.

He was gazing over the expanse of the green, idly wondering what the village pageant that the children had informed him would be held there the following week would entail, when a flash of bright blue in the lane drew his eye.

A lady in a kingfisher-blue pelisse, with a fur-trimmed bonnet and a matching muff in the same fashionable shade of blue, was walking purposefully up the lane toward the Cockspur Arms.

Christopher focused on the marching figure, then softly swore, narrowed his eyes, then, dumbfounded, simply stared.

How the devil did she find me here?

Self-preservatory instinct had him shifting into the shadow cast by the wall while he continued to watch as Marion Sewell—he was willing to wager the lady was her—paused and glanced around.

He didn't breathe again until she faced forward and walked on. Relief flooded him. Thank God she hadn't seen him!

She walked past the inn's front yard, then turned toward the stable arch, where another woman, taller and older in a dun-colored coat, stood waiting. Marion joined the woman, and they spoke, then Marion led the way into the stable yard, with the other woman following in a manner that suggested she was Marion's maid.

Christopher waited, and a few minutes later, Marion emerged, driving a gig, with the other woman perched beside her.

Marion turned the horse to her right along the lane—away from the manor—and drove smartly on through the village.

Christopher strained his ears and tracked the clop of her horse's hooves, relieved to hear the sound slowly fading as the gig rolled out of the village and on up the lane.

Relief swamped him, deeper than before, while something rather like panic pranced along his nerves.

His first thought was to regain the relative safety of his mother's house, but he no longer wished to risk crossing the open green. "Just in case the damn woman turns around and drives back down the lane," he muttered. He swung onto the path he'd taken with the children two days before, following the wall at the rear of the vicarage garden to eventually reach the back of the church.

He strode around the church and started down the drive. Nearing the lane, he slowed, listening for any hint of a carriage. Eventually creeping to the edge of the lane, he looked right and left. On seeing no sign of anyone at all, he strode quickly across the lane and along the few yards to the entrance to the manor drive. He turned up it and increased his pace. Only once he'd rounded the first bend and was out of sight of the lane did he slow his strides.

His chest felt tight. "Damn it—what is she doing here?"

He'd been wallowing in bucolic peace, then she'd appeared and put an end to that.

But did she actually know he was there, staying with his mother?

"Heaven help me if she does!" He wouldn't put it past her to come driving up, knock on the door, and ask to speak with him. Marion Sewell was nothing if not determined.

His thoughts skittered in every direction as he tried to come to grips with what her appearing in Little Moseley might mean. Grimly, he strode along. She had to have followed him there, but how? Both he and Drummond had been sure no one had tracked them out of London.

"Of all the villages in all of England..." For some reason, she'd chosen to come there. He was incapable of imagining that to be any innocent coincidence.

She must have figured out that he'd gone to ground in Little Moseley, but if she had, who else might have guessed?

An even more unnerving thought had him pausing for a second, then he clenched his jaw and strode on. If any agent had been following him in London closely enough to have noticed Marion's pursuit of him, when he'd vanished from the capital... Had some canny agent thought to switch to following her, hoping that she might lead them to him?

He wished he could dismiss the idea as utterly fanciful, but for an experienced agent, the notion wasn't that far-fetched.

"If so..." The thought that some French agent's mission might have become intertwined with Marion's personal quest to hunt him down without her being aware of it left him decidedly uneasy. That she might be being used as an unwitting stalking horse was beyond concerning.

He reached the front door, opened it, and went inside. Closing the door behind him, he thought of how relatively settled and straightforward his world had seemed when he'd left the house only an hour before. Even thinking about what he would need to do when he returned to London had been a distant prospect; in terms of the present, he'd started to feel rather relaxed.

Now, he felt under siege. Indeed, until he knew more—a lot more—he resolved to remain inside the house.

He shrugged out of his coat and handed it to Crimmins, who had come through the green baize door with a welcoming smile.

"Good morning, sir. I've just set out breakfast in the dining room."

"Good morning to you, too, Crimmins." Christopher handed the butler his gloves and unwound the muffler from about his neck. As he handed the scarf to Crimmins, Christopher fervently hoped that, in coming to the manor, to the sleepy village and his mother and the children, he hadn't inadvertently brought danger in his wake.

Crimmins accepted the garments and said, "I'll bring in the coffeepot immediately, sir."

"Thank you—I would appreciate that." Christopher walked down the hall, stepped into the short corridor leading to the dining room, and forced himself to halt. He drew in a deep breath, hauling air past the constriction about his lungs, easing the tightness.

He was overreacting. He knew better than to do so, but clearly, he was rusty. He needed to reassess and, this time, stick to the facts. Coffee would undoubtedly help.

He might have seen Marion. She might be searching for him or be in the vicinity for some other reason entirely. Even if she was hunting him, the only threat she posed was that of a matrimonial snare. Given who she was—who her father was—he could be absolutely certain that she was not acting hand in glove with any French agent, no matter how charming or convincing; he was reasonably certain that she was far too intelligent to be taken in by any façade. Indeed, he'd heard her described as a dragon-in-the-making, and given that propensity, he couldn't imagine any French agent being so foolish as to even approach her.

He *could* imagine a French agent following her.

Being followed aside, Marion otherwise posed no insurmountable problem; even in a quiet country village with his mother in residence, he felt confident in his ability to avoid any matchmaking trap. All he had to do was continue to avoid any and all situations in which she might corner him in private.

The clatter of crockery and cutlery reached him, and the mouthwatering aromas of bacon, sausage, ham, and eggs teased his nostrils.

Surprised at the thought that his mother was already down, he continued toward the dining room. The notion of mentioning Marion's presence to Drummond bloomed, but he promptly quashed it; he could handle the threat Marion posed without assistance, and he would really rather not advertise the interaction between them to anyone else, especially not to others in the firm. Aside from all else, that would not be the action of a gentleman.

He entered the dining room to discover that it was not his mother at the table but the three children.

"Good morning, Uncle Christopher," they chorused, waving knives coated with egg and crumbs.

"Good morning, scamps. What are you doing here?"

"There's no nursery here," Lottie informed him, "so we have all our meals in the dining room."

"I see." He crossed to the sideboard and picked up a plate. "What are the sausages like?"

"Mrs. Haggerty makes them," George mumbled around a mouthful.

Christopher tipped his head. “Enough said.” He helped himself to two sausages and some of the succulent ham as well as two poached eggs, then went to join the children.

He drew out the chair beside Lottie and sat.

“Your hair looks damp all over,” Jamie, sitting opposite, observed. “Have you been outside?”

“Just for a quick walk.” He’d forgotten how sharp-eyed the trio were. Seeking to avoid any questions as to where he’d been and what he’d been doing, he smiled at them. “I have to admit that I’m unaccustomed to sharing my table with others who talk. My lodger, Fredericks, isn’t a morning person. If he deigns to show up at the breakfast table at all, the most I get out of him are grunts.”

“That must be terribly lonely,” Lottie said.

Christopher refrained from mentioning that he found silence over breakfast restful, and as he’d hoped, without further prompting, the children launched into a recitation of their plans for the day. Those included playing on the green with the other local children who were free to do so in the morning, and in the afternoon, the trio informed him, they would have their first choir practice in preparation for the carol service.

Intrigued by how immersed in the village activities they were, he questioned them about the hymns usually sung.

“Of course, this year,” George said, “as Melissa didn’t come, she won’t be there to sing with Dagenham.”

“I wonder whether he’ll sing it as a solo,” Jamie said.

“This year, Melissa decided to go with Mandy and Aunt Henrietta to some shooting party in Scotland,” Lottie informed him. “They’ll only be back in time to come to Winslow for Christmas.”

Christopher calculated that Melissa was now sixteen years old; that she might prefer the company of other youngsters her age rather than joining the household in Little Moseley didn’t surprise him.

“Perhaps they’ll see a stag,” Jamie said. “That would make Scotland in December worthwhile.”

Christopher grinned. He and the children applied themselves to cleaning their plates, but for him, the habit of decades was difficult to suppress. Recalling the number of children he’d seen the Skelton three playing with in the graveyard after church, he asked, “How many children do you think will come to play on the green?”

A quick discussion between the three ensued, then Jamie declared, “At least ten, I expect.”

"From all around or just from the village itself?" Christopher asked.

"Oh, all around," George assured him. "Most live on the farms."

"I see." Ten extra pairs of eyes and ears scattered over the surrounding area, let alone the three in the manor itself, was a temptation he found impossible to resist. "I don't suppose you could ask your friends if they've happened to see a lady I thought I glimpsed in the village this morning?"

The three looked at him with eager eyes. "What did she look like?" Lottie asked.

"The lady I saw was wearing a bright-blue pelisse, with a bonnet and muff in the same blue. I'm not sure the lady was the one I know, who lives in London, but if it was her, then she's not that young—"

"But younger than you?" Lottie asked.

He nodded. "Yes, several years younger than I am, but she's a few years older than Henry and his friends. She's tallish and has blond-brown hair that she usually wears swept up in a knot on the top of her head." He shifted, then added, "Her eyes are quite distinctive—a bright aquamarine."

"Is she pretty?" Lottie asked. "The lady you know?"

He thought, then nodded. "She is quite pretty, and she has highly polished ton manners."

He looked at the children and hoped that would be enough of a description. After all, how many not-so-young ladies in fashionable kingfisher-blue pelisses could there be in such a tiny village? With any luck, via their friends, they would be able to learn where Marion had come from and, most importantly, where she had gone.

The children's eyes narrowed as they thought, then all three looked at him, and Jamie asked, "What's her name—the lady from London?"

He knew them well enough not to trust their innocent expressions, but he couldn't think of any good reason not to answer. "If it is her, then her name is Miss Marion Sewell."

The smile that bloomed on Lottie's face made him uneasy, but the answer otherwise satisfied the three. They nodded, and Jamie said, "We'll be sure to ask around this morning. If she's staying anywhere near, someone is sure to know."

"Excellent." Christopher rose and walked to the sideboard. While helping himself to another serving of kedgeree, he wondered if indulging the impulse to involve the children had been wise.

As he returned to his place, having cleared their plates, the children pushed back from the table.

"We have to go," George said, "or the others will start a game without us."

Christopher nodded and reached for yesterday's news sheet. "I'll see you later. Let me know if you learn anything about the lady, whoever she might be."

"We will," they sang and rushed from the room.

Christopher heard the clatter of their footsteps as they raced upstairs, presumably to fetch their coats and gloves. A few minutes later, the three clattered back down, then the front door opened and shut.

Silence descended. With an inner sigh, Christopher settled into the familiar comfort, focused on the news sheet, and proceeded to address Mrs. Haggerty's quite excellent kedgeree.

Later that morning, Drummond stood staring out of the dormer window of his small room in the attic. He'd spent the past half hour pacing back and forth from the window to the door, ruminating on his current mission.

He'd been an active field agent for the past decade and more, and his instincts were pricking, while the pervasive sense of safety engendered by the sleepy village contrarily left him leery over giving in to the temptation of growing comfy and lowering his guard. He needed to remain alert to ensure no French agent sneaked up on his charge.

He'd been standing, staring out over the front lawn at nothing in particular, for uncounted minutes when he spotted the three children running and skipping up the drive.

A half-formed plan coalesced in his brain, and he nodded, turned, and headed for the door.

The children were his best way forward. He'd come to that conclusion after spending the past two nights in the Cockspur Arms, settling in with the locals as best he could. Sadly, his chosen cover of superior valet-cum-groom wasn't as useful as he'd hoped; it set him too far apart from the farmworkers, laborers, and even from the lower-level staff from the village's larger houses. As matters stood, if any French agent was lurking, they'd spot Drummond in an instant and ensure he didn't see them. A country bumpkin persona would have been more to the point, but it was too late to change identities.

He had to make the best of the hand he'd been dealt, and that meant recruiting the children.

He hovered at the end of the first-floor corridor. When the trio came thundering up the stairs, ruddy-cheeked from the cold and laughing, they saw him, and he beckoned.

They shared a quick glance, then walked down the corridor toward where he waited by the alcove beside the servants' stair.

From comments made by the patrons of the Arms, he'd realized the three were embedded in the village. Even though they were only there for a few weeks every year, everyone knew them. Indeed, the locals seemed to view them as seasonal fixtures, much like their grandmama. Even more importantly, the trio were regarded with affection and a degree of respect quite noteworthy for youngsters. Most important of all, the locals were accustomed to the three asking questions about this or that. Drummond had had his ears filled with tales of missing geese, a hunt for some Roman coins, and a misplaced book of carols. He'd heard the children labeled "the village's Christmas sleuths," and their successes were clearly a source of some pride.

For scouting around Little Moseley, he wouldn't find better eyes and ears.

The three approached, curiosity alive in their eyes. They halted facing him, and the eldest, Jamie, asked, "What is it?"

Confidence oozed from his and his siblings' pores. In a flash of insight, Drummond recognized that when they were grown, all three would be formidable.

He drew in a breath and began, "I've been hearing about your adventures here, in the village, over the past years." All three smiled with evident pride, and he continued, "Given that, then in the current circumstances, it seems to me that I couldn't do better than to recruit you three to the government's cause."

Three pairs of eyes in different shades of blue opened wide. "Oh?" the girl, Lottie, asked.

Drummond didn't trust such overtly innocent looks, not in light of the intelligence he'd glimpsed in all three, but maintaining a serious air, he went on, "It's like this—I'm here guarding your uncle's back to make sure no French agent gets close."

"You've already told us that," the younger boy, George, said.

Drummond nodded. "But I'm hardly invisible, and in a village like this, I stand out as someone who doesn't belong. If any foreign agents are lurking, thinking to kidnap your uncle, if they set eyes on me before I see them, they'll make sure I get no chance to catch even a hint of their presence. Should that happen, and they subsequently mount some sort of attack on your uncle, neither I nor he will have any warning, which will make keeping your uncle out of their clutches that much more difficult."

The children's faces had clouded; it was clear they were taking in his words and following his argument.

He drew breath and plunged on, "So I wondered if you three would undertake to be my eyes and ears about the village. The more pairs of eyes we have keeping watch, the better, and you three can go rolling around anywhere, both with the other children and on your own, and the villagers won't give you a second glance, so any French agent loitering about won't, either. Those agents will hide from me, but they won't hide from you."

His gaze unfocused, Jamie nodded. "They'll think we're just rowdy children so won't care if we notice them."

"Exactly!" Drummond eagerly went on, "So what I hope you'll agree to do is to keep your eyes open and let me know if you or your friends see any strange man loitering about—any man at all you don't recognize."

"Even if they seem to be English?" George asked.

Sobering, Drummond nodded. "Some of Napoleon's agents can pass as Englishmen or even other sorts of foreigners. So I need to know about any strange man at all."

Lottie lifted her big blue eyes to his face. "What about ladies?"

Drummond thought, then shook his head. "Ladies are sometimes foreign agents, but in this case, we only need to worry about men. Men of any class." The approach a female agent might make simply wouldn't work in a small village.

Instead of nodding, Lottie batted her long lashes twice, then without shifting her gaze, asked, "Not even if the lady is chasing Uncle Christopher?"

"What?" Drummond stared at the little girl. "What lady?"

As if to confirm the wisdom of engaging them in his mission, the three explained about their uncle's sighting of Miss Marion Sewell in the village early that morning and how Osbaldestone had asked the three to discreetly learn more about what she was doing there.

Drummond recognized the Sewell name; from that, it wasn't difficult to guess that the lady was pursuing Osbaldestone in the social sense of the phrase. He was unmarried, after all, as was she. Given their families, some would no doubt consider it a good match. It was hardly a wonder that Osbaldestone hadn't mentioned the matter to Drummond; he would want to handle it himself, on the quiet.

Out of curiosity, Drummond eyed the three bright faces before him and asked, "So have you learned anything about her?"

Jamie grimaced. "Not much as yet. Just that she's staying somewhere close, but not in the village itself. She and her maid bought ten pork cutlets from Bilson's and some milk from Mountjoy's, so they can't be staying too far away."

Drummond was impressed. He could wish some of his more mundane sources were as quick-witted and efficient as these three.

Nevertheless, he took pity on Osbaldestone and shook his head. "She won't be a foreign agent—she's a distraction, one we can leave your uncle to deal with. In terms of identifying any nosy foreign agent, we need to concentrate on any man—gentleman to navvy—who arrives and isn't connected to the village." He looked from one face to the other. "So, can I count on you to keep your eyes peeled and let me know if any man like that shows his face?"

The three exchanged a glance, then looked at Drummond and nodded.

"We will," George declared, and it sounded like a vow.

The gong for luncheon rang through the house. The three glanced down the corridor toward their rooms, then looked back at Drummond.

He nodded. "You'd best be off, but if you please, keep this conversation under your hats, at least for now."

They flung him grins that held far too much understanding for his peace of mind, and then they were off, pelting along the corridor and swinging into their rooms to wash and tidy themselves before appearing at their grandmother's table.

~

Minutes later, hands clean, faces scrubbed, and their hair quickly brushed, the children clattered down the stairs in a rush.

As they started down the last flight, they saw their uncle waiting to waylay them. He beckoned them to join him just inside the front door.

When they lined up before him, with one eye on the corridor leading to the dining room, he lowered his voice and asked, "Have you learned anything about Miss Sewell?"

As one, they stepped closer, and also lowering his voice, Jamie reported, "She's definitely not staying in the village or even in the cottages nearby."

"But," George said, "she bought pork cutlets and a pint of fresh milk."

"She wouldn't be carrying those back to London or anywhere far away," Lottie said.

"So," Jamie concluded, "we think she must be staying somewhere around about, possibly in one of the nearby villages, but we don't know exactly where."

With something like awe, Christopher studied the three faces turned up to his. That they'd managed to ferret out even that much so quickly was nothing short of remarkable.

Studying Christopher's face, Jamie tipped his head. "Do you want us to see if we can find out where, exactly, she's staying?"

Instinct prodded; surely the more he knew about Marion, the better. He definitely didn't want her turning up at the manor or—heaven help him—encountering his mother in the village. There was no doubt in his mind that his mother would instantly comprehend Marion's interest and, viewing Marion as an exceedingly suitable bride for him, would channel her energies and unrivaled talents into playing matchmaker.

That was the last thing he needed. Especially as he harbored no illusions whatsoever over his ability to defend against his mother's machinations. The only reason he'd remained a bachelor for so long was because he'd assiduously avoided giving her any chance to meddle in his social life.

But now he was there, living in her house…

He set his jaw. If there was any way to warn Marion off, he needed to seize it, and locating her was the obvious first step.

He focused on the children and, endeavoring to conceal the grimness of his thoughts, nodded. "If you can learn where she's staying *without* her getting wind of you, then yes, please. I would like to know."

The three shot him faintly affronted looks, and Jamie assured him that Miss Sewell wouldn't have any inkling that they were investigating her.

Investigating her? Hmm.

"But," George put in, "we have choir practice this afternoon, so it'll be tomorrow morning before we can ask around."

Jamie nodded. "We'll hunt around before the skating party tomorrow."

Christopher was conscious of inwardly chafing at the delay—now he knew the danger Marion represented was looming, he wanted to take whatever steps he could to push her away before his mother learned she was there—but the delay seemed unavoidable. He accepted it with outward equanimity and waved the children toward the dining room.

They swung around and hurried toward the corridor. He followed rather more slowly and soberly.

He didn't like admitting, even to himself, that he felt a sense of urgency over locating Marion, yet the instincts he hadn't used for years—those of a highly successful field agent—were all but second nature, and they were definitely stirring. And for some ungodly reason, those instincts were focusing more and more unrelentingly on Marion Sewell.

Given she was now a constant itch in the back of his brain, the impulse to learn where she was staying was rapidly transforming into an obsession. He needed to speak with her, if only to put paid to the outlandish yet niggling notion that there might be something more, something other, behind her pursuit.

~

Later that afternoon, several miles away, Marion paced before the window in the large chamber she'd been given at the old manor house, where she and her party had taken refuge, and mentally castigated Christopher Osbaldestone. Chasing him halfway across the country—well, at least into the depths of the countryside—was not how she'd imagined spending the second week of December. She'd had engagements arranged with friends before they all scattered to their country homes, and she'd yet to finish buying her Christmas gifts. She didn't want to be spending her days in a tiny hamlet, trying to run Christopher to earth in an only slightly larger village nearby.

There was, however, no other option, not if she wished to fulfill the promise her twin had made on her behalf.

That morning, she'd called in at the village—Little Moseley—but had yet to set eyes on her quarry. Luckily, eavesdropping in the village shops had elicited sufficient information to confirm that Lady North's guess had been correct. Christopher had, indeed, come to stay with his mother, Lady Osbaldestone, at her house in Little Moseley. Apparently, he'd arrived on Saturday, along with a rather large valet-cum-groom named Drummond.

"I suppose," Marion said, her arms folded and her gaze on the polished boards before her hems, "that this Drummond person's presence supports Lady North's suspicion that Christopher's been sent into hiding because some French agents are hunting for him."

"Oh? How do you figure that?" Marion's maid, Glennis, seated on a chair by the dresser, didn't look up from her careful mending. Having been in service to the Sewell family for most of her life, now in her late thirties, Glennis was accustomed to Foreign Office intrigues and, consequently, saw little in them to become excited about, although Marion suspected that, in this instance, Glennis was rather chuffed to be actively involved.

Marion turned and paced once more across the window. "It seems likely that Drummond's a guard sent to protect Christopher. Carter—the fellow who was going to help me in London—thought so, too. Given how critical Christopher apparently is to the country's diplomatic intelligence, that's just the sort of thing Powell and Castlereagh would order." She swung around and, frowning, paced back. "I hope Drummond isn't going to be a problem."

Glennis straightened and shook out the petticoat she'd been hemming. "But surely this Drummond is with the FO, too, so he won't mistake you for a French spy." Glennis huffed dismissively. "That would be absurd!"

Marion inclined her head. "True. But Drummond will likely be trying to keep Christopher's whereabouts a secret. He won't appreciate me turning up and insisting on speaking with a man who isn't supposed to be there."

"Ah." After setting the repaired petticoat aside, Glennis lifted the next garment from her mending basket. "There is that, I suppose."

After learning from Carter that Christopher had quit the capital for parts unknown, Marion had wracked her brains and concluded that her only possible source of information as to where he had gone was his older sister, Lady North. Lord North was also in the Foreign Office, his position on a par with that of Marion's father. Consequently, it was no surprise that Marion's mother was acquainted with Lady North; the pair had known each other for many years.

Marion had had to weave a convoluted tale about the message from Robbie that he'd insisted she deliver to Christopher in person, face-to-face, because said message was far too sensitive to be passed through official channels, even via her own father. Even via Lord Castlereagh himself, or so Robbie had instructed. Her story had made her mother raise her brows, but ultimately, being well aware of the way matters played out in Foreign Office intrigues, her mother had agreed to see what she could learn from Lady North.

Subsequently, along with other members of the ton lingering in the capital, she and her mother had attended Sunday morning service at St. George's and, afterward, amid the usual social gathering on the church's colonnaded porch, had approached Lady North.

Looking back on those moments, Marion had to admit that her mother had finagled the interrogation with aplomb. As it transpired, Lady North was well aware of her youngest brother's reputation as one of the FO's master intelligencers. Consequently, she accepted the tale of Robbie wishing to deliver a secret message to Christopher via Marion without question. She had then communicated her belief—a belief not being a substantiated fact—that Christopher had been sent out of London with orders to lie low while some threat to him in the capital was investigated. Apparently, information from a reliable source had led Powell and Castlereagh to conclude that French agents were taking too great an interest in Christopher.

That such a thing might happen, especially given the current situation on the Continent, surprised no one. Accepting that, her mother had wondered whether there was any chance of contacting Christopher so that Marion could pass on the message Robbie had entrusted to her.

To Marion's discomfort, Lady North had turned her dark gaze on Marion; she'd been hovering at her mother's elbow, attempting to appear inconspicuous. Lady North had studied her for several seconds, then her ladyship had smiled—it had seemed to Marion in a rather smugly satisfied way—and asked, "Do you envisage delivering the message directly to Christopher, my dear?"

Given the social strictures, that had been something of a tricky question, but Marion was her parents' daughter; she'd chosen her words with care. "My twin…" She'd raised her head and firmed her chin. "Well, he trusts me to carry out his wishes in his stead, as it were, so to keep faith, I really feel I must." Greatly daring, she'd pressed, "Do you have any idea where Mr. Osbaldestone has gone?"

After a second more of studying her, Lady North had glanced swiftly around. Reassured no one about them was paying any attention to their exchange, she'd looked back at Marion and, her voice low, said, "Our family usually gathers at Winslow Abbey for Christmas. I expect most people would assume that Christopher had simply gone there a few weeks early."

Marion had studied Lady North's expression. "But," she'd ventured, "you don't think that's where he's gone."

As if, by divining that, she'd successfully passed some test, Lady North had smiled. "No. Christopher knows that Celia—our sister, the Countess of Winslow—likes to have most of December to prepare for the family descending. She and her household won't welcome visitors at this time, not even Christopher. However, in pursuit of her sanity, nowadays, Celia dispatches her three older children—two boys and a girl—to stay with their grandmother, our mother, the Dowager Lady Osbaldestone, in Hampshire. Christopher is the children's favorite uncle, and he enjoys their company and their antics. On top of that, our mother commenced using her dower house, Hartington Manor in Little Moseley, four to five years ago, and I believe Christopher hasn't previously visited the place." She'd paused, then, her gaze steady on Marion's face, had said, "Christopher's always one to kill two birds with a single stone. It's simply how he thinks. If I were the betting sort, I would wager he's gone to see Mama's dower house."

Marion had had to make arrangements in a tearing rush, but thankfully, her mother, fully understanding the peculiar connection that existed between twins, being one herself, had stepped in and helped. She'd organized for Marion to use the smaller family coach and had agreed to fob off everyone—Marion's father included—with the fiction that Marion had been called to attend the sickbed of a friend, provided that Marion had taken Glennis, her coachman, Foggarty, and her groom, Simon, with her.

Having no wish to find herself mired in scandal, Marion had readily agreed. She might be twenty-eight years old and definitively on the shelf, but she wasn't about to risk her reputation or bring social opprobrium on her family no matter how urgent or critical the message she had to relay to Christopher seemed.

She kicked her skirts around and swung about. "At least now I know for certain that's where he is."

"Assuming," Glennis said, concentrating on her stitching again, "that he stays put."

Marion frowned. "I can't see why he would move again, not before leaving for Winslow, which I gather Lady Osbaldestone does much closer to Christmas. And even if he sees me before I see him, he's not going to imagine that I'm colluding with the French."

At least he hadn't fled London to avoid her; given that, there was still hope that she could simply engineer an unremarkable meeting and complete her task for Robbie.

She paused in her pacing to look out of the window, across the lawns to the shrubbery beyond. A silver glint showing through the encircling trees gave evidence of the river nearby.

Once she'd told the gentlemen for whom, thanks to Robbie, she was supposed to organize a secret meeting with Christopher where Lady North thought he had gone—avoiding any mention of lurking French agents, deeming that one complication too many—the pair had acted with remarkable speed. Through their contacts in the émigré community, they had arranged for the use of Parteger Hall in East Wellow. The old manor house was located in a bend in the river and had been left with a skeleton staff by the wealthy owners, who habitually wintered at another of their properties.

The manor afforded far better accommodations than Marion had expected they would be able to secure on such short notice, which only served to underscore how highly connected her charges were.

So they were there, and she'd established that Christopher was only a few miles away. "Now I just need to find some way to capture his attention long enough to explain why he needs to come here."

"Couldn't you take the gentlemen to meet him there, in Little Moseley?" Glennis asked.

Marion grimaced. "That might have been possible before, but now there's the possibility that French agents are lurking about. I don't know what our gentlemen wish to propose to our government via Christopher, but I'm certain they won't want Napoleon to get wind of it—or even learn they're here."

Parteger Hall was secluded yet easy to reach from Little Moseley; as matters stood, it was the perfect venue in which to host a secret meeting between Christopher and her charges.

Marion felt sure that once she'd managed to gain Christopher's attention long enough to tell him who she was representing and that they wished to speak with him, he would come to the Hall hotfoot. The question facing her was how best to approach him in a way that wouldn't send him ducking and running. "All I need is three—even two—minutes of his time."

Christopher's apparent misapprehension regarding her reasons for wishing to speak with him in private was a hurdle neither she nor her brother had imagined might crop up. Now that it had… Another complication her brother had failed to grasp was that, as a well-born female, she had to deal with many more constraints regarding how she behaved toward any man, well-born or otherwise.

Her options for contacting Christopher were limited. "I don't want to risk sending a note—not to his mother's house." She almost shuddered at the thought of his mother intercepting such a missive. "Even if I manage to get it directly into his hands, given how little I can put in writing, two to one, he won't act on it. He'll just ignore it, thinking I mean to importune him by luring him into a private meeting." She pulled a horrendous face. "And I can't simply walk up the drive, knock on the door, and explain to his mother, who is a truly terrifying sort, that I want a private meeting with her unmarried son." She could just imagine how that would go.

"No, indeed." Glennis shook out the chemise she'd been working on, then carefully folded it. "You'll need to meet him with others about, just like you tried at that soirée."

Marion huffed. "The only way I'll get to speak with him is if I approach him from behind and he doesn't see me coming."

"There's bound to be some opportunity in a village like that." Glennis set aside the chemise and looked up at Marion. "Didn't they say that there was some big village party to be held tomorrow?"

Marion was already thinking of that. "There's to be a skating party on some lake."

"Well, then!" Glennis said bracingly. "Just as well I packed your skates."

CHAPTER 6

The following afternoon, flanked by the children and Drummond, Christopher walked across the village green toward the rise beyond which lay the lake. About them, coming from all points and streaming over the green, other families, many with excited youngsters, were heading in the same direction.

The day was overcast and cold, with a bitter breeze constantly strafing past, icy enough that no one would worry about the ice thawing.

As the group from the manor neared the foot of the rise, the children, all but bouncing with excitement, waved and called to others, then with a gay "We'll see you on the ice, Uncle Christopher!" rushed ahead to join their friends.

Smiling at the sight of the small army of children racing up the rise, with his own skates hanging by their knotted laces slung over one shoulder, Christopher trudged upward beside Drummond; as they climbed, he swiftly glanced around, scanning the crowds for any glimpse of kingfisher blue.

Marion's fashionable pelisse would, he felt sure, make her easy to spot. As it was, rapidly surveying the surrounding crowds a second time, he felt certain she wasn't there.

Drummond, who had also been scanning the throng for any threat, had noticed Christopher doing so. "Damn fool excursion, this," he grumbled. "Why on earth you want to leave a warm house and expose yourself to any lurking Frenchie just so you can slide about on ice is beyond me."

Mildly, Christopher replied, "In all seriousness, you have to admit it's highly unlikely that any French agent would follow me into Hampshire. And if they have, it stands to reason they must already know I'm here. Regardless, the pertinent point to note about a skating party is that I'll be surrounded by well-disposed locals at all times." Smiling easily, he glanced at Drummond's sour and unconvinced expression. "I'll be in no danger of being kidnapped, not least because I intend to spend most of my time on the ice."

He loved skating and, in recent years, had had far too few opportunities to indulge. As they neared the crest of the rise, he glanced to left and right again, but saw no sign of Marion.

In truth, he was more than half hoping she would attend. If her intentions were, indeed, matrimonial, her approaching him while they were whizzing about on the ice surrounded by villagers would be no more dangerous for him than at a London soirée. Yet if she turned up and seized the moment to speak with him, at the very least he would learn if the disconcerting niggle that pricked and poked at the back of his mind, fueled by concern that there might be something other than matrimony behind her wish to engage with him, was justified or not.

Once he'd thought more about it, ascribing her attempt to approach him at Lady Selkirk's soirée to matrimonial ambition hadn't meshed well with what he remembered of Marion. Admittedly, she'd been all of eighteen back then, yet she'd always struck him as a lady courageous enough to be open and direct; ten years ago, he would have sworn she didn't have a duplicitous bone in her body.

Now? He honestly didn't know. But what he did know was that she now possessed significant experience of diplomatic circles, especially with respect to the Russian and Austrian courts. Given that, he had to wonder if there just might be something else behind her pursuit of him, and he wasn't at all comfortable with the scenarios his ever-fertile imagination was throwing up, not with French agents possibly lurking.

On reaching the crest, he paused and looked down on the small valley containing the lake. From that elevation, it was clear that even if French agents materialized out of the flanking woods, if he was out on the ice, he would be out of their reach. He doubted any French agents would have thought to pack their skates, so from their point of view, appearing at the party would achieve nothing beyond showing him and Drummond their faces.

He really wasn't concerned over being confronted by French agents that afternoon.

Unbidden, his thoughts returned to Marion. Her apparent fixation on speaking in relative privacy with him to the extent of chasing him into Hampshire—assuming she had, and if she had, how had she learned where he was?—left him uneasy, precisely because such an act was so blatantly brazen. On the one hand, if she was motivated by matrimony, then such an act was rather shocking; he wouldn't have expected the Marion he'd known to be so forward. *But* on the other hand, if she had some other motive, chasing him into Hampshire spoke of urgency and even desperation. Certainly determination of an adamantine nature.

What he couldn't at that moment fathom was how she'd managed to convince her parents to allow her to race into Hampshire. Or had her mother come with her?

That possibility left him floundering even more.

Shoving the tangle of his thoughts to the back of his mind, he focused on the villagers congregating in loose groups along the lake's nearer shore. A few eager souls were already skating in wide loops on the silvery-gray ice.

He'd caught up with the children in the front hall before they'd set out, and while they'd waited for Drummond and several of the staff to join them, he'd asked if the trio had learned anything more regarding Marion's whereabouts, but other than confirming that she definitely wasn't staying in any of the village's more far-flung cottages, they hadn't yet learned where she was laying her head.

As he stood on the crest, looking over the cheery winter scene and hearing the calls and occasional shrieks as several village children started out on the ice, his mind eased, and it occurred to him that it was possible that Marion had been on her way somewhere else and had merely stopped in the area for a day or so before continuing on her way.

He blinked and considered the notion. On reflection, given how few people had known to where he'd elected to retreat, it was far more likely that she *didn't* know he was presently in Little Moseley, and therefore, her appearance in the village was pure coincidence rather than that she'd somehow learned where he was, had determinedly chased him there, and was remaining in the area to continue her pursuit.

Once he thought of the matter in that light…

He grinned, and relief flowed through him. He'd been worrying over nothing.

Feeling as if a weight had been lifted from his shoulders, he scanned the shifting throng below and located Jamie, George, and Lottie seated on logs by the shore. Together with a bevy of village children, they were busily strapping on their skates. As Christopher watched, Jamie stood, tottered to the edge of the ice, and pushed off. George followed on his heels, and Lottie was only a heartbeat behind. The three instantly fanned out, skating in elegant arcs, then they straightened up and whizzed faster around the lake. Even from the top of the rise, he could make out their ecstatic laughter.

Smiling indulgently, he started down the slope. Drummond grunted and fell in behind.

Assuming his latest, more rational assessment of the Marion situation was correct, then it was likely that she was already far away. Christopher decided to speak with the children and call them off, but given the number of people all around, that could wait until later.

Breathing deeply, he felt his enthusiasm for the party, his eagerness to experience this aspect of a Little Moseley Christmas, swell to fresh heights. It had been a long time since he'd felt such simple unalloyed anticipation; he hadn't had this sort of Christmas for more years than he cared to count.

Over the past decade, his customary Christmas had involved leaving his desk on the morning of Christmas Eve and making a mad dash north to Winslow Abbey, there to kiss a large number of female cheeks and wring his brothers', brothers-in-laws', and nephews' hands, eat a sumptuous feast, then go to church on Christmas morning in the Abbey chapel before sitting down to an even bigger feast, after which he, his brothers, and his brothers-in-law would retreat to the earl's library to sink into deep armchairs and sip fine brandy or whiskey and pray the rest of the family forgot they were there.

He would do his best to relax and enjoy the subsequent few days, but immediately after the first of the year, he would rush back to London.

Winslow was often snowed in, or sleet made going outside unappealing. Only rarely did they emerge for the children to build snowmen or skate on the lake. Throughout his youth, his home had been Osbaldestone House in Berkeley Square; he'd rarely had the chance to enjoy traditional country Christmas events, only on the few occasions when, his parents being away on overseas postings, he'd spent Christmas with school friends at their country homes, but that had been literally decades ago.

Now, of course, he was seeing the Little Moseley traditions through his nephews' and niece's eyes, and he had to admit to feeling an almost childlike excitement.

He glanced at Drummond, now lagging a few steps behind him, then grinned, faced forward, and called, "Come on."

Reaching the groups of adults clustered just back from the shore, he was impressed by the turnout, and the enthusiasm and happiness enveloping the crowd was infectious and uplifting. He could understand why the children insisted on returning to the village year after year.

Weaving between the groups, he smiled and nodded greetings to everyone he recognized, receiving the same in return. His mother had declared her knees were giving her too much trouble for her to attend and had delegated him as her representative. Conscious of that and her expectations, he located the Colebatches, the Swindons, the Longfellows, and Mrs. Woolsey gathered in a group to one side, exchanged greetings all around and conveyed his mother's regrets at missing the event, then stood chatting for several minutes, putting his memory for details to good use by asking after the Longfellows' children, both too young as yet to attend, and charming Mrs. Woolsey by complimenting her on a new scarf.

Finally, along with the Longfellows and the Swindons, he strapped on his skates and took to the ice.

Within seconds, the children spotted him and came swooping in to circle him. They were accomplished skaters, but so was he; although he hadn't skated in years, he hadn't forgotten how. He laughed and, when the children teased him, chased them around the lake. They played a riotous game of tag for a short time, then settled to weave complicated patterns around each other, trying to outdo each other in sheer elegance of movement.

Eventually, they came upon Henry, Dagenham, Kilburn, Carnaby, and George Wiley somewhat languidly skating along. Finding himself rather breathless, Christopher waved the children on and joined the younger gentlemen on their rather more sedate circuit. The children laughed and waved, then raced off to find their friends.

Christopher asked Henry, "How long has the village held a skating party as part of the Christmas celebrations?"

Henry thought, then shook his head. "I don't know. For all of my life, there's always been a skating party, provided, of course, that the lake freezes well enough." He shot a glance at Dagenham.

The viscount smoothly said, "There was an incident four years ago. That was our first year here and also Jamie's, George's, and Lottie's. The lake wasn't, in truth, sufficiently frozen. We—the five of us—were horsing around at the northern end when the surface cracked and a little girl fell through, but Longfellow and Eugenia—she was just Henry's sister then—organized a rescue and managed to get Annie"—with his head, Dagenham indicated a young girl twirling ahead of them with her twin brother—"out in time."

"Since then," Henry said, "Dick Mountjoy's been extra careful over assessing how solid the ice cover is."

Christopher's brows rose. "Excitement, indeed, perhaps rather more than anyone wished for."

Kilburn replied with feeling, "Very true."

Their conversation moved to lighter matters, and they continued to follow the majority of adults in slowly circumnavigating the lake.

Several moments later, Dagenham, on Christopher's left, asked, "I vaguely recall that you have older brothers. Are they in the FO, too?"

Christopher laughed. "Heaven forbid. I suspect the FO is grateful to have only one Osbaldestone in their ranks. Monty, the eldest, is in the Home Office now, although he started in the FO." He glanced at Dagenham, but the viscount's face was something of an aristocratic mask and difficult to read. "I'm surprised you haven't come across Monty."

"Ah, but I'm only a lowly undersecretary, and with all the bustle about the Irish desk, I haven't had much chance to wander the halls and meet others."

Christopher nodded in understanding. "Monty's involved in overseeing various aspects of our trading capabilities at ports as well as the movement of goods around the country. Dry stuff, in the main. Lionel, the second of us, is in the War Office. His work is usually hush-hush, even more so these days."

"From what I've gathered about what you do, I suspect your work is equally classified," Dagenham returned.

Smiling, Christopher inclined his head. "Just so."

"And one of your sisters is Lady North, isn't she?"

Christopher nodded. "As North holds one of the senior posts in the FO, you might say Henrietta and I work for the same firm."

They skated on, then Dagenham said, "I mentioned that they were talking of sending me to Ireland, and I wondered if things would be different were I in the FO." He glanced at Christopher. "From what level are ambassadors and envoys drawn—those who are sent overseas?"

His gaze on the skaters ahead, Christopher shrugged. "Overseas posts range over a spectrum from junior aide to ambassador, so really, all levels might serve overseas. I have in years gone by."

"But surely not the upper echelon—Powell, North, and so on?"

"Not in general, but even Castlereagh might be dispatched overseas for short periods, for treaty negotiations, that sort of thing."

Dagenham nodded his understanding. "Just short-term journeys for specific missions. So where do ambassadors sit in the hierarchy?"

"Essentially one rung below the divisional heads like Powell, North, and Sewell." Christopher considered, then went on, "Sewell is a case in point. He was our ambassador in Russia, then in Austria, then he returned last year and stepped up to head the embassies division, more or less on a par with North and Powell and reporting directly to Castlereagh."

Dagenham's features eased fractionally. "Ah, I see."

"Uncle Christopher!" Jamie called as the three children swooped in to circle tightly around Christopher, displacing the young gentlemen.

"You have to come and help." Lottie caught his sleeve, then George seized the other, and determinedly, they towed him away.

With a laughingly helpless glance at Dagenham and the others, who grinned and waved him off, Christopher allowed the three to conscript him as judge for a race between the village children.

A stretch of ice close to one hundred yards long was duly cleared and delineated by spectators. The children lined up, then Dick Mountjoy, standing behind the line, clapped loudly, and the pack shot off. Parents and friends cheered from the sidelines, and to everyone's surprise, Lottie zoomed past in first place.

She was ecstatic, and another race was called for ladies, and a third for gentlemen. The children insisted Christopher take part in the latter, and he, Henry, and Dagenham vied for first place, only to be overtaken at the last gasp by George Wiley.

Everyone was laughing, joking, and clapping each other on the back. With a smile stretching from ear to ear, Christopher looked around, feeling the exhilaration of the race slowly fading, leaving a warming glow of simple happiness behind.

It had been a very long time since he'd set aside all else in life and enjoyed himself like that.

~

Marion stood on the rise above the lake and surveyed the boisterously gay crowd. At least half the village appeared to be out on the ice, laughing and calling as, having just completed a race, the gathered skaters broke into smaller groups and started to circle the lake.

Christopher wasn't difficult to spot. His dark head and even more the graceful elegance with which he glided over the ice caught her eye. Relief slid through her at the confirmation that he truly was there. Now she just had to get close enough to speak with him.

She watched him for several minutes, noting the three children who interacted with him in a familiar manner that suggested they were the nephews and niece Lady North had mentioned. Deciding that her next step was to get out on the ice, Marion unobtrusively walked down the slope. Skirting the clusters of onlookers, she made her way to the shore.

From the glances thrown her way, it was clear she'd been identified as a stranger, but she met the looks with polite smiles and nods and received the same in return. She doubted anyone would view her as any sort of threat—except perhaps the man, Drummond, assuming he was, as she suspected, a guard sent to watch over Christopher.

As she had yet to learn what Drummond looked like and seriously doubted that Christopher would have warned the man against her, she dismissed the guard from her mind; she would worry about him interfering if and when he did.

She found a vacant log by the lake's edge, sat, and strapped on her skates. While she tightened the straps, she studied her quarry, noting the group of younger gentlemen and the other adults with whom he exchanged smiling comments. He seemed relaxed and at ease, far more so than she'd ever seen him, and the way he smiled at the children and they at him testified to a close connection. Indeed, the three children were his most frequent close companions, shooting away to talk to other children, then sweeping back to circle Christopher before heading off once more. They were in constant motion, like satellites orbiting a planet. She would need to choose her moment to approach him.

She picked her time now, and when he was skating away from where she sat, heading toward the far side of the lake, with her skates secure, she stood, wobbled two steps forward, and stepped onto the ice. After her years in Russia and Austria, she was an expert skater and merged easily with the circling throng, eventually settling into position about twenty yards behind Christopher's greatcoated back.

Taking care to keep several groups of skaters between him and her, just in case he glanced behind him, she skated slowly in his wake, waiting for the right moment to approach him.

~

Jamie, George, and Lottie were talking with the Bilson twins when Jamie spotted Drummond, who'd been sitting on a log on the bank, on his feet and waving at them.

When Drummond saw Jamie looking his way, he beckoned frantically, clearly wanting them to come to him.

Jamie tweaked George's and Lottie's sleeves. When they looked at him, he nodded toward Drummond. "I don't know what, but something's up, and he wants to speak with us."

The other two looked, then the three of them said goodbye to the twins and streaked over the ice to pull up in a shower of flakes by the edge where Drummond waited.

Lottie peered at Drummond's face. "What is it?"

Drummond crouched with the toes of his boots on the edge of the ice and beckoned them close. When they'd crowded in, he met their gazes. "There's a lady who just arrived and joined the skaters. She's circling about fifteen or so yards behind your uncle." They turned and looked, and Drummond went on, "She's not that young, with blond hair and wearing a bright-blue pelisse and matching bonnet trimmed with fur. See her?"

Jamie did and said so, and the other two nodded.

"Is she from the village or from round about?" Drummond asked.

"She's definitely not from the village," Lottie said.

"She looks like the lady Uncle Christopher told us about," George said. "Miss Sewell."

Jamie nodded. "She matches the description."

They all stared across the ice at the lady in the bright-blue pelisse.

"It looks like she's focused on Uncle Christopher," Jamie said.

Drummond nodded. "Seems that way."

"Look!" George pointed. "She's moving through the other skaters toward Uncle Christopher."

"She's closing in on him." Drummond rose. For a second, he stared at the scene unfolding before him as the lady steadily closed the distance to his charge, then he glanced at the children. "Your uncle might appreciate some help."

They looked at him inquiringly.

He waved them out. "Go and get between them and give him a chance to escape."

They turned and were gone, skates flashing as they darted out to where the lady had almost reached her target.

Watching from the shore, Drummond huffed. "He can't say I'm not watching out for him."

Keeping her gaze fixed on Christopher's broad shoulders, Marion carefully skated closer and closer. She'd seen the children skate off to one side and settle to chatter with two others, and she'd decided to seize the moment.

She pushed closer, her skates softly shushing on the ice. To her relief, Christopher appeared oblivious, skating slowly and looking about but, thankfully, not looking backward.

Inch by inch, she drew nearer, then she reached forward, gripped his sleeve, and lightly tugged, as a friend might to get another's attention.

Registering the contact, he slowed and started to spin her way.

Marion drew breath, the words of her many-times-rehearsed speech leaping to her tongue.

"Uncle Christopher!"

Startled, she released Christopher's sleeve as the three children streaked in at speed, skidding to halts that threw up ice shavings and pushing between her and Christopher, their small bodies jostling her.

"Sorry!" one cried, although he didn't sound repentant in the least.

"Excuse us!" the little girl piped.

Before Marion could gather her wits and react, the three, all gabbling ten to the dozen about some game, locked hands, forming a cordon between her and Christopher, and skated forward, pushing him ahead of them.

Marion halted and stared at the children.

Then she raised her gaze to Christopher's face and found him staring at his young relatives, plainly as stunned by their intervention as she. Then he raised his eyes and met hers, and for an instant, their gazes locked. She saw an expression of shocked surprise, almost horror, fade from his eyes, to be replaced by a faintly hunted expression that was almost regretful.

Then he looked down at the heads of his nephews and niece, and his expression hardened.

Facing forward, he allowed them to urge him into a faster glide, ultimately merging with the still-circling crowd.

~

Christopher inwardly cursed, but there was no way he could turn back the clock and rescript the past moments.

As much as he now wanted to.

Obviously, Marion was, in fact, pursuing him, for some reason he'd yet to determine. She had to be staying somewhere nearby and might well have come to the skating party specifically to contact him—as he'd originally hoped earlier that day. More, she'd approached him circumspectly, in a way that should have allowed her and him to exchange at least a few words without drawing anyone's attention.

Unfortunately, the children had picked up on his initial wish to avoid her, and he hadn't yet explained that he'd changed his mind.

The truth was he hadn't been entirely certain of his change of heart until he'd seen her standing there, knocked off-balance by the children's forceful intervention and at a loss to recover from it.

When her eyes had met his, he hadn't glimpsed any hint of frustrated desire. What he had seen had been more in the realm of burgeoning disbelief and welling irritation.

If his niggling suspicion was correct and she'd been trying to contact him for some non-personal reason in a way that would appear unremarkable, then welling irritation made sense.

If she'd been chasing him for personal reasons, then stubbornness would be more her style.

Sadly, given there might be French agents lurking and watching him from concealment, the children's intervention had made refusing their rescue, explaining he'd changed his mind, and stopping to speak with Marion impossible; that would have caused too much fuss and attracted too much attention. If he was being followed and watched, the last thing he wished to do was draw Marion into the spotlight and direct the French agents' attention to her.

If they were after him, they might go after her as a way to lure him into their net.

He wasn't about to risk that.

The children steered him on. He didn't dare glance back to see what Marion was doing. Then they drew level with Henry, Dagenham, and company, and the children patted his arms and his back, as if reassuring him he was safe.

He sighed inside, but something of his reaction must have shown in his expression, and the children looked at him in concern.

"Is something wrong?' Lottie asked.

Even more than before, he needed to learn how to contact Marion. He found a smile and directed it at the three. "I was just thinking that I really need to find out where that lady is staying."

Lottie exchanged a look with both her brothers, then Henry and Dagenham realized he was near and hailed him.

Resuming his relaxed mien, Christopher responded, then felt the children pat his arm again.

He looked their way in time to see them streaking off across the ice.

"They're very quick," Roger Carnaby commented.

Christopher nodded. *In more ways than one.*

~

Marion had remained stock-still, more or less in the middle of the lake, glaring at Christopher's departing back.

Compressing her lips, she'd wished she could curse. Had he actually warned the children to rescue him if she appeared and approached him?

Several curious looks from those skating past had reminded her that remaining stationary would make her stand out, and she'd started to slowly skate again, merging into the stream of adults lazily cruising around the lake.

She was, she'd decided, disgusted. She hadn't had time to tell Christopher anything—not a single word!

Surreptitiously scanning the skaters, she'd found him, still in the care of the children, approaching a knot of five younger gentlemen, no doubt reasoning that if he were with that group, he would be safe from her marauding presence.

Reliving the scant few moments when she'd managed to capture his attention, she'd grown even more annoyed at the memory of the alarmed and hunted look that had infused his eyes. She could guess what had occasioned it. In typical arrogant-male fashion, he thought she was pursuing him for his beaux yeux!

"Ha!" She skated on. No matter how much she might have been drawn to him—and in light of his present stupidity in believing of her what she suspected he did, she was highly inclined to revise that long-ago opinion—her purpose in being there was serious, indeed, righteous.

Her burgeoning temper pushed at her to race across the ice and insist he hear her out—she would love to see his face when he realized what she had to say—but the count and the kapitan had insisted from the first that it was absolutely imperative that contact be made without drawing any attention. Neither the count nor the kapitan had any way of knowing who was watching Christopher, but given his position, they had every reason to suspect that some enemy agent would be. That was why Robbie had nominated her as the person to make the critical first contact with Christopher.

Inwardly sighing, she reluctantly consigned to the realm of fantasy the appealing notion of having a face-to-face argument with Christopher on the ice and refocused on where she now stood.

Given they didn't know who might be watching Christopher or, even in this tiny village, who might be the sort they wouldn't want to know about their secret embassy, much less who might prove dangerous were they to get wind of it, her options were severely limited. She couldn't risk creating any sort of ruckus by openly approaching Christopher and insisting they discuss what she needed to bring to his attention.

"Damn!" She'd uttered that expletive more frequently while on this mission than at any other time in her life.

Irritated and frustrated, she glanced at Christopher one last time, then peeled away from the other skaters and headed for the shore. Forced to retreat, yet again.

She reached the edge of the ice, clumped onto the grass, found a log, sat, and stripped off her skates. She knotted the laces, then yanked the knot tight.

For a second, she paused, staring at the knot. Given Christopher's apparently entrenched aversion to giving her even a few minutes of his time, she had to question whether, despite her twin's confidence, she was the right person to prosecute this mission.

She grimaced, then gripped the skates' laces in her fist, rose, turned away from the lake, and started up the rise. She'd left Foggarty with the gig in the lane. "Time to go back to the manor and face the count and the kapitan."

By the time Marion reached Parteger Hall, she'd progressed to feeling dejected and disheartened.

Entering the house from the stable, she left her pelisse and bonnet with Coles, the butler, and slipped silently up the stairs to her bedchamber. She opened the door, saw Glennis sitting by the window, and walked in, closed the door, and dropped her skates on a corner of the rug.

Glennis looked up expectantly. "Success?"

Glumly, Marion slumped into the armchair before the fire. "Disaster."

"Oh."

"Oh, indeed. I'm seriously questioning whether I'm the right person for this task." She thrust her fingers into her hair. "Christopher is now not only intent on running from me, he even has his nephews and niece actively shielding him from me!"

Unperturbed, Glennis shook out the flounce she was hemming. "You'll manage. You always do. I've yet to see a hurdle you haven't succeeded in overcoming, one way or another."

"Humph!"

Glennis peered at her stitching, then clipped a thread. "Besides, Robert is relying on you, so no matter what happens, you won't give up."

Slumped in the comfort of the armchair, Marion was tempted to sniff disparagingly, but in her heart, she knew what Glennis said was true. She wasn't the sort to give up, not if her quest was worthwhile.

In this case, her quest—the task entrusted to her by her twin—was vital to the country's future.

No, she wouldn't give up.

She allowed herself several minutes to wallow in disaffection, then refocused her mind on what came next. What options she had to move forward.

Eventually, she rose, shook out her skirts, and went downstairs to speak to the count and kapitan.

She found the pair in the drawing room, a pleasant chamber on the ground floor. Two wide bay windows faced the south lawn, and the sun, which had finally broken through the clouds in the hour before it set, poured slanting beams across the room, making it seem quite cheery.

Count Gregor Leonski sat in the armchair closest to the hearth while his countryman, Kapitan Solzonik, appeared to have been pacing the room, as he was wont to do. The kapitan was a military man, and the enforced waiting with little to do was not sitting comfortably with him.

Both men looked up, hope in their faces, as Marion walked in and shut the door.

Solzonik started forward. "Did you meet with Osbaldestone?"

Marion met the count's more-observant eyes and grimaced. She sat on the chaise facing the count. "I found Osbaldestone and succeeded in catching his attention, but sadly, we were interrupted and forced apart before I could say a word, much less explain our request."

Solzonik frowned. "Who forced you away? Are they someone we need to watch for?"

She shook her head. "No—it was Osbaldestone's nephews and niece. I believe they think they're protecting him."

The count's brows rose in quiet amusement. "From you, my dear?"

She humphed. "The London ton is a dangerous place for men like Christopher Osbaldestone."

The count's lips twitched, but Solzonik's frown deepened.

Before the kapitan could lead them off topic, and before she could lose her nerve, Marion fixed her gaze on the count's lined face. He was a portly personage of some dignity, and in the short time she'd known him, she'd grown quite fond of him. "Osbaldestone has fixed it in his head that I'm pursuing him romantically." There. She'd said it. "He therefore runs at the sight of me, which makes it rather difficult to speak with him in any effective, reasonably private, and non-attention-attracting way."

Without giving either man a chance to comment, she rolled on, "I know I previously argued against sending a letter to Christopher at Hartington Manor, asking for a meeting between him and me at which I could verbally explain your presence and arrange for you to meet with him. However, in the circumstances"—*beggars not being able to be choosers*—"that might be the best way forward. I could word the note so he would understand that the subject I wish to discuss with him is in no way personal."

She waited as the count digested that. Solzonik watched the count as well. The kapitan was rather prickly, but Marion suspected that was due to not being comfortable outside his own country and being unsure how things were done, but despite his difficulties, he was wholly and completely devoted to his cause.

From what she knew of the count, he was highly experienced in international diplomatic circles, as one might expect of the Emperor Alexander's personal envoy.

After several minutes, the count, his gaze fixed unwaveringly on her face, said, "Correct me if I err, but as I understand it, the issues you previously raised—the risks in attempting to get a letter directly into Osbaldestone's hands—remain." He arched his brows. "Is that not so?"

Suppressing a grimace, for she could see where this was leading, she nodded. "All I can do is have a letter delivered. There's no way I can see to ensure it reaches Osbaldestone's hands directly."

"And there is still this other man—this Drummond—staying in the house?" Solzonik asked.

Marion nodded. "He was there, at the lake, this afternoon, keeping watch over Christopher." It suddenly occurred to her that Drummond, if he was guarding Christopher, should have intercepted her when she came off the ice, if nothing else to learn who she was…unless Christopher had already warned him about her, which, given the children's intervention, seemed all of a piece. She only just managed not to wince.

"Hmm. And this Drummond hails from your Foreign Office, too?" the count asked.

"I don't actually know, but I suspect so." She paused, then added, "It's the sort of thing they would do if they believed Christopher was being followed by foreign agents."

The count nodded decisively. "In that case, my dear Marion, I believe we need to persevere with our current strategy. We cannot risk others gaining even a hint of my and the kapitan's presence, much less for a note, even one merely organizing a meeting between you and Osbaldestone, falling into other hands. This Drummond is not someone we know, not someone vouched for by anyone we trust. Our mission is too critical to our countries for us to take such a risk."

Solzonik shifted, drawing both the count's and Marion's gazes. "If I could make a suggestion?"

The count nodded in invitation.

Solzonik looked at Marion. "We cannot risk a note that we have to leave to others to pass on to Osbaldestone, but is there some way that you might, perhaps, approach him without him knowing, close enough to slip a note directly into his pocket?"

Marion tipped her head and considered the prospect.

The count eyed her speculatively. "If, as you managed to do today, you could approach him in a crowd or in some other situation where he remained unaware, you could either hand the note over before he flees or, as the kapitan suggests, slip it into his pocket."

Slowly, she nodded. "That might work." Her mind started to evaluate possibilities.

The count cleared his throat. "Sadly, with neither the kapitan nor I daring to show our faces…"

Briefly, she shot him an absentminded smile. "I will have to be the one to deliver the note to Christopher. I do see that."

She straightened on the chaise. "He might well attend church on Sunday. And there's some other village celebration next Wednesday, and as it seems he's intent on enjoying the village's Christmas events with his nephews and niece, the chances are good that he'll attend that as well." She paused, then added, "Other than those two events, I'm not sure there will be another useful opportunity, one where I might be able to use a crowd as cover to get close to him."

After a moment, she refocused on the count, then glanced at Solzonik. "I hadn't imagined it would take this long to set up a meeting between you and Christopher. I suspect you hadn't, either. And I might fail again. Do you have the time to waste another week?"

The count smiled at her. "My dear, during my many long years dealing with government negotiations, I have always found it best not to rush and settle for less than what one needs. We need a private meeting with Osbaldestone, one cloaked in absolute secrecy. Neither the French nor any other government must learn that we are here and speaking with him. If we have to wait another week or even two?" The count shrugged with continental grace. "We will wait."

Marion read his commitment in his eyes. Slowly, she nodded in acceptance. "Very well. I will try on Sunday to, at the very least, slip a note into his pocket."

She rose, and the count inclined his head to her. "Thank you, my dear." He held out a hand, and she extended hers, and he took it and patted it avuncularly. "I and the kapitan and our country are inestimably grateful for your and your brother's assistance with this delicate mission."

She smiled and curtsied, then retrieved her hand. She nodded to the kapitan, who nodded soberly back. "If you will excuse me, I must check with the staff. I will see you at dinner."

With a last graceful nod, she made for the door. As she drew level with the second of the bay windows, she glanced out into the deepening gloom. Shadows danced beneath the tall fir on the opposite side of the narrow lawn.

Marion paused and, frowning, looked again, trying to penetrate the dimness beneath the tree. Had someone been there?

Then she realized the branches were faintly waving. Presumably the chilly breeze was stiffening, tossing the branches and causing the shadows to shift. Reassured, she reached for the doorknob, opened the door, and went to speak with the housekeeper.

CHAPTER 7

Excited and gratified, with twilight edging into full dark, the children clattered into the manor's stable—late, but triumphant.

Inside the stable, they found Simms, whom they'd expected to see, and also Drummond. He was leaning against a stall door and stroking the long nose of one of their uncle's blacks.

The three slid from their saddles, and Simms grunted. He rose from the upturned pail on which he'd been sitting and came forward to take charge of Lottie's pony.

Drummond straightened. "Where did you three skive off to? I saw you running back this way, but when your uncle and I got back here, you'd vanished."

"Came and got their ponies," Simms grumped, leading Lottie's mount into a stall. "Then rode off in a rush."

"We followed the lady in blue—Miss Sewell." Lottie climbed the slats of the stall door and leaned along the side wall to pat her pony while Simms unsaddled the beast and started to brush him down.

Meanwhile, Jamie and George had led their larger mounts into their stalls and were busy tending them. From the stall he was in, Jamie offered, "We waited in the trees on the edge of the green and saw Miss Sewell leave."

"She had a man with a gig waiting in the lane," George said.

"The man drove north along the lane," Jamie continued, "but he wasn't going fast, so we raced back here, got our ponies, and went the other way. When we drew level with Witcherly Farm, we saw the gig turn up the lane toward East Wellow."

"So we followed," Lottie concluded as if that was the most natural thing to do.

Drummond looked at the boys, busy in the stalls, then at Lottie on her perch, stroking her horse's nose, and shook his head. When they volunteered nothing more, he prompted, "So did you learn where she's staying?"

All three children threw him cat-who-got-the-canary grins and nodded.

"They drove toward East Wellow." Jamie vigorously brushed his mount. "But just before the sign, they turned in to a drive that leads to what we think must be an old manor house that sits north of the riverbank, on a piece of land carved out by one of the bends in the river."

His eyes narrowing, Drummond studied the three. "You didn't go any closer than the entrance to the drive?" He couldn't imagine these three being that cautious.

Lottie looked across at Jamie and George, who looked back at her, then she replied, "We tied up the ponies and scouted through the woods a bit, but it was getting dark by then, so we came away."

Drummond narrowed his eyes to slits. "And no one saw you?"

All three emphatically shook their heads.

"We didn't see anyone but Miss Sewell, either," George said.

Lottie nodded. "And we only caught a glimpse of her through one of the windows."

"But," Jamie said, "she was definitely inside the house."

"*And* she'd taken off her pelisse and her bonnet," Lottie said. "So that must be where she's staying."

Jamie and George finished tending their ponies, and Simms had long finished with Lottie's smaller beast. The children, clearly well trained, went to help Simms fetch feed and water for their mounts, then shut the weary animals into their stalls.

In a group, the three turned toward the house, and Drummond and Simms fell in behind.

Once inside the back door, in the short corridor that led past the kitchen, the three exchanged a look, then Jamie said to Drummond, "We need to tell Uncle Christopher." With that, the three clattered up the short flight of steps and pushed through the baize-covered door leading to the front hall.

Simms's smile finally bloomed. He shook his head. "Always up to something, those three."

Drummond grunted. He was quietly impressed by the trio's intelligence-gathering abilities, but it wouldn't do to tell them that. He debated whether or not to follow and see what Osbaldestone had to say, but he hadn't yet let on to his charge that he knew about Miss Sewell, and at the moment, he was happy to leave the man in ignorance. The three could pour out their news to their uncle without his assistance.

Catching a whiff of something that set his mouth watering, he followed Simms into the servants' hall to see what Mrs. Haggerty was preparing for dinner.

~

The children looked into the drawing room, but found it empty. Avoiding their grandmother's private parlor, they trooped quickly upstairs and knocked smartly on their uncle's bedroom door.

"Come in," he called, and Jamie opened the door, and they rushed inside.

George shut the door and joined Lottie on one arm of Christopher's chair while Jamie perched on the other.

Amused, Christopher looked from one to the other. "What's this? And where did you three get to after the skating?"

"You said you needed to know where that lady was staying," Lottie said.

Christopher forgot about the article he'd been reading and searched their joyful faces. "You found out?"

In great good humor, they related their adventures following the gig Marion had left in, then finding the manor house and seeing her inside it, sans coat and bonnet.

The idea of what Celia would say if she learned that Christopher was employing her precious brood to scout for him niggled at the back of his brain, but he quashed the thought; it seemed they'd pulled off a neat piece of surveillance without being spotted. He said as much, concluding with, "And I'm exceedingly grateful."

All three beamed at him, and he realized he was smiling nearly as broadly. "So," he said, "East Wellow. How far away is that?"

Jamie replied, "By the lanes, it's about two miles."

Christopher pondered that. He would dearly love to call on Marion and ask what this was all about, but with the prospect of French agents lurking, he couldn't risk it. If Marion was trying to contact him about something with diplomatic implications, as he now suspected might be the case, then no matter the importance of her information, just by seeking her out, he might put her in danger.

Regretfully, he discarded the notion of going to East Wellow.

He refocused on the children and found them studying him. He smiled. "I'm truly impressed, both by your scouting abilities and your tenacity."

They grinned, then George flicked a glance at his siblings and said, "East Wellow doesn't have Christmas events like the skating party."

"They also don't have any shops," Lottie informed him. "Not like in Little Moseley."

Jamie exchanged a look with the other two, then said, "We thought that perhaps Miss Sewell might just happen to be staying at that house, and she called in at Mountjoy's and heard about the skating party and thought it might be fun, so she came."

"And then," Lottie said, "she saw you and thought to say hello." Growing serious, she went on, "It might have just been that."

Christopher kept his smile in place and inclined his head. "Perhaps." His instincts said otherwise, but there was no reason to involve the children further.

Regardless of Marion's attempts to catch him in London—which he hadn't revealed to anyone at all—if, when she'd approached him on the ice, she'd shown any surprise at seeing him there, he might have allowed the possibility that her presence in the area was simply pure coincidence. But she'd actively stalked him at Lady Selkirk's soirée and had come to the skating party entirely alone and approached him surreptitiously from behind…and there had been nothing but determination in her face, before disbelief and irritation had swamped it.

Short of speaking with her, he was now as sure as he could be that she had some reason for wanting to speak with him. What he didn't yet know for certain was if that reason was in any way personal or something relating to his work.

Or possibly something else entirely, although at the moment, he couldn't imagine what. Guessing what went on in ladies' minds had never been his forte. Give him devious spymasters any day.

He could feel a headache threatening.

Wrenching his mind from the treadmill of trying to fathom Marion's reasons, he thought, then inwardly grimaced. If the children hadn't intervened today, he would have learned what was behind Marion's pursuit of him, but if that reason was connected to matters on his FO desk, even talking to each other apparently innocently might have been dangerous, especially for her and even for him.

The need to confront her and learn what was going on had only grown more urgent. Casting about for ways to approach her, he wondered with whom she was staying.

As if she was following the same line of thought—heaven forbid!—Lottie mused, "I wonder who lives there—at the old manor house."

Before he or the boys could respond, the sound of the gong being struck for dinner resonated through the house.

The children leapt off the arms of the chair.

"We have to get ready, or we'll be late." George led the rush to the door.

Christopher waved them on, then rose, ambled to the door, and closed it. He stood thinking for a moment, then walked to the tallboy, picked up his hairbrush, and as the children were doing, made himself presentable for his mother's table.

~

After dinner, Therese sat in her favorite armchair by the fire in her private parlor and watched her grandchildren attempt to recreate the Battle of Leipzig using a conglomeration of toy soldiers.

Not that any of the three had any real idea where Leipzig was, much less which forces had joined in the battle against Napoleon the previous October, but as a great allied victory, the battle had, unsurprisingly, captured their imaginations. The fact that Wellington and the British forces had been thousands of miles away in the Pyrenees hadn't prevented the lauded general and his valiant troops from making an appearance in the children's version of the clash.

Thoughts of the military engagements on the Continent led Therese's mind to Christopher. At the end of the meal, he'd excused himself and retreated to his room to scour the news sheets delivered that afternoon. She was well aware his position required him to remain abreast of every last detail of the military campaign, and with access to the reports no doubt piling up on his desk in London temporarily cut off, the news sheets, however limited their scope, were his sole remaining source. Of course, the level of information he received would never be available via the news sheets, but no doubt he felt that reading the news reports at least kept him apprised of the generally known developments.

Therese smiled fondly at the children, then on a spurt of surprise, realized they hadn't filled her ears with observations from the skating party beyond confirming that it had been "great fun." Such uncharacteristic reticence was enough to awaken her curiosity. "Children." When they looked up at her, she said, "I'm sure more occurred at the skating party than you've yet told me. Surely something of note occurred?"

Apparently reminded, they launched into a recitation of all those who had been present and recounted the excitement of the races—and that Lottie had won! "George Wiley won the gentlemen's race," Lottie informed Therese, "and Tilly's sister, Jessie, won the ladies' race."

"Uncle Christopher nearly won, but George Wiley whizzed past at the end," Jamie said, clearly in awe of Wiley's prowess.

George eagerly reported, "Uncle Christopher showed us how to skate some really complicated figures."

Lottie bobbed on her knees, clearly captured by remembered events. "But the most exciting moment was when Drummond called us in to the shore and showed us the lady in blue—Miss Sewell—about to catch hold of Uncle Christopher's arm. Drummond was sure Uncle Christopher wouldn't want to speak with her and told us to get in her way, and we raced to the rescue!" Eyes alight, Lottie confided, "We reached Uncle Christopher just in time to tow him away to safety."

Therese blinked. "Miss Sewell?" She wasn't sure she'd heard correctly. "Would that be Miss Marion Sewell?"

Jamie and George shot Lottie surprised glances, but her granddaughter tipped up her little chin and told them, "Uncle Christopher didn't ask us not to tell, only not to be found out while we investigated. And we agreed to be Grandmama's eyes and ears." Having put her brothers firmly in their place, Lottie turned her blue eyes on Therese. "Yes, it was Miss Marion Sewell. Uncle Christopher saw her walking in the lane yesterday morning and asked us to see if we could find out where she was staying."

George volunteered, "She'd bought pork cutlets at Bilson's and a pint of milk at Mountjoy's, so we knew she had to be staying nearby."

Jamie added, "We asked around, but all we learned was that she wasn't staying anywhere in the village or in the cottages that are linked to the village."

"So"—Lottie reclaimed the stage—"after Miss Sewell came to the skating party and tried to speak with Uncle Christopher and we stopped her, Uncle Christopher said he still needed to know where she was staying, so when she left, we followed her."

"I see." Therese was intrigued. That a lady of Marion Sewell's ilk was staying somewhere near Little Moseley and was, apparently, seeking to speak with Christopher raised any number of fascinating questions in Therese's mind. She focused on her intrepid descendants. "And to where did you follow Miss Sewell?"

They told her how they had seen Marion Sewell driven off by a man in a gig, prompting them to race for their ponies and follow hotfoot. Tripping over each other's words in their eagerness, they described the old manor house outside East Wellow and confessed that they had watched from hiding long enough to glimpse Marion Sewell inside.

"She wasn't wearing her coat or bonnet then," Lottie reported, "so she must be staying there."

"It was getting dark," Jamie said. "So we returned to our ponies and rode back."

Therese regarded them with unfeigned admiration. They really were an indomitable trio. "I believe the old manor house south of East Wellow is known as Parteger Hall." The three looked interested, but she had to disappoint them. "I'm afraid that's all I know of it." She studied their faces. "I take it you've informed your uncle of what you've learned."

They nodded.

"And Drummond," George said. "He was in the stables when we rode in, so he knows, too."

She thought, then asked, "Did you see anyone else at the Hall? Any sign of the people Miss Sewell is staying with?"

They shook their heads.

After a moment, Lottie elaborated, "We saw only her through a downstairs window. No one else. But some of the curtains in the upstairs windows were open while other rooms looked shut up, so most likely, there are other people staying there."

"Indeed." Therese couldn't imagine that Marion Sewell would be staying in such a house alone, yet neither could she imagine what family might be living there—a family of sufficient status to host the daughter of Sir Nathaniel Sewell and his wife, Emily, who was a cousin of the Duke of Argyle, on what was, presumably, being passed off as a social visit.

Therese knew Nathaniel and Emily Sewell from the years in which

Therese's husband, Gerald, had reigned supreme at the FO, although they'd all been much younger then. Now, Nathaniel held a very senior post within the FO, as high in the hierarchy as Therese's son-in-law, North, which was to say very high indeed. Therese had been introduced to Marion Sewell years ago, in the year Marion had made her come-out. Although Therese wasn't all that familiar with the girl, she couldn't imagine a daughter of Emily Sewell wandering aimlessly about the countryside.

That left Therese pondering the intriguing questions of what Marion Sewell was doing at Parteger Hall and why Christopher seemed to think she had followed him into Hampshire and was, apparently, fixated on engaging with him.

The more she considered those questions, the more that certain instincts she'd long assumed dead seemed to flicker and flare to life.

Quite obviously, something was going on, but at that point, Therese had no idea what.

Then Lottie leaned closer and asked, "Do you think Miss Sewell might have followed Uncle Christopher to the village to try to meet with him and get him to fall in love with her?"

Therese studied Lottie's earnest expression, then replied, "I have to admit, my dear, that I'm having quite a lot of difficulty believing that."

~

The following afternoon, when the children returned to the house after choir practice, Therese was waiting in her parlor, sipping a cup of strong tea, with a tray loaded with an enticing tea cake on the low table beside her chair.

When Crimmins had brought in the tray, she'd alerted him to her wish to consult her grandchildren as soon as they returned; consequently, hard on the heels of their footsteps clattering into the front hall, the parlor door opened, and Crimmins ushered the three into the room.

In the way of children everywhere, their eyes fell on the cake and promptly grew round.

"Ooh!" Lottie said. "Mrs. Haggerty's special tea cake."

Smiling, Therese waved, inviting them to partake of the treat, and they rushed forward to fall on their knees about the table. Therese watched in supervisory fashion, pleased to see that even among themselves, their manners held firm, and they treated each other with appropriate politeness, even while devouring the cake in ravenous fashion.

Sipping, she waited until the cake was reduced to mere memories, then inquired, "How goes the choir?"

She was assured that the songs were coming along well and that the Moodys—the choirmaster who had conducted the previous year's event and his wife, who was the organist—were living up to the children's expectations.

"The carols are largely the same, of course," Jamie observed.

"Except," Lottie said, "that we all agreed we have to have a new song to replace 'The Holly and the Ivy' because no one else could possibly sing it so beautifully as Melissa and Dagenham did last year."

George nodded. "No one wants to try and end up disappointing all those who come, all of whom would have heard Melissa and Dagenham's version."

Therese nodded. "Yes, I see. That's very sensible of the Moodys. I'm glad you're enjoying working with them again." She set aside her teacup, sat back, and fixed her gaze on the children. "Now, however, I have something of my own to report."

Instantly, all three sat up. "Oh?" came from all three throats.

Therese hid a smile and, maintaining a serious air—as, indeed, befitted the subject—went on, "I've been mulling over all you told me yesterday about Miss Sewell staying at Parteger Hall and trying to catch your uncle, presumably to engage with him."

She paused and studied their attentive faces and spent one last minute weighing up whether asking them to learn more was wise. But she, and very likely Christopher as well, needed to know. "I want you to learn who Miss Sewell is staying with while, simultaneously, exercising an abundance of discretion." She paused, then asked, "Do you know what that means?"

All three nodded, and Jamie said, "We're to do so without being noticed and without making other people too curious."

"Exactly. I—and your uncle, too—need to know who else is currently residing at Parteger Hall. I don't mean the local staff or any children, but I would like to know everything you can learn of all the adults there—all those who might be either the owners or visitors." She scanned their faces. "Without knowing that, we can't make any reasonable guess as to why Miss Sewell is here. But as I said, in gathering those facts, you must not attract undue attention."

She wasn't surprised to see all three faces almost glowing with eagerness; they were delighted with their new mission. "Do you understand?" she asked.

"Yes, Grandmama!" they chorused.

"So you'll do that for me?" When all three nodded like three bobbing-headed dolls, she added, "And be sure, once you have the information, to bring it first to me."

"Yes, Grandmama" came again, then the three turned to each other and started speculating on whom they might ask regarding who lived at Parteger Hall.

Therese allowed their chatter to wash over her while she retrod her conclusions thus far. She couldn't—simply could not—imagine Marion Sewell chasing Christopher into deepest Hampshire on any silly whim. Marion would have a reason, a sound and valid and possibly imperative reason, and it would not be that she was personally invested in becoming more closely acquainted with Christopher. It was simply inconceivable that any daughter of Emily Sewell would be that outrageously forward.

No. There had to be some perfectly sane and sensible reason behind Marion's pursuit of Christopher that Therese could not as yet divine. And it might well have something to do with Marion's twin brother. The pair were understandably close, and after spending the day searching through her copious correspondence, Therese had verified that Robert, Marion's twin, was currently doing duty in the British embassy at the court of Emperor Alexander.

Given Russia was now an active member of the Sixth Coalition…

Therese felt that telltale prickling along her nerves that, in decades past, had meant that something of significance was afoot. Something to do with Russia?

She refocused on the children, still engaged in canvassing the possibilities for learning the vital information. She stirred and, on regaining the trio's attention, said, "My dears, I should clarify that by saying 'who Miss Sewell is staying with,' I'm speaking literally. I would like you to pay particular attention not so much to who owns Parteger Hall but to who else is presently there, residing in the house with Miss Sewell." She held the children's gazes and went on, "It occurs to me that whoever owns the property might not be there—they might well have hired the place out for the season. Consequently, in this instance, the owner is unlikely to be of major interest to us. Rather, please focus on those actually sharing the house with Miss Sewell. Names would be preferable, of course, but if that proves difficult, as it might well do, then a sound description will suffice, at least to begin with."

All three of her grandchildren smiled in ready understanding, then Jamie glanced at the other two and declared, "We'll start our campaign tomorrow."

CHAPTER 8

Two afternoons later, fifteen minutes after choir practice had ended, the children tramped down the church drive, heading back to the manor.

The day had been cloudy and cold, and night was falling swiftly. Bundled up in coats, mufflers, hats, and warm gloves, the three walked steadily, with their gazes fixed on the drive before their feet and frowns on their faces as they reviewed what they'd managed to learn thus far about the current occupants of Parteger Hall. Their first tack had been to talk to all those in the village with relatives in East Wellow. Courtesy of the nearness of the hamlet to the village, there had proved to be several connections.

"It was a piece of luck," Jamie said, "that Betty Butts is the barmaid of the East Wellow inn and she came to visit the Buttses yesterday."

"And that Ben was there to hear the gossip Betty shared with his mother," George said.

Lottie sighed. "At least we've learned that the new people at the Hall are a lady and two foreign gentlemen and their staffs and that they arrived on Monday evening."

"And that they came from London and are supposedly friends of the owners, who don't normally live at the Hall." Jamie kicked a pebble toward the side of the drive.

"Lucky for us," George observed, "that even though the owners aren't at the Hall much, they keep the local staff on."

"They haven't even come to act as hosts for these visitors," Lottie pointed out.

"Hmm." After a moment, Jamie said, "So according to the housekeeper, there's a lady's maid and the lady's coachman and her groom, all of whom are English, plus four foreign staff—two valets, a footman, and a coachman—so seven visiting staff all told."

"That's quite an entourage," George observed. "Even if, as Betty said, they're all quiet and respectful and keep to themselves."

Lottie nodded sagely. "Not even Mama takes that many staff when she travels."

"Yes, but," Jamie said, "the valets, the footman, and the second coachman are foreign, so they must belong to the two gentlemen. They're not all there with the lady."

"Well," George said, "if the three English staff are Miss Sewell's, and the others are the gentlemen's, that suggests Miss Sewell and the two gents are not one group but two."

Both Jamie and Lottie thought, then nodded.

"I'm not sure where that gets us," Jamie eventually said.

The three were accustomed to the vagaries of investigations, to how, at first, information often came easily, but the further they went, the more frustrating things became as they hunted for answers to the critical questions. Sometimes, clues were thin on the ground.

They reached the lane, looked both ways, then crossed. With the temperature dropping and their breaths misting before their faces, they walked on a few yards and turned up the manor drive.

Jamie sighed and glanced at his siblings. "I really don't think the descriptions Johnny and Ginny Tooks got from their cousin Matty are all that much use, not in terms of Grandmama identifying the gentlemen."

Matty Tooks worked in the stable at the inn in East Wellow. He'd called at Tooks Farm for lunch that day, and Johnny and Ginny had come to the carol practice eager to share what their cousin had told them of the pair of foreign gentlemen seen at Parteger Hall.

According to Matty, the younger of the pair was a few years older than the lady, and everyone who had seen him agreed that he had a definite military air. "Struts about all stiff like a soldier" had been Matty's words. Apparently, the military man spoke English with a strange accent, one no one who had heard it could place. Although the staff at the Hall—who often passed a few hours at the inn of an evening—had heard the military man speak French, which language several of them recognized, they were adamant that he did that with a very strong accent, too, and when the military man spoke with the older gentleman, just the pair of them alone, they used some language none of the staff recognized.

As for the older gentleman, apparently Matty had said that he was really old, a bit shrunken and hunched, with dark spots on the backs of his hands and cheeks, and walked slowly using a cane. He would have been a largish man in his heyday and was dressed well, very neat and proper, and the Hall staff reported that he was always very polite to them. "Distinguished" had been the general verdict.

George grimaced. "You're right. We know enough to be able to recognize them if we see them, but it's not enough to take to Grandmama so she can guess who they are."

Determinedly, Lottie stated, "We need names."

Jamie and George nodded.

Lottie tipped her head. "Perhaps the older gentleman is Miss Sewell's grandfather."

"He's not English," Jamie objected.

Lottie persisted, "*Or* a friend of her grandfather's."

"Or her father's or…" George shrugged. "Who knows? All we can say for certain is that Miss Sewell must be acquainted or connected with the two gentlemen in some way." He paused, then more hesitantly said, "I suppose Miss Sewell is not really a *young* young lady anymore, and she does have her maid with her, so presumably that's all right."

Jamie frowned. "If Grandmama knows the Sewells, and Miss Sewell, too, then I suppose we can assume that whatever Miss Sewell does must at least be acceptable."

They neared the house, and the front porch loomed. Lottie glanced at George, then Jamie. "We need to learn more."

Chin firming, Jamie nodded. "Grandmama will want more than we've learned so far." They halted before the door, and he met his siblings' gazes. On seeing his determination and resolution mirrored in their faces, he nodded decisively. "We'll have to go to East Wellow ourselves and see what we can learn."

~

Just before eleven o'clock on Sunday morning, with her pelisse buttoned to her throat against the icy wind and her bonnet dipped to protect her cheeks from the arctic blast, Marion clung to the shadows by the corner of St. Ignatius on the Hill, then as the last of the congregation's stragglers hauled open the main door, she scurried out and slipped into the church on the man's heels.

The door swung closed behind her, leaving the foyer rather dim. She paused and rapidly scanned the church. On spotting a space in the rear pew on the right, one person in from the aisle, she quietly went forward. After excusing herself to the farmwife seated on the aisle, she slipped past, gathered her skirts, and sat, setting her reticule on her lap.

She'd kept her head down, hoping the front of her brown-velvet poke bonnet would shade her face. Having realized that her kingfisher-blue pelisse would make her easy to spot even in a crowd, she'd worn her traveling pelisse, which was in a rich shade of mahogany brown. Glancing to right and left along the pews, she confirmed that the color was much more useful for merging into the Little Moseley congregation.

She exchanged polite nods with the women sitting on either side of her. Judging by their work-roughened hands, both were farmwives.

Then a stir in the foyer heralded the arrival of the minister, and the congregation came to their feet as said minister, tall and thin with tufty white hair and a serene smile, led the choir down the aisle.

Marion seized the moment, and while the entire congregation was looking forward, watching the choir fan out to their places and the minister take up his stance before the altar, facing the congregation, she rapidly scanned the heads, searching for one particular dark one.

The minister raised his hands and intoned, "Let us pray," and just as she was about to join everyone else and bow her head, she spotted Christopher seated by the aisle in the second pew from the front on the left side of the church.

Drawing in a breath, she looked down and allowed a small smile of satisfaction to bloom. As she'd hoped, Christopher was there. Now all she had to do was bide her time and choose her moment to get close.

She responded to the prompts of the service by rote, sitting and rising with the rest of the congregation, dutifully praying and singing the hymns, and listening with an attentive air to the unexpectedly engaging sermon. Meanwhile, she inwardly assessed and evaluated her options for contacting Christopher. Regardless of which tack she took, to make her move, she would need to wait until the end of the service, when the congregation rose and shuffled up the aisle to exit the church via the main door.

The question was whether to risk attempting to speak with Christopher again or whether she should simply resort to surreptitiously slipping into his pocket the note she'd prepared and brought.

If she dallied in the pew and kept her head down, then slipped into the aisle just behind him, it would be easy enough to slip the note into his greatcoat pocket. The only drawback she could see with that scenario was that he might not realize the note was there until some unspecified time later. Who knew how often gentlemen checked their greatcoat pockets? That might result in a great deal more wasted time.

She tried not to frown, at least not outwardly. What if she stepped into the aisle immediately in front of Christopher? He would then know she was there, but would be unable to flee, not without creating an impossible-to-explain fuss. After meeting the minister on the porch and shaking his hand, she could then hover, obviously waiting to speak with Christopher once he finished with the minister, and if she smiled and spoke to Christopher as he was stepping away—making it obvious they were acquainted socially—then under the minister's and other congregants' gazes, surely Christopher would be forced to acknowledge her and listen politely, at least for a few sentences. A few sentences were all she would need to alert him to the reality of why she was there.

She paused, considering, then rose as those about her did. She quickly opened her hymnal to the correct page and prepared to sing the nominated psalm, even as she realized that if she confronted Christopher on the porch, regardless of what words they exchanged, she could hand him her note, and in those circumstances, he would be forced to take it.

Excellent! As the congregation resumed their seats, she shot a glance at Christopher and felt distinctly more confident. Allowing herself the chance to speak with him, give him the note, or both was surely the best way to go.

If she could seize his attention for long enough to indicate that she was, in effect, acting as a verbal courier for her brother, then she and Christopher could stroll on the lawn, as acquaintances might, and they could arrange the necessary meeting then and there.

She was, she decided, glad she'd braved the elements in order to attend the service.

With the rest of the congregation, she rose for the third hymn and, this time, paid attention to the words she, distinctly more joyously, sang. After the last note died, she drew her skirts close, but before she sat, as those in the pews in front of her subsided, she seized the moment to look again at Christopher.

Soon. Soon I'll have successfully completed the mission Robbie entrusted to me.

As she started to sit, she glanced at the spot in the pew beside Christopher, expecting to see the head of his niece or one of his nephews. Instead…

She dropped onto the hard seat and only just managed to smother a heartfelt "Damn!"

In her careful calculations, she'd forgotten all about Christopher's mother. The steel-haired dowager sitting so very upright beside him had to be the revered, famous and feared, and in some circles notorious Lady Osbaldestone.

Struggling to calm her suddenly leaping nerves, Marion shifted and found a gap between the burly shoulders of two men seated in front of her and, through it, peered at her ladyship's elegantly coiffed gray head, topped by a fashionable small beaded hat, while a host of potential scenarios unfurled in her mind.

Given what she knew of the lady, none of those scenarios, not one, was conducive to keeping her mission—hers and that of the count and kapitan—secret.

She knew that Christopher's late father, Gerald, Lord Osbaldestone, had been one of the most-lauded FO mandarins and that, to this day, his wife was regarded with unquenchable awe by those currently serving. Marion's mother had introduced her to Lady Osbaldestone years ago, when Marion had made her come-out, some months before her family had departed for Russia. Despite her ladyship's reputation for having a steel trap of a memory, Marion doubted the old lady would remember her now. Regardless…

Marion inwardly cursed. Courtesy of Lady North, Marion had known that Christopher was staying at his mother's dower property, but she hadn't, until that moment, considered the ramifications of coming face-to-face with that lady herself. All things considered, she was entirely unsure how any such meeting would play out. And she certainly didn't need to introduce an additional complication into a mission that had already proved complex enough.

Can I pretend to simply be visiting some local family for the season?

Which family? Marion had no doubt that would be the first question past her ladyship's lips, and it was one for which she had no viable answer.

The more she thought about meeting Lady Osbaldestone, the more nervous Marion became. It wasn't only the steel-trap memory; she now recalled that the trait was said to be combined with eyes that missed nothing. Absolutely nothing.

Her nice, simple, sure-to-be-effective plan of slipping into the aisle in front of Christopher faded and died. Even the notion of trying to unobtrusively slip into the shuffling queue behind him was fraught with danger. If Lady Osbaldestone was half as observant as her reputation painted her, she wouldn't miss the sight of a well-dressed young lady she didn't recognize standing and waiting to slip into the aisle. She was all too likely to halt in the aisle and speak to Marion, just to find out who she was.

Amid her mental cursing, Marion heard in her mind the count's words as he reiterated that secrecy was paramount and that waiting for the right moment to make contact was preferable to risking exposure. Grimacing, she kept her head bowed as if concentrating on the minister's second reading and accepted that she would have to be guided by the count's experienced wisdom.

She bided her time until the congregation rose for the final hymn, then as unobtrusively as she could, she slipped past the woman at the end of the pew, stepped into the aisle, and walked quietly into the dim foyer. Only then did she risk a glance back, confirming that neither Christopher nor his mother had turned their heads. Reassured on that front at least, she cracked open the heavy door and slipped outside.

Standing together on the altar steps, with their gazes raised as they sang the last hymn, Jamie, George, and Lottie—who, with the other visitors to the village who had joined the choir, had today lined up with the regular choir to test the merging of their voices into a cohesive whole—saw the lady in dark brown slip out of the last pew and make for the door.

Then the lady glanced back.

With her elbow, Lottie jabbed George, who was standing beside her. Eyes widening, George nudged Jamie, who nudged back. He'd seen and recognized the lady, too.

All three looked at their Uncle Christopher, but his gaze was on his raised hymnbook.

As one, the three raked the congregation and spotted Drummond, standing in a place on the aisle farther back.

Although he appeared to be singing, as luck would have it, Drummond was looking at them.

All three signaled frantically with their eyes.

Drummond frowned, then glanced toward the door.

Just in time to see it shut.

To the children's relief, Drummond set down his hymnal, walked quickly and quietly up the aisle, crossed the foyer, and left the church.

Without missing a note, the children shared excited glances, then returned their attention to Mr. Moody, who they discovered was looking sternly at them.

All three smiled beatifically and continued to sing.

The hymn came to an end, and with the rest of the choir, the children resumed their seats. Under cover of the slight fuss that entailed, they saw Drummond come back in and unobtrusively reclaim his seat.

Seeing the children with their gazes trained on him, Drummond nodded once.

The children shifted on their seats, keen to learn what he had found.

They had to possess their souls in patience until the benediction had been bestowed, then as Reverend Colebatch, beaming as usual, led his congregation up the aisle, the children piled into the vestry to doff their chorister's robes, leaving them in Mrs. Moody's care, and spilled out of the church via the vestry door. They rushed to the front of the church and spotted Drummond standing to one side of the forecourt, apparently keeping an eye on those gathering on the lawn. The children made a beeline for him.

They pulled up in front of him, and Lottie fixed him with a sharply interrogatory look. "Did you see her?"

Drummond wasn't sure how much he should reveal to the three scamps, but in this case, they'd been the ones to alert him to Miss Sewell's presence. Without their sharp eyes, he wouldn't have known she'd been there. After a second's inner debate, he replied, "She got into a gig and drove off. Leave it with me—I'll let your uncle know."

All three regarded him through narrowing eyes, but then one of their friends hailed them, and ending their assessing scrutiny, they ran off to join a bevy of local children.

Drummond waited.

Eventually, after the usual chatting with the village gentry, Christopher guided his mother to where Simms stood beside the manor's gig.

Christopher helped his mother into the gig, then stood back as Simms drove off. Then he looked at Drummond and tipped his head down the drive. "Coming?"

Drummond nodded and lumbered forward, falling into step beside Christopher as they set off toward the lane.

"The children ran down a few minutes ago," Drummond volunteered.

"Yes, I saw." Christopher looked down the drive, but the three were already out of sight.

"What I suspect you didn't see," Drummond said, "was your Miss Sewell. She slipped out at the start of the last hymn and drove off in a gig."

Christopher's stride hitched, then he resumed his long-legged pacing and cast Drummond a sidelong glance. "You know about Miss Sewell." He paused, then faced forward. "The children told you."

Drummond nodded. "They did, but I wouldn't hold it against them. I'd asked them to tell me of any stranger they saw about the village, meaning men, but they didn't take it that way, and you hadn't told them to keep the matter of Miss Sewell to themselves." The big man shrugged and glanced to the side. "This is unknown territory for me, and I need to use whatever informants I can find."

Christopher snorted. "I suppose I'm doing the same. I've asked them to find out where she's staying." He frowned. "I wonder why she left without trying to speak with me?" He couldn't imagine why else she would have come, and the gathering on the lawn after the service would have provided the perfect cover—far better than trying to approach him in the middle of the lake. If she'd approached him outside St. Ignatius on the Hill in the same manner in which she'd tried to approach him in Lady Selkirk's drawing room, given he'd stopped stupidly running from her, they could have exchanged a few words in reasonable privacy in a way that would have seemed incidental to anyone watching.

He and Drummond trudged down the drive, then Drummond huffed. "Perhaps she doesn't want your mother to know she's pursuing you?"

Christopher saw the light. His lips tightened. "Damn! That's it."

They reached the lane, strode across, walked the few paces to the manor drive, and started up it.

Puzzled, Drummond looked at Christopher. "It, what?"

Christopher grimaced. After a moment, he explained, "If I was a female of Marion Sewell's ilk intent on tripping me into a matrimonial snare, I'd be eager to attract my mother's attention and do my damnedest to recruit her significantly powerful support." He shook his head. "Initially, I was stupid enough to think that was her purpose, but now… Her whisking away makes no sense unless the reason she's been trying to speak to me is something else entirely."

Her being at the church, but vanishing before trying to contact him was the final proof of that.

Drummond waggled his head. "She's female. Who can tell what she's taken into her head? I wouldn't read too much into that if I were you."

Christopher didn't reply. He was now convinced that Marion was chasing him in order to tell him something, and he was increasingly certain it was something he would want to hear.

Drummond stared ahead at the manor. "She couldn't be…well, caught up in some French agent's scheme, could she?"

Christopher snorted derisively. "Absolutely not. You may put that thought out of your head. The one element in all this that we can be absolutely, unquestionably certain of is that Marion Sewell is not a French spy. Or any other sort of spy." Christopher slanted a glance at Drummond. "You do realize she's Sir Nathaniel Sewell's daughter? He even outranks Powell. He's on the same level as North—one step down from Castlereagh himself."

"I know who her father is," Drummond somewhat impatiently returned, "but that only makes her a juicier target for some sneaky-but-charming French émigré, who doubles as one of Napoleon's agents, to befuddle and seduce." Darkly, he rumbled, "Ladies like her have been known to be susceptible to Continental charm."

Christopher almost laughed. "Trust me when I say that Marion Sewell wouldn't give any charming Frenchman the time of day. She'd look down her nose and cut him dead. She's the least impressionable young lady I've ever met—she's observant, sees people for who they truly are, and is insightful to boot."

Drummond humphed, but after several seconds, tipped his head Christopher's way. "Not being acquainted with the lady myself, I'll have to take your word for it. That said, the way she's behaving strikes me as suspicious, even if her motive for trying to speak with you is something other than appreciation of your charming self. Why not just come up to you in the village street?"

Christopher huffed. "She tried that at the skating party, remember? And it didn't work." Drummond didn't need to know about how Christopher had behaved at Lady Selkirk's; the skating party was example enough. "She's intelligent. She's not going to try simply coming up to me

—innocently bumping into me, as it were—again. She'll assume that if I see her coming—or you do—I'll fling you or the children in her path and hare off at speed."

He couldn't keep self-disgust from his voice. From the corner of his eye, he saw Drummond glance at him curiously, but simply shook his head. He'd allowed his recent brush with matrimonial danger to cloud his thinking regarding Marion; he'd effectively tarred her with the same brush as that other young lady and her matchmaking aunt. Out of sheer self-protectiveness, he—an experienced operative of long standing—had made her mission, whatever it was, much more difficult than it should have been.

If he'd allowed her to come up with him at Lady Selkirk's soirée, he could have learned whatever message she had for him and dealt with it before he left London. Instead, he'd led her there, into an area where French agents might be lurking.

While he had no idea what Marion wished to tell him, he felt certain neither she nor he wanted Napoleon to know anything about it.

As they neared the manor's front door, he was still castigating himself for his abysmal lack of judgment when the patter of flying feet had him pausing on the porch and looking back along the drive.

The children came pelting up.

He arched his brows. "Where have you lot been? We"—he tipped his head toward Drummond—"saw you come down ahead of us."

The trio flowed onto the porch, passing Christopher and Drummond. Close to breathless, George replied, "We went to the green to see Robert Milsom's new sled."

Lottie halted before the door, whirled, and fixed her big blue eyes on Christopher's face. "Did Mr. Drummond tell you about Miss Sewell being in the church?"

"Yes," Christopher said, "but as she left before the end and was long gone before we emerged, then at present, there's nothing further we can do on that front."

The children grinned, then Lottie opened the door, and the trio tumbled inside, followed by Christopher and Drummond.

With a clatter, the children rushed upstairs, and Drummond followed.

Christopher paused to hand his hat to Crimmins, draw off his gloves, and shrug out of his greatcoat, leaving all in Crimmins's hands.

As Christopher headed toward the drawing room where his mother would be waiting, somewhat grimly, he inwardly admitted that with respect to Marion Sewell's reason for trying to contact him, he was growing increasingly concerned.

~

After choir practice on Tuesday afternoon, with the day closing in, the children parted from their friends in the lane and turned up the manor drive.

A few paces along, Lottie glanced behind them, confirming that they were out of sight and hearing of anyone, then faced forward and asked, "So what do we do next to learn the names of the gentlemen staying at Parteger Hall?"

On Monday, the skies had opened, and it had sleeted all morning, but the weather had cleared sufficiently after midday to allow them to ride to East Wellow. There, they'd approached and interviewed every local they'd thought might know more about the visitors at the Hall.

Jamie grimaced. "I can't believe that the people in East Wellow are so uninquisitive that they haven't even bothered to ask the Hall's housekeeper what the names of her guests are."

George shrugged philosophically. "It's probably because the guests' names wouldn't mean anything to them."

"At least we now know," Lottie said, "that the older gentleman is a count and the other one is a captain." She frowned. "Of something."

"'Of something' is right," Jamie said. "For all we know, he could be the captain of a ship. Unfortunately, for Grandmama, who we can be very sure knows lots of counts and captains of all sorts, that's not going to be identification enough."

Soberly, the other two nodded.

Jamie glanced at George. "That was an inspired idea, to ask the deacon. A pity the Hall's guests haven't yet felt moved to attend church."

George wrinkled his nose. "I've been thinking about that. If this count and captain are from the Continent, which it seems almost certain they are, then chances are they're Catholics, and they don't go to our churches, do they?"

Jamie grunted and nodded. "You're right."

After a few more paces, Jamie looked at Lottie, on his right, then at George, on his left. "We're going to have to find some more direct way to learn those gentlemen's identities."

Lottie nodded decisively. "We're going to have to find someone who knows them and ask. That's the only thing we haven't tried."

George pointed out, "It seems the only people in East Wellow who know the guests' names are the staff at the Hall."

Jaw firming, Jamie nodded. "So that's who we're going to have to ask."

The three reached the porch. They climbed the single step and paused before the front door.

Jamie looked at his siblings. "We're going to have to go back to the Hall and hang about without being spotted by anyone until we see one of the staff come out—someone like a stable lad, who we can approach without raising suspicions. We could say that we've lost our way and then get chatting."

The three exchanged glances, then simultaneously nodded.

Jamie opened the door, and they trooped inside.

CHAPTER 9

On Wednesday morning, Christopher quickly climbed the stairs on his way to fetch his greatcoat from his room. He'd spent the past two days haunting the village shops—driving Drummond to grumbling under his breath about damn fool notions—in the vain hope of catching sight of Marion, reasoning that if he approached her himself, she wouldn't turn tail and flee.

Sadly, she hadn't appeared.

Not knowing if, by now, French agents had located him and were watching him, he didn't dare drive out to East Wellow, much less call at Parteger Hall. He didn't even dare risk sending a groom with a message. Any contact between himself and Marion had to appear incidental, at least initially. Any encounter had to appear unplanned and unremarkable until he learned what message she carried.

His worry over what she'd become embroiled in—and what might be happening given she'd yet to successfully contact him—was steadily escalating. But today, he lived in renewed hope. The children were waiting impatiently downstairs to conduct him to witness the village pageant, to be held on the green.

He'd been assured there would be a considerable crowd attending; with any luck, Marion would have heard of the event and would attempt to approach him there.

On the landing, he heard footsteps descending and glanced up, faintly surprised to see his mother coming down, pulling on her gloves as she came. "You're attending this event?"

She met his eyes and smiled. "I might not be as eager as the children, but for the atmosphere alone, I wouldn't miss it, and there's sure to be some unexpected excitement. There always is."

Smile still in place, she stepped onto the landing and, as they passed, waved him on. "Do hurry up—you don't want to keep our intrepid trio waiting."

He laughed and obligingly took the stairs two at a time.

The children had given him a brief description of the pageant, touted as one of the highlights in the village's Christmas calendar. When they'd questioned him, he'd admitted he'd never experienced such an event before. Predictably, they'd assured him it would be excellent fun.

He also prayed it would facilitate an encounter with Marion and thus ease his mind.

He entered his room and found his greatcoat tossed over the chair where he'd left it. He unearthed his muffler from a drawer and wound it about his neck and was shrugging on his coat when a tap on the door was followed by it opening and Drummond sticking his head around the panel.

His gaze raked Christopher. "Going, are you?"

"I'm not sure I have much choice, but regardless, I'm hoping Miss Sewell will seize the opportunity to make contact. With any luck, coming upon me in the thick of a crowd with my nephews and niece in attendance should give her cover enough to do so." He headed for the door. "I daresay she'll attempt to approach me surreptitiously, and a milling throng should be perfect for that."

Drummond eyed him narrowly. "And if she's after you for some personal reason, like you originally thought?"

Christopher was now sure that wasn't the case, but rather than argue, he mildly replied, "We'll see, won't we?"

Drummond snorted. "In case it's slipped your mind, you're supposed to be hiding from French agents who—so our higher-ups believe—could well be intent on kidnapping you."

Christopher lightly shrugged. "I haven't forgotten, but while a large crowd will assist Miss Sewell to approach, no French agent will be able to even show his face, much less get close. At such a gathering, everyone will know everyone else. Miss Sewell's been seen about several times, and she's English, but any foreign strangers will be scrutinized and watched. Such is the parochial nature of small villages, which, I'll remind you, is one of the reasons I'm here."

The more he thought of it, the more he approved of the morning's event as a safe venue for Marion to approach him. Even if French agents were watching from a distance, if she and he came upon each other in a crowd and spoke for a few minutes, it would appear to be an entirely incidental conversation.

He halted before Drummond, who was blocking the doorway, and smiled winningly. "Besides, if any French agents manage to draw near, you'll be there to save me."

Drummond made a rude noise, but consented to step back, out of Christopher's path. "In case anything does happen," Drummond grumbled, "I want it on record that I didn't approve of you wandering about freely in such a public place."

Already on his way to the stairs, Christopher replied, "Nevertheless, you'll come along and enjoy yourself. Best hurry and get your coat. I've been warned not to keep the children waiting."

Drummond huffed and headed for the servants' stair at the end of the corridor.

Christopher joined the children and his mother in the front hall. He accepted his hat from Crimmins, who was also dressed in his outdoor clothes.

His mother claimed Christopher's arm, and they turned toward the door, which Crimmins leapt to open.

As she stepped onto the porch, his mother looked up at the sky, which was blessedly clear. "I intend joining Henrietta Colebatch and watching the event from the end of the vicarage porch." Smiling, his mother met his eyes. "As you'll no doubt discover, the high ground on the green side of the vicarage wall is a favored vantage point for this event, and the spot can get rather crowded. Henrietta and I will be much more comfortable on her porch, which is even higher and affords a clear view of the action."

"That sounds like an excellent idea." Christopher was relieved on several counts, not least that, although her acuity and sharp intelligence remained undimmed, his mother wasn't getting any younger, and he knew her knees occasionally gave her trouble. On top of that, having his mother at a distance, out of his immediate orbit, would, from Marion's point of view, remove another impediment to her approaching him and explaining what was going on.

The children scuttled out of the door and around them. "Come on!" they implored.

"Or we won't get good spots," George ominously chided.

"You have to come with us," Lottie informed Christopher, "so we can tell you what all the different bits mean."

He smiled and waved them ahead. "We'll deliver your grandmama to the vicarage, and then I'm all yours. Let's go."

With a cheer, they led the way, dancing and skipping down the drive.

Still smiling, with his mother on his arm, Christopher followed, and as they walked in the children's wake, virtually all the manor staff came around the side of the house and fell in behind them. Glancing over the heads, Christopher spotted Drummond bringing up the rear, pacing alongside Simms, his mother's ageing coachman.

Facing forward, Christopher felt his smile grow wider.

They soon reached the steps that led up to the vicarage garden gate, where Henrietta Colebatch stood waiting. Christopher steadied his mother up the stone steps, then she dismissed him and, together with Mrs. Colebatch, walked through the garden toward the house and the steps to the porch.

Christopher turned to descend to the lane and saw the children beckoning wildly. With a laugh, he went quickly down, and as soon as he stepped into the lane, they pounced and, with Lottie hanging on one arm, George on the other, and Jamie leading the way, towed him the short distance to the village green. The rest of the staff had gone ahead, except for Drummond, who walked close behind Christopher, plainly scanning their surroundings for any threat—an undertaking that became distinctly fraught when they reached the green and saw the crowd already massing on the sward.

"Good Lord!" Christopher surveyed a veritable sea of heads. "I had no idea this many people call the village home."

"Well"—Lottie gripped his hand more firmly and confidently towed him into the scrum—"there's everyone from all the farms round about as well, and all the staffs at the bigger houses come."

"So," George summarized, "this really is all of the village in one place."

Between them, the children herded Christopher, with Drummond on his heels, up the slope that rose to meet the side wall of the vicarage garden. Once they'd claimed a spot, with all of them lined up with their backs to the stone wall, Jamie informed him, "This is the prime vantage point. We'll be able to see everything, from the start of the procession over there"—he pointed far to the left, where, despite the crowd, it was obvious a mustering area of sorts had been set up in the center of the green—"all the way along the procession's route as it winds through the crowd to the stable in Bethlehem." He'd traced a wending path leading across their line of sight to a rudimentary structure, much like a market stall without any front table, that had been erected some way to their right, about ten yards from the lane. Under the awning stood a large wooden manger with a three-legged stool beside it.

"That's where Mary sits," Lottie explained, "and all the animals come to see Baby Jesus, with the kings and shepherds and all the rest."

George pointed to a small group of choristers, dressed in white robes, who were standing to one side of the "stable." "They're the Heavenly Host."

"That's the angels who sing," Lottie told him.

Christopher tried to keep his lips straight as he dutifully nodded.

A large buxom woman, clearly in her Sunday best with a bonnet sporting dried flowers perched on her gray head, puffed up the slope, turned, and settled into the spot alongside Christopher. She nodded at the children. "Lady Lottie, Lord James, Mr. George. It's nice to see you about the village again."

The children smiled and returned the greeting, addressing the woman as Mrs. Tooks.

The woman turned to Christopher. "Good morning to you, Mr. Osbaldestone, sir. I'm Martha Tooks of Tooks Farm."

Christopher returned her polite nod. "I believe your son looks after the village's flock of geese."

Mrs. Tooks's face split in a proud smile. "Indeed, he does, sir." She tipped her head Christopher's way and confided, "Johnny used to be such a tearaway, but the geese have given him something to do. Settled him right down, they have."

Christopher smiled. "The responsibility has made him grow up?"

Mrs. Tooks nodded. "Just so."

She turned to speak with the two ladies who had followed her up the slope and claimed the positions next to her. Glancing that way, Christopher saw that the entire length of the vicarage wall was now lined with people, and more were steadily settling in ranks before and below them, the better to view the promised entertainment.

Christopher saw Henry, Dagenham, Kilburn, Wiley, and Carnaby in a similar position farther along the wall. He raised a hand, and they waved in reply. Watching them, Christopher got the impression that they considered shifting closer, but the crowd before and between them had grown much denser, and there was no space left along the wall.

Looking out across the green, he had to admit that their position afforded an excellent view. The babel rising from the crowd was approaching deafening when he saw Reverend Colebatch leave the mustering area and stride rapidly along a zigzag path that several helpers had cleared through the crowd. As he passed, the crowd quieted, and an expectant hush gradually fell over the scene.

Christopher had to admit that even he felt a rising sense of anticipation.

The good reverend reached the stable and the Heavenly Host and took up a position before the latter, facing the crowd. Beaming fit to burst, Colebatch raised his hands in a wordless appeal for silence, although that was already approaching absolute. Into the resultant quiet, his voice strong and sure, he welcomed everyone to the event and gave a short introduction, followed by a description of what was to come. Then he reached high and waved in what was clearly a signal to those in the mustering area to begin the procession.

All eyes swung that way, and good-natured claps and cheers rang out as, perched on the back of a gray donkey and swaying rather precariously, a brown-haired girl gowned in blue and with what was plainly a cushion stuffed under her dress came into view. A boy in a white-and-red robe with a banded head covering, presumably Joseph, was urging the donkey along, tugging manfully on a rope attached to the animal's halter. The donkey reluctantly plodded along, then nearing the first curve, halted, lifted its great gray head, and looked around.

The boy tugged to no avail, but then, as if responding to calls from within the crowd, the donkey abruptly started trotting quickly along. The sudden change in gait elicited a shriek from the startled Mary, who now gripped the donkey's mane in both fists. Joseph, meanwhile, had to run to keep up with the now eagerly trotting beast.

"That's Duggins," George said to Christopher. "He belongs to Lord Longfellow and is the only donkey in the village, and he always does something unexpected during the re-enactment of the Nativity."

"I see." Resisting the urge to raise his head and scan the crowd to see if Marion was there, Christopher kept his gaze locked on Mary, doing his best to project the image of an unsuspecting target. Noting how jostled the poor girl was, he observed, "Whoever agrees to be Mary every year should probably get a medal."

The children laughed, but their gazes remained glued to the unfolding biblical scene. Christopher couldn't recall witnessing anything comparable as a child, but judging by the trio's expressions, their enthrallment was absolute. Looking about, he saw the same wonder reflected in every child's face and in the majority of adult faces, too.

Returning his gaze to the action, he could understand the attraction, the absorption, could appreciate the moment as one of shared communal celebration. Were he fanciful, he would say that there was magic in the air.

The almost-galloping couple, borne and dragged along by the increasingly eager donkey, swung around the last bend in their path and rapidly approached the stable. Mary shrieked again, and Joseph drew back on the rope, but the donkey was intent on charging forward. Joseph wrestled, and Mary desperately clung, while the donkey seemed determined to pass by the stable and forge on toward the lane.

Then Longfellow stepped out of the crowd and directly into the beast's path, and the donkey brayed, slowed, then halted, with its head a foot from Longfellow's chest. Mary sagged, then frantically scrambled to climb down, while Joseph wilted with relief. The donkey raised its head and shook all over, effectively dislodging Mary. She slid to the ground, picked up her robes, clutched her cushion to her chest, dodged around the rear of the beast, and raced into the safety of the stable. Joseph handed the rope to Longfellow and followed as fast as he could.

The donkey pranced, light on its hooves, then nuzzled up to Longfellow. His lordship shook his head, then turned and led the now-docile beast off.

Beaming, the children sighed, and Jamie leaned across his siblings to tell Christopher, "Duggins always surprises us."

Christopher realized he was beaming, too. Watching Longfellow lead the donkey off, Christopher caught a flicker of movement at the edge of the crowd. Instantly alert, he did his best to appear not to be looking while, from the corner of his eye, he surveyed the shifting heads.

He'd been hoping to spot Marion, but instead, he picked out a tall, dark-haired man—a gentleman by his attire—who had joined the crowd, yet remained on its periphery.

Immediately sobering, Christopher surreptitiously studied the man.

He didn't recognize the fellow, but he knew his type. Apparently, despite the long odds, an agent had followed him to Little Moseley.

The cut of the man's clothes marked him as English, but if judged by his stature and coloring, he could easily be a Frenchman who'd been in the country long enough to have acquired clothes there.

Alternatively, he could be a minor scion of one of the older English aristocratic houses. Napoleon's agents were known to have been active in recruiting disaffected second, third, and even fourth sons of minor branches, promising them elevation over their more favored relatives in Napoleon's imperial court in return for help in winning the war. Given what Christopher could see of the man's features, that was a distinct possibility.

Regardless of his origins, purely based on the way the man moved, Christopher had no hesitation in labeling him dangerous. If Christopher had needed any confirmation, it was there in the way the man carefully scanned the crowd, in exactly the same manner as Christopher and Drummond had.

Just at that moment, the man looked up—directly at Christopher.

Christopher endeavored to appear to be looking at the scene being enacted in the stable, but the man wasn't deceived. At the edge of his vision, Christopher saw the man deliberately shift behind a large farmer. Although Christopher watched, the man didn't reappear.

Damn! Christopher more openly scanned the fringes of the crowd, hoping to pick up some sign of the man, but saw nothing. He was about to glance at Drummond when he caught a glimpse of rich brown, the crown of an elegant bonnet drifting along the far edge of the crowd, not far from where the dangerous gentleman had been.

Christopher tracked the bonnet, willing the owner to step clear of others so he could confirm that she was Marion. Eventually, he got a clear sight of the lady's face, and yes, it was her. As he watched, she edged into the crowd. Although for a woman, she was of above-average height, in a crowd including many large farmers and their workers, she couldn't easily scan the gathering. She kept pausing and looking around, clearly searching for someone—presumably Christopher—but at present, her search was focused on the large crowd thronging the flat of the green.

Look up. I'm here.

He watched as she methodically quartered the crowd, until at last, she raised her gaze to the slope. Realizing that if she saw him looking directly at her, she might not approach, Christopher shifted his gaze to the re-enactment taking place in the supposed stable, but from the corner of his eye, continued to watch her as she scanned the ranks on the slope, tracking from side to side, steadily moving upward.

Finally, she spotted him, stopped her searching, and stared.

Come on—come up and tell me what this is all about.

In something approaching desperation, he willed her up the slope. It took effort to keep his gaze focused on the activities in the stable and not look directly at her.

She studied him for several long seconds, then he thought he saw her expression harden. The next instant, she frowned direfully—even he saw that clearly—and muttered some word. *Damn?* Then she swung around and slipped away through the crowd.

What?

Christopher gave up all pretense and stared after her. Where was she going?

Away was the answer, and she was moving much more quickly than before.

Christopher tensed. He wanted to push through the crowd and go after her, but before he could manage even a step, he'd realized how hemmed in he was. Trying to pursue her would cause enough upheaval to focus every second eye on him—and ultimately, on her.

He gritted his teeth. He couldn't risk it. Inwardly, he gave vent to a *Damn!* of his own.

Forced to stand and watch her progress through the crowd, he realized that she was walking quite swiftly, and although he couldn't see her expression, he noticed that those in her path, once they'd glanced at her face, quickly moved out of her way.

Damn, damn, damn!

She reached the far edge of the crowd, stepped free, and turned toward the lane.

The dangerous gentleman stepped back from the crowd's edge, directly into her path.

Marion pulled up. Christopher saw the man he definitely didn't trust raise a staying hand.

Then he started to speak, and Marion listened.

Christopher stiffened.

~

Marion was utterly fed up with the hurdles Fate kept strewing in her path. She had intended to approach Christopher surreptitiously and, without him noticing, slip a note into his pocket, but the damned man was standing with his back to a stone wall! More, he'd been watching for her; he hadn't fooled her for an instant. Regardless of whatever angle she might have taken, there'd been no way to sidle up to him unseen. And he wouldn't have let her get within ten feet, not without thrusting his nephews, niece, and his guard at her, which would have created a ridiculous and thoroughly unhelpful fuss.

According to the count, she had to engage with Christopher in an entirely innocuous way, and having every eye in the village trained on her and him would hardly satisfy that stipulation.

If she could have communicated with him mind-to-mind, she would have heaped scorn on his head over his erroneous assumption of the reason she wished to speak with him. The man was arrogance personified! She wished she could give him a piece of her mind. The piece in her note, at any rate.

With no option but to retreat in good order, she'd swiftly made her way across the crowd, only to find her way blocked by a devilishly handsome gentleman she knew she ought to recognize.

He'd held up a hand in a placating gesture. "I come in peace."

She narrowed her eyes on his face while rapidly flipping through the visual catalog in her mind. Then she arched her brows haughtily. "Good morning, Mr. Kincaid."

Stephen Kincaid's eyes widened; he hadn't expected her to recognize one of her brother's FO friends. He was patently made uneasy by her identifying him so readily, but after a momentary hesitation, he half bowed. "Miss Sewell." He straightened and cast a meaningful look at the backs of those nearest, then looked at her questioningly and, with a graceful gesture, urged her to step farther away with him.

She obliged and took two steps. He was still between her and her destination, but she was now exceedingly curious as to why he was in Little Moseley.

He settled before her, studied her expression, then said, "I confess I'm surprised to find you here." He glanced fleetingly at Christopher, then focused rather intently on her. "If I read your actions aright, you intended to approach Osbaldestone. Can I ask what business you have with him?"

No. Rather than baldly state that, she countered with "And why is my business with Osbaldestone of any interest to you?"

Kincaid's lips tightened. He searched her face for several seconds, then, apparently correctly interpreting her stubbornness on the subject, muttered, "I suppose you are Robbie's sister."

She waited, lips shut, refusing to rise to such obvious bait.

Eventually, Kincaid drew breath and confided, "If you must know, I've been delegated to keep an eye on Osbaldestone from a distance, specifically to see who tries to approach him, which you, Miss Sewell, definitely wished to." He paused, then ventured, "May I ask why?"

She held his gaze and, once again, arched her brows. "I'm afraid, Kincaid, that I am not, at this point in time, at liberty to reveal my purpose."

As she'd hoped, the familiar phrasing successfully communicated that in the matter of telling him why she was there, she was not going to be swayed. He frowned at her. "At this point… So you might be able to tell me more shortly?"

"Possibly. However, I can make no promises."

He digested that, holding her gaze all the while. Eventually, he said, "Can you at least assure me that your purpose has nothing to do with the French?"

"The French?" She didn't have to fabricate her shock. Or her concern as she asked, "Have they tracked Osbaldestone here?"

He read her sincerity in her eyes and lightly grimaced. Sliding his hands into his breeches pockets, he admitted, "The short answer is that we don't know. But they are the reason I'm here and"—he tipped his head toward where Christopher stood—"Drummond is there, waiting to see what eventuates."

Marion huffed and glanced at Christopher with rising concern. To Kincaid, she said, "You know perfectly well I would have nothing whatever to do with our enemies."

He acknowledged that with a dip of his head. "So why are you trying to contact Osbaldestone?" His tone held more curiosity than accusation.

Marion studied him. Like her twin, Kincaid had training and experience sufficient to make him potentially useful. Feeling her way, she offered, "I have a message to deliver from a mutual family friend."

She held Kincaid's dark gaze and willed him to extract from that at least an inkling of the truth.

He looked at her for a moment, then his eyes widened slightly, and he straightened. "I see." After a moment of what was clearly some inner debate, he nodded. "All right. So when are you going to meet with Osbaldestone?"

The question reignited her temper. She reined it in enough to keep her tone low as she peevishly snapped, "That's what I've been trying to arrange! A simple meeting to pass on a message I can only deliver verbally and only to him! But the lackwit thinks I'm *pursuing* him, and he's been avoiding me assiduously, so I haven't been able to organize a private meeting, which is the only situation in which I can deliver the message—it's too sensitive to be written down!"

Kincaid fought to keep his lips straight. "Ah. I see."

She had no doubt that he did. Approaches of the sort she was endeavoring to arrange were common enough in diplomatic circles. Tipping her head, she eyed him speculatively. "I've been saying for some time that, with Osbaldestone reacting as he is, I'm really not the best person to set up this meeting. But you…" She narrowed her eyes at him. "Do you think you can get close enough to slip a note into Osbaldestone's pocket?"

Kincaid didn't shift his dark-blue gaze from her face. "How did you come to be involved in this? Who recommended that you be the person to contact Osbaldestone?"

That, she could safely tell him. She huffed. "Robbie, of course." Her brother might be currently in Russia, but his contacts extended throughout their Sixth Coalition partners' administrations, so revealing that didn't tell Kincaid anything specific.

Nevertheless, the information reassured him enough for him to glance assessingly at Christopher, who was still standing against the stone wall on the other side of the green.

When she followed Kincaid's gaze to her frustrating target, she saw that Christopher was now staring fixedly at them, rather than even pretending to watch the ongoing pantomime.

His gaze still on Christopher, Kincaid murmured, "I know Robbie trusts you more than he trusts anyone else, so…"

"So you'll try to get my note to Osbaldestone?" She all but crossed her fingers.

Kincaid looked at her. "Give it to me, and I'll try. Obviously, he's noticed me." Kincaid's swift—quite devastating—smile flashed. "But I am very, *very* good at what I do."

"That's the spirit." Shifting to hide her actions from Christopher, Marion pried open her reticule. "Think of this as a challenge." In her considerable experience of the male of the species, that suggestion usually ensured their best efforts.

She drew out the twist of paper she'd prepared, small enough to be slipped easily into a man's pocket, but also bulky enough to ensure it was discovered later. The message inscribed therein contained several well-chosen and pithy remarks.

Kincaid, too, had shifted, so that as Marion handed him the note, his bulk screened the exchange from Christopher.

"All you have to do," she said as Kincaid slipped the note into his coat pocket, "is to get that to Osbaldestone." She fixed him with a minatory gaze. "Don't read it. Don't try to interfere. There really is rather a lot at stake."

He searched her eyes, then nodded.

To encourage his compliance, she added, "If you play by my rules, I'll tell you all as soon as I can, but the people I'm acting as emissary for are exceedingly nervous, almost certainly rightly so, and they'll retreat if anyone other than Osbaldestone turns up at the meeting, even if that meeting is only with me."

He frowned. "They won't be attending?"

She shook her head. "They want a secret meeting with him—that's what they want me to meet with him and arrange. They'll speak with him—him and no one else, at least at first." Pointedly, she held his gaze. "Do you understand?"

Kincaid took in her expression and, lips thin, nodded. "For the record, you're actually more confrontingly intrepid than your brother. I didn't think that was possible, but…" He shrugged.

She arched her brows. "He's my twin. What did you expect?" With that parting shot, she raised her head, stepped around Kincaid, and continued on her interrupted march to the inn where she'd left her coachman, Foggarty, with the Hall's gig.

As she neared the lane, she swiftly glanced back, but could no longer see Kincaid. Satisfied, she smiled and walked on. With Kincaid busy delivering her note, he wasn't going to be able to follow her.

From what she'd heard about Kincaid, she had every confidence that he would carry out her commission successfully. Thus assured, she crossed the lane and strode toward the inn's stable yard, much happier than she'd been only half an hour earlier—indeed, with a thoroughly satisfied spring in her step.

Instead of watching the re-enactment of the Nativity that had been playing out before him, with mounting unease overriding his frustration, Christopher had stood with his attention unwaveringly focused on the extended exchange between Marion and the dangerous gentleman. As the minutes had dragged by and Marion had seemed to grow more relaxed with the fellow, Christopher's concern had escalated. He'd silently cursed when, noticing him watching, the pair had shifted to screen their continuing interaction from him.

He hadn't liked the implications of that one bit.

He'd stared hard at the man, trying to fix the fellow's image in his memory. He didn't recognize him, not at that distance and perhaps not at all, but to Christopher's mind, the man's type was blatantly evident. If the fellow wasn't one of their own—and why would he be lurking if he was?—the only alternative was that he was an enemy. One of Napoleon's agents, possibly sent to track Christopher.

The thought had chilled him. Had Marion known the man before? Could he be the charming French émigré that Drummond had postulated might have gained Marion's trust?

Christopher had thought back to the moment when the two had met, when the stranger had stepped out of the crowd into Marion's path. Christopher couldn't be certain, yet reviewing what he'd seen, he thought Marion hadn't immediately been sure of the man, not at first. There'd been clear hesitation in her stance, a certain stiffness, but then she'd recognized the fellow, and that telltale stiffness had eased, and they'd begun to talk.

At last, the pair had parted, and Marion had marched off alone, to Christopher's intense relief.

He tracked her, confirming she was making for the inn's stable yard where, presumably, she would have a gig waiting.

She passed under the stable arch, and he finally dragged his gaze from her and looked back at the man—only to discover the fellow had vanished. Christopher mentally flayed himself for operational sloppiness; forced to make a choice, he should have kept the more dangerous person under surveillance. For several minutes, he diligently searched the crowd, but didn't catch sight of the man.

Christopher glanced sideways at Drummond. His guard was standing beyond the children and was as trapped against the wall as Christopher.

From his rapt expression, Drummond was enthralled by the pantomime and oblivious to what had transpired on the other side of the green. Christopher jettisoned the thought of immediately alerting Drummond to what he had seen; to do so would create a fuss and draw too much attention.

He was about to return to scanning the crowd when Lottie tugged his sleeve.

"See?" She pointed excitedly. "Those are the three kings!"

Giving up hunting for the man as a lost cause, at least at that moment, Christopher obediently looked where Lottie had pointed and saw two lads and an older girl swathed in bedsheets with gold-painted crowns balanced on their heads and necklaces of gold-painted tokens draped over their shoulders. "They do look fine."

Lottie nodded in vigorous agreement.

In between glancing at the pantomime, he continued to quarter the crowd, but didn't catch so much as a glimpse of the dangerous stranger.

His attention snagged by the children's comments, Christopher found himself drawn back to watching the re-enactment. When one of the goats decided to eat the straw in the manger under the doll representing Baby Jesus, the chaos made even Christopher laugh.

Then, at last, the pageant was over, and in closing the event, Reverend Colebatch reminded everyone about the village carol service, to be held the following Monday evening.

As, released, the crowd flowed down the slope to the flat of the green, many intent on collecting children and animals and helping to dismantle the "stable," Christopher followed Jamie, George, and Lottie as they scampered down, then wove through the crowd, calling to friends and exchanging their views on the highlights. He paused as the three joined in the chase to recapture an escaped sheep and, finally, found Drummond next to him.

He glanced at his guard. "Did you notice the stranger who was standing over there?" Christopher nodded to the far side of the green. "The one who spoke with Miss Sewell?"

Drummond colored, then cleared his throat. "Miss Sewell was here?"

Christopher turned to stare directly at Drummond. "Yes, she was. As was a gentleman I didn't like the look of at all."

Drummond looked sheepish. "I was caught up in the play. What did Miss Sewell do?" He glanced around as if she might still be hovering.

Succinctly, Christopher told him.

Drummond frowned. "She just stared at you, then turned and went off?"

"Yes. Then she met the dangerous-looking stranger."

"What did this cove look like?"

Briefly, Christopher described the man.

Drummond's frown deepened, and he nodded. "You're right. He doesn't sound like the sort we need hanging around, whether he's after you or Miss Sewell."

"My thoughts exactly." Christopher turned as the children came running back, eyes alight and cheeks rosy.

Lottie grasped Christopher's hand. "We'd better go back to the vicarage and help Grandmama down the steps."

"We need to get back to the manor for lunch," George stated, "and we don't want to be late."

Christopher and Drummond dutifully fell in and, keeping a surreptitious eye out for the dangerous stranger, allowed the children to lead them off the green and into the lane.

~

After a satisfying luncheon, the children rushed out to help tidy the green. In the resultant peace, Christopher sat with his mother in her parlor and allowed himself to be distracted from the implications of the events he'd witnessed on the green by a discussion of the latest political reportage. His mother's extensive experience of the courts of Europe and England combined with her almost unique insight into the people and families in power made her a remarkably useful sounding board for honing his own observations, deductions, and conclusions.

Eventually, however, the need for some privacy in which to review the unexpected events of the morning and decide what, if anything, he could or should do drove him to set aside the news sheets, excuse himself, and climb the stairs to his room.

After shutting the door behind him, he walked to the desk that sat before the window. He looked down at the desktop, debating his options, but the notion of sending a letter to Marion via the local post, arranging to meet at some place like Mountjoy's Store or even the middle of the green—some public spot where they could believably encounter each other and speak in reasonable privacy—still seemed sound.

Lips tightening, he drew out the chair, unbuttoned his coat, and as he stepped across the chair to sit, flicked the halves of his coat wide and heard the crackle of paper. Puzzled, he sat and searched his pockets and, from the left pocket, drew out a twisted note.

He stared at the neat, deliberate twist. Other than to the pageant, he hadn't ventured outside that day, and on the green, he'd worn his greatcoat over his coat. Yet the note had been in his coat pocket, not his greatcoat pocket…

He frowned as he remembered. "I didn't button up my greatcoat." The wind hadn't been strong enough to warrant it. He thought back to when he'd been standing against the vicarage wall with the children, then tried to remember his route down the slope and onto the flat.

When he'd paused to watch and wait for the children as they'd chased the errant sheep, someone had lightly jostled him. He'd barely registered it, and then Drummond had joined him, and they'd started talking. He hadn't thought anything of that fleeting contact, not in a crowd.

Compressing his lips, he shook his head. "Whoever it was, they were good." Had it been the dangerous man? If so, he'd got close. Very close. Indeed, too close.

Grimly, Christopher eyed the note. "Only one way to find out."

He unraveled the crumpled sheet, smoothed it, and read.

Inscribed in a neat, distinctively feminine hand, the message was brief and to the point.

Osbaldestone - Please believe me when I say that I have absolutely no designs on your virtue. You are the most irritatingly arrogant man to assume my interest lies in that direction. Regardless, I have been approached by others, vouched for by one I trust implicitly, and asked to arrange a meeting between you and them. I am not at liberty to reveal more in writing. So please cease being so damned idiotic and meet me on Saturday afternoon at 3:30 pm in the church opposite your bolt hole. As I hope you have by now deduced, the matter for discussion has office implications.

The note was signed "M. Sewell" in the same hand.

Christopher raised his head and, unseeing, stared out of the window. It seemed Marion had entrusted her message to the dangerous man. He couldn't decide what to make of that. Was she in danger, or was he missing something? Or were both those possibilities true?

Returning his gaze to the note, he reread her words. It didn't require any great feat of imagination to hear her speaking the phrases. He had to marvel at the talent that allowed her to cram so much frustrated exasperation into so few lines.

Plainly, she was annoyed with him…and he had to admit that, all in all, he deserved her ire.

He rose, thrust the note back into his pocket, and crossed to the fireplace. He sank into the armchair angled before the hearth and settled to stare at the flames leaping in the grate.

She'd chosen well. At three-thirty on Saturday afternoon, there shouldn't be many, if any, people in the church. More, it was a venue that neither of them should feel trapped inside; there were always multiple ways to exit a church. The acoustics, however, might be a problem; depending on where they stood to talk, it might be possible for someone to hide and still be able to overhear them.

He arched his brows in thought. Perhaps, once he pointed that out, they could go out onto the lawn to exchange whatever information she had for him. The middle of the church lawn would do very well in terms of staging an incidental encounter between social acquaintances.

That decided, he moved on to trying to imagine on whose behalf Marion was acting. "A matter with office implications." She was Sir Nathaniel Sewell's daughter; she would know what that phrase would convey to Christopher.

"Who?" He turned the question over and around in his mind, viewing it from every possible angle. The exercise led him to conclude that she could be representing the interests of anyone at all. Even the French.

As her father's daughter, she'd spent years in both the Russian Imperial court and also the Austrian court. During those years, she would almost certainly have come to the attention of a great many diplomats, attachés, and aides. Given the state of the war, given the seasonal pause in engagements, it was entirely possible that some of Napoleon's generals wished to sue for peace.

He'd seen no sign of that in what crossed his desk and, overall, considered it unlikely, yet he couldn't rule it out. In the diplomatic world, stranger things had happened.

The more he dwelled on the situation—including the tall, dark, and dangerous stranger who had, apparently, dealt himself into Marion's game—the more uneasy he grew. Dealing with the secret side of the FO was never entirely safe.

"Just look at my situation," he muttered. "Hiding in my mother's house with Drummond as my guard."

Still, one point was clear. Given the circumstances as they now seemed, he would definitely be in the church on Saturday afternoon to meet with Marion. The insistent and persistent itch beneath his skin—his mounting concern over her safety and the dangerous waters she'd apparently been drawn into—would allow nothing else.

A light tap on the door preceded Drummond sticking his head into the room. "I was going to nick around to the Arms and listen to the talk about the gathering this morning. Have the youngsters learned anything more about who Miss Sewell is staying with?"

"Not that they've reported." Christopher hesitated for only a second before beckoning Drummond to join him.

Curious, Drummond stepped into the room and shut the door. "This about Miss Sewell?" When Christopher nodded, Drummond came forward and dropped into the second armchair. "Have to say, I can't figure out what she was about in coming this morning, staring at you, then just walking away." Drummond arched his brows. "You have any idea what that means?"

The impulse to defend Marion caught Christopher by surprise, then the answer to Drummond's question fell into his mind, and he grimaced. "I believe she came intending to slip a note into my pocket—or possibly deliver it into my hand if she got close enough to do so. Only I was standing with my back to a high stone wall, and she saw that I'd spotted her." She'd assumed he would bolt rather than allow her to get close. Lips tightening, he said, "So she walked away and met the stranger." He paused, then drew her note from his pocket and waved it. "I assume she gave him this, and he was well-trained and experienced enough to slip it into my pocket."

Drummond's eyes widened. "He got that close?"

Grimly, Christopher nodded and, omitting Marion's more forthright comments on his character, briefly summarized the salient points of her communication. Drummond had, after all, been sent to guard him.

Christopher tucked the note back into his pocket and, before Drummond could offer any opinion, said, "I'm concerned that Miss Sewell might have fallen in with this stranger and that he's someone we would really rather she hadn't drawn into this—whatever this proves to be." He met Drummond's eyes. "While at the Arms, can you keep your ears open for any news of him and then, in the morning, take a thorough look around?"

Drummond studied him. "You going to stay put?"

"Through the morning, yes."

"And on Saturday afternoon, you'll go and meet with her as she asked?"

Christopher nodded. "It seems an explanation of what's been going on will be forthcoming." He looked pointedly at Drummond. "If I could be certain that the man who presumably slipped her note into my pocket wasn't loitering close enough to overhear, I'd feel a lot happier."

Drummond grunted and rose. "You and me both." He paused, studying Christopher. "So you're now thinking Miss Sewell's got more on her mind than marriage?"

"Not more." Christopher couldn't keep his irritation with himself from coloring his tone. "Something other. It seems likely that I misjudged her motives from the first."

Drummond huffed. "If you believe what she wrote." He headed for the door. "Personally, I think you should still exercise all due caution on that front." He paused at the door. "But I'll see what I can learn about our mystery gentleman. Give me that description again."

Christopher obliged, concluding with "He definitely had a dangerous edge. Bear that in mind."

Drummond nodded. "I'll scout around tomorrow and see what I can learn. I'll report back before dinner."

Christopher nodded, but still Drummond paused, frowning into space, then said, "I can't imagine what Miss Sewell's business with you might be, but meeting her in the church surely can't hurt. At least you'll learn why she's been after you. But ten to one, it won't be anything that will actually concern the FO."

On that note, Drummond opened the door and departed.

Christopher watched the door close, then shook his head and murmured, "I really wouldn't wager on that."

Drummond wasn't acquainted with Marion Sewell. Christopher was, and the sinking feeling slowly intensifying in his gut suggested he'd misjudged her in a way that might well have destroyed any regard she'd ever had for him.

Why that made him feel as he did was another development that disturbed him.

CHAPTER 10

On Friday afternoon, as silent as the proverbial mice, the children crept into the shadows beneath the drooping branches of an old fir that grew close to the edge of the south lawn of Parteger Hall.

They'd been keen to come earlier, but in the aftermath of the pageant, during the tidying of the green, they'd found Duggins's leading rope, which had apparently been lost, and had gone to Dutton Grange to return the rope to Lord Longfellow. That and playing with the Longfellows' son, Cedric, who had grown to be a laughing, chortling toddler, had eaten up the rest of their Wednesday. When they'd left the Grange, daylight had been fading fast and the shadows closing in.

Then on Thursday morning, unexpectedly, all the village children had been recruited by Farmer Johnson of Witcherly Farm in the hunt for a missing lamb. Henry, Dagenham, Kilburn, George Wiley, and Roger Carnaby had joined the group and, together with Reverend Colebatch, had organized and directed the search to the west of the village, while the workers from Witcherly and Crossley Farms had searched to the east, the Tookses and their workers had searched to the north, and the Milsoms had beaten the lands to the village's south.

Under Henry's and the reverend's direction, the band of children had split into two. One group had tramped through the woods to the north of the lake, while the other had gone to the south. Finding no sign of the errant beast, they'd all moved into the rising forest that extended beyond the western shore of the lake. Eventually, Lottie's and Ginny Tooks's sharp ears had picked up weak bleating, and the girls had led the rescue party to the missing lamb, which had taken shelter in a hollow under a fallen tree. After a suitable celebration, Robert Milsom had carried the lamb off to reunite it with its mother.

In the wake of all the excitement, the children had dutifully spent Thursday afternoon at choir practice, an obligation they hadn't dreamt of not fulfilling.

Consequently, as they wriggled into place under the old fir tree, their impatience and determination to learn who Miss Sewell was staying with had reached new heights. A blustery sleet storm had blown in that morning, keeping them indoors, but the weather had cleared by lunchtime, and they'd left the manor within minutes of being excused from the table. They'd trotted quickly along the lanes, then had skirted the property, eventually tying their ponies to trees down by the riverbank, away from the Hall and well out of sight of the upper-story windows.

They'd discovered the spot under the fir on their first visit to Parteger Hall. With the area around the base of the trunk screened by the tree's drooping branches, in terms of observing the drawing room and the paved terrace and lawn that the room overlooked, the spot was the next best thing to a hide. More, the ground under the tree was thickly carpeted with old, largely dry needles. The children sat cross-legged on the accommodating cushion and made themselves comfortable as they settled to watch and wait.

There were larger trees to either side, but as they were currently leafless, climbing one to keep watch from a useful branch hadn't been an option. Indeed, in order to reach their place of concealment, they'd had to hug the rear hedge of an overgrown shrubbery, then scurry from one rhododendron bush to the next to make their way around the edge of the lawn to their hidey-hole. Now they were in position, to their left, they could see into the area outside the kitchen door and keep watch over the path that led to the stable block, which stood farther away from the house on that side. The entire southern façade of the Hall faced the lawn and them, while to their right lay the high hedges of the scraggly shrubbery and, beyond that, the woods that rambled over the strip of land above the river.

Jamie, George, and Lottie stared across the lawn at the house. Weak winter sunshine played across the gray stone, occasionally glinting off one of the lead-paned windows. After the earlier storm, the wind had fallen, and the air had grown curiously still, almost as if Nature was holding her breath.

Jamie shifted and looked to the left. They'd come as early as they could, hoping to spot a stable lad returning to the stable after having his lunch. From the fir, a series of bushes followed by a low hedge would provide cover almost all the way to the stable.

"If a stable lad appears," Jamie murmured, "I'll go over and speak with him. I'll say I'm lost and left my horse by the river and came up through the wood to ask directions."

Lottie chewed her lower lip and peered at the stable. "Are you sure he won't recognize you?"

"According to Matty Tooks, the stable lads here hail from families in East or West Wellow, so there's no reason they'll know who I am," Jamie replied.

"Hmm." George, who had fixed his gaze on the kitchen door, grimaced. "I hadn't thought of it before, but it's possible—even likely—that a stable lad won't know the names of the guests. He'll just know them as the count and the captain."

Jamie turned his head and stared at his brother. After a moment, he said, "Perhaps, but he—the stable lad—might have heard the butler or someone else say the names. That's all we need—a name."

George dipped his head. "That's true."

Lottie sighed, then more staunchly said, "Anyway, who else are we to ask?"

The comment put an end to that discussion. The three shifted and wriggled, then settled again, their impatience on a tight rein.

Fifteen minutes or so later, the kitchen door opened, and a lanky lad emerged. Head down, he shoved his hands in his pockets and ambled along the path toward the stable.

Like hounds sighting prey, the children came alert, straightening, their gazes locked on the lad. Expectation infusing his expression, slowly, Jamie started to rise.

The stable lad glanced back at the house, then he spoke, and an older man replied as he pushed through the kitchen door and set off, striding in the lad's wake.

Jamie sank back.

"Ugh." George wrinkled his nose.

The trio watched the man, presumably the stableman, catch up with the lad, who had waited, then the pair walked on together and disappeared around the corner of the stable.

The children stared after the men.

They waited for what must have been another ten minutes, then Jamie shifted and tensed to rise. "I'll have to risk it."

Lottie grabbed his sleeve. "Wait!" she whispered.

Jamie glanced at her and saw that her eyes had widened and she was looking eagerly at the Hall. He followed her gaze to the door leading from the house to the paved area that served as a terrace and saw it open. He froze as Miss Sewell stepped out.

The children watched with bated breath as she was followed by two men.

"Presumably the count and the captain," George breathed.

Jamie and Lottie nodded.

Under the tree, the trio remained motionless and watched as Marion Sewell and the two men, apparently intent on taking advantage of the milder afternoon to get some air, started to amble along the terrace in the direction of the shrubbery.

"Descriptions," Jamie murmured, barely audibly. Together with his siblings, he scrutinized the men, noting every facet of their appearance and committing each detail to memory.

Miss Sewell and the men had been strolling and quietly conversing—too quietly for the children to make out any words. Then the older man—Jamie presumed he was the count—turned toward Miss Sewell so he could study her face, and Jamie saw that the man carried an old yet clearly visible scar. A sword or knife cut that started high on the man's left cheek and ended at the corner of his lips, the scar lightly puckered the skin, especially close to the lips.

His eyes glued to the scar, Jamie grinned. If his grandmother had ever met the count, she would remember that.

Satisfied, Jamie shifted his attention to the younger man. Of much the same age as Jamie's uncle, the man unquestionably possessed a military background. He didn't merely walk—he strutted with a stiff-legged gait. He held himself rigidly upright, without any of the natural ease that generally characterized a tonnish gentleman. The man was tall, but not exceptionally so, had broad shoulders, and his muscled legs were encased in a pair of tight buckskin breeches. He wore black boots with tassels and a form-fitting riding coat. Having seen such men before, Jamie put him down as a cavalryman. Eyes narrowed assessingly, Jamie murmured, "Light cavalry, not heavy," and from the corner of his eye, saw George nod in silent agreement.

Miss Sewell and the men reached the end of the terrace, and Miss Sewell waved toward the shrubbery. The three stepped onto the lawn and strolled on, disappearing behind the poorly trimmed hedges.

The children looked at each other. Jamie widened his eyes in question, and Lottie and George nodded decisively. Keeping a watchful eye on the house's façade, the trio quietly scrambled to their feet and crept toward the wall of green they'd previously used to screen them from the house.

Jamie led, picking his way cautiously around the intervening bushes, then quickly hurrying along the hedge that formed the unbroken rear wall of the rectangular shrubbery. He slowed, head cocked as he listened. His siblings followed at his heels.

Then Lottie, directly behind Jamie, tugged his jacket. He turned to see her crouching against the hedge, her ear pressed into the soft new growth. She glanced up, pointed into the shrubbery, and mouthed, "They're here."

Jamie and George both crouched and copied her; everyone in the family knew she had the sharpest hearing.

Sure enough, through the hedge, Jamie heard Miss Sewell's voice, followed by the rumble of what he thought had to be the voice of the military man. It sounded as if they were pacing slowly along the inside of the hedge; their voices reached Jamie quite clearly.

He pressed closer, leaning into the greenery, and tried to make out the words. He grew puzzled that, although he could hear the pair quite well, he couldn't work out what they were saying. Then he realized why.

Eyes wide, Jamie looked over Lottie's head at George and excitedly mouthed, "French!" He'd started lessons in the language with his tutor over a year ago, and George had recently joined in. Excited, Jamie leaned hard against the hedge. Now he knew they were speaking in French, he could pick up words here and there, but although he concentrated and tried his best to parse out the words, in general, all three were speaking too rapidly for him to make head or tail of what they were saying.

From George's frown, he was having the same problem.

Lottie had been listening closely, too. She looked up and caught Jamie's eye and breathed, "The men have funny accents."

Jamie blinked, then listened more intently. Although Lottie couldn't speak the language, she knew what it should sound like, and she was correct. The men definitely had strange, rather gruff diction.

After listening some more, Jamie decided that both men had similar accents—harsh and slightly guttural, with an odd intonation for some of the vowels. The pair might be speaking French, but they weren't French. Of that, Jamie felt sure.

To his ears, of the three, Miss Sewell seemed the most fluent and smoothly spoken and, therefore, the clearest. Judging from what he could make out from her slick, polished phrases, she and the men were discussing something. The exchange wasn't an argument but seemed to involve suggestions, followed by a back-and-forth leading to another suggestion. Could they be planning something?

Then Miss Sewell's words slowed, as if she was stressing some point; although she spoke in French, Jamie's mind immediately translated the words. "My dear Count Leonski, I assure you there's no danger whatever in me meeting with Osbaldestone. More, if Kapitan Solzonik were to attempt to follow me in a protective capacity, in such a small, out-of-the-way village, the chances of him being seen and recognized as foreign are very real." Miss Sewell paused to draw breath, then continued in the same measured—clear and translatable—fashion, "At this point, I would strongly counsel that we have no reason to court such a risk."

The old man—Count Leonski—sighed, loudly enough for the children to hear, then replied with a barrage of what, to Jamie, sounded like garbled French. However, judging by the overall tone and that of Miss Sewell's reply, it seemed the count had accepted Miss Sewell's point.

Crouched hard by the hedge, the children listened to the ensuing discussion, but once again, Miss Sewell spoke too rapidly for Jamie to follow. Then the voices started to fade, and he realized the three in the shrubbery were walking away, back toward the house.

He drew his ear from the green wall and sat back on his heels, and Lottie and George did the same. They'd heard "Leonski" and "Solzonik" repeated several times, clearly enough to be certain they'd deciphered the names correctly.

Catching George's and Lottie's eyes, Jamie whispered, "We've got what we came for. Time to go."

Lottie nodded. "We should take what we've learned back to Grandmama."

Without more ado, they crept farther along the rear of the shrubbery, then retraced their steps to where they'd left their ponies.

In the manor's drawing room, Therese smiled encouragingly at Ermintrude Woolsey, who was seated on the chaise, and held out the plate containing the last slice of Mrs. Haggerty's famous fruitcake.

Mrs. Woolsey hesitated, clearly tempted, but then she shook her head with a regretful sigh. "Such a rich combination of tastes. I really don't know how your Haggerty manages to conjure such an explosion of flavors. However, my lady, I really should be on my way."

In her usual ineffectual manner, she commenced gathering the various shawls and scarves draped in haphazard fashion about her and threw a vague smile at Viscount Dagenham, who sat elegantly at ease in the second armchair angled before the hearth. "Although I must say, these days, Henry and his university friends—although, I suppose, as they're no longer at university, they're just his friends now—do manage to keep themselves amused. So helpful!"

From their earlier conversation, Therese had gathered that, this year, lacking any mystery with which to engage, the five young gentlemen were wont to gather in the billiards room, potting balls while discussing their lives. Given that all five were now twenty-two years old or thereabouts, Therese wasn't surprised to hear of them taking tentative steps toward defining their futures. All hailed from good families and doubtless had opportunities opening before them and, consequently, decisions to make.

As one of Henry's no-longer-university friends, Dagenham had volunteered to drive his hostess from Fulsom Hall to the manor. Now, he rose and came forward to assist Mrs. Woolsey. "Allow me."

Therese watched him—tall, dark-haired, and every inch the ineffable aristocrat—patiently untangle three of Mrs. Woolsey's scarves. Ever since the pair had arrived on her doorstep, Therese had been waiting to glean some inkling of Dagenham's ulterior motive—the one that had led him to find a reason to present himself at the manor; his kind heart notwithstanding, she felt perfectly certain that he had one.

Finally free to move, Mrs. Woolsey grasped Dagenham's proffered hand and allowed him to draw her to her feet. "Thank you, dear boy." Slightly flustered, she released his hand and gushed, "You're most kind." After gathering her abundance of shawls, she paused, then looked about her, faintly puzzled. "Where was I?"

Dagenham smoothly replied, "We were about to leave for Fulsom Hall." Gallantly, with an encouraging smile, he offered her his arm.

"Oh yes—of course!" Smiling again, Mrs. Woolsey laid her hand on his sleeve. "Such a gentleman!"

Therese was aware that Mrs. Woolsey was growing increasingly forgetful, and to their credit, Henry and his friends, all of whom seemed sincerely fond of the old lady, supported her as and when they could. Therese had watched with approval as, throughout the hour-long visit, Dagenham had consistently shown himself to be quietly attentive to his elderly hostess's needs.

As he turned to Therese and, with maturing sophistication and his customary languid grace, took his polished leave of her, she found herself spontaneously smiling with very real appreciation. Dagenham was fast becoming the epitome of the complete ton gentleman.

Alerted by the children's report concerning Dagenham questioning Christopher about how the FO operated internally, Therese had, apparently idly, inquired of Christopher, and he'd confirmed the subjects in which Dagenham had shown an interest—all precisely what others might expect from one now rising in the ranks of the Home Office. However, while Dagenham's questions might reflect genuine interest, Therese seriously doubted that FO arrangements were what he'd truly wanted to know—what he'd actually been angling to learn. That had left her wondering just what the handsome viscount, heir to the earldom of Carsely, already suspected his future might hold.

And given Dagenham's presence in her house that day, Therese had to wonder if her granddaughter Melissa, who had not come to Little Moseley as she had over the past two Decembers, was likely to play any further part in the viscount's future.

Ever the gracious hostess, Therese walked with her visitors into the front hall.

There, they paused to allow Crimmins to help Mrs. Woolsey into her winter coat.

Dagenham turned to Therese and, somewhat to her surprise, baldly asked, "How is Melissa?"

Therese met Dagenham's pale-gray gaze and glimpsed rather more than he, she felt sure, had wished her to see. "She's well and presently accompanying her parents on a trip to Edinburgh." With barely a pause, she continued, "She's sixteen now, and I understand it's been decided that she'll wait two more years before plunging into the whirl of her come-out."

Stating that was a straightforward way of reminding Dagenham that, socially speaking, Melissa would remain out of bounds for at least the next two years.

His expression impassive, he inclined his head. "When next you see her, please give her my best." His gaze shifted to Mrs. Woolsey, who was still fluttering and fussing in settling her scarves and shawls over her coat. He hesitated, then voice low, said, "I'm in line to be sent to Ireland, and the higher-ups are keen."

Therese knew that being posted to Ireland was currently regarded as important training for those of whom the Home Secretary entertained high hopes. She allowed her eyes to widen slightly. "Career-wise, that will be an important step for you."

"Indeed." His tone was flat. "I daresay it will be."

Mrs. Woolsey was finally ready, and Dagenham briefly bowed to Therese. "My lady."

Straightening, he smiled at Mrs. Woolsey and gave her his arm.

Therese nodded to Crimmins, and he opened the front door.

She trailed behind Dagenham as he led Mrs. Woolsey, who waved gaily and called a farewell, out to his curricle, which Simms had brought around.

Dagenham helped Mrs. Woolsey up to the seat of the gleaming carriage, then rounded the horses, exchanged a word with Simms as he collected the reins, then climbed up and sat beside his passenger.

With a brief glance Therese's way, Dagenham raised his whip in salute, then flicked the reins and set his matched bays trotting down the drive.

Therese stood on the porch and watched the carriage roll away. She thought of that glimpse she'd caught of what lurked behind Dagenham's storm-cloud eyes and felt her heart pinch, but not even she could manipulate the future, at least not in any way that might help.

Dagenham's curricle had reached the bend in the drive. Therese was about to turn and retreat inside when she saw the carriage veer to the right. Dagenham and Mrs. Woolsey waved at three small riders perched on ponies who came rapidly trotting up the drive.

The children returned Dagenham's and Mrs. Woolsey's greetings, but didn't pause, and with a flick of his whip, Dagenham urged his pair on, and the curricle swept out of sight.

As the children neared, one look at their faces was enough to tell Therese that they'd uncovered something momentous. She waved them on to the path to the stable. "Take the ponies to Simms. I'll be waiting in my parlor."

Three bright, eager faces smiled at her. "Yes, Grandmama," all three chorused in that way she never tired of hearing.

Smiling, she walked into the front hall, waited until Crimmins shut the door, then ordered more tea and slices of fruitcake. "And three glasses of milk."

She was waiting, curious and expectant, when the trio, rosy-cheeked and with their hair windblown, came tumbling through the door.

"Grandmama!" Lottie sang. "We learned the men's names!"

"Did you, indeed?"

"And," Jamie added, with the superior air of a firstborn, "we have good descriptions." His eyes had already gone to the plate bearing slices of fruitcake sitting on the low table before Therese.

As if drawn by some elemental attraction, their gazes locked on the cake, the children closed in on the table. Then all three halted and looked at Therese hopefully.

She laughed and waved them on. "Eat, drink, and then you must tell me all about your adventure."

While they fell on Mrs. Haggerty's cake, she reached for the teapot. She poured herself a cup, then sat back, sipped, and watched with amusement as the three appeased their apparently voracious appetites while obviously and very consciously endeavoring to maintain the manners of polite gentlemen and ladies.

Soon enough, all that remained of the cake were a few stray crumbs, and they'd drained the dregs of their milk.

Therese nodded approvingly and set down her teacup. "Excellent. Now, start at the beginning and tell me what you've learned."

They commenced their tale at the point where they'd arrived on the riverbank south of Parteger Hall. Therese listened in dawning wonderment as they related what they'd seen and, subsequently, done. She'd known for years that they were an intrepid bunch, but even so, she was surprised at how close they'd managed to get to the unknown gentlemen. "So you were on the other side of the hedge?"

Sensing her concern, Jamie rushed to reassure her, "They didn't see us. Not even a glimpse."

"They didn't hear us, either," Lottie very seriously added. "We were very quiet."

George nodded. "We'd already learned from the East Wellow villagers that the gentlemen were referred to as a count and a captain."

"But Miss Sewell said it differently," Lottie reported. "She called him a kap-i-tan."

"Kapitan Solzonik." Jamie pronounced the name carefully. "They—Miss Sewell and the two men—were talking. I think they were discussing something, but they were speaking in French and far too quickly for us to make out the words."

"Especially not with the men's funny accents," George said.

Therese was intrigued. "What sort of accents?"

The boys tried to explain, then Lottie piped up, and Therese discovered that her granddaughter was a rather talented mimic. Although Lottie couldn't manage a sufficiently deep register, her rendering of the men's gruff and harsh consonants and odd-sounding vowels was enough for Therese to be certain of the men's origins.

When Lottie stopped speaking, Therese sat back. "I see." She thought she might, finally, be glimpsing light through the mists. After a moment, she asked, "What did this kapitan look like?"

Their description of a dark-featured, dark-haired man with very pale skin, solidly built with the figure of a cavalryman and a strikingly military gait, had her raising her brows. "I suspect, my dears, that Kapitan Solzonik is a Russian—a captain in their Hussars." She narrowed her eyes. "And the other gentleman—the count. What did he look like?"

Between them, the children built a word picture of an older man, possibly old enough to be Miss Sewell's grandfather, of no more than average height and with a portly figure, yet fashionably dressed in a faintly foreign style. Then Jamie described the scar on the man's face, and Therese blinked.

She managed to keep her dawning delight from her face as she asked, "Did you hear his name?"

"Count Leonski," George replied. "We heard Miss Sewell call him that twice."

Relaxing in her chair, Therese regarded her truly amazing grandchildren. "My dears, you are—collectively and individually—remarkable. Your ability to gather information is second to none."

Unsurprisingly, they preened.

"Now!" She got to her feet, bringing them scrambling to theirs.

"Since you've successfully completed your mission, I want you three to stand down, at least for the moment, while I consult my other sources."

All three looked uncertain whether to feel disappointed or unperturbed.

Taking due note of that, she waved them to the door. "Come along now—upstairs with you. It'll soon be time for dinner, and as you know, I prefer to see clean hands and faces and neatly brushed hair around my table."

"Yes, Grandmama!" they sang and allowed her to herd them to the door.

She went with them up the stairs, eager to see what she might turn up in the hour before she went down to the drawing room.

Predictably, it was Lottie who, slipping her hand into Therese's, looked into her face and inquired, "What 'other sources' do you have, Grandmama?"

Therese glanced at Jamie and George, who likewise trained encouragingly inquisitive looks on her.

She smiled. "Why, my memories and my correspondence, my dears, but I will admit that, with the latter, accessing the relevant period might take some time."

~

Later that evening, after Therese and the children had left Christopher in the dining room, savoring a glass of fine brandy, and the four of them had settled in her parlor before the roaring fire, she listened to the wind howling about the eaves and caught the splatter of sleet against the windows.

The children had fetched books and settled to read, sprawled like puppies on the rug before the hearth.

She studied them, then seized a moment when they stirred and asked, "My dears, am I correct in thinking you have carol practice tomorrow afternoon?"

All three nodded. "From two o'clock until we finish going through all the carols," Jamie said.

"It's our last practice before the carol service," Lottie added, "so we're doing a proper rehearsal."

"I see." She smiled benevolently upon them. "You are to be

commended for continuing to contribute to the village celebrations. I'm very pleased to see it."

They smiled back, then returned to their books.

Therese watched them settle again, then shifted her gaze to the leaping flames and turned her mind in a different direction.

CHAPTER 11

An hour after leaving the luncheon table on Saturday, Christopher quietly let himself out of the manor's front door. After carefully closing the door behind him, he paused to wrap his muffler around his throat and turn up his collar against the icy breeze.

Although the skies were an unrelieved gray and the sleet of the previous evening had converted to a light smattering of snow, the day was fine enough, at least for midwinter. Christopher glanced back at the house. He fervently hoped that the other occupants would remain indoors. He'd gone to his room after luncheon and stayed there to avoid the children, who had rushed off immediately the meal was over. He didn't know where they currently were but hoped they would be too busy and distracted to notice his absence.

He pulled out his fob watch and checked the time. He had nearly twenty minutes before meeting Marion. Time enough to reconnoiter the church to ensure they had no unexpected observers, then pick the best position from which to watch the main door.

After tucking his watch into his pocket, he resettled his coat, then stepped off the porch and started down the drive. Beneath his outward calm, he was conscious of a clawing impatience to set eyes on Marion, to speak with her and, most important of all, assure himself that she was safe and would remain so.

Drummond hadn't turned up any hint as to the identity of the mystery man or even where he might be staying, which only increased Christopher's uneasiness over what might be going on.

He'd taken only a few paces down the drive when he heard gravel crunch. Glancing over his shoulder, he saw Drummond lumbering around the house from the direction of the kitchen door. He had on his coat and was clearly intending to follow Christopher.

Lips setting, Christopher halted at the intersection of the main drive and the path to the stable and waited for Drummond to catch up. When he neared, Christopher stated, "I don't need protection for a meeting such as this."

Drummond halted. "I'm here to make sure no harm befalls you. You'll have me at your back whether you want me there or not."

Christopher tried to keep his tone reasonable. "For all I know, Miss Sewell will balk if she sees I've someone with me."

"Did she say that in her note?"

"No, but I doubt she would imagine that I would come with a guard. Not to meet with her."

Drummond's jaw set. "Well, then, I'll just have to make sure she doesn't see me."

Christopher gritted his teeth. "You've seen inside the church. If you're hiding close enough to save me from any danger she might pose, she'll almost certainly see you."

"It's not her I'm worried about." Drummond jabbed a stubby finger at Christopher. "Don't forget there's Frenchies after you. Who knows if she's some sort of lure?"

"She's not!" Exasperated, Christopher glared. The last thing he wanted was for Drummond—another FO operative, no less—listening in to a conversation that might include some rather caustic personal observations. If matters were as Christopher now suspected, he would have to apologize and, depending on Marion's reaction, might even have to grovel. No matter where Drummond secreted himself, the acoustics of the church made it likely he would be able to hear all that was said, and if Christopher and Marion moved outside, onto the lawn, Drummond might not be able to hear but would almost certainly be seen.

His jaw clenched, Christopher ground out, "I don't want you there."

"Bad luck." Drummond glowered belligerently. "I'm coming anyway—it's my job."

"One you didn't want."

They went around and around. The more Christopher resisted, the more Drummond pushed, with neither willing to back down.

Abruptly, Christopher cursed and hauled out his watch. He stared at the face. "Damn it! I'm going to be late!"

He thrust the watch back and, ignoring Drummond entirely, whirled and strode rapidly down the drive. If Marion was already furious with him and he didn't turn up at the appointed time, she might not wait.

Blocking his ears to the sound of Drummond's boots thumping in his wake, Christopher walked as rapidly as he dared, knowing that running would catch the attention of anyone who saw him.

He reached and crossed the lane without spotting any other living soul and started up the church's curving drive. He rounded the bend and saw the church ahead, sitting squarely on the crest of the rise, then heard the sound of carriage wheels coming along the lane.

Christopher paused and listened.

The carriage slowed and turned up the drive.

Christopher ducked left, beneath the trees of the wood bordering the drive on that side. He glanced back and could no longer see Drummond; he assumed his guard had likewise taken cover.

Concealed in the shadows, Christopher watched as a gig came smartly up the drive. As it drew level with where he stood, he saw the unknown gentleman—tall, dark, and dangerous—managing the reins.

Christopher inwardly cursed. *What's he doing here?*

Had Marion invited the fellow?

Christopher remained where he was and watched the mystery man halt the gig by the side of the church—where Christopher now saw several other carriages left waiting.

He frowned. What sort of meeting was taking place? He wasn't going to go in and speak with Marion if that man and God knew who else were there as well. She hadn't written or even intimated that she expected anyone else to be there. Much less several others.

Confounded, Christopher stealthily moved forward beneath the trees until he reached a position from where he could watch the front of the church as well as the carriages. The mystery man had descended and was busy securing his horse.

The breeze shifted, and Christopher heard singing.

The choir. Practicing.

He cursed anew. He'd forgotten about the choir practices the children invariably attended. He hadn't realized there would be one that afternoon, and of course, Marion couldn't have known.

Damn! No meeting in the church, and not on the lawn, either, not with the mystery man hanging about.

Christopher drew out his watch and checked the time. What with arguing and hiding and wondering what was going on, it was now fifteen minutes past three-thirty.

He glanced at the mystery man. Instead of entering the church, the man was loitering between the porch and the carriages. Christopher frowned. Was the man now working with Marion? If so, in what capacity? He had, after all, arrived alone.

Christopher heard a twig crack some way behind him. He glanced in that direction and spotted Drummond inching around the bend in the drive, keeping under cover.

Drummond saw Christopher and paused. Realizing that, from where Drummond stood, he couldn't see the mystery man, Christopher signaled Drummond to stay out of sight and directed his attention to the mystery man's position.

Drummond understood and nodded, then melted deeper into the wood's shadows.

Returning his attention to the church, Christopher assessed his options. Despite the ongoing choir practice, he had to assume Marion was already inside. If he didn't show up soon—

The church door was hauled open, and Marion stalked out.

One look at her face told Christopher that he was definitely too late and no longer had any options at all, not with regard to the scheduled meeting. Marion's fine complexion was lightly flushed—a result of heightened temper, he felt sure—and even from that distance, he could see her jaw was set and her lips were compressed to a thin line.

She was furious with him, and given how many times she'd tried to contact him only for him to deny her, he could understand her anger.

For one second, straight and tall, she stood on the church porch and glared down the drive, then from where he'd been waiting at the corner of the building, the mystery stranger stepped forward and spoke, drawing her gaze. She studied him for several moments, then stepped down from the porch and walked to where he stood.

A conversation ensued. Christopher was too far away to hear even the tones of their voices, much less any words. All he could read were their gestures, and from those, it seemed the stranger was pleading his case, trying to persuade Marion to do something. She, however, was exercising sensible caution and appeared distinctly unconvinced. The exchange went back and forth. Then abruptly, Marion flung up her hands and, it seemed, gave way and agreed to whatever the man had been suggesting.

Far from looking smug or even satisfied, the man, Christopher noticed, looked relieved. That seemed odd.

Before Christopher could make any sense of that, let alone work out what was happening and what he should therefore do, Marion waved the man toward the carriages and took the lead. She marched to a gig, and the man took her gloved hand and helped her climb to the seat. He unhooked the reins and handed them to her, and she said something to him, then flicked the reins and turned the horse down the drive.

The man rushed to retrieve his own gig and, within seconds, was briskly tooling it in Marion's wake.

First Marion, then the man, drove rapidly down the drive, without a sideways glance passing the spot where Christopher hid.

Before he could reach the drive, the pair had vanished. He stalked out from the trees, halted in the middle of the drive, and stared after them. "What the devil's going on?"

"Beats me." Drummond emerged from the trees and joined him. "I take it that's the cove you saw on the green?"

Grimly, Christopher nodded.

"I see what you mean about him having a dangerous edge," Drummond said. "Any idea where they might be going?"

"That old manor house in East Wellow would be my guess." Christopher was about to stride off to fetch his curricle when the patter of feet and an "Uncle Christopher!" brought him up short.

He turned to see Jamie, George, and Lottie pelting down the drive, closely followed by Henry, Dagenham, Wiley, Kilburn, and Carnaby.

The children reached him, and George blurted, "Did you see her?"

"Miss Sewell." Lottie fixed her gaze on Christopher's face. "She was in the church, sitting in the rear pew."

"She left a few minutes ago," Jamie said.

Jaw clenching, Christopher explained, "I was supposed to meet her, but I got held up." Curtly, he exchanged nods with the five younger men, then looked down the drive. "We saw her drive off, followed by a man we're not sure it's safe for her to know."

He turned back in time to see the children biting their lips and looking at each other in the way they did when silently communicating. "What?" He tried not to bark.

Jamie wordlessly consulted with George and Lottie, then raised his gaze to Christopher's face. "Grandmama asked us to learn the names of the men who are staying at Parteger Hall with Miss Sewell. Yesterday, we learned they were a Count Leonski and a Kapitan Solzonik. Grandmama said they were Russians."

"Russians?" Christopher stared at the children as several pieces of information fell into his brain simultaneously, and he finally got an inkling of what might be going on…

"Oh God." He whirled to look down the drive. "She's been trying to arrange a meeting between me and some Russians."

Along with all the others, Dagenham stared at Christopher's horrified expression. "The Russians are members of the Sixth Coalition. They're our allies, aren't they?"

"Yes." Christopher couldn't help his strangled tone. *And I've been avoiding her, and therefore the meeting, for weeks!*

And now, in a snit with him, Marion had driven off with a potentially dangerous man. One she was presumably taking to meet her Russians. *Damn, damn, damn!*

Christopher set his jaw and started walking. "I have to get to Parteger Hall."

"Yeah." Drummond fell into step beside him. "I really think *we* do."

Christopher didn't argue but broke into a run. Drummond huffed, but kept pace.

"We'll come, too!" Henry called after them. "We have our curricles here. We'll wait for you in the lane."

"We'll come!" Jamie declared. "We can all cram into your curricle, Uncle Christopher."

Christopher glanced around and found the children running to catch up. He slowed, intending to forbid their participation, but George pointed out, "You'll need us to show you the fastest way."

"And the best way to sneak up to the house." Lottie was running flat out beside her brothers.

Christopher glanced at Drummond, hoping for support.

Instead, the big man shrugged. "They've already been close and know the lay of the land, which is more than we do."

That was unarguable. Christopher gritted his teeth and increased his pace.

He and Drummond reached the stable and flung themselves into harnessing his blacks—bored and very ready to run—to his curricle. The boys ran to help Simms drag the curricle into position.

The instant the blacks were secure between the shafts, Christopher seized the reins and leapt to the seat. Drummond sat beside him, and the children squeezed into the box seat. "Ready?" Christopher asked.

"Yes," the three chorused.

Drummond nodded. "Let's go."

Christopher trotted the blacks down the drive. In the lane, they found Dagenham behind a pair of high-stepping bays, with Kilburn up beside him, and Henry in his curricle with Wiley beside him and Carnaby behind.

Christopher swung into the lane, but slowed and turned to the others as they fell in behind. "You don't have to come." He glanced at the children; he fully intended to sideline them after they'd shown him the approaches to Parteger Hall. "I can't vouch for how safe this might be."

Henry, his friends, and the children all grinned, and Henry said, "For all of us"—with his gaze, he included the children—"this had been an unusually quiet lead-up to Christmas. We're used to much more excitement. In short, you won't stop us from following you no matter how hard you try."

In truth, Christopher had no idea what plot Marion might have got herself tangled in or what danger they might find at Parteger Hall. Extra help might be welcome. Tersely, he nodded. "Right, then." He glanced at the children. "What's the fastest way to this place?"

"To the left at the end of the village lane," Jamie promptly supplied. "Then north up the main lane to the turnoff to East Wellow."

Grim-faced, Christopher led the way, with Dagenham and Henry following close behind.

~

They reached East Wellow and Parteger Hall in good time, ten or so minutes, Christopher estimated, behind Marion.

Taking the children's advice, their party left their curricles in a clearing off the lane leading to the Hall, then in single file, they followed the children through woodland, skirting several blackberry thickets to reach the rear of the house's rather neglected shrubbery.

Jamie, who had led the way, hugged the hedge and turned to whisper to Christopher, "This is the closest we can get to the house without risking being seen."

Christopher nodded and moved silently past Jamie. He edged to the corner of the hedge and peered around it. From that position, he had an excellent view of the entire southern façade of the house, with its twin bay windows and garden door opening to the paved terrace and the lawn. Sadly, he was too far away to see with any clarity through the multipaned windows that overlooked the terrace, but at least those windows were uncurtained, and he glimpsed movement enough to be certain there were people in the room beyond. Given its location, that room was most likely the drawing room.

Drummond had sidled up and now peered around Christopher's shoulder. After a second, he murmured, "We need to get closer and get a better look at what's going on in there."

Christopher nodded. After raking the scene one last time, he drew back and signaled to the others. "We need to circle around the shrubbery to the corner closest to the house."

He led the way. It had been years since he'd been in the field, but he hadn't forgotten the art—or the thrill—of making up plans as one went along. He rounded the shrubbery with Drummond on his heels, then halted at the next corner and peered past.

From there, he looked directly along the building, down the length of the paved area toward the stable block beyond the house. The light from the westering sun fell at an oblique angle across that face of the house, leaving the corner closest to him and the nearer window of the drawing room in shadow. Christopher turned and murmured to the others, "Wait here. I'm going to take a look."

He stepped past the shrubbery corner and carefully walked forward. Should anyone come out of the garden door, or even along the path from the stable, he would be in plain sight, but the garden appeared deserted. Most importantly, he wouldn't be visible to anyone inside until he drew level with the window.

After passing the entrance to the shrubbery—an archway cut into the front hedge—he continued on to the flagstone pavers. Setting down each foot carefully so as not to make a sound, he approached the first bay window. Each of the five panels that made up the bay contained ten individual panes. He crouched beside the edge of the nearest panel, then inched forward until he could just see through the lower corner of the bottom pane.

It took several seconds for the scene inside to resolve into its component parts.

Marion was sitting on a sofa facing the window. Her hands were clasped in her lap, and she was leaning forward slightly, with her gaze locked on the occupant of a wing chair that had its back squarely to the window. The tall, dark, and dangerous stranger who had followed Marion from the church stood behind her, as if holding himself ready to react if she sprang to her feet. He, too, had been looking at the person in the wing chair, but as Christopher watched, the stranger shifted his gaze to a military-looking man standing stiffly to one side of the fireplace. Christopher pegged the second man as the children's Kapitan Solzonik.

Solzonik spoke, then together with the stranger, glanced toward a distinguished-looking older gentleman, who occupied an armchair on the other side of the hearth. Christopher squinted and studied the older man, presumably Count Leonski. The count made some comment, then all three men, along with Marion, who had tracked the exchange, refocused on the occupant of the wing chair. All four expressions Christopher could see suggested a degree of deference.

From his position, Christopher could make out nothing at all of whoever was sitting in the wing chair.

He lingered for a moment more, enough to confirm his reading of the situation, then silently retreated and returned to where the others waited, in and around the arched entrance to the shrubbery.

With wary eyes trained on the distant stable, from which, thankfully, no one had yet emerged, the company closed around Christopher. "Well?" Drummond demanded, his voice a low rumble.

"Miss Sewell is in there, along with four others." Succinctly, Christopher described the scene inside the drawing room. "Miss Sewell is watchful. The stranger is a touch tense. The kapitan is unsure, while the count is more relaxed, but also…curious. The critical point is that all four keep returning their attention to whoever is sitting in the wing chair."

"They—that person—must be the leader, the mastermind behind this escapade, whatever it is." Drummond frowned, then looked at Christopher. "Do you have any idea what this caper is?"

Christopher grimaced. "None." He paused, then went on, "I'm fairly certain Miss Sewell has been attempting to contact me to arrange a meeting between me and the count and possibly the kapitan as well. But who the dangerous stranger is and how he connects to our supposed mastermind in the wing chair and what their involvement in all this is, I have no clue."

"What now?" Henry asked.

Christopher glanced at Drummond. "I think we need to go in."

Drummond nodded. "Only way to learn what's going on and, hopefully, take charge."

"How?" George Wiley asked. "Do we just knock on the front door and ask if anyone's at home?"

"Not quite." Christopher frowned. "I would dearly love to know who the person in the wing chair is before we barge in."

Dagenham had drifted off and now returned. "I just checked. Other than the two big bays along the terrace, there are no other windows in that room, so no way to see who is in that chair."

"Were there any pistols or other weapons on show?" Kilburn asked.

Christopher shook his head. "Not that I saw. If there's any degree of coercion being brought to bear, it appears to be purely by threat at this stage."

"Well," Drummond said, "whoever the person in that chair and the dangerous fellow are, it's plainly our duty to learn their identities and, if they can't explain themselves, take them into custody."

In his mind, Christopher juggled the possibilities. "The most likely scenario is that whoever's in that chair is working with the stranger to interfere with and disrupt the opening of a dialogue between the British government and the Russians. It seems fairly clear that establishing such a dialogue is why the Russians are here."

Frowning, Henry asked, "Why aren't they talking to someone in London?"

"They tried to approach me in London, but didn't succeed in making contact, and when I came down here, they followed." Christopher frowned as well. "But as to why they didn't simply approach someone else at the FO…" He tipped his head consideringly. "I can only conclude that they want to keep their approach a secret, and there could be several excellent reasons for that." He arched his brows. "It might even be that a major reason for such secrecy is or is connected to the person in the wing chair."

"All right." Drummond looked at Christopher. "So what's our next move? Weapons on show or not, how do we get Miss Sewell and the Russkies out of there in one piece?"

An excellent question. "We don't go in aggressively, but we need to be prepared." Christopher rapidly weighed their options, then looked at Drummond. "You and I are FO—unless the discussion in there has progressed much further into threats than it currently seems, having two officials of the FO arrive should be sufficient to allow us to take charge and send whoever it is packing."

"Not if our mystery man and the mastermind are Frenchies." Drummond set his jaw pugnaciously. "We'll need to take them into custody, and I can't see how we'll do that easily if we go in softly-softly."

He had a point. Christopher thought, then said, "What about this?" Rapidly, he outlined a plan that, by deliberate design, gave everyone in their company a role and a goal. He wasn't deluded enough to attempt to exclude his nephews and niece or leave them with nothing to do. In terms of props, Henry kept a fowling piece under his curricle's seat, and Dagenham had a brace of pistols locked in his curricle's boot. At Christopher's suggestion, the pair raced back to the carriages to retrieve the guns and returned with all three loaded. Meanwhile, Drummond had pulled out his own serviceable pistol and loaded it as well.

"I hope it won't come to that," Christopher said, eyeing the pistol.

"Just as well to be prepared," Drummond rather grimly returned.

Christopher watched Dagenham hand his second pistol to Kilburn, then looked around the circle of eager faces. "Right. You all know what you have to do. Stick to the plan, and we'll see everyone safe, including all those in the drawing room."

Especially Marion Sewell. Christopher continued to mentally rail at himself for avoiding her for so long. What had he been thinking? Sadly, he knew what he'd been thinking, but he'd been a coward, and now, courtesy of his stupidity, Marion was facing who knew what danger and having to deal with a situation his misjudgment had allowed to develop.

Given that, it was up to him to put matters right.

After a final glance over his troops, he nodded. "Let's go."

He turned and strode along the path that led around the house toward the front door, which, according to the children, was located on the north side of the house, facing the drive. Gravel crunched softly under Drummond's and Kilburn's boots as they followed. Rather more quietly, the three children obediently walked behind Kilburn. The trio were under strict orders as to what they were to do. Christopher prayed to every deity he knew that they would stick to his script.

He turned the corner of the house. Given the thickness of the old house's walls, they hadn't been concerned that anyone in the drawing room would be alerted to their approach. The front porch lay a little way along, past two windows. As he walked past the windows, Christopher looked in and saw what appeared to be a study, presently deserted.

He paused to allow the rest of the company to pass his group and carry on around the house to the kitchen door; Drummond, Kilburn, and the children were slated to remain with him. Once the others had slipped around the far corner of the house, Christopher stepped onto the porch, strode to the bellpull hanging beside the door, and tugged it. They all heard a bell peal inside and quickly got into position.

Several seconds later, the door opened, revealing an elderly butler. He looked inquiringly at Christopher. "Yes, sir?"

Christopher stepped back, and Kilburn stepped forward, the pistol in his hand pointing at the butler's chest.

The butler's mouth fell open, and his eyes flew wide.

"Don't say a word," Christopher said, his voice even and low. "Just step back and let us in."

Kilburn took half a step forward, and his eyes now as wide as saucers, the butler hesitantly backed into the hall. Kilburn followed, directing the man to one side, allowing Christopher, Drummond, and the children to walk in.

After one quick glance around the foyer, Christopher crossed to what had to be the drawing room door. He paused and looked at Drummond. "Ready?"

When Drummond, his pistol in his hand, nodded, Christopher gripped the doorknob, opened the door, and strode boldly inside.

The murmur of voices halted.

The glare from the bay windows cast much of the scene before him in shadow. Three paces into the room, he halted and blinked.

And blinked.

Then he stared.

It took several seconds for his mind to reconcile his expectations with what he was seeing, then reality crashed over him. *"Mama?"*

"Grandmama!" The children rushed past him, confirming that he wasn't hallucinating. The trio dashed across the room to the wing chair.

Jamie asked, "What are you doing here?" for which Christopher was grateful.

"Everyone thought you might be a French agent." George glanced curiously at the others in the room.

With the seriousness only a little girl could achieve, Lottie informed

Christopher's mother, "We thought you might be a dangerous mastermind."

His mother's brows had risen progressively higher with each damning revelation. "Dangerous?" She raised her obsidian gaze to Christopher's face. Transparently amused, she continued, "I will own to half that description, but as to the rest… Really, Christopher, I had no idea you had such an active imagination."

Conscious of a flush rising in his cheeks, Christopher decided to concentrate on his relief—which was significant—although it was difficult not to feel deflated and distinctly foolish.

He glanced at Marion, still seated on the sofa. When he'd walked in, she'd swiveled to stare at him and now regarded him with what he interpreted as poorly concealed exasperation. He promptly returned his gaze to his mother and half bowed. "I regret, Mama, that I was forced to operate with an incomplete grasp of the situation."

He hadn't properly looked at the three men—the dangerous stranger and the kapitan, both of whom had straightened but otherwise remained where they'd been, and the count, who, apparently unperturbed, continued to observe the action from his chair—but from his mother's approving expression, he sensed he'd taken the right tack.

"So it seems," Therese returned.

Other voices reached them from the hall, then Henry and Dagenham walked in, followed by Carnaby, Wiley, and Kilburn.

"It's all a hum, Osbaldestone." Henry smiled and nodded to Therese.

Dagenham half bowed to her, then informed Christopher, "We found Simms in the kitchen, and he told us it was her ladyship who had called."

Noting that poor Christopher was looking beyond awkward, Therese took pity on him; what was a mother for, after all? She waved toward the count. "Christopher—and everyone else—allow me to present Count Leonski. The count is the personal envoy of Emperor Alexander."

Christopher immediately bowed. "Count."

While the gentlemen who had accompanied Christopher exchanged bows with the count, Therese blithely continued explaining to her son, "I've known the count for more years than either of us care to recall, indeed, since the days your father and I spent at our embassy in Moscow. Trusting in our name and discovering that there was still an Osbaldestone at the Foreign Office—namely, you—the count came to London intent on gaining an audience with you."

Smoothly, Therese indicated Solzonik. "And this is Kapitan Solzonik, who has accompanied the count. The kapitan bears communications from Alexander's generals as to the ongoing advance against our mutual enemy in France."

She paused to allow Christopher and the other newcomers to exchange bows with Solzonik before adding, "The count and the kapitan are here in the hopes of commencing informal discussions with our government." She felt sure Christopher would have no trouble guessing what details the Russians wished to discuss.

Finally, she directed her attention and that of Christopher and company to the gentleman now standing beside Solzonik. "And this is Mr. Stephen Kincaid, a colleague of yours and Mr. Drummond's."

Christopher's brows rose. "You're FO?"

Preserving a commendably straight face, Kincaid nodded. "Powell dispatched me to keep an eye on you from a distance in the hope that I would identify and apprehend whoever was following you."

"Unfortunately," Therese cut in, pulling Christopher's attention back to her, "we have just established that the man the FO took to be a French agent watching your house was, in fact, the kapitan, who had wished to assess if there was some viable way of contacting you directly other than through Miss Sewell."

When Christopher looked at him, Solzonik shrugged. "I tried, but I could see it would be difficult to simply speak with you and expect to gain your confidence. So I agreed with the count to allow our approach to you to go forward as arranged." He nodded at Marion. "Which is to say, via Miss Sewell."

"It was thought," Marion distinctly dryly remarked, "by my brother and the count, that it would appear perfectly unremarkable were I to approach you socially and arrange to meet in secret and, at that subsequent meeting, explain the count's request for a face-to-face meeting with you."

Scrutinizing Christopher's expression, Therese easily read the supreme self-consciousness he was attempting to conceal and drew her own conclusions about why it had taken Marion so long to make a seemingly simple contact.

Kincaid said to Christopher, "So it seems there never were any French agents following you."

Therese noted the faint disgust with the situation that colored Kincaid's tone and expression and Drummond's expression as well. It seemed the pair had, from the first, been wasting their time keeping their eyes peeled for foreign agents in Little Moseley.

Beside Therese, George, who with his siblings had remained clustered about her, suddenly shifted to stare out of the bay window at her back. She noticed and looked his way, just in time to see him stiffen.

"I say," he exclaimed. "There's someone outside."

Jamie promptly moved to stand beside his brother. "Where?"

His gaze fixed, George nodded beyond the window. "Beneath the tree we hid under yesterday."

Christopher exchanged a swift look with Drummond and Kincaid, then with outward calm, walked around the sofa to where the boys stood, laid a hand on George's shoulder and, over his nephew's head, looked out. "The fir?" he asked in an even tone.

George nodded. Lowering his voice, he said, "There's two of them. They're lying down under the tree. I think they have a spyglass."

Christopher could just distinguish the darker, denser shapes cloaked in the shadows beneath the tree.

"They've noticed us looking at them!" Jamie's voice rose. "They're running away!"

Christopher, too, had seen the sudden movement. He whirled and raced for the door.

Kincaid and Drummond vied for the position at his heels—with Drummond being closer, but Kincaid more nimble—and Solzonik proved to be no slouch, beating the younger men and the children through the doorway.

Therese and the count watched with mild interest as all their juniors tore out of the room.

Marion, too, had leapt to her feet, but hesitated. As the children ran past her, she cast an uncertain look at Therese.

Therese promptly waved her on. "Do please follow and make sure no one does anything foolish. Lottie's too young to exert sufficient control on her own."

For a fleeting second, Marion stared at her, then grinned, spun around, and raising her skirts, rushed after the others.

Amused, Gregor Leonski caught Therese's eye and smiled. "One thing about you English diplomats—you rarely lead boring lives."

Therese snorted. "You can talk, old friend. Now, as we are happily alone, tell me how my son can assist you."

CHAPTER 12

Marion followed the children. They seemed to know the area around the Hall better than anyone else. As she ran in their wake, she couldn't help but think, *What next?* The supposedly simple business of arranging a secret meeting was proving to be an exhausting exercise. One step forward, two steps back, then racing off to prevent some unknown party from spreading the news of a secret meeting between mysterious Russians and FO officials. Never mind that the meeting hadn't yet occurred!

The children followed the stream of men toward the river, then the line cut sideways, angling into the woods.

Marion wondered who they were chasing and, more importantly, who had sent them to spy on the Hall.

Ahead of her, the children slowed, then joined their men, who were milling, apparently aimlessly, in a small clearing from which three paths led onward.

The children slowed only to weave through the company. "They'll have gone this way!" the older boy insisted, pointing to a path that led deeper into the wood.

The children raced on down that path.

The men looked at each other, then several shrugged, and they all pounded off in pursuit. Marion paused to catch her breath, then set out once more in the men's wake.

The land sloped downward, and she found she could track Christopher's dark head as he moved at the front of the pack of adult males. Despite her very real exasperation with him, she'd felt hugely relieved when he'd walked into the Hall's drawing room; she'd been so on edge over having to deal with his terrifyingly omniscient-seeming mother that the instant she'd swung around and set eyes on him, a little voice in her head had chirped, *At last!* and she'd felt the weight she'd carried for the past weeks slide from her shoulders.

The land leveled, swinging once more toward the river, and she lost sight of Christopher. She slowed, keeping her eyes trained on the back of the young gentleman who was now at the end of the line, directly in front of her.

The track they were following wound through the wood for another thirty yards, then she rounded a curve and found the entire company standing silently along the path ahead of her. She peered forward and caught sight of Christopher. From the front of the line, he and Kincaid signaled for everyone to keep silent.

After a moment, the group crept forward again, then those ahead of her crouched and, following hand signals from Christopher and Kincaid, silently drifted to either side of the path. Marion followed the others' lead. From her position at the end of the line, slightly higher than those in front, she peered over the heads along the path to where it ended in a clearing by the river and saw two rough-looking men arguing vociferously.

The wind was blowing off the river, and the men's voices carried clearly.

"Come on, Dave!" The taller, lankier man gripped his mate's sleeve and tried to haul the shorter, heavier man along the bank to the right. "We need to get back to that chevy-bloke and tell him what we saw!"

His mate's jaw set. He dug in his heels, caught his friend's arm, and tried to drag him in the opposite direction. "No, Donny, you daft beggar. Those people saw us! We need to get out of here and save our skins!"

Donny resisted. "But then we won't get any money! We've done what he asked—we should get paid."

"I don't care! It's not worth it!"

Marion realized that Kincaid and Solzonik had circled to the left, and Christopher and Drummond had drifted like ghosts to the right. Now all four leapt to their feet and charged Donny and Dave.

Donny squawked.

Dave whirled and threw a poorly directed punch.

The five younger gentlemen leapt up and dashed into the ensuing fray.

Marion was relieved to see that the children had the good sense not to join their seniors. Instead, they danced around the periphery of the ensuing melee, calling encouragement and, in the little girl's case, directions.

The result was never in doubt. Dave and Donny were quickly overpowered.

The pair's hands were tied behind their backs with twine sourced from Christopher's nephews' pockets, then the captives were marched back to the Hall, with the rest of the company following, more or less in single file.

In charge of the prisoners at the head of the line, Christopher and Kincaid steered the men onto the south lawn and ordered both to sit, which they did, sullenly crossing their legs and glowering, but without much heat.

The count and Christopher's mother emerged from the house and joined everyone else in a semicircle arrayed in front of the pair. Christopher took up a position directly before the captives and stared down at them.

From her position at one end of the semicircle, Marion surreptitiously studied Christopher. His face was set in a way she'd never seen before—like granite, unforgiving. He appeared unexpectedly strong and distinctly commanding.

After a long moment of silence during which Donny and Dave grew obviously more nervous, Christopher folded his arms and, still regarding them unwaveringly, said, "On the bank, you argued about returning to report to someone, presumably to tell them what you had seen, and you expected them to pay you for that information. Who is that person?"

When the pair stared back, then shifted nervously and glanced to left and right, Christopher's voice hardened, and he demanded, "Who hired you? Who are you working for?"

Donny licked his lips. "'Ere"—he glanced at Solzonik and the count—"how'd we know that you lot aren't working fer the Frenchies?"

Dave jabbed a stubby finger at the count and the kapitan, who was standing beside his countryman. "Them two is furriners—we heard 'em jabbering."

Christopher glanced at the count and the kapitan, then looked back at Donny and Dave. "They are, indeed, foreigners. They're Russians." He caught Donny's and Dave's eyes. "The Russians are our—Britain's—allies. They're fighting alongside us against Napoleon as we speak."

Both men looked skeptical, but also wary.

After a moment, Donny admitted, "We don't know nuthin' about that."

"Fer all we know, you could be double-dealin' with them—that's what the other blokes said." Eyes narrowing, Dave thrust out his chin pugnaciously. "We're no French spies, but you're here with them furriners, and no matter what you try to tell us, how'd we know you're telling the truth? How'd we know fer sure you ain't workin' fer the French, heh?"

Marion noted that everyone around the semicircle looked faintly shocked and rather offended.

Then Lady Osbaldestone heaved a dramatic sigh—one communicating a degree of long-suffering that only an aristocratic ton hostess of the highest caliber could command. She leveled her black gaze on the hapless pair sitting cross-legged on the grass. "My dear good man." The weight of eons of aristocratic forebears resounded in her voice. With a sweeping gesture, she waved to either side, indicating the assembled company. "Just cast your eyes about you." Her tone hardened, growing distinctly quelling. "For your information, I am Lady Osbaldestone. Among other postings, my husband was the British ambassador to the Russian Imperial Court, which is how I came to be acquainted with this gentleman"—she indicated the count—"who is Count Leonski. I can testify that he is, indeed, the personal envoy of the Emperor of Russia."

Next, she pointed to Christopher. "That gentleman is my son, and he works for the Foreign Office, as does my son-in-law, Lord North. My eldest son is in the Home Office, and my middle son is in the War Office. Mr. Kincaid over there is also with the Foreign Office, as is Mr. Drummond." She pointed to each man.

"And then," she went on, imperious and commanding, "we have Viscount Dagenham, who is heir to the Earl of Carsely and currently with the Home Office, and Mr. Thomas Kilburn, heir to Lord Kilburn, Mr. Roger Carnaby, heir to Lord Carnaby, and George Wiley, heir to Viscount Worth. And of course, a gentleman you might recognize, Sir Henry Fitzgibbon, of Fulsom Hall in Little Moseley. As for my intrepid grandchildren, the eldest is James, Viscount Skelton, heir to the Earl of Winslow. And I must not forget Miss Sewell, whose brother is currently serving overseas with the Foreign Office, and whose father, Sir Nathaniel Sewell, holds a very high rank in that department."

Lady Osbaldestone brought her obsidian gaze once more to bear on the hapless captives and, in an awful voice, inquired, "Do you seriously imagine that a group such as this would be consorting with our country's enemies?"

Both Donny and Dave looked stunned, no doubt reeling under the barrage of titles and affiliations. Marion rather thought their state was the definition of being rolled up, horse, foot, and guns.

After a long, pregnant pause, during which no one on the lawn so much as twitched, Lady Osbaldestone, who had continued to hold the pair immobile with her piercing gaze, imperiously demanded, "Well?"

Staring at her as if at a much larger and dangerous predator, both men slowly shook their heads.

Both swallowed, then the heavier, possibly older Dave nervously glanced at Christopher. "Seems we might've been told a bit of a story."

Unrelentingly grim, Christopher nodded. "It seems so. So I ask again—who is the man who hired you? The one you expected to pay you?"

Donny squirmed, but Dave stared at his friend until Donny mumbled, "They're two gentlemen."

"French?" Christopher asked.

Donny bit his lip and nodded.

Dave rushed to explain, "They said they were refugee-émigrés. That they lived here now and were working with our government to expose Napoleon's spies."

"You called one of them 'that chevy-bloke,'" George said. "Is he a chevalier?"

"Yes!" Donny bounced. "That's it!" He looked at Dave, then tried to get his tongue around the name. "Chevalier Hoostace Demill."

Solzonik stiffened. "Chevalier Eustace De Mille is one of Napoleon's most senior agents." The kapitan looked at Christopher. "De Mille was sighted in Russia before we left. We thought he was still there."

The count had paled. "He must have followed us here."

Kincaid refocused on their captives. "What did De Mille set you to do?"

"We was to watch the two furriners." Dave nodded at the count and the kapitan. "He—the chevalier—told us they were French."

"We was to keep watch and see who came to visit," Donny elaborated. "And if any London-looking gentleman came to call, we was to let them know as soon as may be."

"We usually watch from the other side of the house," Dave explained, "but we'd seen the tykes"—he nodded at the children—"sneakin' about, so we decided to come and see if there was somewhere on this side of the house to keep a better watch, given we had the spyglass and all. We'd worked our way around and just got into position beneath that tree when you lot walked in."

The count and Christopher exchanged a glance. Donny and Dave's information confirmed that De Mille already knew the Russians were there. However, he hadn't had his watchers follow Marion, most likely deeming her inconsequential, indicating that he hadn't realized it was she who was delegated to make first contact with Christopher. Instead, De Mille had focused on learning who—which government official—turned up to meet with the count and the kapitan.

Marion felt chilled at the thought of what might have happened if she'd succeeded in contacting Christopher at Lady Selkirk's soirée. Or anywhere in London. Concealed by the teeming hordes constantly filling London's streets, De Mille would most likely have been able to keep watch himself, and if he'd been watching the Russians from the time they'd left their country, he would have seen Christopher when he met with the count and kapitan and would have followed him…

Who knew to what lengths De Mille might have gone to disrupt and discourage closer cooperation between London and Moscow?

Before she could dwell further on that, Christopher returned his attention to the captives. "You wanted to go and meet with them just now. Where?"

Donny looked at Dave, who shrugged. "We ain't goin' to get paid nohow now, so you might as well tell 'em."

Donny grimaced and looked at Christopher. "There's an old boat shed up the stream a ways. They told us if we saw anything, we'd find them there, and they'd pay us handsome-like. We usually stop by there of an evening, and they pay us for our time."

Instantly, an eager discussion erupted. The younger men were all for rushing down and rounding up the Frenchmen, but to Marion's relief, older and wiser heads prevailed.

"We need a plan," Christopher insisted. "If, as we suspect, it is De Mille and we corner him, he's not going to surrender without a fight."

"And he'll be armed for sure," Drummond added.

"De Mille is a favorite of Le Petit Corsican," Solzonik said. "If he is here, then it is a duty for us all to make every effort to capture him. That, in itself, will strike a real blow against Napoleon. News of De Mille's capture will demoralize Napoleon's more junior agents and hearten ours and our generals as well."

Christopher, Kincaid, Drummond, and even the count nodded in ready agreement.

Drummond pointed out, "Powell will have conniptions if we have a bead on De Mille, but allow him to slip through our fingers. He's a real prize, that one."

"Agreed," Christopher said. "And De Mille's presence here says a great deal about how much importance the French attach to scuppering the count and the kapitan's secret embassy." Christopher looked to the west. The afternoon light was already fading. Soon they would be plunged into winter's brief twilight. "We don't have much time to devise our plan and execute it."

Drummond looked at Donny and Dave, who had been listening to the discussion with rather startled expressions. "This old boat shed—does it have walls and a roof?"

Donny and Dave nodded.

"Describe it," Kincaid said.

The pair obliged, drawing a word picture of a run-down but still useable abandoned shed on a lonely stretch of riverbank, screened from sight of the surrounding fields by encroaching woods.

"You said two gentlemen," Dagenham reminded everyone. "De Mille is one. Who's the other?"

They described a weaselly, wiry man, also a Frenchman. "Didn't hear his name," Dave said.

"Something like Corbu," Donny offered.

"Corbeau?" Solzonik suggested.

Donny nodded. "That's it."

Solzonik looked at Christopher. "Jacques Corbeau is De Mille's long-time henchman. He obeys De Mille's orders, but is dangerous in his own right." Solzonik looked at Donny and Dave. "You are lucky to have been caught. If Corbeau is with De Mille, that pair is more likely to slit your throats than pay you for anything."

Donny and Dave blanched.

Christopher shifted, drawing everyone's gazes. "Did De Mille and Corbeau have horses waiting? Or did they come by boat?"

Neither Donny nor Dave knew.

"*Could* they have a boat waiting in the boat shed?" Drummond asked.

Donny and Dave shared a glance, then Donny admitted that was possible.

"We've never seen inside," Dave explained.

"So what's our plan?" Kincaid looked around the semicircle.

Suggestions were flung about. Bright ideas were tempered by experienced counsel, and reasonably rapidly, the outline of a plan took shape. There was only one stumbling block. No one wished to trust Dave or Donny to play any part in the action.

"Unless we find horses tethered nearby, we have to assume they have a boat in that shed." Christopher looked at the others.

His expression hard, Kincaid nodded. "We can't risk either of them using a boat to escape. We need to lure at least one of them—preferably De Mille—away from the riverbank. Far enough away that we can send some of us across, in between the pair of them, to prevent him reaching the boat."

Despite cudgeling their brains, none of the men came up with any viable way to lure De Mille away from the boat shed. Marion noticed the three children huddling together whispering, then they broke apart, and the eldest said, "What about this?"

Their proposition was really rather clever, but lacked a vital touch—namely, a way to tip the scales toward it being De Mille rather than Corbeau who responded to their lure.

Seeing a way in which she could contribute, ignoring the attempts by the assembled men to dismiss the children's suggestion as too dangerous—as they had no alternative to offer, said attempts weren't convincing anyone—Marion raised her voice and announced, "We already know that De Mille discounts females. He didn't bother ordering Donny and Dave to follow me when I left the Hall. If I go with the children, playing the role of, let's say, their aunt, then if we follow the script the children have suggested, there's every likelihood it will be De Mille who will leave the riverbank and come to assist us."

Predictably, all the assembled gentlemen were horrified by her suggestion, but with the light fading rapidly and no workable option—and with Lady Osbaldestone and Count Leonski rather unexpectedly speaking in support of the revised plan—Christopher and the others had to grit their teeth and reluctantly acquiesce.

With a sense of building urgency, they knuckled down to work out the necessary details to give their plan the best chance of succeeding.

Fifteen minutes later, Christopher, Lottie, Drummond, Solzonik, Kilburn, and Wiley slid into positions around an old oak tree in the largely leafless wood thirty or so yards from the river.

With his eyes fixed on the run-down boat shed on the bank a little to his left, Christopher sank into the space between two evergreen bushes. On the grassy area before the shed's sagging doors, two tall, lean, faintly swarthy men sat on upturned barrels. They appeared engrossed in a card game, using a third barrel set between them as a table.

Not by a flicker of a glance did either man show any awareness of movement in the wood. Christopher filled his lungs, feeling tension cinch about his chest. He hadn't been out of the field for so long that he'd forgotten what the gripping alertness of an active mission felt like, yet he couldn't recall ever feeling so on edge, and he was very aware that the extra anxiety stemmed from Marion's role in the upcoming drama. The notion of her deliberately attracting the attention of a supremely dangerous agent like De Mille…threatened to freeze Christopher's faculties. When it came to the issue of Marion being in danger, he felt far—*far*—too much.

Waiting, silent and still, for the action to commence required significant effort.

To keep his mind from wandering into unhelpful speculation, he focused on De Mille. Darkly handsome in a rakish, rather piratical way, the man possessed a natural expression that was so superciliously arrogant that no one could doubt he was a Frenchman. He was tall and leanly muscled in a way that suggested strength combined with power. In any physical clash, Christopher suspected De Mille would be a formidable opponent.

Corbeau, on the other hand, was a sharp-featured man, whip-thin and wiry, but in a fight, he would probably be stronger and more dangerous than he looked.

For today, Corbeau wasn't Christopher's concern. Kincaid had led Henry, Dagenham, and Carnaby through the wood, making for the spot where the trees encroached close to the riverbank a little farther east of the boat shed. That group had been delegated to deal with De Mille's henchman, and Christopher and the others about the oak were to wait for Kilburn's signal before initiating their plan.

Christopher glanced down to his left, to where Lottie hunkered beside him. Her small body was all but quivering with suppressed excitement. Initially, he'd assumed she was nervous, but then she'd looked up at him and smiled, and he'd seen the eagerness and impatience shining in her eyes.

He tried not to wonder how good her acting talents truly were. Her brothers had vowed she could pull off the necessary deception, but if De Mille caught sight of her face as it was now, he would never believe she was consumed by fear.

By raising his head, Christopher could see the section of wood in which Kincaid and his small troop should be. Even though he scanned the area carefully, he detected no sign of anyone being there, much less that four largish men were sneaking through the bushes, trying to get as close to the river's edge and the boat shed as humanly possible while remaining under cover. Christopher not being able to spot them was all to the good; if even knowing they were there, he couldn't see them, then De Mille and Corbeau wouldn't, either.

Finally, the plaintive cry of a curlew rose from that section of the wood. Kincaid had suggested that particular birdcall as being one everyone recognized, and they'd decided that it was unlikely De Mille or Corbeau would register the oddity of hearing a bird normally found on the coast or marshland in a country wood.

Christopher's tension ratcheted one notch tighter. He looked at Lottie, who had come alert like a scenting hound quivering to be let off her leash. She looked eagerly up at him. Feeling his face harden into grim lines, he forced himself to nod. "Off you go," he breathed.

She flashed him a beaming grin and slipped away.

He tried to track her progress, but almost immediately lost all sight of her. He shifted his gaze to the old oak that they'd chosen as their centerpiece for the upcoming charade. Even though he was watching, he almost missed the flash of a small booted foot as Lottie swiftly climbed the tree. She obeyed his instructions and, as far as she was able, moved up the far side of the wide trunk, out of sight of the men on the riverbank.

Even when she settled on the selected branch, one higher than a man's head, all Christopher could see of her was a small section of her red coat.

With Lottie in place, Christopher swiveled and looked toward the path that ran from the smattering of dwellings that was the hamlet of East Wellow to the river. The path ended in a small clearing that lay about fifty yards to his right, around a bend and out of sight of the boat shed.

Christopher prayed Kincaid's curlew's cry had carried far enough to reach Marion, Jamie, and George.

He waited with bated breath. A minute passed, then he heard Marion call from within the wood between the small clearing and the old oak. "Lottie? Come along—we need to head home."

Given dusk was closing in, that much was entirely believable. Christopher hoped the uncertain light would aid them more than De Mille.

Both Frenchmen had raised their heads at Marion's call. They waited—as did everyone else hidden in the woods.

"Lottie, you little beast—come on!" Jamie's voice rang with the exasperation of an older brother running out of patience.

Seconds later, Jamie and George came into view as they noisily pushed between the trees, plainly searching for the missing Lottie. Marion followed rather more sedately along the path, looking searchingly to left and right.

"It's too late to play hide-and-seek," George complained. He paused and, his hands on his hips, looked around. "It'll be dark soon, and we have to go home."

Jamie leapt in to add, "You don't want to be left out here all alone, do you?"

Promptly on cue came an entirely believable wail, one that, for a fleeting instant, nearly pushed Christopher into responding. He only just managed to suppress the impulse to stand. He looked at De Mille.

The Frenchman had come to his feet, as had Corbeau.

Both slowly laid aside their cards, their attention wholly fixed on the old oak and the little drama being enacted expressly for them.

Then Lottie wailed again, the sound breaking on a sob. "Don't leave me! I can't get down. I'm st-stuck!"

Christopher jettisoned his earlier doubts as to Lottie's acting skills—or that of her brothers as the pair immediately thundered through the wood toward the tree, missing Drummond and Solzonik by inches along the way.

"Wait where you are," Marion ordered as, catching her skirts in both hands, she hurried after the boys. "We'll get you down."

At no time had Marion, Jamie, or George so much as glanced toward the river. Even as they drew near the oak, their attention remained riveted to the tree and Lottie, who was clutching the trunk as if it were a lifeline.

The boys circled the oak's trunk, then took up a stance directly below where Lottie huddled on her chosen branch.

Jamie held up his arms. "Jump. I'll catch you."

Lottie gave vent to a distrustful noise and vehemently shook her head. "You'll drop me. I'm too heavy for you."

Marion reached the boys and stepped up behind Jamie. "It's all right, Lottie. I'll help Jamie—we'll catch you together."

Christopher switched his gaze to De Mille. As if drawn by magic, the Frenchman started across the narrow strip of grassy bank, heading toward the wood and the oak. From the indulgent, charming smile spreading across De Mille's face, he'd swallowed the lure whole.

The fact that De Mille's so-charming smile was trained on Marion set Christopher's teeth on edge.

The three gathered about the base of the tree gave no sign that they were aware of the Frenchman's approach. Marion, George, and Jamie pleaded with Lottie to simply jump, assuring her all would be well, while Lottie continued to shake her head and shrink back against the trunk, clutching as much of it as she could in a death-grip embrace.

"No, no, nooo!" She ended on a hiccup. She screwed her eyes tight shut. "I can't! I just *can't*!"

Incipient hysteria quavered in her voice.

De Mille halted five yards away. "Might I be of assistance?"

Marion and the boys startled in believable fashion. The boys immediately sidled closer to Marion, and she summoned a weak smile. "Oh, hello. I'm afraid we didn't see you there."

She peered past De Mille toward the boat shed, where Corbeau stood, hands on hips, watching. She looked at De Mille. "I apologize if we disturbed you."

De Mille's teeth flashed in a smile. "Think nothing of it, madame." He looked up at Lottie, who stared back at him, suspicion writ large all over her small face. De Mille's smile grew more charming. "You are at an impasse—yes?" He glanced briefly at Marion, then looked back at Lottie. "If you will permit it, I might be able to help. I believe I can almost reach her."

Marion bit her lip and looked at Lottie. "We really do need to get home. Lottie, will you let the gentleman lift you down?" To De Mille, she said, "If you can manage it, we'll be in your debt."

De Mille smiled encouragingly at Lottie. "She is your daughter?"

Marion laughed lightly. "No, she's my niece." When De Mille glanced her way, she waved at Jamie and George, who had taken up positions on either side of her. "These are my nephews."

Both boys were regarding De Mille with transparent reservation. If

Christopher had been in De Mille's shoes, he would have thought the scene genuine, too.

De Mille's smile didn't waver. He transferred his dark gaze to Lottie. "It is getting dark, ma'moiselle. By the time your pretty aunt returns to your house and brings help, it will be as black as pitch and cold as well. So better you let me lift you down, no?"

Lottie regarded him unblinkingly for several long seconds before saying, "You won't drop me, will you?"

De Mille smiled reassuringly. "I am generally held to be very strong. On my honor"—he placed a hand over his heart and executed a half bow—"I will catch you and set you safely down."

After another moment of deliberation, Lottie nodded. "All right."

His gaze on Lottie, De Mille moved closer to the trunk, set his feet, and held up his arms.

Lottie hesitated, then flung herself at him.

With an "Oof!" De Mille caught her, but the sudden impact made him stagger back. Marion thrust out her booted foot, and De Mille tripped, tipped, then crashed onto his back.

Lottie rode him down, then as instructed, went to roll free, but De Mille's fingers snagged in her coat, and he clutched and held her.

Christopher, Drummond, Solzonik, Kilburn, and Wiley all leapt up from their hiding places and rushed to close in around De Mille.

Simultaneously, down on the riverbank, Kincaid, Henry, Dagenham, and Carnaby burst forth, cutting Corbeau off from De Mille and forcing him back toward the river.

But De Mille wasn't a feared operative for no reason. In a flash, he rolled to his feet. Clutching a now-squirming Lottie to his chest, in a single comprehensive glance, he took in his situation—his and his henchman's. De Mille saw the men closing in on him, saw Christopher in the lead.

De Mille flung Lottie at Christopher, whirled, lunged, and seized Marion's hand. Then he charged past Christopher, ducking his shoulder and knocking Christopher even farther off balance as he barreled past and raced into the wood, dragging Marion with him.

Marion had been backing away when De Mille had seized her, and he'd yanked her forward so viciously, almost off her feet, that no matter how much she wanted to resist, as he tore on, under the trees, she found herself helplessly stumbling in his wake.

He gave her no chance to regain her balance, dig in her heels, and pull back. His fingers felt like steel manacles, wrapped about her wrist in an unbreakable grip, and he hadn't lied. He was strong. His momentum as he plowed through the undergrowth, dodging trees, bushes, and brambles, was akin to that of a bull. She could do nothing to even slow him.

Frantically, she tried to track where he was going, but she didn't know the area, and given the way he kept looking every which way, she didn't think he did, either. Barely seeming to register the effort of hauling her along, he started to cast back and forth, as if searching for some path, some sign.

She was gasping for breath and desperately trying to think of a way to escape when De Mille abruptly halted in a small clearing.

He paused, head rising as he plainly tried to pick up any sounds of pursuit.

His grip on her wrist didn't ease. Half bent forward, her lungs laboring, over the thudding of her heart, Marion strained her ears, too.

From a distance came the sounds of men calling and crashing through the wood. The promise of rescue seemed very far away.

Apparently, De Mille came to the same conclusion. His shoulders lowered fractionally, and his fingers eased about her wrist as he turned to her.

Christopher surged out of the bushes, a wicked-looking knife in his hand.

Reacting instinctively, De Mille released Marion and leapt back to avoid Christopher's slashing thrust.

With barely a fleeting glance at Marion, Christopher seized her arm and shoved her behind him. His relief on seeing her unharmed had already been swamped by geysering fear for her safety and an instinctive, compulsive need to engage and vanquish De Mille.

He refocused on De Mille to discover the Frenchman had taken a step back and now held a pistol in his hand. His very steady hand.

Slowly, Christopher straightened, lowering the knife.

De Mille arched a black brow. "Osbaldestone, yes?"

Puzzled by the question, Christopher frowned.

De Mille responded with a faint smile. "I like to know the names of those I kill."

"No!"

A rock the size of a cricket ball flew past Christopher's head, pitched with force toward De Mille's face.

The Frenchman saw it coming, but too late. Instinctively, he swung aside, but the rock clipped his ear.

The pistol discharged, splintered the side of a nearby tree trunk.

Christopher flung himself at De Mille, hoping to take the Frenchman to the ground, but De Mille was nearly as tall and undeniably stronger. He set his feet and, although they swayed, managed to remain upright as he caught Christopher's knife hand and forced it away, to the side.

Christopher dropped the knife and grappled with the fiend.

They wrestled, their boots shuffling across the ground as first one, then the other, got the upper hand, then De Mille tripped Christopher, and they both crashed to the ground with De Mille on top.

Since shying the rock at De Mille's face, Marion hadn't taken her eyes from the fighting men. Earlier, while De Mille had been focusing on Christopher, she'd armed herself with the rock and a nice sturdy branch. She still held the branch. Hefting it, tightening her fingers around it, she circled the desperately wrestling men, her eyes darting between Christopher and De Mille.

Then De Mille succeeded in pulling back enough to raise his fist, intending to smash it into Christopher's face.

No you don't! With the branch already raised high, with all the force she could muster, Marion brought the solid piece of wood down on the back of De Mille's head.

The branch broke.

The Frenchman froze. Then he slumped on top of Christopher.

Christopher froze for a second, too, then he grunted and pushed, struggling to get free of De Mille's dead weight.

Marion stared at Christopher as he staggered to his feet, then, his chest swelling, he straightened. He stared down at De Mille, apparently cataloguing the man's state while absentmindedly brushing off his coat.

Relief poured through her in a torrent, and she felt herself teeter—literally swaying forward on her toes—driven by a near-overpowering compulsion to fling herself at Christopher and cling…

The strength of the reaction shocked her. Confused her. Enough to have her reining it in.

Then Christopher looked at her and met her eyes. "Thank you. That was very well-timed."

She swallowed and managed, "No—thank you. I couldn't have—wouldn't have—got away from him if you hadn't come."

For an instant, all she could see was his eyes and the warmth in the rich brown. Then still holding her gaze, he quietly said, "I'm sorry. For everything." Without shifting his gaze, he waved at De Mille. "Not just for this, but for all the rest that led to it. I should have known—"

Drummond pounded into the clearing, then skidded to a halt. He stared at the fallen Frenchman, then doubled over and wheezed. "You got him! Thank God." Hands on his knees, Drummond shook his head. "He led us all over." He glanced up at Christopher. "How did you know he would come this way?"

Christopher's lips had thinned at the interruption, and Marion wasn't pleased by it, either. His features impassive, Christopher replied, "I guessed he would make for the lane." He glanced at Marion, then bent to retrieve De Mille's pistol and moved on to pick up his own knife. "Corbeau?"

Drummond hauled in a deeper breath and, his hands on his hips, straightened. "Kincaid has him well and truly trussed up." With his chin, he indicated De Mille. "It was this one who was the truly slippery character."

Christopher studied the still-unconscious De Mille, then his lips twitched, and he glanced at Marion. "Still, I fancy that the story of how Napoleon's most famous agent was persuaded to walk into a trap by an eight-year-old girl, her brothers, and her supposed aunt will be doing the rounds for a long time in FO circles."

Drummond chuckled and smiled at Marion. "I'll confess I wasn't sure our little company of players could pull it off, and I certainly never imagined you would do it so slickly. He didn't have a clue—not a one—until he landed on his back and saw us closing in."

Looking down at De Mille, Christopher ambled across and halted by Marion's side. "You were right. Men like De Mille are so busy being devious themselves that when presented with an apparently normal scene, they see only what they expect to see. They never imagine others might be equally devious."

When he looked up, she met his eyes. She looked into his—plain brown, apparently unremarkable, yet with alluring hidden depths—and saw faint hope and a nascent possibility she found herself eager to explore. "Indeed." Her heart was slowly returning to its customary rhythm. Boldly, she linked her arm in his. "And now that our plan—mine and the children's—has, with the help of all concerned, succeeded so brilliantly, I suggest it's time for us to take our prize back to Parteger Hall."

Dagenham and Solzonik came clomping through the wood. Delighted to find their coconspirators well and De Mille laid out on the ground, the pair pulled rope from their pockets, secured De Mille's hands, then between them, rolled the Frenchman onto his back.

They'd just completed the task when the others arrived, Kincaid and Kilburn pushing Corbeau, who was sporting a black eye and looking as malevolently furious as a trussed cat, before them.

Seconds later, De Mille stirred. When he realized his hands were tied, he quickly came to his senses.

He glared at them all, but unlike less experienced villains, he didn't waste breath protesting. He made to sit up, and Carnaby and Wiley stepped forward and hauled him to his feet. The instant they released him, De Mille surreptitiously started to scan the surroundings.

They all saw it; despite their delight over their success, they remained on guard as they set off through the wood on the trek back to the Hall.

Their way lay mostly along untended tracks, most too narrow for two to walk abreast. They ended strung out in single file, with Christopher in the lead, followed by Marion, Dagenham, and Solzonik. Next came De Mille. Initially, he'd been closely followed by Drummond and Henry, but as the company tramped along, the three children wove like eels between the men and slipped into position in front of Drummond. He looked at them, grunted, and reasoning that their reflexes were faster than his and their beady eyes probably sharper, allowed them to dog the Frenchman's steps.

Behind Henry, Wiley and Carnaby sloped along, followed by Corbeau, being herded by Kincaid and Kilburn, who brought up the rear.

They marched steadily on through the deepening gloom.

The edge of the woods neared, and they caught their first glimpses of Parteger Hall through the trees.

De Mille tensed.

Drummond picked up his pace and started to reach for their prisoner, but the children were before him.

De Mille lifted one foot, about to dart to the left where a break in the trees beckoned, but the children timed their rush-and-shove perfectly. In concert, they struck, and off-balance, the Frenchman twisted and teetered helplessly, then fell into a huge bramble bush on the path's right.

Uttering a sound very much like a screech, De Mille landed on one side amid the thorny canes. Then he cursed loud and long, but as he'd reverted to French, although highly inventive, his curses failed to have any effect on his tormentors-in-chief.

The trio stood on the path, safely out of reach, and grinned unrepentantly at the French agent.

Of course, Corbeau tried to capitalize on the distraction his master had caused, but Kincaid and Kilburn had been waiting for exactly such a move and dealt with it without compunction, temporarily depriving Corbeau of the ability to speak.

As for De Mille, he wriggled and threshed and only succeeded in snaring himself deeper in the brambles' embrace. The company were in no hurry to rush to his aid, but eventually, with night coming on, Christopher directed Drummond and Solzonik to haul the man out.

With their prize prisoner back on his feet and their company feeling thoroughly in charity with the world, they continued to the Hall.

"Not far now," Christopher murmured as the trees around them thinned.

As the track had widened, Marion had moved up to walk alongside him, and when he'd offered her his arm, she'd taken it and had gifted him with a smile. Scanning the way ahead, he prayed she'd forgiven him, but he wasn't sure if her new softness was any indication of that; they were both recovering from heart-pounding shocks, so their present comfortable detente might not mean what he hoped it did.

Glancing over his shoulder at the line of people behind them, he caught De Mille, undeterred, still searching for any chance to escape.

Solzonik, who had dropped back to walk beside De Mille, had noted the chevalier's plotting, too. Before Christopher could speak, Solzonik leaned closer to the Frenchman and spoke conversationally, "Trust me, Chevalier—all three children still have their eyes glued to you, and they have more tricks up their sleeve than you, I, or anyone else here might dream of. First, the oak tree. Then, the bramble bush. Next…" The Russian shrugged. "Who knows?"

De Mille blinked, then shot Solzonik a startled look and found the kapitan nodding approvingly at the three children—who had plainly heard his commendation and were grinning ear to ear. De Mille turned his head to look at them, and they raised their gazes to his face. Even in the dim light, their eyes were alive with eagerness, and all three were transparently waiting to prove the kapitan's assessment correct.

De Mille stared for a moment—and the children stared back—then Napoleon's most famous agent faced forward and kept his gaze fixed straight ahead.

Christopher grinned and faced forward, too. For the moment at least, De Mille had given up plotting his escape.

CHAPTER 13

"Victory is ours!" Beaming, Count Leonski raised his glass high. "I give you our fearless band of heroes, who have managed to apprehend the slipperiest of French spies—a favorite of Napoleon's, no less—who has plagued all our countries for many years." With his glass, he saluted the assembled company. "Congratulations to you all. To your health!"

"Hear, hear!" Lady Osbaldestone raised her glass as well. She smiled fondly at her grandchildren, then benignly included the rest of the company. "I own to being thoroughly impressed."

The children all but glowed, and everyone else grinned and drank.

Solzonik promptly did the rounds with another bottle of the champagne the butler had unearthed from the cellars. The kapitan refilled the glasses, all except those of the children; in recognition of their sterling contribution, they'd been allowed a small sip, but her ladyship had warned them of the dangers of becoming tipsy.

They were all once more gathered in the drawing room of Parteger Hall. Relaxing in chairs and on the sofa or lounging against the mantelpiece, having regaled the count and Lady Osbaldestone with a full report of how their plan had unfolded, all were savoring the resultant relief and the concomitant elation.

Patently satisfied with the outcome, from his position beside Solzonik by the hearth, Kincaid observed, "The capture of an agent of De Mille's caliber doesn't happen every day." Many murmured in agreement, and

Kincaid raised his glass to Marion and the children, who were sitting beside her on the sofa. "And there's no question about it—you four are going to be the talk of the FO."

Appearing decidedly chuffed and happy, the four exchanged satisfied smiles. Christopher watched Marion raise her glass to the children in a silent toast, and they grinned and returned the tribute.

On reaching the Hall and finding themselves faced with having to arrange suitable accommodation for their prisoners, Christopher had pointed out that, with Parteger Hall being the only large house in the immediate area, it was likely past owners would have served as local magistrates. He and Kincaid had inquired of the staff, and consequently, De Mille and Corbeau had been left languishing in a small cell in the cold and rather dank cellar.

Donny and Dave, who had been locked in a room off the scullery, had been left where they were for the moment. Kincaid and Solzonik had volunteered to warn the pair before releasing them later.

Subsequently, the company had gathered in the drawing room and described the exciting capture to the count and Christopher's mother, in the process filling in the others who hadn't seen the action that had, ultimately, brought down De Mille.

The cheers and crows of appreciation elicited by Christopher's account of Marion's expertise with rock and branch had made her blush delightfully.

But now night had fallen, and with dense clouds covering the sky, the darkness outside was absolute. Christopher saw his mother swivel to look out of the window behind her chair, then she turned back to the company and, with her usual aplomb, swept her black gaze over the entire group, causing everyone to regard her attentively. "My dears, while I appreciate that there is rather a lot of important discussion still pending, with De Mille and his companion secured and all threat, therefore, removed, might I suggest it will be significantly more comfortable for us all if those necessary discussions were put off for tonight and, instead, taken up tomorrow, perhaps after luncheon at Hartington Manor?"

Kincaid had already offered to relocate to the Hall from the inn in West Wellow where he'd been staying, the better to assist Solzonik and the Hall staff in overseeing De Mille and Corbeau's incarceration. Despite that, Christopher noted that his mother had plainly extended her luncheon invitation to everyone present.

Still beaming, Count Leonski acquiesced with the graciousness of a longtime diplomat. "My dear Therese, what an excellent suggestion. You are entirely correct—given the hour, we will do better to savor and digest the triumphs of today and leave all business for tomorrow." The count arched a brow at Christopher.

He half bowed. "I agree." Smiling, he glanced at Marion. "As we have now made contact, we can afford at least one night to absorb the day's events before commencing our discussions on what might lie ahead." He returned his gaze to Solzonik and the count. "Aside from all else, the existence of De Mille's mission has implications we should perhaps consider."

The count nodded approvingly. "You are right. A little time for each of us to dwell on such matters would be wise."

"Wonderful!" His mother rose. "In that case, you are all"—with a gracious gesture, she included everyone there—"invited to partake of luncheon at Hartington Manor tomorrow after church." To Solzonik and the count, she added, "We keep country hours. I will expect you at half past twelve." She glanced at the rest of the company and smiled. "I'm sure Mrs. Haggerty will rise to the occasion once I inform her we have a triumph to celebrate."

Everyone accepted with alacrity.

"We'll definitely be there," Henry assured her.

"You couldn't keep me away." Drummond hiked up his breeches and looked at Kincaid. "Trust me, Kincaid, you won't want to miss one of Mrs. Haggerty's spreads."

Smiling, Kincaid inclined his head to Drummond and then to Christopher's mother. "Thank you, ma'am. I believe the staff here are more than capable of holding the fort for the requisite hours to permit me to attend."

"Excellent!" Christopher's mother swept the gathering with one of her grande-dame glances, then focused on Jamie, George, and Lottie. "Come, children. It's time we returned to the manor. You must be quite famished."

Naturally, the trio agreed with that suggestion. They promptly gathered around their grandmother and moved with her as she led the way into the front hall.

Marion followed, conscious that, in the same way that the children had moved with his mother, Christopher kept pace with her as she crossed to the front door and spoke with the butler, Coles, instructing that the visitors' carriages be brought around. Earlier, her groom and the various coachmen had been dispatched to fetch the carriages from where they'd been left.

All the other men, including the count and Solzonik, drifted into the hall in Marion and Christopher's wake. While the others congregated and chatted, reliving various moments of the recent action, Christopher shifted slightly to one side, drawing her attention.

When she looked inquiringly at him, he cut a glance at the others, including his mother, who was once again engaged with the count. Then Christopher focused on her face, drew breath, and said, "I owe you an apology of such comprehensive magnitude that I have absolutely no idea where to start." He caught and held her gaze. "Regardless, for all my…"

He plainly searched for the right word. When he couldn't seem to find it, she arched her brows. "Silliness? Dimwitted dimness?"

His lips tightened, but he nodded. "Yes. For all that, I truly am sorry. I had no foundation for the assumption I made. I was wrong—I freely admit it. More"—his gaze locked with hers, he lowered his voice—"I should have known better."

Should have known you *better. I should have trusted you.*

In his patently unshielded brown eyes, she read the words he didn't say.

Quietly, he concluded, "I hope you can find it in your heart to forgive me."

He paused, searching her gaze, then in an even lower tone, added, "I truly do want that."

The next breath he drew was definitely tight. He let it out with, "If you're willing, I would like to wipe the slate between us clean and start anew. Start afresh."

She heard more than saw the absolute sincerity behind those words. She blinked, but didn't shift her gaze from his. While she was unutterably grateful that he'd followed her and De Mille and had rescued her from the fiend's clutches—and that she'd been able to return the favor—what weighed more heavily in her mind was his initial arrival at the Hall, when with no encouragement from her, he'd stormed the house intent on, as he'd thought, rescuing her from Kincaid's machinations.

He'd thought she was in danger, had been walking into danger, and without pausing to learn more or consider the situation and weigh up the pros and cons, he'd come riding to her rescue.

He might not appreciate being compared to a knight on a charger, but for her, without thought for what such a response might cost him, he'd embraced the role.

That, more than any other action, had opened her eyes. Gentlemen of

Christopher Osbaldestone's ilk were far too well-trained to turn aside from their missions and, instead, ride off to rescue damsels in distress, not unless…

Not unless, behind all his avoidance, beneath all his obfuscation, there was something undeniable drawing him to her. A something powerful enough to compel him to an action he wouldn't normally take.

And now he was asking to start afresh.

What do I want? The question occurred only to be answered in the next thought. She wanted to learn what that "something powerful" was and where it might lead.

She studied his eyes for a second more, then held out her hand. "A clean slate. We start afresh."

His smile was the epitome of intense relief shot through with hope, so clear and unequivocal that she couldn't doubt that, at some point during the past days, he'd been struck by an epiphany.

She smiled back. She was willing to admit that she might have been, too.

It was an effort to drag her gaze from his, but she managed and glanced around—and discovered that his mother was watching them, a faint and far-too-knowing smile curving her lips.

Then her ladyship cast her gaze over the assembled company and declared, "Today has seen revelations on several fronts." She returned her gaze to Marion and smiled encouragingly. "I look forward to seeing you tomorrow, my dear."

Marion hoped she managed not to look self-conscious or, indeed, blush. Training and experience came to her aid, and she murmured something appropriate. She was nevertheless cravenly grateful that her ladyship's coachman chose that moment to draw up before the porch steps.

Her ladyship took the children with her, and the other carriages rolled up one by one.

Marion stood in the Hall's doorway and watched Christopher—with a last lingering look and a stylish flourish of his whip—drive away.

The count and the kapitan, both pleased and already eagerly discussing what was to come, walked inside.

For one last minute, Marion stood alone on the porch and looked out, surveying not the black sky of the winter night but the prospect of a future that, until the past half hour, she hadn't allowed herself to even imagine, much less dwell on.

The following morning, escorted by Kincaid, Marion walked into the nave of St. Ignatius on the Hill in good time for the service. Deeming it prudent, both she and Kincaid had wished to give thanks for the capture of De Mille, but had discovered that the smaller church at East Wellow hosted services only on alternate Sundays and, today, would remain empty.

Dressed in her favorite kingfisher-blue pelisse and with Kincaid at her back, Marion walked down the aisle. She should have been casting about her for empty places, but her gaze had fixed on Christopher's dark head. A second later, as if sensing her presence, he glanced around and saw her. The smile that lit his face, reaching all the way to warm his brown eyes, made her heart leap and flutter.

Nonsense, of course, but as he came to his feet and, still smiling, beckoned and held out his hand, she felt faintly giddy, and hope and expectation fizzed in her veins.

She walked forward and placed her gloved fingers in his palm, and he closed his hand around hers. "Good morning," she whispered. "The church in East Wellow isn't holding services today."

His smile bathed her in welcome. "East Wellow's loss is our gain." He indicated the space at the end of the pew.

His mother—who caught Marion's eye and smiled and nodded in approval—had already slid farther along, leaving more than enough space for two.

Warily, Marion returned her ladyship's nod, then glanced back to find Kincaid slipping into a pew two rows behind. As he sat, he grinned and nodded to Marion and Christopher.

Christopher gently squeezed her fingers, then released them and waved her into the pew.

Mentally girding her loins, she sidled in and, gathering her skirts, sat beside his mother.

"Good morning, my dear," her ladyship murmured.

Quietly, Marion returned the greeting as Christopher sat beside her.

He leaned closer and murmured in her ear, "I'm glad you thought to join us here."

She glanced up and met his eyes, in which sincerity shone bright and clear.

Then a stir rippled through the congregation, and in a rolling wave from rear to front, everyone rose to their feet as the minister, followed by his deacon and quite a large band of choristers, paced ceremoniously down the aisle.

Marion saw the three children and, with rather more surprise, noted that the five younger gentlemen who had assisted the day before were also members of the choir. Apparently having read her thoughts in her expression, as the choristers streamed to either side of the altar, Christopher dipped his head to hers and murmured, "For the children and also our five gentlemen acquaintances, joining the choir in the weeks before Christmas is, I gather, something of a tradition."

She let her surprise show in her eyes, then the minister launched into the first prayer, and she and Christopher bowed their heads.

The service rolled on, comforting and, indeed, soothing in its predictability. When the congregation rose to sing the first hymn, Christopher offered to share his hymnal. She'd brought her own hymnbook, but rather than hunt it out of her reticule, she met his eyes and smiled in acceptance. She discovered that he sang in a rich baritone that twined with her alto in quietly pleasing harmony.

For a small country church, the choir was impressive, and the sermon gently yet definitely uplifting. As the service drew to a close, Marion was conscious of feeling buoyed.

As the congregation followed the minister up the aisle, and she and Christopher walked slowly in his mother's wake, he offered her his arm, and she smiled and took it.

He dipped his head to hers and said, "The children and our fine young gentlemen join the choir through these weeks as part of the preparation for the annual carol service." He caught her eyes as she glanced up questioningly. "It's one of the village's regular Christmas events, and I've been assured it's quite something. It's certainly highly anticipated by everyone round about." He held her gaze for a second, then went on. "It's to be held tomorrow night. Would you be interested in joining me for the event, Miss Sewell?"

She smiled—no, she glowed. She couldn't hold back a soft laugh. "As it happens, Mr. Osbaldestone, I'm rather partial to well-sung carols. I believe I'll accept your kind invitation."

His smile bloomed; for a man who habitually played the diplomat with an expression that was rarely informative, when he relaxed his guard, he had the most generous and genuine smile, and she happily basked in its warmth.

They paused at the door to greet the minister. Christopher introduced her to Reverend Colebatch, who beamed benevolently on them both, then she and Christopher crossed the snow-dappled lawn to where several of the company from the day before had gathered. As they joined the group, the children and the five younger gentlemen came skipping and striding up.

After greetings were exchanged all around, Kilburn asked Kincaid, "How are our captives faring?"

Kincaid replied and had them all laughing with the story of how De Mille and Corbeau had reacted to being served the typical countryman's breakfast of porridge. "I can't be sure because they were muttering in French, but I think they thought it was a peculiar English soup."

"What happened to Donny and Dave?" Sir Henry asked.

"The staff took pity on them and fed them dinner, then Solzonik and I had a chat and sent the pair off with fleas in their ears." Kincaid grinned as he added, "I doubt they'll help any foreigner again."

The discussion veered into speculation of what might be learned from De Mille and his henchman.

After listening for some moments, Therese excused herself and circled to speak with the Colebatches, the Swindons, the Longfellows, and Mrs. Woolsey, confirming the arrangements for her now-traditional Christmas dinner to be held after the carol service the following evening. That accomplished, she returned to the younger crew, rounded them up, and gave them their marching orders. "Count Leonski and Kapitan Solzonik will be arriving at the manor shortly. I suggest we should be there to greet them."

With the promise of one of Mrs. Haggerty's meals as enticement, the group readily fell in with Therese's direction and obediently followed her down the church drive.

On reaching the manor and going inside, after handing her coat, hat, and gloves to Orneby, who had arrived to assist Crimmins in the front hall, Therese led the company into the drawing room. She took possession of her favorite armchair and directed the others to various seats. Noting the tentative progress of Christopher and Marion toward developing a deeper understanding, Therese took charge of the wider conversation and endeavored to keep the attention of all others focused away from the pair on the sofa.

She was determined to—unobtrusively but effectively—foster the unlooked-for yet highly desirable connection for all she was worth.

Even if it was she who said so, in that respect, she was worth a great deal.

Less than five minutes after they'd all settled, the count and the kapitan arrived and were shown in. Therese rose with the others and, after the customary greetings were exchanged, waved the count to the armchair alongside hers. Solzonik took up a position behind the chair, close to where Kincaid was standing by the mantelpiece, and the pair fell into an easy exchange.

Therese and the count, both old hands when it came to sitting back and observing the dynamics of people in a room, watched as Drummond sauntered over to join Kincaid and Solzonik. Shortly after, the five younger gentlemen joined the circle. A moment later, someone said something, and the group laughed.

Smiling, the count turned to Therese. "Everyone is happy, it seems."

"Indeed." She leaned closer and murmured, "Initially, both Drummond and Kincaid were not best pleased to be put on guard duty, especially not when that looked likely to amount to kicking their heels in a quiet country backwater with no prospect of any meaningful action." She smiled and sat back. "Now, however, with one of Napoleon's senior agents in custody, they're much happier with their stay in Little Moseley."

The count chuckled and met her eyes. "I will confess to being very relieved that matters have played out as they have. Not only have the kapitan and I succeeded in making the required contact with your Foreign Office son, but because you, too, are here, through you and your family, the ramifications of that contact will be much more valuable. To Alexander and Russia, to the British, and to our allies as well."

Therese inclined her head. "I'm sure Lionel and the War Office will be delighted to confer with the kapitan." When her old friend had learned that she was, in truth, in residence at Hartington Manor, he'd debated whether to approach her in order to reach Christopher, but a deep understanding of "the way things were done" and the possibility that the manor had been under surveillance had—Therese suspected wisely—dissuaded him from that course. Nevertheless, he'd been very glad to see her when she'd called at the Hall.

After a moment, she continued, "I can feel it in my bones, Gregor. This time, we will send the Corsican monster running." She focused on her old friend's face. "What think you?"

Gregor Leonski nodded. "I agree." After a moment, he added, "As you and I and those like us, who have been in service to our countries for decades, know, when countries work together in good and genuine cause, great things are achievable."

Therese dipped her head in regal agreement.

Crimmins appeared to announce the meal, and they repaired to the dining room. Mrs. Haggerty had outdone herself, and the compliments rained thick and fast. The conversation was lively, moving from recollections of the day before to observations on the village's celebrations to date. The children took great delight in describing the local events to the count, the kapitan, and Marion and, naturally, concluded with the upcoming carol service.

Christopher asked the Russians about their Christmas events, and the count, aided by the kapitan, recounted the festivities that occurred on their estates.

Therese was happy to respond to the blatant appeal in her grandchildren's eyes and invite the count, the kapitan, and of course, Marion, to attend the carol service with her. "And afterward, you must come to dinner. It's something of this household's own Christmas tradition—the Hartington Manor dinner following the carol service." Therese waved down the table. "All these gentlemen will be present, as will others of the local gentry." She met the count's eyes and smiled. "It's a relaxed affair, but courtesy of our choristers, always entertaining."

The count and the kapitan exchanged a look, then both readily accepted.

"We are missing our Christmas events," the count informed the table, "so we will be delighted to be included in yours."

Everyone smiled, and the conversation rolled on, but as the dessert plates were removed, Therese noted that the count and the kapitan were growing restive. Their glances down the table, to where Christopher sat at its foot with Marion on his right, spoke volumes. Having finally reached their quest's end, both Russians were eager to speak with Christopher and embark on the discussions they had traveled from Moscow in the hope of instigating.

Therese clapped her hands, and the table fell silent as everyone expectantly looked her way. "Now that we have dealt with Mrs. Haggerty's delicious offerings as they deserve"—grins bloomed all around the table, and Therese focused on her grandchildren—"how do you propose to spend your afternoon?"

Somewhat to her relief, Dagenham glanced fleetingly at the count and the kapitan, then looked across the table at the children. "On our way to church, as we passed the green, we spoke with Johnny Tooks and some of the other children. They'd decided that the drifts of snow on the green were iced enough to hold an impromptu snowman competition after lunch."

"Yay!" came from three throats, and the children looked at Therese.

"May we go, Grandmama?' Jamie asked.

Therese directed a grateful look at Dagenham—who clearly possessed the right instincts for one in the civil services—then looked at the three children and nodded graciously. "But remember, you must return before dark or if the weather grows foul."

The trio vowed compliance and, at her nod of dismissal, pushed back their chairs.

She returned her attention to Dagenham to see him gathering the four other younger men with a glance, then all five rose and half bowed to Therese, and Henry said, "As always, your ladyship, we're honored to have been invited to lunch at the manor, and with your permission, I think we'll join the scamps and see what excitement is brewing on the green."

Therese smiled. "That sounds like an excellent idea, Henry."

She came to her feet, bringing everyone else to theirs. As the company filed into the front hall, most calling for their coats, Drummond and Kincaid paused beside her.

With his gaze on the Russians, now speaking with Marion and Christopher before the drawing room doorway, Drummond bobbed his head to Therese. "Kincaid and I thought we might go and keep an eye on the doings on the green."

Kincaid's lips lifted. "We thought the front window of the Cockspur Arms might well be the perfect vantage point."

Therese laughed. "Indeed, gentlemen. That's another excellent notion." She inclined her head as they bowed, then they went to fetch their coats as well.

As the bulk of the company streamed out of the front door, Therese joined the small group before the drawing room doorway and waved them into the room. "Shall we?"

They settled comfortably, with Therese in her armchair, but she directed Marion to its mate on Therese's right, leaving the count and the kapitan to take the sofa, facing Christopher in the third armchair, which sat to Therese's left.

Having presided over many such meetings, Therese knew how best to facilitate useful discourse.

At Christopher's inviting look, the count opened proceedings with a statement from his master and old friend, Alexander. Christopher responded in classic FO fashion, forcibly reminding Therese of his father.

Without looking at Marion, Therese tipped her head toward the younger woman. Their armchairs were sufficiently distanced from the three men to permit a low-voiced conversation. "In meetings such as this," Therese murmured, "it best serves to keep the line of sight between the two sides as direct and as uncluttered as possible."

Marion shot her hostess a careful look, but she wasn't averse to learning from a master. After a moment, she murmured back, "I take it a meal—or even a tea tray—would be a distraction?"

Her ladyship nodded. "Indeed. Best to avoid all situations that might interfere with their mutual concentration on the exchange."

Marion watched as Christopher, rather subtly, encouraged the count to fully describe the scope of the Russians' hopes and expectations and outline all the areas the Russians wished to address during this visit. It was clear that the Russians believed Napoleon would be defeated soon and wished to reach an in-principle agreement with the British government regarding the approach to the reorganization of much of Europe that inevitably would follow. "For as we all know," the count concluded, "we will have to meet, all the allies and some of the other states as well, and agree on many things."

Christopher nodded. Once the count had fully defined the Russian position, he suggested various ways of furthering the Russian aims, tangentially alluding to where those ran parallel to the likely British aspirations and touching only very lightly on those points that might prove more contentious.

The discussions went back and forth, and eventually, a consensus was reached regarding their next steps. It was agreed that Christopher would return to London and report to Castlereagh and Powell, and a more formal yet still highly secret meeting would be arranged. Meanwhile, through Christopher, Kapitan Solzonik would be put in touch with Christopher's brother, Lionel, who all agreed was the perfect contact through whom Solzonik could deliver his intelligence on vital aspects of Napoleon's military situation.

Throughout, via private asides, her ladyship drew Marion's attention to various aspects, often interpreting comments the count or the kapitan made, very much reading between the lines. Marion was amazed at the degree of the older woman's skill in identifying all the little nuances, the telltale reactions and gestures that, she felt sure, half the time, the one under observation didn't know they were making, yet once those signs were pointed out, she could appreciate the accuracy of what Christopher's mother had deduced.

As the deliberations drew to a close, her ladyship looked at Marion and smiled. "You'll pick up the knack with time, my dear."

Reading the encouragement in her ladyship's normally impenetrable black eyes, Marion managed a nod. When, still smiling gently, Lady Osbaldestone looked back at the men, Marion quietly exhaled. For a moment, she cast about in her mind, trying to decide what it was she'd sensed behind that encouraging look, then she realized. Her mother had trained her to be an FO daughter. Christopher's mother was intent on training her to be an FO wife.

She was still grappling with that realization when the gentlemen ended their meeting. The count and the kapitan rose. They'd come in the count's coach and were eager to return to Parteger Hall to write reports and dispatch them to Moscow via their embassy in London.

Marion glanced at Christopher—she didn't want to leave—and found him waiting to catch her eye and smile encouragingly. She smiled in reply. "I came with Kincaid, and I find I'm rather curious over learning the results of the snowman competition."

The curve of Christopher's lips deepened. "I'm sure the children will return with the news by teatime."

Muting her own smile, she captured the count's attention and explained that she would return to the Hall with Kincaid.

The count nodded benevolently and said to Christopher, "The kapitan and I and our people will, I believe, leave Parteger Hall on Tuesday morning. We will travel to Southampton and spend our Christmas with Russian connections there, then in the new year, as arranged, we will meet with you in London."

Christopher nodded. He smiled at the kapitan. "You know where I live. If you leave a message there as to where you're staying once you've returned to London, we can proceed from there."

"Excellent!" The count clapped his hands.

Christopher thought to ask Solzonik, "Has Kincaid spoken of his plans to take our prisoners to London?"

The kapitan nodded. "I understand that he and Drummond will escort the pair thence on Tuesday as well."

Christopher looked inquiringly at his mother, as did Marion, the count, and Solzonik.

Her ladyship smiled. "On Tuesday morning, the children and I will set out for Winslow Abbey." To the count and the kapitan, she added, "That's some way to the north. We'll be taking a route that bypasses London—faster for a traveling coach and less noisy." She turned her black gaze on Marion. "And what about you, my dear?"

"I came down in my parents' second carriage. I have my coachman, groom, and maid with me." She dipped her head to the count. "I, too, will leave on Tuesday morning and rejoin my family in the capital."

She glanced at Christopher and found him regarding her.

"If you would rather travel more quickly," he said, "albeit in an open carriage, weather permitting, I could take you up in my curricle. I have to call in at the office and bring Powell and Castlereagh up to speed on what's happened here before I head for Winslow. I could easily drop you off."

The journey suddenly appeared a lot more appealing. "Thank you. I'd like that." An open carriage didn't necessitate having a maid or groom with her. *I just hope it doesn't sleet or snow!*

Christopher smiled, as did everyone else. "That's settled, then. I'll call at the Hall on Tuesday morning."

Crimmins appeared to announce that the count's coach was outside. The count and the kapitan donned their thick coats, then as a group, the five of them walked out onto the porch.

After waving the count and the kapitan off, her ladyship left Marion and Christopher to their own devices while she dealt with some household matter. After returning to the drawing room, Marion reclaimed her preferred position on the sofa while Christopher, after hesitating for an instant, resumed his seat in the armchair opposite.

Marion looked at him and sighed happily. When Christopher arched his brows in question, she said, "You must have guessed that it was my brother—my twin, Robbie—who asked me to act for him in arranging a meeting between you and the count."

"I wondered if that was so, and the count more or less confirmed it."

"Yes, well, you know how you would feel about a request one of your brothers made of you. No matter how much you might grumble, you would do your best to deliver whatever was required—to meet the expectation, not just their expectation of you but yours of yourself."

When Christopher nodded, she went on, "With a twin, take that expectation and double—no, quadruple—it. I couldn't possibly let Robbie down." She added, "In all fairness, he'd feel the same way in reverse." She met Christopher's eyes and let her feelings show. "That's why I'm so relieved, grateful, and happy that I've succeeded in getting the count and you together. And trust me, the relief is very real—there were so many points along the way when I really thought I would fail."

Christopher grimaced ruefully. "And that was entirely my fault. Your brother's request should have been easy enough to achieve. It was my stupidity that threw hurdles in your path."

To his relief, she laughed. "That might be true, but given we ultimately achieved the desired end result, I'm willing to forgive you."

He met her bright eyes and slowly smiled, delighting in the softness in her aqua-blue gaze. In truth, he felt gratified and satisfied—indeed, buoyed—on so many counts. That the Russians had approached him would be a feather in his cap career-wise, and quite aside from the advance the count's embassy would make on the diplomatic front, if he'd correctly understood the type of information Solzonik had to offer, the advance on the military side would also be significant, while the capture of De Mille and Corbeau would confer an advantage in several respects.

Yet the achievement that warmed him most—that wrapped closest about his heart—was knowing that, once he'd overcome his idiocy, he'd helped Marion achieve what had essentially been her mission, one she'd just confirmed had meant a great deal to her.

His gaze rested on her as those thoughts whizzed through his head. Those were the accomplishments he could point to, yet over the past weeks, the actions forced upon him and even more his reactions to unfolding events had compelled him to recognize and face his own personal wants, needs, and desires.

Now, as he gently smiled at Marion, he realized just how wrong his original view of her pursuit had been. Far from cursing him, in sending her after him, Fate had conferred a very real blessing.

Despite moving in similar circles, he doubted their paths would have crossed, at least not for long enough for him to glimpse and appreciate the reality of what she truly could mean—and now did mean—to him.

Sounds from the front hall drew their attention, and in the next instant, the children rushed in, followed by his mother and Crimmins, bearing a loaded tea tray. Christopher sat back and listened as the adventuresome trio babbled about how Ben Butts had arrived with the most amazing buttons, supplied by his ancient grandmother, with which to decorate his snowman. In the end, there'd been no competition but, instead, everyone who had come to the green had contributed in some measure to what had been declared the communal village snowman.

"There really wasn't enough snow for lots of snowmen," Lottie said. "They would have ended up being very small."

"Instead"—Jamie sprang to his feet and waved his hand high above his head—"the one we all made is huge!"

"The Tookses found an old shepherd's crook in the ruined cottage at Allard's End, so we had that as well," George reported in between licking honey from his fingers. Mrs. Haggerty had supplied crumpets fresh from her griddle, along with fruitcake, which was rather more to Christopher's, Marion's, and his mother's tastes.

Eventually sated, the children, sitting on the floor, slumped against the edge of the sofa and sighed. "We only have one more day here," Jamie said. "And then we'll be off to Winslow."

Christopher caught the sense of a holiday—a special time—drawing to a close.

He sat in comfort with Marion and his mother and chatted about whatever came to mind while the children nattered between themselves, and he couldn't stop his mind from imagining a life filled with the sort of activities that day had held. A life with Marion beside him. Enjoying those simple activities, sharing those moments.

After Crimmins fetched away the plundered tea tray, his mother rose and looked out of the window. "The day's fading, and here come Kincaid and Drummond."

Marion caught Christopher's eye, and he and she rose. While his mother shooed the children out of the room and up the stairs to wash their sticky fingers, Kincaid and Drummond came into the front hall. After greeting Christopher and Marion, Kincaid asked Crimmins to have the gig brought around.

Christopher glanced at Marion and found her watching him, the faint smile on her lips reflected in her eyes. He arched his brows, then crossed to where Crimmins had hung the coats. He carried Marion's kingfisher-blue pelisse and her bonnet to her and held the coat as she slipped her arms into the sleeves. While she settled and buttoned the pelisse, then donned her bonnet, he glanced at Drummond and Kincaid; the pair were engrossed in a discussion of the logistics of their journey to the capital. When, ready to depart, Marion looked Christopher's way, he waved at the front door. "Let's wait outside."

She smiled in ready acquiescence, and he opened the door, and they walked out onto the porch.

She tugged on her gloves, then turned up her fur collar against the stiffening breeze. "After the excitements of yesterday, today has been quietly satisfying, a day of gratifying outcomes."

Standing beside her, he drank in her profile. "Indeed." Then he sobered and said, "I can't thank you enough for persevering in your attempts to contact me."

She glanced his way and arched her brows faintly. "Indeed." Her eyes danced. "Acting as conduit for the count will unquestionably gain you significant kudos within the FO."

He grinned in acknowledgment, then the grin, too, faded.

She tipped her head, trying to read his face. "What is it?"

He hesitated, then looked over the snowy lawn. "Kudos, true enough, but it's not really something I earned. I owe it to my father—to my illustrious name—rather than any effort of my own."

She considered that, then said, "Up to a point, that might be true, but ultimately, you were there to be approached, and what's more, the count's an extremely canny and experienced diplomat. He would have asked any number of contacts about you, and what he heard must have convinced him you were the right person to approach." She met his eyes, her own gaze direct and clear. "You might have done something entirely different with your life. You might not have bothered to join any of the services at all—I'm quite sure you don't need the income—but instead, you've followed in your parents' footsteps, and that's not something every man will readily do. So you were there to be approached and viewed as capable and trustworthy, and *that* is entirely due to you."

He blinked, absorbing the words—her view—as she went on, "Indeed, from what I've gathered of the nature of the Russian request—its sensitivity and the need for utter secrecy—I suspect they wouldn't have even approached our government if the ability to connect via an Osbaldestone hadn't been there. They might have turned to Prussia or even Austria instead, and that would have been to our country's detriment."

She met his eyes and smiled, serenely assured. "I'm perfectly certain the Osbaldestone name and the reputation it carries, even now that the mantle rests solely on your shoulders, is what tipped the Russian scales our way. I do know that the count and the kapitan are deeply relieved to have, via you, gained the access they sought, all without any formal contact and the resultant diplomatic fanfare." Her eyes twinkled. "Despite the difficulties encountered in gaining your attention, I'm certain you'll find them both exceedingly grateful for your assistance."

He held her gaze, then, his features relaxing, murmured, "'Difficulties encountered.' You're being very kind."

One brow rose higher, and still holding his gaze, she tipped her head. "I am, aren't I?"

He laughed, and she did, too. Then Simms appeared with the Hall's gig, and no doubt hearing the clop of hooves, Drummond and Kincaid came out.

Christopher took Marion's hand and led her to the carriage, then helped her into it. Kincaid climbed up and sat beside her, and Christopher smiled and stepped back. He nodded to Kincaid as the agent flicked the reins, then Christopher saluted Marion, and she raised a gloved hand in farewell.

Christopher stood and watched the gig—and Marion—roll away down the drive.

From the window of her private parlor, Therese watched her son watch the gig—or more accurately, the lady in it—until the carriage rounded the bend in the drive. Only then did he turn and, looking down, his mind clearly elsewhere, walk inside.

Entirely content with the way that matter was progressing, Therese turned away from the window and discovered that all three children had crept up until they, too, could see outside.

Now all three beamed at her, and Lottie declared, "All is well for everyone!"

Therese smiled, reached out and smoothed Lottie's hair, then waved the three back to the rug before the fire.

EPILOGUE

The carol service, Christopher was given to understand, was the ultimate highlight of the Little Moseley Christmas calendar and, therefore, a must-attend event.

That explained the crowd streaming up the church drive. Inside, while people waited for the usual occupants of pews to take their places before squeezing in, many others lined the walls and stood clustered in the foyer, behind the rear pews. His mother led the count and the kapitan forward to the pew she usually occupied, whispering that it was the Hartington Manor pew, and Christopher led Marion in their wake.

Drummond and Kincaid, both large and tall, had signaled that they would remain with the crowd in the foyer.

A babel of voices came from all directions—some calling greetings, others talking avidly. His mother stopped several times to touch hands and exchange comments.

Eventually, they reached the pew, filed in, and sat.

From her position nearest the aisle, with Christopher beside her, Marion looked around in amazement. "I had no idea there were so many people in the area."

"It's the farming community, my dear," Christopher's mother remarked from his other side. "They often can't attend village events because of their animals or harvesting, planting, and tending, but this is the one evening of the year on which every last one comes with their children and neighbors to join in the celebration."

Christopher scanned the crowd and had to admit the enthusiasm was impressive.

Then the chatter faded, and an expectant hush descended. A moment later, the doors were drawn open, and sweet voices rose on the wintry air as the choir gave voice a cappella as they followed Reverend Colebatch down the aisle.

Over Marion's bonnet, Christopher watched his niece and nephews pace past, their faces alight with the purest joy as they sang a paean to the heavens. On reaching the altar steps, the choir fanned out to form two long rows on the lower steps. Behind them, Reverend Colebatch ascended his pulpit. When the choir sang the final note and fell silent, leaving the entire congregation in a state of awe, the good reverend looked out over his packed church and smiled benevolently.

It was a magical start to what proved a magical evening.

After Reverend Colebatch had welcomed them, the service commenced with a carol sung by all, led by the choir. The following carol was sung by the choir alone, and subsequently, the pieces alternated between being sung by the whole congregation or only the choir.

Without exception, everyone was swept up by the music, by the power of the singing and the upswell of joy it evoked. It was amazing. Christopher slid a glance at his mother's face and found it softened by profound emotion. Beyond her, the count and the kapitan were similarly affected, and as Christopher scanned others around about, he realized it was a universal response to the power of the carols, delivered with such blinding sincerity.

Finally, he looked at Marion. Her face was radiant, her expression alive with the uplifting emotion carried on the swelling notes as the choir built in a rousing crescendo to deliver a final and emphatic hallelujah.

And then it was over, and despite the feeling of not having wanted the magical interlude to end, the delight and joy and simple pleasure engendered by the carols and the singing continued to illuminate everyone's faces and glowed in everyone's smiles.

After Reverend Colebatch led the triumphant choir, followed by the choirmaster and the organist, up the aisle, the congregation followed more slowly, neighbors greeting neighbors, kind words and accolades being freely bestowed on all the members of the choir.

His mind still awash with glorious sound, Christopher escorted Marion to where Reverend Colebatch waited by the door, beaming with unalloyed delight as he shook his parishioners' hands and bade them a

Merry Christmas. After sincerely congratulating Colebatch, Christopher steered Marion onto the lawn to where his mother was already holding court.

Out of ingrained habit, Christopher had been idly monitoring the conversations of those about them as they'd shuffled up the aisle and crossed the snowy lawn. That part of his brain that only stopped working when he slept continued to listen and take notes even while he introduced Marion to his mother's village friends and he and she found themselves the cynosure of a number of speculative glances.

Marion, he noticed, braved the attention without turning a single blond hair.

Then the children came pelting up, all but leaping with excitement over their performance. They were followed by Henry, Dagenham, Kilburn, Wiley, and Carnaby, all lightly flushed from their exertions and every bit as thrilled as the children with how the singing had gone. The others in the group promptly showered accolades upon them all. Christopher wondered how long it would be before any of them, himself included, managed to stop smiling.

Mrs. Woolsey flapped and wrapped her shawls more tightly about her, then asked Lady Longfellow, "And how is little Edgar, dear?"

From what followed, Christopher understood that the Longfellows had been blessed with a recent addition, another son to join Cedric, their young toddler.

"Oh!" Mrs. Swindon said. "Before I forget, I have news of Richard and Faith."

"And," Christopher's mother stated, "I also have news from Callum and Honor and Professor Webster, but as the temperature is falling rather precipitously, perhaps we should adjourn to the manor and share our glad tidings there."

Everyone was quick to agree. The iciness in the air was intensifying by the minute.

"There'll be a hoar frost come morning," Henry prophesized.

No one disagreed.

Allowing the elders of the group to lead the way, Christopher offered Marion his arm, which she happily took, and they dawdled in the others' wake until they were the last of those headed for the manor and the dinner table no doubt presently groaning under the weight of Mrs. Haggerty's offerings.

He shared that vision with Marion and added, "I've been assured that, for tonight, the redoubtable Mrs. Haggerty pulls out all stops, and we both saw what she considered appropriate for a celebratory luncheon."

Marion laughed. "But it's all so delicious."

Christopher nodded with feeling. "Indeed."

Between them and their elders walked the group comprised of the children, Henry and his friends, Drummond, Kincaid, and Solzonik. The children, Henry, and the other younger men were entertaining the older three with, it seemed, tales of Christmases past.

Christopher slowed a fraction more, until he and Marion were sufficiently far behind that, in terms of conversation, they were effectively alone. He looked up at the sky, tonight entirely clear, with the moon and shining stars casting a silvery wash over everything.

As it sometimes did, his mind finished processing all the snippets he'd overheard and jolted him by serving up its conclusions. He considered those for a minute, found them sound, and murmured, "There's real hope. Did you sense it? People here"—he gestured at the woods and land beyond—"tucked away in the country though they are, have sensed that the winds are shifting, and we stand on the cusp of major change."

"I noticed that most here are truly looking ahead to next year—as if they're certain it'll be better than the last." She paused, then murmured, "Do you think they know what's happening in France?"

He considered that, then replied, "Not with any degree of specificity. But in the way of countrymen, they've heard from so-and-so that her son has written with hope. That someone else's son-in-law has written of coming home soon. It's that sort of knowledge."

"And are they correct, do you think?"

He smiled. "Oh yes. This time, they are. After all the years of war, the end is finally in sight." He met her eyes. "If nothing else, Alexander's approach signals that the end truly is nigh."

She smiled and squeezed his arm. "I'm glad—so glad. We've had enough of war."

There were people all around, walking home in the starlight, yet as they reached the lane and idly followed the others along, then turned in to the manor drive, it seemed the perfect moment to bite the bullet and confess, "When you first tried to approach me, at Lady Selkirk's soirée, the reason I"—*face it*—"turned tail and ran was because, just the week before, I'd been told by a young lady at a ball that she had important information to relay to me. She asked me to meet her in a folly in the garden." He paused. From the corner of his eye, he could see he had

Marion's undivided attention. He went on, "I was so caught up in my work—at times, it consumes my thinking to the exclusion of all else, and that was one of those times—I accepted what she said. I was half expecting a message from one of my contacts in one of the embassies. I swallowed her story whole."

She was studying his face; he could feel her gaze. "What happened?"

He sighed and fleetingly glanced at her. "I was on my way to meet her, but there were others looking out over the terrace. To avoid their notice, I took a roundabout route that had me approaching the folly from the rear. As I neared, I spotted the young lady's gorgon of an aunt and several of her cronies."

"What did you do?"

"I swung on my heel and walked away. I don't think they saw me."

Her tone turned wry. "And a few days later, you noticed me hunting you."

He tipped his head. "Just so."

They were nearing the manor. The others had already vanished inside. As they stepped onto the porch, Marion glanced at him. "Why did you tell me that?"

He found the answer waiting on his tongue. Lowering his arm, he grasped her hand and gently squeezed. "Because while it's no excuse"—he met her gaze—"I should have known better, known *you* better, enough to trust you. I wanted you to know that it wasn't *you* I ran from, but the memory and the fear of falling into some snare that your approach unknowingly evoked."

Marion searched his face, his eyes. She knew enough to appreciate what such a revelation had cost him. He was used to being in control of his life, assured and confident, yet he'd nearly slipped and found himself trapped. She knew her brother, knew men like him and Christopher quite well. That he'd revealed that weakness purely to soothe her pride... augured well for their future.

Still holding her gloved hand, his thumb lightly stroking her knuckles, he shifted under her scrutiny, then asked, "Are you willing to overlook my rank stupidity and carry on and see where this"—with his free hand, he gestured between them—"leads?"

He wasn't going to fight it or even attempt to deny it. Her heart gave a little leap.

Surrendering to the impulse that reaction provoked, she slipped her fingers free of his, then placing her hands palms down on his chest, she stepped closer, stretched up on her toes, and kissed him.

He hesitated for only an instant, then his hand rose to frame her face, and he took charge and steered the kiss into deeper waters.

His lips moved on hers, confident and assured. She assumed he'd had numerous lovers, that he would know how to capture her senses purely with a kiss, and he didn't disappoint.

She lost all sense of time, all sense of where they were. Stopped thinking entirely when his tongue cruised the crease of her lips and she opened to him, and he smoothly surged in and claimed.

Heat bloomed and spread, licking deliciously beneath her skin, luring her on.

But then he made a soft sound and, patently reluctantly, drew back.

He looked into her eyes, and she looked into his, and she would have sworn what she saw mirrored in his warm brown eyes was the same emotion that had flowered inside her.

His lips curved, just a touch, and somewhat ruefully, he said, "We have to go inside, or they'll wonder where we are and come looking."

Sadly, that was true. She sighed and stepped back, only then realizing his arm had banded about her and immediately regretting the loss of the sensation of his long, hard frame pressed against her softer curves.

He took her hand again and looked at her in question, and she nodded and allowed him to usher her through the door.

Inside, it seemed that no one had missed them, but glancing at his mother, who appeared oblivious, Marion seriously doubted that.

She and Christopher had barely had time to join one of the groups filling the drawing room before dinner was announced. She wasn't at all surprised to find herself seated once again on Christopher's right, opposite Solzonik.

Far from being provincial, both in quality and style, let alone taste, the dishes placed before the company would have done credit to a London hostess's table. Given the manor's owner, perhaps that shouldn't have been a surprise.

The tone of the gathering was distinctly festive, with good cheer and good wishes abounding. The company shared tales of others who had been present in previous years, fostering a sense of continuity, of this place, this day, this event—just as for the carol service—being somehow critical to the proper observance of the season.

Marion found herself—and Christopher, too—drawn in to the shared joy of the company, enveloped in the warmth of communal understanding, and lifted up by the very real hope everyone seemed to hold for the coming year. At one point, looking up the table, she noticed his mother watching her and Christopher with a knowing air. Before Marion could shift her gaze elsewhere, her still-terrifying hostess raised her glass to her in a silent toast, sipped, then smoothly turned her attention to the count, on her right, engaging him with some comment.

Marion looked at Christopher, chatting animatedly with Solzonik, then let her gaze roam the table, drinking in the faces lit with happiness, the laughter, and the excited chatter, then she looked again at Christopher, smiled, and let herself sink into the moment.

Under cover of taking another sip of her wine, Therese glanced at Marion, saw she was distracted, and smiled to herself. Letting her gaze sweep her guests, she was conscious of a feeling of quiet elation. All those she considered her regulars were present, including Dagenham, with whom she'd decided she needed to have a quiet word. Later. For now, everyone was enjoying the food, the wine, and the company, and at this point in the evening, that was her principal goal.

"My lady." Henrietta Colebatch leaned forward to look up the table. "Did you say you'd heard from Mr. Goodrich?"

Instantly, the majority of eyes swung Therese's way. She nodded. "Indeed. I received a letter from Callum yesterday. He wrote that he, Honor, and their new daughter, who they've named Charlotte—" She paused to allow the various versions of "Ooh, Lottie, they named their baby after you!" to subside, then went on, "Are spending Christmas in North Yorkshire, with Callum's family, and the professor will be with them. I gather he's moved to live with them in a small manor house outside Oxford. Callum sends his regards to everyone, with special mention to those he termed 'his Little Moseley crew.'"

The children beamed, as did Henry and his friends, who had been involved in the adventures of the previous year.

Sally Swindon, seated farther down the table, waved to get everyone's attention. "Richard and Faith sent their best wishes as well. They're in Somerset, of course, and report that little Horry is growing apace."

Jamie and George, with assistance from Lottie, explained to those who hadn't heard the tale about the missing book of Christmas carols, the loss of which had threatened to disrupt the carol service two years before.

Thoroughly content, Therese sat back and surveyed her guests. This event might not hold a candle in any way to the dinners she'd once hosted in London, but now, in this time of her life, entertaining these people to the top of her bent, in the way most satisfying to them, was important to her. Being a hostess had long ago become a part of who she was. More than anything else, however, on this particular evening of the year—at this particular dinner party—she'd come to feel as if her roots were sinking just a little deeper, year by year, into Little Moseley's rich and fertile soil.

When the last morsel of the brandy-soaked pudding had been consumed and everyone was comfortably replete, she inquired and had it confirmed that the gentlemen saw no reason to linger about the board but would happily take their brandies in the drawing room. With an approving nod, she pushed back her chair and got to her feet, bringing the company to theirs, then she led the way to the drawing room, where everyone sat or stood in groups and continued to chat in animated vein.

Instead of claiming her usual armchair, Therese drifted in hostessly fashion from one group to another. Finally, she cornered Dagenham—literally in one corner of the room. He eyed her somewhat warily, but ever the gentleman, refrained from bolting.

Therese stood a little to the side so that it appeared they were idly watching the room and commanded, "Tell me about this Irish posting of yours."

From the corner of her eye, she saw his handsome face harden and his long fingers tighten about the glass he held in one hand. A moment passed, then, like her, apparently surveying the assembled guests, he replied, "They're talking of sending me over in May."

"For how long?"

"Initially two years, but in the circumstances, I've been warned that might be extended for up to five years."

"Your father's in good health, I take it?"

That got a half smile out of him. "Indeed."

Therese now understood why he'd been fishing for information—he'd wanted to know what the chances were of Lord North and, presumably, his family being posted overseas. "Dublin isn't all that far."

"Far enough."

She had to admit that in terms of participating in the social whirl of a London Season, Dublin was, indeed, too far away. Dagenham was, therefore, facing the prospect of not being in London, indeed, being well out of it, when Melissa made her come-out.

The fact that was dragging him down, as she could see it was, confirmed her suspicion that he remained seriously and genuinely smitten with her granddaughter. That said, given their characters and their relative youth, enforced separation wouldn't necessarily be a bad thing.

But how to explain that to him?

"I last saw Melissa two months ago, and she gave me to understand that, at present, she's entirely unsure of what she truly wants of life, let alone even approaching the stage of considering with whom—or even if—she wishes to share said undefined life."

He glanced at her. Incredulity—and a touch of horror—sharpened his tone. "She's not thinking of taking the veil?"

Therese blinked. "No, of course not." She paused, then added, "Although I daresay the thought will cross her mind at some point, I think we may be certain she won't take that path."

"Thank God for that," he muttered.

Therese paused. She'd told him what she'd felt he needed to hear, to have confirmed. Not being able to pursue something he definitely wanted—being blocked by social stipulations from doing so—was undoubtedly a bitter pill for a nobleman like him to swallow. She strongly suspected that as the Earl of Carsely's heir, Dagenham had, in the main, had his every wish accommodated, yet in this one thing—a matter that meant a great deal to him—he was helpless. He couldn't bend Fate to his will.

She was tempted to leave it at that, to allow him to escape, yet found herself saying, "One last thing. If at any time in the future, you should find yourself dealing with members of my family, do remember that you can call on me, and that I will remain… What's the phrase you young people use? Ah yes—firmly in your corner."

He looked at her then, openly studying her expression, and after several seconds, surprise was superseded by understanding. After a further moment's hesitation, he inclined his head. "Thank you, ma'am."

She nodded in dismissal, he half bowed, and they parted.

She circled the room, checking on her other guests, smiling and exchanging comments here and there while she considered Dagenham and his situation. She suspected he was coming to believe—moving inch by painful inch toward accepting—that courtesy of his duty to his country, his name, and his station, what had come to be between him and Melissa had no future. Given who he was and who Melissa was, she was still too young for him to even call on.

Therese inwardly sighed. She should have let it go, but it seemed she was unable to suppress her matchmaking instincts. She was, it seemed, incapable of turning her back on the possibility of a match made in Heaven.

Then Henry approached, with Kilburn, Wiley, and Carnaby on his heels. "Your ladyship." Henry bowed, and the others followed suit. "As always, it's been a pleasure, my lady." Henry straightened and cast a beaming glance around the room. "Another wonderful carol service followed by a magnificent feast at the manor." His gaze came to rest affectionately on Mrs. Woolsey. "But now, I fear it's time we rounded up Cousin Ermintrude and rolled on home."

Therese thanked them for the pleasure of their company, which thanks were quite sincere. She'd come to appreciate all five of the group. Her oldest male grandchild was Henrietta's son, Christopher, younger than Melissa and just fifteen, so Henry and friends fell into an age group with which she otherwise hadn't had much interaction; over the past three years, she'd been pleasantly reassured by her observations of them.

She was unsurprised when the Fulsom Hall party's departure started an exodus. She took up station in the front hall, farewelling each group and wishing all a Merry Christmas and a prosperous New Year.

The Parteger Hall party was the last to leave. Therese spent a few minutes with the count, making plans to meet again in London in January. She studiously pretended not to overhear—as did the count—when Christopher confirmed that Kincaid would return to the Hall with the count and Solzonik in the count's ponderous coach, but that Christopher would ferry Marion thence in his curricle. Apparently, the night had remained clear, and although it was distinctly frosty outside, the journey was, after all, only a few miles.

Therese and the count rejoined the group at that point.

After ensuring Marion was well rugged up against the cold, attended by the children and Drummond, Therese walked out onto the porch and, with the others, watched while the last of their guests climbed into the waiting coach and Christopher handed Marion into his curricle and climbed up beside her, then with final farewells ringing in the frosty air, the group on the porch waved the carriages off.

Therese lingered on the porch as the clop of hooves faded, then smiled to herself, turned, and shooed the children inside.

Drummond followed, and Crimmins shut the door.

Therese smiled at Crimmins. "Well done. You and all the others can stand down and go to your well-deserved rests."

Crimmins smiled. "Thank you, ma'am. Mrs. Haggerty instructed me to convey that breakfast would be ready at seven o'clock on the dot"—his gaze drifted to the interested children—"so you'll have plenty of time to fill up before you pile into the coach and are on your way."

The children beamed. "To Winslow!" they cheered.

"And Christmas," George somewhat unnecessarily added.

"Well, children, in light of Mrs. Haggerty's decree, you had better hie off to your beds." Despite knowing it was highly unlikely, Therese added, "I don't want to hear any grumbling in the morning."

"No, Grandmama!"

"You won't!" Jamie assured her.

She smiled and bent so that they could kiss her cheek, then the three galloped up the stairs.

Crimmins smiled, then bowed and retreated.

Therese turned to her son's now-redundant guard. "Well, Mr. Drummond. I understand that you'll be traveling back to London with Mr. Kincaid. Dare I hope you've enjoyed your time in Little Moseley?"

Drummond met her gaze rather sheepishly and, in a rumble, admitted, "Rather more than I'd thought I would, my lady. It's a pretty little place, and we certainly haven't wanted for excitement, even though the excitement was mostly due to your son and your Russian friends."

Therese held out her hand. "I might see you at breakfast, but possibly not. So farewell, Mr. Drummond, and do take care."

Drummond gripped her hand lightly, then swept her a surprisingly decent bow. "Thank you, my lady. And I hope you and all your family and this household have a lovely Christmas." Releasing her hand, he glanced at the stairs, then looked at her. "One question, if you don't mind me asking?"

Therese widened her eyes encouragingly.

Drummond looked rather self-conscious. "I'm aware of your reputation, ma'am. Well, everyone in the office is. But one thing in all this puzzles me. When you went to the Hall, you already knew what was going on." He looked truly confounded. "How?"

Therese smiled gloriously. "Why, the children, Mr. Drummond. One can always rely on the children."

Drummond blinked, then looked chagrined, and Therese laughed, waved to the stairs, and led the way up.

Marion sat beside Christopher on the seat of his curricle and listened to the rattle of the wheels as they left the village behind. The count's coach had gone ahead via the more direct route, but at her suggestion, Christopher had turned right out of the drive, and they'd rolled slowly through the village, noting the inn, still open with golden lamplight streaming out of the lead-paned windows, the lone snowman standing sentinel on the otherwise empty starlit expanse of the green, and the sleepy shops, closed and shuttered, as if to imprint the village scenes on their memories.

In truth, she felt rather fond of Little Moseley and sensed that Christopher felt that way, too.

The shadows of trees closed around them as they followed the lane around a curve, and the intersection with the lane to East Wellow appeared ahead. By her calculation, by now, the count's coach would be well ahead.

Christopher turned his sleek blacks north, onto the main lane. The horses' breaths plumed in the icy air as the curricle rolled smoothly on.

Although Marion had driven that way several times in the Hall's gig, she hadn't previously had time to appreciate the scenery. Even at night, it was somehow comforting, tranquil and serene.

They approached the river—the same one that, farther to the west, looped around the Hall—and the narrow stone humpback bridge that spanned it.

Christopher slowed his horses, then started them up the rising curve of the bridge.

Marion looked out to the left, then clutched Christopher's arm. "Oh—oh, look! Stop!"

Christopher pulled back on the reins, bringing his blacks to a stamping halt, then drew on the brake and looked at what had caught—and transfixed—Marion's attention.

She was staring…at a magical sight.

Along that stretch, the river normally meandered lazily. Tonight, under the moon and stars, the surface appeared like black glass. Smooth and gleaming, it reflected each and every star that winked and twinkled in the firmament above.

The wind had died. There was not so much as a whisper to ruffle the surface of the silent water.

In that moment, as they both sat and stared, it felt as if time had suspended and the entire world stood still.

For long moments, they sat silent and unmoving, absorbing the magic, letting it touch their souls.

Then Christopher reached for Marion's hand. Her gloved fingers immediately twined with his and gripped. A spontaneous smile curving his lips, he returned the pressure, and they continued to simply sit, side by side, drinking in that ageless vision of a frosty, starry night.

Eventually, she sighed, a contented sound that sent her breath misting before her face. "It's so very peaceful here, in our green and lush England."

He nodded. "It is. And it's that, I think—sights like this and what they mean to us—that moves Wellington, his officers, and all our troops to fight so doggedly, so far from home, to ensure that home remains like this."

"An oasis of hope," Marion murmured. "We all felt that tonight in our discussions of the war, that there was, finally, hope. For the coming year and the future it will, at long last, bring."

Again, he nodded. "An end to the war."

After a moment, Christopher ventured, his tone lower, more private, "Hope." He waited until Marion looked at him, then met her eyes and simply asked, "Dare I feel it?"

She searched his eyes, then quietly replied, "Although I hope so, I don't know." She tipped her head, her eyes on his face. "I'm as new to this—whatever this is between us—as you are."

He felt his lips lift. "Perhaps we can go forward together and find our way."

She drew in a deeper breath, then leaned closer. "Let's see."

This time, she only lifted her face, offering her lips, inviting his kiss, and without hesitation, he bent his head and set his lips to hers.

The kiss itself was tinged with magic. A moment caught in the web of time, the caress spun out and on, slowly, gradually, deepening, until she moved closer, raising a hand to cup his nape and draw him to her.

He fumbled and secured the reins, then shifted and drew her closer still. Nearer. Deeper into his arms, into his embrace.

Around them, the quiet sounds of the night—the barely audible murmur of the river, the rustling of the reeds, the plop as a frog returned to the water—soothed and reassured as they explored and sensed and felt and wondered.

And with every second that passed, hope bloomed ever brighter.

Eventually, reluctantly, they drew back on soft gasps. Their breaths fogged the air, and they caught each other's eyes and laughed.

Smiling, she said, "I do believe we'll manage."

His smile lit his face. "Come hell or high water, I suspect we will." He eased her back onto the seat, freed a hand, and held it out to her. "Pax, Marion Sewell, and truce. And I propose we explore the possibility of an alliance."

She laughed again, a magical sound, and gripped his hand and shook it. "Incidentally, I got the impression your mama has already decided on that last."

He grinned and retrieved the reins. "Very likely, but I have to point out that she exercised commendable restraint throughout the past weeks, for which I, for one, am deeply grateful."

Marion nodded. "I did notice, and I appreciate her tact." As they settled once more on the seat and Christopher reached for the brake, she observed, "One of the pros of an alliance between us is that your mother could teach me so very much that, as the wife of a diplomat, would be extremely useful."

"She could and would—she would enjoy that immensely." Christopher tipped his head in thought, then added, "I daresay she would view that as an appropriate enduring legacy."

He glanced at Marion, saw she was still smiling, and returned the gesture. Together, they looked one last time at the star-spangled river, then he flicked the reins and drove off the bridge and on toward their now-much-desired future.

~

~

Dear Reader,

What fun I had writing this book and dabbling in Lady Osbaldestone's past history with the Foreign Office. I hope you enjoyed getting a glimpse of that, too. I also had to refresh my knowledge of the years leading up to Napoleon's defeat and the state of the military campaigns at the end of 1813, which proved something of a trip down memory lane. Most of all, of course, this book allowed me to find a match—a suitable match—for Lady Osbaldestone's unmarried youngest son. That she, of all the grandes dames, still had an unmarried adult child was clearly not a situation that could be allowed to continue unaddressed! Crafting the perfect wife for a gentleman such as Christopher was fun, as was imagining how our intrepid trio of James, George, and Lottie would act in their favorite roles of Cupid's assistants.

Avid readers will note that Dagenham is clearly continuing to hold a candle for Melissa, further setting the stage for what will eventually evolve between them. Their story is currently slated for release in July 2022.

I should add that, eventually, Jamie, George, and Lottie will also have their stories told.

I hope you enjoyed following Therese and her grandchildren through their latest unexpected adventure in Little Moseley in the lead-up to Christmas.

My next release will be the latest in the Cynster Next Generation novels, *The Games Lovers Play*, Therese and Devlin's story scheduled for March 18, 2021.

As ever, I wish you continued happy reading!

Stephanie.

For alerts as new books are released, plus information on upcoming books, exclusive sweepstakes and sneak peeks into upcoming novels, sign up for Stephanie's Private Email Newsletter http://www.stephanielaurens.com/newsletter-signup/

Or if you don't have time to chat and want a quick email alert, sign up and follow me at BookBub https://www.bookbub.com/authors/stephanie-laurens

The ultimate source for detailed information on all Stephanie's published books, including covers, descriptions, and excerpts, is Stephanie's Website www.stephanielaurens.com

You can also follow Stephanie via her Amazon Author Page at http://tinyurl.com/zc3e9mp

Goodreads members can follow Stephanie via her author page https://www.goodreads.com/author/show/9241.Stephanie_Laurens

You can email Stephanie at stephanie@stephanielaurens.com

Or find her on Facebook
https://www.facebook.com/AuthorStephanieLaurens/

COMING NEXT:

THE GAMES LOVERS PLAY
Cynster Next Generation Novel #9
To be released March 18, 2021.

Lord Devlin Cader, Earl of Alverton, married Therese Cynster five years ago. What he didn't tell her then and has assiduously hidden ever since, for what initially seemed excellent reasons, is that he loves her. For her own misguided reasons, Therese decided that the adage that Cynsters only married for love only meant that the Cynster involved loved, not that they were necessarily loved in return. Consequently, given she loved Devlin, she accepted the half love-match he offered and, in her usual managing, not to say bossy, fashion, set about organizing to make their marriage the very best it could be. There's only one problem. Devlin is no longer content with the half love-match he himself engineered.

Pre-orders available by January 1, 2021.

RECENTLY RELEASED:

The fourth and final volume in the Cavanaughs
THE OBSESSIONS OF LORD GODFREY CAVANAUGH

#1 New York Times *bestselling author Stephanie Laurens concludes the tales of the Cavanaugh siblings with the riveting story of the youngest brother and his search for a family of his own.*

The scion of a noble house who is caught in a storm and the lady who nurses him back to health strive to unravel a web of deception that threatens her family and ensnares them both, forcing them to fight for what they hold most dear—family, each other, and love.

Lord Godfrey Cavanaugh has no thoughts of marrying as he drives into North Yorkshire on a plum commission for the National Gallery to authenticate a Renaissance painting the gallery wishes to purchase. Then a snow storm sweeps in, and Godfrey barely manages to haul himself, his groom, and his horses to their destination.

Elinor Hinckley, eldest daughter of Hinckley Hall, stalwart defender of the family, right arm to her invalid father, and established spinster knows full well how much her family has riding on the sale of the painting and throws herself into nursing the initially delirious gentleman who holds her family's future in his hands.

But Godfrey proves to be a far from easy patient. Through Ellie's and her siblings' efforts to keep him entertained and abed, Godfrey grows to know the family, seeing and ultimately being drawn into family life of a sort he's never known.

Eventually, to everyone's relief, he recovers sufficiently to assess the painting—only to discover that nothing, but nothing, is as it seems.

Someone has plans, someone other than the Hinckleys, but who is pulling the strings is a mystery that Godfrey and Ellie find near-impossible to solve. Every suspect proves to have perfectly understandable, albeit concealed reasons for their behavior, and Godfrey and Ellie remain baffled.

Until the villain, panicked by their inquiries, strikes—directly at their hearts—and forces each of them to acknowledge what has grown to be the most important thing in their lives. Both are warriors, neither will give up—together they fight to save not just themselves, not just her family, but their futures. Hers, his, and theirs.

A classical historical romance set in North Yorkshire. Fourth novel in The Cavanaughs—a full-length historical romance of 90,000 words.

ALSO RECENTLY RELEASED:

THE INEVITABLE FALL OF CHRISTOPHER CYNSTER
Cynster Next Generation Novel #8

#1 New York Times *bestselling author Stephanie Laurens returns to the Cynsters' next generation with a rollicking tale of smugglers, counterfeit banknotes, and two people falling in love.*

A gentleman hoping to avoid falling in love and a lady who believes love has passed her by are flung together in a race to unravel a plot that threatens to undermine the realm.

Christopher Cynster has finally accepted that to have the life he wants, he needs a wife, but before he can even think of searching for the right lady, he's drawn into an investigation into the distribution of counterfeit banknotes.

London born and bred, Ellen Martingale is battling to preserve the fiction that her much-loved uncle, Christopher's neighbor, still has his wits about him, but Christopher's questions regarding nearby Goffard Hall trigger her suspicions. As her younger brother attends card parties at the Hall, she feels compelled to investigate.

While Ellen appears to be the sort of frippery female Christopher abhors, he quickly learns that, in her case, appearances are deceiving. And through the twists and turns in an investigation that grows ever more serious and urgent, he discovers how easy it is to fall in love, while Ellen learns that love hasn't, after all, passed her by.

But then the villain steps from the shadows, and love's strengths and vulnerabilities are put to the test—just as Christopher has always feared. Will he pass muster? Can they triumph? Or will they lose all they've so recently found?

A historical romance with a dash of intrigue, set in rural Kent. A Cynster Next Generation novel—a full-length historical romance of 124,000 words.

And if you haven't already indulged:
PREVIOUS VOLUMES IN LADY OSBALDESTONE'S CHRISTMAS CHRONICLES

The first volume in Lady Osbaldestone's Christmas Chronicles
LADY OSBALDESTONE'S CHRISTMAS GOOSE

#1 New York Times *bestselling author Stephanie Laurens brings you a lighthearted tale of Christmas long ago with a grandmother and three of*

her grandchildren, one lost soul, a lady driven to distraction, a recalcitrant donkey, and a flock of determined geese.

Three years after being widowed, Therese, Lady Osbaldestone finally settles into her dower property of Hartington Manor in the village of Little Moseley in Hampshire. She is in two minds as to whether life in the small village will generate sufficient interest to keep her amused over the months when she is not in London or visiting friends around the country. But she will see.

It's December, 1810, and Therese is looking forward to her usual Christmas with her family at Winslow Abbey, her youngest daughter, Celia's home. But then a carriage rolls up and disgorges Celia's three oldest children. Their father has contracted mumps, and their mother has sent the three—Jamie, George, and Lottie—to spend this Christmas with their grandmama in Little Moseley.

Therese has never had to manage small children, not even her own. She assumes the children will keep themselves amused, but quickly learns that what amuses three inquisitive, curious, and confident youngsters isn't compatible with village peace. Just when it seems she will have to set her mind to inventing something, she and the children learn that with only twelve days to go before Christmas, the village flock of geese has vanished.

Every household in the village is now missing the centerpiece of their Christmas feast. But how could an entire flock go missing without the slightest trace? The children are as mystified and as curious as Therese—and she seizes on the mystery as the perfect distraction for the three children as well as herself.

But while searching for the geese, she and her three helpers stumble on two locals who, it is clear, are in dire need of assistance in sorting out their lives. Never one to shy from a little matchmaking, Therese undertakes to guide Miss Eugenia Fitzgibbon into the arms of the determinedly reclusive Lord Longfellow. To her considerable surprise, she discovers that her grandchildren have inherited skills and talents from both her late husband as well as herself. And with all the customary village events held in the lead up to Christmas, she and her three helpers have opportunities galore in which to subtly nudge and steer.

Yet while their matchmaking appears to be succeeding, neither they nor anyone else have found so much as a feather from the village's geese. Larceny is ruled out; a flock of that size could not have been taken from the area without someone noticing. So where could the birds be? And with the days passing and Christmas inexorably approaching, will they find the blasted birds in time?

First in series. A novel of 60,000 words. A Christmas tale of romance and geese.

The second volume in Lady Osbaldestone's Christmas Chronicles
LADY OSBALDESTONE AND THE MISSING CHRISTMAS CAROLS

#1 New York Times *bestselling author Stephanie Laurens brings you a heart-warming tale of a long-ago country-village Christmas, a grandmother, three eager grandchildren, one moody teenage granddaughter, an earnest young lady, a gentleman in hiding, and an elusive book of Christmas carols.*

Therese, Lady Osbaldestone, and her household are quietly delighted when her younger daughter's three children, Jamie, George, and Lottie, insist on returning to Therese's house, Hartington Manor in the village Little Moseley, to spend the three weeks leading up to Christmas participating in the village's traditional events.

Then out of the blue, one of Therese's older granddaughters, Melissa, arrives on the doorstep. Her mother, Therese's older daughter, begs Therese to take Melissa in until the family gathering at Christmas—otherwise, Melissa has nowhere else to go.

Despite having no experience dealing with moody, reticent teenagers like Melissa, Therese welcomes Melissa warmly. The younger children are happy to include their cousin in their plans—and despite her initial aloofness, Melissa discovers she's not too old to enjoy the simple delights of a village Christmas.

The previous year, Therese learned the trick to keeping her unexpected guests out of mischief. She casts around and discovers that the new organist, who plays superbly, has a strange failing. He requires the written music in front of him before he can play a piece, and the church's book of Christmas carols has gone missing.

Therese immediately volunteers the services of her grandchildren, who are only too happy to fling themselves into the search to find the missing book of carols. Its disappearance threatens one of the village's most-valued Christmas traditions—the Carol Service—yet as the book has always been freely loaned within the village, no one imagines that it won't be found with a little application.

But as Therese's intrepid four follow the trail of the book from house to house, the mystery of where the book has vanished to only deepens. Then the organist hears the children singing and invites them to form a special guest choir. The children love singing, and provided they find the book in time, they'll be able to put on an extra-special service for the village.

While the urgency and their desire to finding the missing book escalates, the children—being Therese's grandchildren—get distracted by the potential for romance that buds, burgeons, and blooms before them.

Yet as Christmas nears, the questions remain: Will the four unravel the twisted trail of the missing book in time to save the village's Carol Service? And will they succeed in nudging the organist and the harpist they've found to play alongside him into seizing the happy-ever-after that hovers before the pair's noses?

Second in series. A novel of 62,000 words. A Christmas tale full of music and romance.

The third volume in Lady Osbaldestone's Christmas Chronicles
LADY OSBALDESTONE'S PLUM PUDDINGS

#1 New York Times *bestselling author Stephanie Laurens brings you the delights of a long-ago country-village Christmas, featuring a grandmother, her grandchildren, an artifact hunter, the lady who catches his eye, and three ancient coins that draw them all together in a Christmas treasure hunt.*

Therese, Lady Osbaldestone, and her household again welcome her younger daughter's children, Jamie, George, and Lottie, plus their cousins Melissa and Mandy, all of whom have insisted on spending the three weeks prior to Christmas at Therese's house, Hartington Manor, in the village of Little Moseley.

The children are looking forward to the village's traditional events, and this year, Therese has arranged a new distraction—the plum puddings she and her staff are making for the entire village. But while cleaning the coins donated as the puddings' good-luck tokens, the children discover that three aren't coins of the realm. When consulted, Reverend Colebatch summons a friend, an archeological scholar from Oxford, who confirms the coins are Roman, raising the possibility of a Roman treasure buried somewhere near. Unfortunately, Professor Webster is facing a deadline and cannot assist in the search, but along with his niece Honor, he will stay in the village, writing, remaining available for consultation should the children and their helpers uncover more treasure.

It soon becomes clear that discovering the source of the coins—or even which villager donated them—isn't a straightforward matter. Then the children come across a personable gentleman who knows a great deal about Roman antiquities. He introduces himself as Callum Harris, and they agree to allow him to help, and he gets their search back on track.

But while the manor five, assisted by the gentlemen from Fulsom Hall, scour the village for who had the coins and search the countryside for signs of excavation and Harris combs through the village's country-house libraries, amassing evidence of a Roman compound somewhere near, the site from which the coins actually came remains a frustrating mystery.

Then Therese recognizes Harris, who is more than he's pretending to be. She also notes the romance burgeoning between Harris and Honor Webster, and given the girl doesn't know Harris's full name, let alone his fraught relationship with her uncle, Therese steps in. But while she can engineer a successful resolution to one romance-of-the-season, as well a reconciliation long overdue, another romance that strikes much closer to home is beyond her ability to manipulate.

Meanwhile, the search for the source of the coins goes on, but time is running out. Will Therese's grandchildren and their Fulsom Hall helpers locate the Roman merchant's villa Harris is sure lies near before they all must leave the village for Christmas with their families?

Third in series. A novel of 70,000 words. A Christmas tale of antiquities, reconciliation, romance, and requited love.

ABOUT THE AUTHOR

#1 *New York Times* bestselling author Stephanie Laurens began writing romances as an escape from the dry world of professional science. Her hobby quickly became a career when her first novel was accepted for publication, and with entirely becoming alacrity, she gave up writing about facts in favor of writing fiction.

All Laurens's works to date are historical romances, ranging from medieval times to the mid-1800s, and her settings range from Scotland to India. The majority of her works are set in the period of the British Regency. Laurens has published over 70 works of historical romance, including 40 *New York Times* bestsellers. Laurens has sold more than 20 million print, audio, and e-books globally. All her works are continuously available in print and e-book formats in English worldwide, and have been translated into many other languages. An international bestseller, among other accolades, Laurens has received the Romance Writers of America® prestigious RITA® Award for Best Romance Novella 2008 for *The Fall of Rogue Gerrard.*

Laurens's continuing novels featuring the Cynster family are widely regarded as classics of the historical romance genre. Other series include the *Bastion Club Novels*, the *Black Cobra Quartet*, the *Adventurers Quartet,* and the *Casebook of Barnaby Adair Novels.*

For information on all published novels and on upcoming releases and updates on novels yet to come, visit Stephanie's website: www.stephanielaurens.com

To sign up for Stephanie's Email Newsletter (a private list) for heads-up alerts as new books are released, exclusive sneak peeks into upcoming books, and exclusive sweepstakes contests, follow the prompts at http://www.stephanielaurens.com/newsletter-signup/

To follow Stephanie on BookBub, head to her BookBub Author Page: https://www.bookbub.com/authors/stephanie-laurens

Stephanie lives with her husband and a goofy black labradoodle in the hills outside Melbourne, Australia. When she isn't writing, she's reading, and if she isn't reading, she'll be tending her garden.

www.stephanielaurens.com
stephanie@stephanielaurens.com